About the author

aty ... is an award-winning writer, comedian, actor and journalist. She has appeared in numerous films, TV shows, radio programmes and live events, including the Edinburgh Festival and a UK tour in 2010. In 2008 she won Best Female Newcomer at the British Comedy Awards for *Katy Brand's Big Ass Show*, which ran for three series on ITV. Katy has written extensively across all genres for herself and others, including screenplays, sit-coms, sketch shows and for national newspapers and magazines. *Brenda Monk is Funny* is her first novel.

For anyone who has ever made someone laugh and liked it.

1

August, and London is empty. Or at least empty of anyone that really matters: the comedy world is in Edinburgh, sharpening its wits and claws, pacing anxiously, avoiding newspapers, blogs and anyone else and instead seeking out only the company of other members of that fragile fraternity called 'the comedians'. Attempts by comedy clubs across the capital to keep their venues running are half-hearted, booking acts that would usually struggle to gain traction on even a Tuesday night for their weekend shows. Everybody knows the centre of the universe has flipped on its axis and gone north for the summer. If you have anything to do with comedy, for this one month of the year, you do not want to be here.

For these four weeks Soho has no glamour and those that remain must be doing something wrong. The media industries have flown to Mexico, France, Italy or are at home either pretending to be in Mexico, France, Italy, or telling themselves that the 'stay-cation' was a deliberate decision and not the result of a bad year. Nobody is at work, that's for sure. Soho does not make stars in the summer. The heat of the sun doesn't suit the pavements for a start – it only shows up the dirt. The West End belongs to tourists visiting M&M's World and trying to book tickets to a family show from the cut price booths on Leicester

Square. The established clubs north and south of the river that usually hum with nerves and the low rumble of laughter close their doors and sit still, waiting for September. In short, there isn't much going on.

It was the fifth weekend in a row that Brenda was spending alone in London. To be fair, Jonathan had been disarmingly upfront at the beginning of their relationship that he would not be the 'usual kind of boyfriend'. Of course, for the first six months, this didn't matter at all – couples often spend the first six months of a relationship finding all the things they have in common, and the second six months finding all the things they don't. And for Brenda and Jonathan, this was quite firmly the second six months.

Jonathan's stand-up comedy career was going extremely well. He was now an established headline act for the larger clubs and making good money. Never mind that his twenty-minute set largely consisted of jokes about his relationship with Brenda. The fact was they were good jokes. One or two were even great jokes, possibly classics. But still, the irony that Jonathan spent most of his time miles away from Brenda whilst talking about her to a roomful of three hundred strangers was not lost on her. Last weekend was Glasgow, the week before had been Birmingham and before that had been... Somewhere... Belfast? Maybe Belfast. And now he had gone to Edinburgh for the whole month with the hour-long show he had been working on (and not working on) for the past twelve weeks.

Brenda had suggested she ask her newspaper editor about covering the Festival for the whole month and then accompany Jonathan to Edinburgh to 'look after him'. But he had rejected her offer. She would 'distract him', he said. He needed 'space to feel powerful'. And so, another weekend stretching out in front of her. What to do with it? Go swimming? Again? A yoga class perhaps? Something, she had to do something. Call a friend? Pretty much all Brenda's friends were either on holiday, or in relationships that were still new enough to want to exclude others at the weekend, choosing instead to remain in bed together drinking Cava and talking about where they stood on private education – a good way of disguising the inevitable 'do you want kids?' chat, a conversation that had been attempted once between Brenda and Jonathan and swiftly shut down with a highly contrived and deliberately diversionary pillow fight. The only friends she had that were married and therefore possibly desirous of new company, Laura and Susie, were on some kind of spiritual retreat and according to their joint Facebook page, not to be disturbed for the next few days.

Last weekend had been a particular low point as Brenda had spent it sitting in her flat, alternating restlessly between playing the piano badly, watching day-time TV (supposedly ironically) and then, in a fit of frustration and self-loathing, going out to purchase all the necessary ingredients for home-made hummus, which she had then abandoned half way through upon realising dried chickpeas require twenty-four hours soaking. And who the hell has time to soak chickpeas for twenty-four hours? Well, Brenda actually, but that was part of the problem. Jonathan would often tell Brenda to capitalise on the freedom his absences gave her, talking romantically about how missing one another actually brought them closer together and prevented them from getting into a 'rut'. Brenda's suspicion, buried for now but apt to flare up at inappropriate and embarrassing moments, such as his friends' birthday parties, was that it was any degree of commitment at all on his part that constituted a so-called 'rut'. For Jonathan was the kind of man who could see entrapment in a three course set-menu, and could barely commit to taking a shit – he always had to be doing something else on the toilet as well as emptying his bowels lest his colon get too comfortable and try to tie him down.

Brenda looked at herself in the mirror as she cleaned her teeth for the second time that morning – she wanted to get rid of the taste of the sour cream and chive Pringles she had eaten for breakfast. The combination of artificial cheese powder and toothpaste curdled in her mouth for a moment, and then was overpowered by the mint flavour. She could start afresh and forget the crisps. She could have had anything for breakfast now: eggs benedict; fresh fruit; a warm croissant with French butter and seedless raspberry jam. Anything.

The reflection in the mirror reminded Brenda that she really didn't like her hair this way. It made her look older. Older than twenty-nine anyway. It made her look downtrodden. It made her look like she had given up. Maybe if she had her hair cut, coloured even, Jonathan wouldn't treat her this way. She pulled her hair off her face and piled it on top of her head, Bardot style. That was better, but it wouldn't stay up that way.

Suddenly seized with the desire to change something, anything, Brenda opened the bathroom cabinet, grabbed a pair of scissors, pulled her hair back into a rough ponytail and chopped it off at the base. It took three purposeful hacks, and she was detached: hair in one hand, scissors in the other, head in the middle. The remaining bush sprang out in shock, ends blunt, layers accidental. Brenda smiled.

'I'm going mad,' she thought, and her immediate instinct was to call Jonathan and tell him she was going mad. At least it was something new to say.

She picked up her phone and pressed the redial button. It went straight to voicemail. She had hardly expected anything more, and waited for the automated message (no personalised outgoing message here. Too much like commitment for Jonathan

– how could he predict how long he was going to keep this phone?) to finish before she spoke at the tone.

'Hi, it's me. I've just cut off all my hair and I think I'm going mad. It's good though. Give me a call. When you can. OK, bye.'

She hung up. Alone again. And now with really bad hair.

Brenda grabbed her wallet, phone and keys and left in a hurry. She wanted to be out now, out in the world. In the street she could feel the warmth of the sun on her newly exposed neck – it was nice. It felt hopeful. Where to? Where to... Freedom felt like a prison sometimes, but suddenly it was unexpectedly delicious. She felt a little reckless but had yet to find anything to point it at. She would walk from Hackney to Islington and see poverty give way to affluence in less than a mile. Passing nail salons advertising shellac tips and gel polish designs, Jamaican food shops selling patties and jerk seasoning and maybe more under the counter, Brenda started to sweat. Checking her phone and finding no missed call, no text and no voicemail, she picked up the pace. The smell of spice, hot rubber and bus exhausts made the air lively but she wanted to get to the cool, indifferent, tree-lined residential streets of Canonbury sooner rather than later.

Crossing over the junction of Essex Road and Newington Green Road and continuing up St Paul's Road, she made a left turn into Canonbury Park North and at once the world was completely different. In the spring the trees were thick with pink blossom and you could stand beneath one and look up and imagine oneself as part of an old Japanese painting. But right now they were green and leafy and a high, light breeze rustled the uppermost branches. It was a good sound, a clean sound, and the shade was welcome. Surrounded by expensive houses with Farrow and Ball front doors and discreet alarm systems on the wall, Brenda felt calmer. Her pace slowed. She liked to be near rich people as long she couldn't hear them talking, and these streets were silent now, their occupants filling villas and gites instead, private pools full of private school children. She stopped at a small newsagent and bought a cold can of ginger beer, downing half of it in one before she even exited the shop.

Standing on the pavement outside, she considered her options: continue to Upper Street to browse the endless eye-poppingly expensive interior design shops and boutiques? Get a bus into town? Bend back round on herself and go to Highbury Fields to watch other people's dogs? The world was her oyster. Of course, what she really wanted to do was get on a train to Edinburgh, take a taxi straight to Jonathan's rented flat, get into bed with him, have excellent sex and then go to his show before heading out into the night for all the booze and comedy chat anyone could ever possibly want, but she couldn't do that. He had said she couldn't and he wouldn't be pleased to see her. Well, he would be pleased to see her but against his own will and that would annoy him. It wasn't going to happen. She would have to think of something else to do.

*

Brenda wasn't sure how she had ended up on the Royal Caledonian Express as it broke free of Greater London and ran north as fast as it could, but she was certainly enjoying her gin and tonic. Brenda didn't hold with the view that the first drink is the best. She always found the third gin and tonic to be the most enjoyable, and this one was slipping down very nicely. She was even feeling more confident in her decision (made after an hour or so in a pretentious Islington pub) to hail a taxi, ride it to King's Cross, buy a ticket to Edinburgh and get on the next train, which had left the station exactly six minutes after she arrived.

Jonathan always told her she should be more spontaneous and stop trying to plan everything, and what could be more spontaneous than this? Crisps, she needed crisps. And one more G&T, but only one more. After the fourth all her courage would disappear in a plume of ethanol vapour and she was likely to panic, or start crying, or both.

The trolley was clinking its way down the aisle with a sour-faced train attendant attached to the back. Brenda ordered her second crisp-based meal of the day and her drink. Her phone buzzed on the table. Jonathan. She stared at it, paralysed – should she answer? If she told him she was on her way wouldn't that spoil the surprise? He might tell her to go home. On the other hand, she didn't know the address of his Edinburgh flat (and neither did he for that matter) and at some point she was going to need it. She didn't answer. Their relationship was best conducted face to face, or at least face to groin, and so she silenced her phone and the train sped on.

Arriving into Edinburgh Waverley Station some four hours later, Brenda was now experiencing wave after wave of nauseating self-doubt. Gin based elation was long gone and she needed to buy a toothbrush. She had already decided to kill a couple of hours shopping for nice underwear and a change of clothes before heading to the Pleasance in time for Jonathan's show. His manager Lloyd would be there and would let her in and she could just settle somewhere at the back, out of Jonathan's eye-line and then surprise him afterwards. If the show went well he would be delighted to see her. If the show went well he would be delighted to see anyone, frankly. And if it went badly she would take him away and comfort him with all the attention he needed. It was win-win. Probably.

Walking up the long, wide, tarmacked slope that led out of the station and into the fickle Edinburgh sunshine (you know what they say, if you don't like the weather in Scotland, hang around for twenty minutes) the smell of yeast filled Brenda's nostrils and she felt nostalgic, though for what, she did not know. It was a smell that was unique to this place, created by the breweries that still lay around the edge of the city. All the buzz that had drained out of London was here, and the air was thick with its electromagnetic current. Anything could happen, literally anything. Brenda smiled. She had done the right thing. Even if Jonathan told her to fuck off she would rather be here than there. If push came to shove she could always crash on the floor or sofa of one of Jonathan's charmingly disloyal friends for a couple of nights and enjoy herself – see some shows, catch up with friends and even make a few more in the teeming bars and pubs that overflowed into the streets all night, every night.

Brenda had been to the Festival before, several times. The first many years ago, with a university comedy group called *The Gifted Amateurs*. She had played a few small parts, got a few laughs and then given it up in favour of a career in journalism. Later visits had been social more than anything else: a long week-end with friends, seeing shows for free on borrowed press passes and Festival staff tickets. Brenda had always been a comedy geek and for the last couple of years she had been reviewing comedy shows for various online blogs and magazines which had given her an 'in'. She reviewed fairly and knowledgeably and although she was not paid, and the publications she wrote for were not impressive enough to be used as poster quote material for more established acts, she had given a good few novice comedians a personal boost with her constructive criticism, made plenty of friends in the process, and was now reasonably respected on the comedy scene. In fact, it was how she had met Jonathan in the first place. She had given him a broadly positive but considered review twelve months earlier and then let him pursue her for a few weeks before she dumped the boyfriend she hadn't really been that into anyway and took up with 'this comedian person', as her father called him.

A gust of wind picked up and blew past her ears without warning, taking the last of the gin with it. Brenda felt excited again. Screw Jonathan (and she certainly would, of that there was no doubt, their relationship wasn't that old yet) she was her own person and could do as she pleased. Who was he to banish her from the entire city of Edinburgh? This was her (not quite) professional domain as much as it was his. Indeed, she had been invited to come up for the first two weeks to review for a comedy website (at her own expense of course) but had declined out of respect for Jonathan's wishes to be left alone. Well, she was here now, and had as much right to be as anyone.

Turning right out of the station and onto Princes Street, Brenda stood for a moment to admire the castle, punched straight out of the ground by some ancient giant, thrusting sky-wards on its rock. A crash round H&M saw her with three days' worth of clothes and a quick stop at Boots took care of her personal hygiene needs. She turned towards North Bridge and fell in step with the crowds of day-trippers, tourists and Festival-go-ers eager to make the most of the atmosphere. Brenda paused half way across the bridge to admire the view – on one side the gothic city spread out beneath her and on the other it seemed to simply stop in its tracks and abruptly become open country-side, all watched over by the mountain they call Arthur's Seat, the threat of dark clouds behind it.

'I'll climb Arthur's Seat this year,' thought Brenda, like every-one else who comes to the Festival but never seems to rise early enough to make it genuinely viable.

And then on she went, down the brief, steep, narrow descent of Old Fishmarket Close, along Cowgate, and then up the steep, brief ascent of the Pleasance, to the cobbled courtyard that still remains the spiritual centre of the whole dirty, delicious, deranged Comedy Festival.

Brenda walked through the stone mouth of the Pleasance courtyard and immediately saw three people she knew. On the yellow and black chalkboard to the left were the names of the shows that had sold out that day. Right in the middle '*Jonathan Cape*' had been written in large, capital letters, implying that it had sold out so early in the day that space had not been at a premium at the time of writing. As the evening crept in, the board had become full and names were being squeezed into the remaining gaps. One had even been written inside the 'o' of Jonathan, such was the space his name occupied. Jonathan had that elusive, maddening buzz, it seemed. He was going to have a very good Edinburgh, that much was clear. This could take him from top range circuit player into the realms of TV panel shows, televised stand-up specials, arena tours and... And well there wasn't really anything after that, history seemed to show, but that didn't bother anyone too much. It was more than enough, for a stand-up comedian anyway.

'Brenda!'

A small man with red hair was making his way between the pub tables that took up most of the available space inside the courtyard. Brenda recognised him immediately. Jim John was a promising comedian with a nicely original line in songs about girls he had fancied at primary school.

'Brenda, I didn't know you were coming up.'

Brenda examined his face to see whether he looked concerned at her appearance. Had Jonathan been telling people they were 'on a break' again? But no – she must stop being so paranoid.

'Hi Jim. Spur of the moment thing. London's empty.'

Jim John rolled his eyes. 'God, what I wouldn't give to be back in London right now, away from all this.'

He gestured round to the packed courtyard, filled with punters, players and comedians waiting for shows to start or winding down after shows ended, and drinking, drinking, always drinking.

'Oh fuck off, Jim. You love it. You wouldn't be anywhere else and you know it,' Brenda said, smiling. 'How's it going? I saw a nice review in *The List*.'

Jim covered his ears with pleasing melodrama.

'No! Don't tell me. I'm not reading them, any of them.'

'Of course you're reading them. The first sign that someone's definitely reading their reviews is them saying they're not reading them.'

Jim dropped his hands and shrugged.

'It said I was "still finding my voice". I mean, fuck off, really.'

'Well, I thought it was good. You should be pleased.'

'Jonathan's all over it, as per fucking usual. He's the courtyard celebrity this year, no doubt about it. And look, here he is...'

Brenda instinctively ducked behind Jim as she followed his gaze to where Jonathan had just entered the courtyard. She felt the molecular structure of the whole place shift. People started nudging each other and already a small, shy crowd had gathered round him. Edinburgh has the ability to create these microcosmic celebrities for the space of four weeks in any year, where a handful of comedians who are not remotely famous, except to the most devoted of comedy fans, for the remaining eleven months, are suddenly treated as if they are Jack Nicholson. Men fawn, women flirt, they can do no wrong. Some go on to become truly famous and rich beyond their wildest dreams, some only last one year and then go back to their old lives headlining the larger comedy clubs around the country, and some enjoy this same Edinburgh celebrity for a few years in a row before sinking without trace or going to live in Australia or to 'try their luck in LA', usually after an horrifically abortive TV debut where every vulnerability and weakness both professional and personal is brutally exposed, leaving a trail of bruised executives wondering what they had seen in them and vowing never to do coke again.

Watching Jonathan now, Brenda's principal sensation was lust mixed with anxiety – a heady combination and one that reminded her she had not had sex for three weeks. Standing at least a head above all those around him, with soft brown hair that flopped appealingly, a small wooden stud in one ear, broad shoulders encased in a soft, brushed cotton lumberjack shirt that fell down over his perfectly distressed jeans, he was that rare thing – a genuinely physically attractive comedian. In fact, it had been suggested that he was too good-looking to really make it in comedy. People didn't warm to stand-up comedians who appealed to the eye as much as the mind, at least in the UK they didn't. Which was why Jonathan was keen to go to New York in the autumn and begin what he saw as his 'real career' in America. As Jonathan made his way to his venue entrance, Brenda felt her guts turn to liquid. No matter how well she knew this man was not good news, there was no way she could give him up just yet. Sex with Jonathan wasn't always amazing, but he did have a par-ticular gift for oral and he was very generous with it.

'Is it normal to hide from your own boyfriend?'

'I'm not hiding. It's just nice to watch him the way, you know, a stranger would sometimes...'

'He doesn't know you're here, does he?'

Brenda ignored Jim's question. She had one of her own.

'Who's that woman?'

A slightly dumpy but striking looking woman was walking alongside Jonathan. Her manner was proprietorial.

'Julia, I think she's called. She's American, maybe from some agency out there? I can't say we've been "officially introduced."'

Brenda didn't like it. Women like this attached themselves to Jonathan at an alarming rate, and Jonathan let them attach themselves with alarming ease. Brenda would become jealous and Jonathan would become outraged at her distrust. They would argue, Brenda would storm out and then come back later and apologise. Jonathan would then spend a couple of hours deciding whether to accept her apology while she sat meekly in his living room. Once he had calmed down they would have sex and Brenda's initial questions would remain unanswered. It was a shitty, dysfunctional pattern but so long as it continued to end in sex it would barrel on in this manner.

'Look, I have to go but come to the Attic Bar later, OK? I'll be there from around midnight. I can sign you in.'

'Jonathan can sign me in,' replied Brenda, a little too sharply. 'Of course.'

Brenda came to her senses.

'What time is your show?'

'10.30. You want a ticket?'

'Yeah, can you leave me two on the door? I'll bring Jonathan.'

'No problem. You'll have around thirty seats to yourself so you can stretch out.'

Brenda smiled sympathetically.

'You'll be a sell out soon, just wait for people to catch on. I've heard good buzz about you for a Newcomer nomination.'

Jim brushed aside any feeling of being condescended to and looked grateful.

'Enjoy the show. I mean, you know, as much as you can...'

Jim left and Brenda frowned. 'As much as you can' – that was unsettling. She hadn't seen much of Jonathan's show when it was previewing in London as he had asked her to stay away and there had not been any reviews as yet. Given how easily he was selling out reviewers were attending other shows first that might need a boost.

Brenda had the best part of ten minutes before the start and so she made her way over to the bar. Already thick with people, she had to wait seven minutes just to get served. Holding her pint in its plastic glass she walked over to the venue entrance. As she had anticipated Lloyd was standing in the doorway, watching Jonathan's audience file in: a healthy mix of young and middle-aged, with as many women as men. He saw Brenda just as she saw him and his face betrayed him momentarily – a shadow of concern passed over his eyes and then, ever the professional, he smiled brightly.

'Brenda! Naughty Jonathan didn't tell me you were coming. Let's find you a nice seat. You're coming in? Lovely.'

Brenda relaxed. Lloyd always made her feel important, and welcome. He placed a guiding hand on her back and gently propelled her round the edge of the large, cabaret style room to a stool at the back.

'You've got a drink? Wonderful. I'm so glad you've come. It's a great show, real buzz this year. We've got a bit of business to do after the show but Jonathan needs a bit of R&R if you know what I mean.'

Lloyd winked warmly, that strange combination of camp and heterosexual, and a brief image of an orgasming face crossed Brenda's mind. It was too fast to identify it, but she felt certain that it was her own.

Brenda's expert eyes swept the room. People were sat in groups of three or four at small round tables. There was noisy chatter, a good sign – they were already drunk. 7.45pm was a great time to be on. People would have had a good few drinks, but didn't tend to have dinner beforehand, meaning they were nicely tipsy but not sleepy. They also had a sense that this was the start of their evening, bringing with it the energy and anticipation of a good night. A slot in this venue at this time was the holy grail for most stand-up comedians of Jonathan's level and he was the man to beat this year. You could feel it in the room. These people had already decided they were going to have a good time and all Jonathan had to do was keep them onside. It would take a lot to lose them. Brenda shivered with anticipation. This was still a thrill for her. She sat at the back, in the connoisseur's spot. She felt secretly important. Nobody here knew that Jonathan Cape's actual girlfriend was in tonight. Not even Jonathan.

The lights dimmed and a hush followed.

'Ladies and gentlemen, please welcome to the stage Mr Jonathan Cape!'

Loud walk-on music boomed through fat speakers – a thumping, funky, dirty old soul track – and a spotlight illuminated a microphone in its stand in the middle of the otherwise empty stage. On the back wall a banner that read 'Jonathan Cape' in graffiti-style letters had been pinned to a black curtain and had a 3D effect. In the tight fifteen-minute turn-around between shows there wasn't time to do much more than this but it looked good and effective and was more expensive than anyone could have guessed, having been designed and built by an expert with care and understanding of the constraints of this Festival. Less experienced acts demanded complicated stage sets and consequently kept their audiences waiting and found them grumpy before the show even started. Not Jonathan though. He had good management behind him with an eye on the money as it moved in both directions.

The man himself now loped on to loud applause and a couple of whoops. Pushing his hair out of his eyes and assessing the front three rows before he had even made it to the mic, he couldn't have looked more on top of his game. Brenda's head spun – she had an adrenaline rush perhaps almost as strong as his. His confidence never failed to impress her. She studied him closely, she saw all his tricks, but the execution was so perfect you couldn't help but marvel. As he reached the mic stand, flicked the mic out of its cradle and moved the empty stand behind him in one easy move, you knew already that this was going to go very well.

'Good evening, good evening, good... evening.'

First laugh.

Jesus, he could get a laugh off 'good... evening' these days. The audience were at pre-orgasm stage before he even opened his mouth, all he had to do was tip them over the edge and keep them coming. His mouth curled up at one side into a smile that said, 'I am in full control.' It was sexy – he was feeling sexy and it showed. A woman near the front let out an involuntary yelp. Manna from heaven. Jonathan, who had been strolling along the front of the stage, stopped dead in his tracks.

Second laugh.

Brenda shook her head. This was too easy, even for Jonathan. He'd be irritable later, complaining that he might as well have not written any material at all, although you'd never know it to look at him now. He turned his head and gave the woman his full attention.

'Good *evening*,' he said straight to her pink face.

Third laugh.

'Are you going to let me do this show, or should I just take you outside and show you all my jokes at once?'

The audience erupted. The woman buried her face in her hands. Her friends laughed enviously, faces upturned, white throats exposed, ready for kiss or kill and both equally welcome.

Brenda felt a dead weight in her stomach. She'd forgotten that this is what happened when he didn't know she was in.

'Of course, I shouldn't let you flirt with me, madam – I do have a girlfriend.'

Pause.

'Four hundred miles away.'

Fourth laugh.

Brenda swallowed hard and steeled herself for the hour ahead. The roller-coaster ride had begun and she was trapped behind a metal bar of her own making. She couldn't leave without attracting his attention, and in any case she knew she wouldn't even if she could. She was in it now.

'Anyone here in a relationship?' A world-weary tone. 'Isn't it *wonderful*? So, my girlfriend is amazing, but she's an arsehole. No, no, she'd love hearing me say that, she agrees with me. In fact, she told me she was an arsehole on our first date. It's one of the reasons I went back for a second...'

Fifth laugh.

'But I could never leave her. She makes the best "come noise" I've ever heard. No, seriously, listen...'

*

Brenda and Lloyd stood in the bar waiting for Jonathan to join them.

'It's a great show,' Brenda said, then sipped her drink carefully. 'Really great – the best I've seen him, really.'

Lloyd smiled warmly. 'Well, he's got you to thank for the material,' he joked with some small but well concealed discomfort.

Brenda nodded and smiled, although the nausea had not yet subsided. She had just sat through exactly fifty-five minutes of hellishly detailed, comedically brilliant observations on her relationship with Jonathan; her own relationship with her parents and how it affected her relationship with Jonathan; a run-down of her sexual preferences with notes on each by Jonathan; a compendium of her personal body neuroses and an eloquent and at times actually quite moving speech from Jonathan on how he didn't mind any of them; a story about the first time she farted in front of him and how it made him feel, and, by way of a finale, an extended fantasy set piece about their future together which brought the house down. It was a lot to take in and the fact that Lloyd was standing less than a foot away from her, furnished with the knowledge that she liked to stand naked facing the wall with her arms outstretched, hands on the plaster, legs slightly apart and be felt up by Jonathan from behind before sliding to the floor, did not fill her with joy.

Of course Jonathan had used her as material in the past, but this was beyond anything he'd done before. She was the whole show, for god's sake. It now seemed perfectly clear why he had kept her away from his previews and tried to prevent her from coming to Edinburgh. The overall impression was of a man delightfully and desperately in love with a needy, neurotic, nymphomaniac lunatic, whilst still conveying a sense of being very much on the market for any extra-curricular female attention that may come his way. He had pulled this difficult balancing act off perfectly and Brenda's feelings were complicated by the fact that she was profoundly impressed at the sheer level of skill he had displayed. If she had not been the subject of the show, she would have given it five stars. Hell, she'd probably give it five stars anyway. It was a bona fide five star show and they didn't come along too often.

'Ah, here he is,' Lloyd announced, looking up from his Black-berry.

And for the second time that day, Brenda was able to observe her boyfriend unobserved. He had the swagger of a man who had tasted triumph. People thrust themselves forward, offering to buy him drinks or just wanting to shake his hand or take a picture. He accepted all with good grace. He was in no hurry to get to the bar, he was already a little drunk from the drinks he had consumed backstage before, during and after the show, and high from the large joint he usually smoked out of the window of his small, shared dressing room whilst making small talk with the comedian who would inherit his venue for the hour that followed. Brenda knew Jonathan's habits well.

Brenda felt a surge of pride. She should squash down these bourgeois feelings of having had her honour compromised in some way. There could be no betrayal in art, she thought. She was the muse; her place was surely unassailable, even as she watched a plain young woman with enormous breasts make unexpectedly appealing eyes at her man. Jonathan smiled down at the woman, clearly planning to engage her in conversation, but Lloyd whistled to get his attention.

Jonathan looked up, saw Brenda, was momentarily stunned and then grinned from ear to ear. The plain woman with the enormous breasts was brushed aside and he took large, confident strides to the other side of the packed bar area.

'Here you are,' he whispered in Brenda's ear as he wrapped her in a hug. 'You came – I hoped you would but I didn't want to pressure you.'

He pushed her away from him gently and stared deep into her eyes.

'Did you like the show? Are you upset?'

Brenda, legs jellied and head fuzzed by primal desire, shook her head.

'It's brilliant. It's a brilliant show. You'll definitely win this year.'

Jonathan permitted himself a small smile and then shrugged.

'Awards don't mean anything. It's about the comedy, the comedy is what's important. So you really liked it. God, you are a sight for sore eyes. I love this.' He fingered her hair. 'It's very subversive.'

Brenda was warm from head to toe and she was approaching giddiness when 'Julia' the dumpy American joined them.

'Jonathan, that was just... ahhh. That was just great. Really great.'

'Thanks Joan, really appreciate it. This is "the girlfriend" Brenda.'

Joan gave Brenda a cursory look and pushed out a 'Hi' before turning back to Jonathan.

'I cannot wait to get back to LA so I can start selling you. In the meantime, let me buy you dinner and tell you how fucking great you are.'

Jonathan smiled his version of bashful.

'Sounds like my kind of evening. Is that OK, Bren? I'll catch up with you later.'

Joan took Jonathan by the arm and led him off, speaking in confidential tones. Lloyd and Brenda looked at each other, only the merest hint in Lloyd's eyes that he was thinking about Brenda in his newly acquired knowledge of her favourite sexual position.

'Drink?' asked Lloyd.

Brenda was sure he was taking in her breasts, which he now knew, thanks to Jonathan, that Brenda was worried were slightly lopsided when cut loose from lace and elastic.

'Thanks, but I said I'd go to a friend's show. I'll see you later.'

Lloyd nodded and smiled, turning away as she left, forgetting her already.

2

Alone in Edinburgh, then. Still better than being alone in London. Brenda descended the Pleasance and tacked over to the collection of venues known as the Underbelly, where Jim John's show was due to start in less than half an hour. Passing a row of men pissing in the dark up against the mossy wall of the viaduct that towered above, Brenda had a moment to process her day. It was certainly not as she had imagined when she awoke that morning, full of heaviness at the inevitable boredom and loneliness that lay ahead. She had taken action. She touched her hair. Had it started with that chop, chop, chop? She felt exhilarated. She had taken charge, nothing less than that. And Jonathan was pleased to see her. And she was pleased to see Jonathan. Or if not pleased, then relieved. When she saw him she could stop thinking about seeing him, and that gave her a break. She knew this was not how relationships were supposed to work, but for now she didn't care.

Feeling a light drizzle start to descend around her, she quickened her pace. The dank caves that made up part of the Underbelly's network were before her and she stepped inside just as the rain really began to pour. Pinned to a wall ten feet high to the right of the entrance were dozens of photocopied and printed reviews of acts appearing within. Only the good reviews of course, anything less than a three star was not included. Brenda scanned it briefly, picking out names she knew. In one small area she found Jim John's write ups, three in total thus far, including the one from *The List*. They were fine, good even for someone who had only been in the game for a couple of years. They were nothing compared to what Jonathan would receive in due course and Brenda felt that familiar rise of ego by proxy she enjoyed whenever she consciously acknowledged that she was going out with the current king of stand-up. There were comedians above him in the pecking order, of course: TV names who flew in for a short run in a massive 'super venue' and then flew out again. But in terms of the clubbing comics who enjoyed niche celebrity among genuine comedy fans, Jonathan was at the top of the tree. And there was a certain romance to that, a 'just before-ness' that gave him a glow, his potential still 'shimmering on the horizon' as Peter Cook had once put it. Brenda smiled to herself – it made the exposing nature of his show worth it. And in spite of herself, she was flattered that he had devoted a whole hour to talking about her. She couldn't even pretend to be cross. It gave her kudos, and she didn't mind that at all.

Moving deeper inside, she bought a drink at the pink lit bar, tried to get used to the smell of damp, checked her reflection in the mirror – her hair did look kind of cool – and found her way to Jim's tiny venue. Exchanging her name for a ticket, she moved into the auditorium. Just fifty seats and less than half full. The ceiling was low and craggy, an old cellar of some sort or possible ex-torture chamber. The room was hot and airless. This being a late show in a venue that had turned over every hour since 12pm, the moisture caused by sweating bodies moving in and out rocking with laughter had hit the ceiling, condensed and now fell onto Jim's audience as a fine, misty rain. Even inside you could not escape Edinburgh's weather. Brenda took her seat, the lights dimmed and she heard Jim's voice announce himself into an offstage microphone. The twenty-two members of the audience applauded as he bounced out from behind the curtain with his trusty guitar and commenced his hour.

*

'That was great. I loved it. Can I get you a drink?'

'Yeah, well, I'm no Jonathan Cape, am I?'

'You're different, that's all. It's a completely different style. It's great, though.'

'Yeah, well.'

'What do you want to drink?'

'A blue WKD. And a shot of Aftershock.'

Brenda hesitated. An odd order, but Jim sometimes did have the predilections of a teenage girl.

'OK.'

She walked away from him, glad to have a moment to rearrange her face. The show was fine, but not amazing, and *The List* was right, he did still need to 'find his voice'. It was too timid, too polite, and yes, despite the difference in style and genre, it suffered greatly by comparison with Jonathan. It was a different league. But she had enjoyed it and it was a relief to hear a load of material about women other than herself. She felt a tap on her shoulder and turned to find Jim.

'Let's not stay here. Let's go to the Attic Bar. It's better and everyone will be there. I'll say you're my agent.'

Brenda nodded and checked her phone. There was a text from Jonathan.

'Attic Bar. Then home. Then you and me...'

Brenda smiled to herself and linked arms with Jim.

The gate-keeper to the Attic Bar was a medium sized security

guard who clearly expected trouble at some point, but nothing
he couldn't handle. Anyone who ate real food regularly and
attended the gym more than twice a year could more than control
a malnourished, drug-infused comedian who couldn't bear to
fall out with anyone anyway. Jim flashed his performers pass
and Brenda entered with him with no comment from the guard
– women were always welcome. Down a narrow corridor which
bent and then opened into a large bar with an even larger roof
terrace, the place was heaving. It was close to midnight by now
but in Edinburgh time this was the equivalent of around 9pm.
This was one of the three main bars in the city available exclu-
sively to performers and their hangers on. Comedians hardly
ever went drinking in the pubs and clubs open to the public.
These bars were an excellent place to talk shop, and the late
licences didn't hurt either. Brenda scanned the room and the
terrace outside – where was Jonathan?

'What do you want?'

'To find Jonathan.'

'No, to drink.'

'Oh a Jack Daniel's and coke, please.'

Jim nodded and walked away. Brenda caught sight of Jonathan outside, lounging on a chair under a large umbrella, flanked
by Joan and Lloyd and with a small gang of comedians and their
various people sat around. Brenda approached the group.

'Hey babe,' said Jonathan with a casual tone, 'you got my text.'
'Yeah.'

'Hey, move over Lloyd, I want my girl next to me.'

Lloyd dutifully moved and Brenda sat down next Jonathan
who kissed her full and long on the lips.

'Mmm... it is very good to see you. Did I mention that?' He
leaned in to whisper, 'Hey, we've all done some MDMA, want a
bit?'

'Sure.'

'OK, good.'

Jonathan turned his body towards hers in some parody of discretion, deftly took a small crystal out of his pocket, wrapped it in a Rizla paper and handed it to her. Brenda swallowed it down with a gulp of his beer and grinned. Jonathan beamed back.

'You look so great tonight, B. I'm so glad you came.' He leant in again. 'I'm gonna suck you dry later.'

Everyone heard, but who cared? They were as far from the grip of respectable suburban values as you could get, and surely this was just the life they wanted. They prided themselves on being unshockable. Brenda snuggled down into Jonathan's armpit as Jim arrived with the drinks.

'Ah, Jim James, very nice to meet you at last,' said Jonathan, with less mockery than he had obviously intended.

'Jim John, actually, and we've met before.'

'Jim John, Jim John. I'm sorry, why can't I ever remember that?'

'I don't know. Brenda, here's your drink. Ruth's over there so I'm going to catch up with her, OK?'

Brenda nodded and sipped her Jack Daniel's and coke. Jonathan shook his head as he watched Jim retreat.

'Odd guy.'

'He's OK.'

'Brenda likes him, so I like him,' Jonathan announced to the group.

Brenda looked around at the faces in front of her: three men and two women. All three men were comedians, and of the women, one was a junior TV development researcher who would pretty much sleep with anyone who had ever thought of a joke. The second was the wife of one of the comedians. She looked tired. The oldest of the male comedians, an American named Linus, was approaching his fifties. Already a legend in some respects, he had gained true notoriety five years previously by piercing his foreskin live on stage with the earring of an audience member during a late night show and since then his once legendary promiscuity had dropped off even if his dick hadn't. He had once performed with Bill Hicks, a fact he never tired of referencing, and at one stage in his career it looked as if he would go all the way. He could have been George Carlin, he liked to say, if he'd worked a little harder. Jonathan considered him a kind of mentor, even though he mostly pitied him now. Linus's commitment to stand-up as 'art' gave him an almost mystical aura and even though he was more interested in the theory rather than the practice of stand-up comedy these days, his taste was impeccable and he was always engaging. Right now, though, he was engaged in rolling a joint on his lap using some of the finest medical marijuana money could buy, which he quietly explained he'd managed to bring all the way from LA in a very expensive designer candle he had carefully melted and reformed around the packet of green buds.

Brenda watched him lick the cigarette paper shut and twist the end, remembering how he had once propositioned her outside a disabled toilet while Jonathan was onstage. He couldn't promise full intercourse, he had cautioned, but he could promise everything else. She had declined and he had smiled – their friendship was sealed. In the land of the amoral, the man (or woman) with one scruple is king.

Linus sparked the end of the joint, took three deep drags and passed it straight to Brenda. She took it and pulled once before passing it to Jonathan. Then came the whoosh of the MDMA high, pushing up through her body and breaking a warm wave over her brain. She felt perfect, she felt that this was the only right place on earth to be. She felt her tongue push against the back of her front teeth and tried not to clench her jaw.

'Brenda is fucked,' said Linus, grinning, 'her pupils are like fuckin' dinner plates.'

Brenda giggled and Jonathan's arm tightened around her shoulders.

'So, Linus, I'm working on this bit about the new censorship,' started Matt, an eager, ambitious comedian in his mid-twenties who clearly couldn't believe who he was hanging out with.

'You referencing Carlin's seven words you can never say on TV?'

'Yeah, I guess, I mean, that's the thing, the words have changed now so...'

'Sure, the words have changed, but the ideas haven't. You got anything new to say? Anything original to add?'

'Well, I was going to start in with some stuff about how women can say some words, but men can't...'

'So it's a "differences between men and women" bit?'

Linus didn't bother to hide his contempt. Jonathan smirked and Matt blushed. Brenda watched on as the tired wife discreetly tugged on the sleeve of her husband, Mike.

Brenda knew, as everyone knew, that this forty-four-year-old comic had settled into a nice, quiet stand-up career consisting of a solid twenty-minute set he performed for decent money around the country. He wasn't at the Festival to perform an hour long show, although every year he said he would, if he could just find the time to write one. She also knew, as everyone knew, that somewhere deep down, as much as he loved his wife and kids, Mike clearly felt that they had ruined his once promising career. The pressure to make money had led him onto the relentless B-list club treadmill, driving around the country performing the same twenty minutes, collecting his money and going home. He was just up for a long weekend to 'see what's happening' and do a few late night gigs in the compilation shows that hoovered up time and audiences from midnight to around 3 or 4am. Hannah, his wife, looked exhausted and Brenda sympathised. It took a while for a person's body-clock to adjust to the nocturnal Edinburgh time zone, and it was not helped by the fact that she was clearly bored out of her mind. Brenda let her mind wander, imagining the decade over which Hannah had heard these same conversations happening around her, and although she sat quietly, patiently, pleasantly, she had also grown used to being entirely ignored for hours at a time.

The TV girl, whose name no-one seemed to know, was draped around Matt, her chosen target for the night – a fact that had not gone unnoticed by Linus who was trying to conceal how painfully aware he was that there would have been a time when she would have been draped over him. Joan stifled a yawn and stood up.

'Well guys and gals, it's been emotional but I can't do it like you kids anymore. Linus, good to see you again. I have to say, I honestly thought you were dead.'

Linus smiled thinly.

'And Jonathan, I will call you in the morning, we have much to discuss. Lloyd, we'll talk, yes?'

Lloyd nodded and Joan left, walking through the crowd and out of view.

'She's such a bitch,' Linus murmured reverentially, watching the space her departing back had just occupied.

'Actually, that's one of the words I wanted to talk about in my new bit,' Matt started again, 'how come women can say bitch, but men can't?'

'Well, I'm a man and I just said it, didn't I?'

'Yes, but it's OK for you to say it here, around comedians. We're not going to get offended, but if you said it to normal people, I bet all the women would call you a misogynist.'

'Young Matt, I am a misogynist. My mother taught me everything I know.'

Brenda laughed and Linus turned his eyes to her, full of warmth. Hannah tugged at Mike's sleeve again and he turned to her, irritably.

'What?' he hissed.

'I'm tired. It's nearly one in the morning.'

'Well, this is when things start to happen. Do you want to just go back to the hotel and I'll join you later?'

Hannah shook her head miserably. She doesn't trust him, thought Brenda, with a burst of MDMA fuelled clarity, and then recalled Jonathan telling her that Mike had been unfaithful once many years ago and though they had stayed together, it haunted their marriage. So, for now and forever, Hannah would rather be here with him, exhausted, than sat in the cheap, depressing hotel where she wouldn't sleep anyway until he returned.

Brenda watched this interaction with interest. Somewhere in her drug-addled mind a connection fired, but it wasn't one she wanted to look at directly, so she allowed the MDMA to push it to one side – a useful drug indeed. She hadn't come all this way to feel depressed. She decided to concentrate instead on Matt and the TV girl who were now kissing, oblivious to everything. His hand was already inside her skirt. Brenda watched them as if through a fish-eye lens, the rest of the world falling away at the edges. Lloyd was now snoozing lightly, his head tipped back on a cushion. She could dimly register voices but they were fuzzy.

'So, old Joanie's going to be your earthly representative in LA, is she?' Linus was already rolling another joint.

'I think so. I mean, she seems the right person for me at the moment.'

Jonathan stretched luxuriously and then settled back into

position with his arm around Brenda, his fingers resting very near the top of her cleavage, stroking her skin with micro-movements designed to turn her on. Which it was.

'What's your view of her?'

Linus shrugged.

'She's connected to the hilt, and if she likes you, she really likes you. If you try to leave though... I mean they don't call her Hotel California for nothing.'

Jonathan absorbed this information carefully – like a fox, he needed to check his exits before he entered into anything.

'Thanks for the advice. I appreciate it.'

'De nada, pal.'

Jonathan turned to Brenda and gave her the full force of his attention. The kissing and fondling hadn't escaped his notice either.

'You ready to leave?'

Brenda nodded.

'OK, good. Linus, Matt, Matt's new friend, Mike and his good lady wife, we will see you tomorrow no doubt.'

Jonathan stood up, and so did Brenda, a little unsteadily. He took her hand and kissed the back of it.

'When Lloyd wakes up, please tell him he's fired.'

He winked to show he was joking. Brenda gave a little wave – she seemed to have lost the ability to speak. This was stronger MDMA than she was used to. Linus waved back.

'Take care, sweet Brenda.' Jonathan led her away.

As they passed from the outside roof terrace to the indoor bar area, someone caught Jonathan's attention and he grimaced. Standing right in their path was an extraordinary looking woman who was talking loudly and making everyone around her laugh in great gales of appreciative noise. Jonathan's pace slowed imperceptibly to everyone but Brenda, and she too took in the sight of Fenella Lawrence. Tall and lean, she had dark shiny hair cut into a Liza Minelli in *Cabaret* micro-bob, complete with perfectly geometric points that lay in front of both ears and served to outline her cheekbones. She had matt red lips and heavily kohled eyes, and a black, tight fitting polo-neck jumper she wore clung to her impressive and incongruous breasts. A short black leather miniskirt turned into black leggings which turned into a pair of pristine, classic black Doc Marten boots, laced up nicely.

She saw Jonathan.

'Jonathan Cape. Here he is, the man of the moment. How are you Jonny? Having a good Festival?'

Jonathan dropped Brenda's hand and adopted the most casual pose he could.

'Can't complain? And you? Reviews from God, as usual?'

'Can't complain either, Jonny. And this is?'

Fenella stared straight at Brenda.

'This is my girlfriend.'

'Oh, hello, Jonathan's girlfriend. Do you have a name?'

'Brenda,' Brenda said.

'Brenda what?'

'Brenda Monk.'

'I like it. A good, strong name. So you're the one old Jonny-boy here is exploiting for laughs. I did wonder if you were even real, but here you are, clear as day...'

Brenda was startled, but it was blunted by the drugs dancing through her veins. Jonathan still didn't take her hand.

'You know Fenella, it must be nice to be you and know everything all the time.'

Fenella looked straight at Jonathan, unblinking, eyes a cold, pale blue.

'Yes, it is.'

'Well, see you Fenella. I'll try and check out your show on my off night. We're on at the same time, so it'll be my only chance.'

'Be glad to have you in, Jonny. And Brenda, just let me know if you'd like to come along. I'll leave you a ticket at the door. Given that you've basically written his sell out show, I'd love a little help with mine.'

Jonathan pulled Brenda away as Fenella turned back to her group to continue their conversation.

Once outside, Jonathan lit up a cigarette.

'She's such a cunt.'

Brenda was slow to respond, her mind working to turn over what had just been said inside.

'She's just threatened by you,' she said automatically and Jonathan pulled her to him.

'You're amazing, Brenda. You understand everything. Let me take you home and ravish you right now.'

Jonathan hailed a passing taxi and gave his address to the driver. It seemed he did know it after all.

Once back at the high-ceilinged, wood floored flat Lloyd had rented for himself and his about-to-be-huge client, the kissing that had started in the taxi continued with some aggression.

'Strip,' said Jonathan as they entered the living room and Brenda did as she was told.

'That's good. Now you want an inspection, don't you? Dirty girl.'

Brenda nodded and her eyes glinted with anticipation. She walked over the wall and turned to face it, an arm's length away. She placed her hands on the cool, painted surface and spread her feet a hip's width apart. Jonathan stood behind her and started to move his hands up the front of her belly until they cupped her breasts. Brenda breathed in. The MDMA made every stroke an exquisite explosion.

'Did you like hearing about what a dirty girl you are tonight?

Did you like me telling all those people?'

Jonathan whispered in her ear as one hand moved round her torso and down her back, and the other played with her nipple.

'Yes,' Brenda breathed. And then remembered the show.

'Jonathan...'

'Yes babe?'

'Do I really make that noise when I come?'

'Yes babe. And I fucking love it.'

Jonathan's hand slid under her buttocks and he slipped two fingers between her legs. She was already wet. Brenda's hands slid down the wall and she sank into his lap just as he undid his fly. Lying back on the floor, Jonathan guided her on top of him, into her favourite position which, as everyone in Edinburgh now knew, was the reverse cowgirl.

3

Brenda awoke to the smell of grilling bacon. The midday light melted soft and buttery through the gold curtains and she stretched luxuriously in the large, wood framed bed. The come-down blues vultures were circling, but she knew from experience that a good Bloody Mary and a cooked breakfast would solve that. And if the sun was shining too then the MDMA blues could be effectively banished by the time it got dark. Don't try to outrun them, she thought, just stay still and they'll get bored and go and bother someone else. She pulled on Jonathan's dis-carded dirty T-shirt and found the knickers she had bought the day before. The cheap but sexy underwear lay undisturbed in its carrier bag, tags still on and Brenda found this pleasing. They didn't need incentives for sex, they just needed each other. And a wildly successful show, and some Class A drugs.

She wandered into the hall and followed her nose to the kitchen. Jonathan was cooking breakfast, which in itself was pretty amazing. When they spent the night together at home he was rarely up before her.

'Good morning, my dear, you slept very well.'

'Yes, did you?'

'No, I was up most of the night.'

'Oh, what were you doing?'

'Just replying to messages, catching up on this and that. Things I've ignored while I was working on the show.'

'Oh. Messages from who?'

Brenda knew this was dangerous territory but she had just woken up and her jealousy crushing equipment was not operating at optimum level.

'My nosey girl. Just stuff to do with gigs and things. It's not worth me going into detail about.' He kissed her on the lips to indicate that the conversation was closed.

'That bacon smells very, very good.'

'Yes, it does. I went out and hunted it down for you as soon as the shops opened this morning.'

Jonathan placed it on a plate and added two fried eggs and toast. He set the plate down in front of Brenda, with cutlery, ketchup and a large cup of sweet tea. He then sat opposite her at the table to watch her eat.

'You're not having any?'

'No, I just had a juice. I need to keep on a good regime, need to stay strong.'

Brenda nodded, suppressing the memory of the sheer volume of booze and drugs Jonathan had consumed the night before, and took great mouthfuls, chewing and smiling as the salty grease rolled down her throat.

'So, Bren, how long were you thinking of staying?' Jonathan asked lightly, as if he had been rehearsing that question all morning, which of course, he had.

'Uh, well, I don't know. It's Sunday, so maybe 'til Monday... or... or Tuesday?'

Jonathan nodded.

'Monday's good.'

Brenda was momentarily winded, but sucked it up. She had arrived unannounced and uninvited after all and she didn't want to push her luck.

'OK, tomorrow it is, then'.

'Great. There's a fast train around 1.20, I think.'

'Great.'

Brenda suddenly lost her appetite, but not wanting to hurt Jonathan's feelings she continued eating. One of the vultures settled in a tree to watch. The comedown blues may not be so easily averted.

'I need to meet Joan and Lloyd for lunch and then I thought we could spend the afternoon together. I'll have a nap around five and then we can go down the venue in time for my show.'

Brenda took this in.

'Actually, I thought I might take Fenella Lawrence up on her offer of seeing her show tonight.'

The room froze over instantly.

'Sure. No problem.'

Jonathan took her empty plate to the sink and walked out of the kitchen.

Brenda stepped out into the grand, gently sloping Georgian street and turned left towards Princes Street. She walked automatically, feeling a little out of sorts, turning over the previous twenty-four hours in her mind. Was there anything she could have done differently that would have made Jonathan want her to stay until Tuesday? Or even until the end of the week, or month? She couldn't see where she had gone wrong. He had seemed delighted with her until this morning and then this abrupt indication that she should leave tomorrow. She was already starting to regret the slightly rash decision to announce her intention to see Fenella Lawrence's show. It had been an attempt to convey her independence. She had thought he would like that, but it had had the opposite effect and he had left for his lunch appointment with barely a word, just a gruff 'See you later, then' but with no accompanying specific arrangement.

It was a warm and humid lunchtime, with the ground soaked from earlier rain. A heavy layer of cloud trapped the moisture, and though you could feel the sun's heat, you could not see the source. Still full of Jonathan's breakfast and without much of an appetite, Brenda had no specific place to be. She felt spare, dispensable, surplus to requirement. Her significance only existed in Jonathan's reflected glory. When he was not next to her, she was of no importance. Did this make her feel good or bad? Brenda didn't know – she oscillated between the two. On the one hand she loved the sense of everything before her, she had yet to break the surface of any sizeable collective consciousness and yet somehow she felt that one day, she would. On the other hand, she had no idea how this would happen and she was acutely aware of all the as yet unknown bodies humming in this city right now, each tightly packed with dreams and ambitions and not sufficient space in the world for all them to come true.

But what were Brenda's dreams? She didn't know, she had nothing to aim herself at. So for the time being she piggybacked on Jonathan's naked ambition and kept faith in the idea that the right thing would reveal itself before too long.

She meandered across North Bridge and turned onto the Royal Mile, but instead of almost immediately turning off it again she continued, away from the castle, past the cashmere shops and old pubs, dodging students with bundles of flyers and crowds gathered around silver painted mime artists and street theatre groups singing medleys from various musicals it was easy and cheap to get the rights for. The Royal Mile was running out, and so she made a sharp right and dipped down to Cowgate, but instead of then turning up to the Pleasance she walked on, under a dripping railway bridge, past a couple of bars that had yet to open and on to the outpost of the Festival square mile.

Suddenly the road widened and a big, washed sky appeared. A breeze had picked up and blown some of the clouds away. It was refreshing and Brenda turned her face towards it gratefully. A small supermarket on the left, and a depressing looking council estate to the right, and then a modern development of flats with no soul.

Brenda walked on. By now she had some inkling that she was heading towards Arthur's Seat. She saw the Scottish Parliament building and knew that a curl round it to the right would lead her to the start of the path and the ascent to the top. She smiled. Why had she brought herself here? Interesting. Was she going to climb it? She still didn't know, but she had a strong feeling she might. She tried to admire the Assembly Building but her heart wasn't in it. She could see now that the sky behind Arthur's Seat was clear and coming her way. By the time she got to the top, the bad weather would be gone and the view spectacular. She breathed in deeply. She saw the start of the path. She knew from the accounts of others that there was an easy climb and a hard climb – you could stop half-way up and still get the view. She thought that if she got to that point and wanted to stop she would allow herself to feel some small sense of achievement before descending. And so, by tiny increments, she began to climb.

The path was easy and shallow at first, and was nothing more than a light Sunday afternoon walk. Brenda kept a decent pace and reaching the half-way mark was no hardship. She knew she wasn't stopping – she barely paused to look. If Brenda was going to climb Arthur's Seat, she was going to do it properly, otherwise she wouldn't have started. She may have given herself the illusion of a get out, but the first step up meant that every step would be taken until there was nothing left to do but fly.

After the half-way point, which was heavily populated, the path got steeper and harder and Brenda became more aware of her inadequate footwear. The light breeze from the road was now a stiff wind and she was thirsty with nothing to drink. She had no intention of turning back, though. Up she climbed, up, and when the path became more vertical, Brenda breathed harder and deeper, life filling her lungs and nature healing her mind. She felt the vultures that had been threatening her since she awoke flap their great wings and soar away, in search of another carcass – god knows they wouldn't go hungry in this city in this month. Brenda paused to catch her breath – the blood was pumping hard now, pink in her cheeks and burning in her chest. She wondered if she wished Jonathan was here, and found that she didn't. She was sated, and it hadn't taken much – just one night of premier league shagging and she could feel clearly again. She could see the end now, peaking above her. Another ten minutes and she'd be there, looking out over everything.

Push, push, push and stop. Stop, and stare. Stand, and stare.

The view was better than she had imagined, and the stark and abrupt end to the city that she had observed from the bridge below the day before was now writ large. She turned so that Edinburgh was behind her, and looked across to the Firth of Forth, its huge red iron bridge stretching out, trenchant, commanding, secure. The water was a steely blue with the surrounding countryside scrub green broken with stripes and rounds of rust coloured thorny undergrowth. Some clouds scudded high and made rippling shadows on the ground below. Brenda was exhilarated, cold air caught in her nostrils as she pulled a breath in hard and then pushed it out through her wide open mouth. She felt good. She felt healthy. Yes, healthy, inside and out, as if a great knot had been untwisted and now she could grab the ends and hold onto them, tying herself securely to her own mountain, attached and stable and grounded. She checked her watch. 3.45. Shit.

Brenda took one last look, drinking it in, trying to fill her batteries for later, knowing somehow that this would keep her going and prepare her for something she could not yet articulate. Then she turned and strode back down the mountain. She couldn't help but smile to herself, even though with every step misgivings about the rest of the day rose in her stomach.

By the time she had reached the base and was making her way back past the Parliament building, past the soulless new flats and the depressing council estate, she was nervous. There was no text or call from Jonathan, but that wasn't unusual. He may still be at lunch, he may have bumped into someone he was interested in and forgotten their plan to spend the afternoon together, he may be assuming she would turn up whenever she was ready, or he may be punishing her for the Fenella Lawrence gaffe she had made that morning. That was the thing about Jonathan, his change up was so fast and unpredictable it was impossible to adequately foresee what would happen next. Which of course was part of the thrill. Brenda didn't want to take any chances though. Jonathan was quite capable of abandoning her entirely if he felt so inclined and although she could entertain herself, she felt bleak at the prospect of a whole night in Jonathan's Kingdom with no Jonathan by her side.

She hailed a passing taxi and arrived back at the flat less than ten minutes later. She rang the buzzer, and the door wordlessly snapped open. Climbing the concrete stairs, she found the flat door ajar and walked through.

Lloyd stuck his head round the kitchen door.

'Oh, I thought you were Jonathan.'

'Easy mistake to make. Is he not here?'

'He was. He said he was just popping out for a minute. I don't know where he went. If he's not back in twenty minutes, I'll have to just see him at the venue. I've got a show to see at 5.'

Brenda nodded.

'Are you coming along tonight?'

Brenda hesitated, but one of those mountain batteries was enough to provide her with enough will to stick to her instincts.

'Actually, I thought I'd see Fenella Lawrence. We bumped into her last night and she said she'd put my name on the door if I wanted to come.'

Lloyd nodded slowly, scrolling through his phone, processing this information.

'Do you have a number for her? I don't know how to let her know I want to come tonight.'

'Of course. Easily done.'

And to prove his point, Lloyd tapped out a quick text. Brenda put the kettle under the tap, and by the time it had filled, Lloyd's phone had buzzed its answer.

'Done,' said Lloyd, pleased with his influence.

Brenda smiled, and flicked the switch on the kettle.

'Tea?'

'Oh, no – I really should go. Tell Jonathan I'll see him later, if he ever comes back...'

Lloyd busied off in the direction of his bedroom and called 'Bye' before pulling the front door shut behind him.

The flat was quiet. The huge sash windows in the kitchen created the kind of natural, light filled space that could gladden the darkest of hearts. Brenda made herself a cup of tea and sat down to think. She noted that she didn't care as much as she thought she would that Jonathan had mysteriously gone out. Usually this kind of behaviour was the fastest route to nuts for Brenda, and often resulted in an unexpectedly violent row when he returned. But Brenda found she was enjoying this moment to herself. She felt quietly powerful and now that the Fenella Lawrence tickets had been sorted and she had a plan of her own the panic at the prospect of an evening without Jonathan was receding. Maybe it wasn't quite Jonathan's Kingdom after all, and she didn't have to be anyone's subject.

The door slammed a second time, and Jonathan was before her.

'What happened to you?'

'I climbed Arthur's Seat.'

Jonathan was momentarily surprised.

'I didn't think anyone ever actually did that.'

'Well, they should. The view's amazing.'

Jonathan nodded.

'Tea?'

'Nah, I'm OK thanks. Listen, Bren, I think I'm just going to sleep this afternoon. Are you still going to Fenella's show?'

Brenda nodded.

'Lloyd's arranged me tickets. He said he'd see you at the venue.'

'You alright, then?'

Brenda nodded again.

'OK, good.'

'I'll probably head out while you're asleep so I'll catch up with you at the Attic Bar later or something.'

Jonathan adjusted to this newly carefree tone.

'I'm doing *Late n Live* tonight, actually, so maybe come there...'

'OK, cool. Can you put my name on the door?'

'Yup. I'm on third.'

'OK.'

Jonathan kissed her on the head and went to his bedroom.

Brenda felt a new reality opening up at her feet, a tentative crack in the earth. Was this the kind of exchange Jonathan wanted when he complained that she was 'too intense'? It certainly felt cool and detached but there was no love in it, no need or passion, no relationship that you could find any expectation in.

Brenda was disconcerted and part of her felt a lurch to go straight into Jonathan's room and snuggle up to him, apologise for being weird and ask if she could come to his show after all, to re-establish the connection between them or at least to revive the usual dynamic they were now so used to. But Brenda didn't. Maybe a week ago, she would have. Maybe even a day ago. But for some reason she was sitting still, staying put. Why, she did not know. It made her feel a little sick but she still had three batteries full of cool mountain air inside her and that was enough for her to power on with, whatever this was.

*

Brenda was excited about Fenella's show. She arrived in good time to the venue: a theatre space set on three sides, with a sunken stage in the middle. The Box Office had issued her ticket with no trouble and she now sat on the back row, as the excited babble of her fellow audience members bubbled around her, rising and popping in vertical streams.

The stage was bathed in a dimmed amber glow, waiting to be occupied, dominated. The music had a low, thumping bass line but Brenda could not hear the top line because of the chatter. She felt a brief sensation of vertigo at the thought that Jonathan was less than a hundred metres away in his own venue, starting his own show, and once again itemising her sexual proclivities to strangers as she, herself, Brenda, sat right here. Not just an idea, a set up-punch, but actual flesh and blood with agency and autonomy. She stifled an urge to get up and run over to Jonathan's show, to take her 'proper place' at the back as part of his 'team'. As she pictured some other version of herself there, right now, waiting with docile loyalty to hear her life laid out for the laughter of strangers, another universe of possibilities borne out of the choices she did and did not make was instantly created and she felt so out of bodied that her stomach actually twisted. She shook her head and to her surprise said, 'No.' But not so loud that anyone could hear it. Then suddenly all the lights went out, and a voice boomed,

'Ladies and Gentlemen and everyone else, please welcome Fenella Lawrence into your lives.'

The crowd burst into applause and Fenella bounded onto the stage, already miked up with a radio device clipped round her ear that sat along her cheek and stopped next to her mouth. She wore exactly the same outfit as she had before and her hair gleamed like dark, silky melted chocolate under the lights. Brenda wondered if it was a wig, but then Fenella started talking and she forgot about her hair. She forgot about everything except Fenella Lawrence and the master-class that was unfolding before her eyes.

Fenella had easily as much command of her audience as Jonathan, and to Brenda's mind, even a little more. The material was good too – sharp and relevant, punchy without being crude and without that reliance on sexual charisma that Jonathan often fell back on, although she certainly had sex appeal and wasn't hiding it. She didn't flirt though, that was the difference. There were no biddable women on the front row imagining, even planning, their accidental encounter and subsequent seduction with every minute that passed. And so, unlike Jonathan, there was nothing to distract Fenella, no easy route to an easy laugh. Fenella didn't have to play to the Gag Hags – the one solid gold advantage of being a woman in comedy.

Brenda laughed more than she usually did in stand-up comedy shows which showed that Fenella's jokes had the ability to surprise and wrong-foot even the most committed comedy fans. Her gloriously ironic, self-mocking riff on how her rape jokes were morally superior to male comedians' rape jokes was a joy.

'I used be so against comics that did jokes about rape, I'd be like, how could you? Don't you have any self-control? I said rape gags would never happen to me, I'm not that kind of comedian. But then I got drunk at a gig and one just came out, so I guess I have to take responsibility. No really, I shouldn't have had that extra pint of Bailey's. I was asking for it. I had it coming. Yeah, I'm now doing material against my own consent, so this may be a bumpy ride...'

No wonder her audience was in raptures. Every slight piece of improvisation or audience participation was dealt with deftly and would be used to enhance the show, indicating a comedic architectural ability to structure on the fly that eluded most comedians. This skill was the difference between goodness and greatness and what was clear was that Fenella was soaring into this league with barely a flap of her wings. She had found a comedy thermal and was riding it, curling up and up. Tangible effort minimal; effect maximised and total domination the result. This was a top predator in full health doing exactly what she was designed to do. By the time the show finished Brenda felt high as a kite.

Standing outside as Fenella's audience poured past her, Brenda wondered where she should go to catch Fenella after the gig. Her mind was buzzing, a new horizon seemed to suddenly stretch out before her though what was beyond it she couldn't say. She didn't have to wonder long, however, as Fenella appeared right behind her as the last couple left the building. The tight turnaround of shows every hour meant that there was no hiding backstage for the performer. The venue spat you out as the last seat flapped up on its hinges, leaving comedians blinking and sputtering in the real world as the tide of one they had spent an hour delicately creating rolled back to reveal fresh sand for the next act to draw on.

'Brenda Monk. I'm so glad you came.'

'Thanks for the ticket. I loved it. I mean, shit, I don't have the vocabulary to say how much I loved it. There is nothing original to say, only clichés, I can't...'

'Let me buy you a drink.'

'No, let me buy you a drink.'

'You can buy the second one.'

Fenella walked away without looking back.

In the bar at the back of the second small Pleasance court-yard that lay behind the main courtyard, Fenella bought two pints of cider and set them down on the table they now occupied. People were keeping a respectful distance from Fenella, but the nudging and looking was rife.

'So, you honestly don't mind Jonathan raping you for material, then?'

Brenda spluttered her cider back into its glass.

'He doesn't *rape* me.'

'No, not literally, I mean figuratively. Did you give your consent for him to talk about you like this?'

'He says it's implied when you're in a relationship with a stand-up comedian.'

'Jesus.'

'You're not a fan, then.'

'I think he's a great comedian. I think he's an awful man. I am able to tell the difference. Sadly, not everyone can.'

'He's not awful, he's...he's...'

Fenella cocked her head.

'He's a genius.'

'Oh please. You've got it bad, haven't you? Listen, I know he's good in bed...'

'Uh, OK.'

Brenda adjusted, absorbed, adapted and did not ask. She had got good at this. Fenella continued, oblivious.

'But that does not make him a genius. If he was a genius, he wouldn't pick his shirts quite so carefully.'

'You don't pick your outfits carefully?'

'Of course, but I am a genius so it doesn't apply to me.'

Brenda laughed in spite of herself.

'Look, Brenda Monk, I'm not here to split you and Jonathan Cape up. I just saw his show and I thought, I'd like to meet this woman. And now here you are. If you're happy with what he's doing – if he's convinced you that you are part of some important art project and you believe it, then that's your business. I just think if he needs you that much for material then maybe it's you that should be onstage. You perform you and let him figure out how to fill the gap, you know?'

Brenda drank her cider and looked at the cobbled ground, trying to keep calm. This was a giddying new perspective, and not one that had been terribly forthcoming from Jonathan's group of comedian friends. Linus had ineptly hinted at it once, but the integrity of his concern was slightly undermined by the fact that he was clearly trying to brush her breast with his knuckle as he spoke. Fenella looked straight at Brenda.

'Am I freaking you out?'

'A little.'

'OK, well, forget I said it then. What do you do?'

'I'm a journalist. I write pieces on women in media, mainly. And I review comedy for fun for online blogs and stuff like that.'

'So you're a writer then.'

'I wouldn't go that far.'

'How far would you go?'

Brenda started to feel that Fenella was possibly coming on to her. She shifted slightly in her seat, crossing her arms in front of her chest.

'I'm not a lesbian, Brenda Monk, so don't panic.'

You can't hide anything from a comedian at the top of their game, Brenda reminded herself. They read micro-signals like Derren Brown and if they don't expose your thoughts out loud it's because they are choosing not to. She uncrossed her arms self-consciously.

'I wasn't panicking.'

'OK. Not every comedian you meet will want to fuck you, you know.'

'No, it's just you don't meet the 1% very often.'

Fenella laughed.

'We do exist in a world of priapic schoolboys, it's true.'

Brenda noted the 'we' and liked it.

'It's not even flattering in the end. You realise that with some of them you only have to be warm and wet and you're in. I mean, where's the struggle?'

'Oh you like a struggle?' asked Fenella.

'Once you've picked all the low hanging fruit, what's left?'

Fenella nodded and drank half a pint in one mouthful.

'My round,' Brenda said and rose to go to the bar.

Standing at the bar, looking back at Fenella who was now studying her phone and trying to look inconspicuous, Brenda had a chance to consider their conversation.

She hadn't met a real woman comedian before. She had met female comics who talked loudly and crudely to impress their nihilistic male colleagues, but she had always found their noise jarring. The brash confidence hid insecurity and a need for the approval of men that was off-putting to Brenda, and depressing too. Jonathan had accused her of being an unsisterly bitch when she had hinted at her misgivings so she had never raised it again. But Fenella was quite different. She seemed genuinely confident.

It was calming rather than spirit rattling. Brenda had met female journalists through work who had this same aura, and admired them, was drawn to them, but never until this moment had she seen it in the female comedians she had met. She knew they were out there but they didn't hang around with Jonathan and his friends and so she had almost decided they didn't exist. She had always assumed it was the women's loss. Jonathan and his friends were, by their own assessment, at the cutting edge of stand-up comedy and anyone who didn't want their company must therefore have sold out or couldn't hack it. This was the received idea Brenda had been carrying around inside her for a year now, since she had been admitted to the inner sanctum. But this crack of the new reality was widening a little and she felt at some point she might have to decide which side of the crack to jump to, lest she plunge straight down the middle and into the abyss. You have to stand for something, or you'll fall for anything, Brenda recalled being told by a drunk political journalist one Christmas, before he was sick into his own inside jacket pocket.

Brenda brought two fresh pints of cider back to the table and took her seat. Fenella immediately put her phone down and gave Brenda her full attention.

'So, have you ever reviewed me?'

'No, I haven't.'

'Why not?'

'I don't know. No particular reason.'

'Were you scared I wasn't any good and you wouldn't look very sisterly giving me a slagging off?'

'No. Maybe.'

'We ladies must stick together, eh?'

Brenda conceded defeat.

'I don't believe in that, but...'

'Good, neither do I. None of that "women in comedy" bollocks, thanks. I don't need a special disabled person's permit, I don't need a special parking space near to the laughs, I don't need anything they don't need.'

'I know. But it's hard, isn't it? I mean, it is harder.'

'The more we talk about it, the harder it gets. That's their trick, see. If we keep having to talk about it, it cements the problem in people's minds and then it doesn't go away. You have to ignore it. I'm not saying it doesn't exist – I'm not an idiot – but the strategy is to ignore it.'

'You have a strategy? Like a planned strategy, with other people?'

'Of course. If you don't have a strategy how will you know when you're going wrong?'

'But what if the strategy's wrong?'

'Then you change it.'

'But if you can just change it any time, what's the point of the strategy?'

'So you know if you need to change it.'

'That's not an argument. That's just some weird circular logic that eats itself.'

Fenella shrugged.

'Perhaps you're right, but that's the way we're doing it.'

'We?'

'Yes, me and a few others. We meet for drinks every now and again, to shoot the shit.'

'Just women? Women in comedy?'

'Yeah.'

'Then doesn't that rather disprove your point? I mean, if it's women only, how is that ignoring it?'

'We ignore it in public. In private we do whatever the hell we want. That's the strategy. Why don't you come along?'

'I'm not a woman in comedy.'

'No. Not yet. Are you funny?'

'Yeah.'

Fenella let out a shriek of delighted laughter.

'You played that perfectly. That was great. Just deadpan and...
yeah, great.'

Brenda blushed.

'I don't know if I'm funny, I mean, compared to Jonathan
and...you...and...'

'No, don't spoil it. That was funny. That was a nice instinct.
Tells me a lot.'

'You comedians are so intense all the time.'

'Only the great ones.'

'Don't you get exhausted, analysing, picking apart everything
all the time?'

'Yeah – that's why we all have substance abuse problems.'

'What's yours?'

'Hash. The finest Lebanese Black money can buy. What are
you doing the rest of the evening?'

'Jonathan's on *Late n Live* third...'

'So around 1.30 or so?'

'Yeah, I guess.'

'OK, let's go down for the start of the show. I might do a bit too.'

'Are you booked?'

'No, but if I turn up I'm sure Diarmuid will squeeze me on
somewhere.'

A sharply consumed hot dog, another show. This time a
promising twenty-four-year-old woman Fenella wanted to see
who had some good jokes at the start but ran out of material
twenty minutes in. (A common problem according to Fenella –
a circuit honed twenty minutes then dissipates over the forty
minutes still left to run to a full hour.) Then on to *Late n Live* at

midnight. Fenella was waved through by a smiling ticket collector and Brenda followed in her wake. Sliding round the side of the auditorium through a damp, winding corridor, and they were in one of the few green rooms of established comedy nights that Brenda had never entered before.

Jonathan had not yet arrived. In fact the room was half-empty. In one corner Diarmuid Coyle sat hunched over a tiny notebook. Heavily bearded and dressed in the uniform of slightly too tight flowery shirt, brown cords and converse trainers, this Irish comedian's appearance was misleading in that he looked like some kind of gentle, harmless indie kid. His winsome Dublin accent also helped conceal the rapier mind and sharper tongue that had taken many victims by surprise throughout his time as a professional comedian.

He smiled as he saw Fenella.

'You want ten minutes?'

'Yeah, why not?'

'OK you can go on fourth, after Jonathan Cape.'

'Thanks. How's it going for you?'

'Good. The main show's fine, the more experimental one is... more experimental.'

Brenda knew Diarmuid to be a man not content to let a career based on the path of least resistance take its course. A stand-up of rare accomplishment, he had shunned the call of the TV panel show and branched out instead into more theatrical ventures which were reviewed incredibly well and selling OK. You had to kill for a ticket to his main stand-up show, however, and his hosting of this legendary late night comedy compilation show where anything could happen was a draw in itself. He had power and status most could only dream of. This was his room, this most feral of rooms – he had made it his own.

'This is Brenda Monk.'

'Hi Brenda Monk. Have we met before?'

'Yeah, I go out with Jonathan Cape.'

Diarmuid hesitated for a second but Fenella and Brenda both caught it. Brenda knew what it meant: he had seen Jonathan looking cosy with some woman or other and assumed he was single.

'Oh so his show is based on a real... I mean, it's actually a... person.'

'Yes, and the person is me.'

Diarmuid took this in but his distaste was written across his face. Brenda could tell that Diarmuid fancied his material was of a higher order than Jonathan's and he had a point. The hierarchy expanded again, the perceived horizon was further and wider. The crack at Brenda's feet opened some more.

'Well, nice to meet you. Is it all true?'

'Every word.'

'So do you get a co-writing credit?'

'No, but I get paid for the sex.'

Diarmuid blew air out quickly through his nose – as close as he got to an actual laugh these days – and his eyes suddenly turned interested. Fenella gave a gentle snigger herself. Brenda felt dizzy and disloyal.

'Excuse me, I need to get back to this. Help yourself to the extremely poor selection of drinks and snacks.'

Diarmuid gestured to an old splintered table to one side which had bowls of nuts and crisps on it, along with a box of beer cans and two bottles of white wine. There were no cups. He bent back over his notebook. A member of the backstage team stuck her head round the door.

'We'd like to start in five. Is that OK, Diarmuid?'

'Yup,' Diarmuid said and snapped his book shut.

Two more comedians entered the green room: Rich Joyce,

an old circuit veteran who was liked by everybody because he posed no significant threat, and Matt from the previous night at the Attic Bar. They greeted Diarmuid and Fenella and shook Brenda's hand courteously. Matt had clearly completely forgotten her, and was eager to make an impression on Fenella.

The thrumming from the main auditorium could be heard and felt through the gap in the wall to one side of the room which was the portal to the black painted but brightly lit stage. Once you were out there, there was nowhere to hide. No curtain, no set, no band, no chair, just a deep stage with a black brick wall at the back. And in front, four hundred people in various degrees of drunkenness waiting for the show known affectionately as 'the bear pit' to begin. The intro music played and the walls vibrated to a piece of thrash metal carefully selected by Diarmuid. He leapt up, through the gap in the wall and was gone, like some barbed Mr Tumnus.

A huge cheer, which Diarmuid enjoyed for a few moments and then quietened down.

'Hello cunts,' said Diarmuid into the microphone.

First laugh.

Brenda was drawn to the gap in the wall. She loved watching stand-up from this angle, the performer and audience in profile, either side of some invisible dividing line that would either get stronger or weaker depending on the comedian. You could capture both in the same shot from here, you could watch individual audience members unobserved by anyone, you could see how they reacted to each joke and predict how they would react as the gig went on. Close up, you could see Diarmuid evaluating everything he said and making minute by minute adjustments according to what went well. Sometimes he would lovingly berate the audience, sometimes he would compliment them. Every inebriated interruption hurled his way from the darkness visibly delighted him even when he pretended it didn't. This was a man in his own room. The more confident he was the more confident the audience was in him, and so the more confident he became and on and on into a prolonged simultaneous orgasm across the footlights.

It was always fun to watch each successive comedian come on and play to this exact same crowd and yet not necessarily elicit the same response. The mounting frustration of a comedian dying on his arse in front of an audience he had seen eating out of Diarmuid's hand not five minutes earlier was always compelling but awkward viewing.

And it was about to happen now, as Diarmuid asked the crowd if they were ready for their first act of the evening. They shouted, 'NO!' and Diarmuid obliged them with five more minutes of affectionately mocking material of his own.

Back in the green room, Rich Joyce was cursing Diarmuid and somehow managing to pace on the spot.

'Why does he fuck us over like this, every time? Jesus.'

He wiped damp hands on the tops of his denim thighs as he hovered by the gap in the wall, waiting to go on.

'Fucking bastard.'

A crescendo of delighted laughter, and then without further warning Diarmuid announced Rich from the stage.

'Fuck,' muttered Rich and bounced on.

'Thanks buddy,' he said as he took the mic from Diarmuid's hand, and that was the best received two words he said for the next ten minutes. But Brenda paid no attention because at that moment, Jonathan walked in with Lloyd and Joan and a woman Brenda had never seen before.

He clocked her immediately.

'Hey Bren, you made it. I put your name on the door but I see you didn't need me to.'

This was delivered amiably enough, imperceptible to the untrained ear. But Brenda knew him well enough to understand that he was put out. Something contrary rose within her.

'Fenella got me in,' she said, and instantly regretted it. That was too much.

'Hey Jonny Boy,' Fenella called from the other side of the room, her mouth full of nuts.

'Fenella Lawrence, comedian extraordinaire. How nice of you to take care of my girlfriend while I took care of business.'

Brenda saw the unknown woman adjust to this mention of Jonathan's girlfriend.

'Oh, no problem. We had a great time.'

Jonathan turned to Brenda with a question mark over his head. Brenda just smiled beatifically. Fenella immediately immersed herself in conversation with Matt, who tried to be cool.

'Who's on now?'

Jonathan's antennae had already sensed that whoever it was was not having a good time.

'Rich Joyce,' said Diarmuid. 'Having a rough one.'

'Sounds like he's wrapping up.'

'He won't get off until he gets one big laugh. He's a stubborn old bastard.'

At that precise moment the audience blew a decent gust of laughter into the green room, and they all heard, 'Well, I've been Rich Joyce, and you've been a rucksack of arseholes, good night!' Rich had clearly decided that was the best he was going to get tonight and Diarmuid moved swiftly to the gap and disappeared once more.

'Rich Joyce, people. Give him a clap, he's as old as your grandad, remember.'

Rich grimaced as he reappeared.

'Tough lot, Rich?'

'Bit slow, yeah.'

A huge laugh from beyond. Rich flinched.

'Think I'm gonna call it a night.'

He grabbed a shabby old leather bag and his old bomber jacket and left the room. Everybody relaxed.

'I don't know why he still does it,' said Matt.

'What else would he do?' said Fenella, and there was a small pause as they all acknowledged the brutal truth of it.

'Without further fucking about, here's Matt Linton to entertain and inform.'

A disappointed round of applause for the unknown comedian, but the young one ran on with all the confidence of youth. Diarmuid tag teamed him and then left him to his fate.

Brenda took a bottle of white wine off the table and looked around for a glass.

'Just drink it out of the bottle, no-one else will want it,' Fenella said and Brenda unscrewed the cap. Jonathan had settled himself in one corner on a chair that had been stacked. Lloyd, Joan and the other woman pulled their own chairs off the pile and sat down around him.

'Why does he always need an entourage?' Brenda heard Fenella mutter to Diarmuid as she walked over to join Jonathan.

'Bren, this is Ruby. She works in Joan's London office.'

Ruby stuck on a smile and stuck out her hand.

'This is Brenda, my girl.'

Brenda swallowed – Jonathan always called her 'his girl' as opposed to his 'girlfriend' when he wasn't feeling especially committed.

'Did you enjoy Fenella?' Lloyd asked politely.

'Yes, she was great. Really great.'

This was greeted with a brief silence, broken only by a peel of laughter from Fenella on the other side of the room as Diarmuid showed her something on his phone. The tension in the room was getting pretty tasty.

'Jonathan, you're on next, OK? Then Fenella, then I'll wrap it up,' Diarmuid called over.

'I thought I was closing.'

'Yeah, you were, and then Fenella turned up and I thought she could do ten as a surprise guest.'

Fenella scented a weak spot.

'I don't mind going on before you, Jonny, if you'd rather close. Just don't blame me if they're so weak with laughter by the end of my set that there's none left for you.'

An extremely deft move by Fenella. There was now no option Jonathan could take without looking weak.

'Let's leave it as it is,' he said with great nonchalance, 'I'm not bothered either way.'

'OK, Fenella closes then.'

Brenda was now sitting next to him, and he placed his hand on her knee. Ruby shifted in her seat.

'I think I'll head out and watch from the front,' Joan said, indicating that Ruby should go with her. Jonathan watched them leave, paying particular attention to Ruby's leather-clad departing behind, as it seemed to Brenda.

The door closed. Lloyd leaned in.

'She's just shit hot at the moment. She was named as one of LA's top deal closers in the *Hollywood Reporter* in April. It's going to be an interesting autumn out there for us.' Brenda pricked up her ears. So Jonathan was planning on being away for the whole autumn? He had mentioned a couple of weeks gigging in New York, but clearly the plans had got bigger. She didn't have the stomach to tackle it now, though, and she knew better than to be needy just before Jonathan went on stage. She also knew better than to be needy when he came off stage too. And when he was resting on a day off. In fact, there was never a good time to be needy with Jonathan, so she tried to never to need anything. Which worked to a point, except that there would be an inevitable explosion every few weeks over something apparently bafflingly small, that in fact constituted far less than one eighth of what was lurking below the surface. She just squashed the prospect of no Jonathan for three months and used two whole Arthur's Seat batteries in the process. She had one left.

Matt Linton re-entered the green room without burning up and it was clear he'd had a good gig. He was glowing. He helped himself to a beer and drank silently, still inside his adrenalised bubble of triumph. There was nothing wrong with the world as far as Matt Linton was concerned and he would shortly leave to go round to the public bar, certain as a man could be that some sort of sex would find him tonight. Jonathan slapped him on the back as he walked out and Matt sent him an appreciative look, cub to bear. Diarmuid was back onstage, re-marking his territory before he brought on a big beast. Jonathan was still sat, apparently relaxed, in his chair. Lloyd was scrolling, always scrolling.

'Jonathan Cape!'

A burst of applause, a scream from an over-excited woman. Jonathan rose from his chair, walked in no particular hurry to the gap in the wall and ambled into the light. Diarmuid, Brenda noted, hovered in the wings to watch for the first time that night. And Fenella was clearly listening too – they couldn't help themselves.

Jonathan knocked it out the park, but Fenella knocked it further, a fact that was apparent within two minutes of her set which was also, coincidentally, the precise time Jonathan decided he wanted to leave.

Lloyd and Brenda dutifully trooped after him, and the

mood was not improved by Joan signalling from the back of the audience that she wanted to stay and watch the end of the show. The cab ride back to the flat was silent, save for a single outburst by Jonathan who shouted, 'Fuck,' and then continued to stare out of the window for the rest of the journey. Once inside, Jonathan went to his bedroom, and Brenda followed him.

Jonathan lay down on the bed and closed his eyes. Brenda lay down next to him and stared at the ceiling.

'You still leaving tomorrow?'

'Uh, yeah. Unless you want me to stay...'

'No, don't worry. You go, you go. I don't want to take up your time.'

'You're not taking up my time. I can stay if you want me to.'

'No, it's OK.'

A pause where Brenda tried to figure out the right way to be. Jonathan had got used to being the best at any gig he went to. It had been that way for eighteen months now. It was strangely fascinating to see him dealing with this.

'Do you mind if we don't have sex tonight?'

'Er, no, that's fine. Don't worry about it, it was great last night, so...'

A light snore. Jonathan, it seemed, was already asleep.

*

The 13.20 from Edinburgh Waverley to King's Cross left on time and the Festival slid away from Brenda. Or rather, perhaps she slid away from the Festival. There was much thinking to do and instead of feeling gnawed from the inside at the prospect of four hours alone with nothing to do but examine her life, or try to distract herself from this pursuit, Brenda felt glad of the time. Getting up that morning had been as if in a dream. Jonathan had been sleeping deeply and she had hesitated over whether to wake him. In the end she had, feeling that leaving without saying goodbye would seem a more dramatic statement than she intended to make. So she had gently leant over his face and kissed him on the lips. He had jumped unexpectedly violently at the touch of her lips, and then tried to focus on her face, as she whispered she was leaving now to get her train. He had nodded and smiled and was whiffling again before she even left the room. Oddly, this had not bothered her as much as it usually did. She felt there was some strange membrane around her now, flesh coloured and transparent but shielding her from anything that would get under her skin.

Brenda put her hands round the cardboard cup of cappuccino, drew it up under her chin and settled back into her seat. As the train gathered speed, she tried to look inside herself. What was going on in there? Why was she not obsessively checking her phone to see if Jonathan had called to a) see if she had got her train OK or b) beg her to come back and stay a little longer?

She pulled her phone out and looked at it, but more out of habit than feverish need. Nothing. Of course. And now it hit her quite hard – there would always be nothing. Then when the nothing became too much to bear she would turn it into something by calling or texting him herself, so that there was not an abyss of nothing to stare into but the weight of expectation. Which at least reminded Brenda that she existed and was alive, even though ultimately she felt worse when the return message was vague or so impersonal you could almost suspect it had been sent from the list of pre-written templates that came with Jonathan's phone, or worst of all, when it was clearly intended for someone else.

Again, Brenda asked herself whether this version of herself was what Jonathan really wanted, and further, whether she could in fact provide it. She didn't have to break up with him after all. She could just coast along like this for some time and see how it felt. She didn't want drama, contrary to what Jonathan liked to tell her. In fact she wanted excitement, and these two were very different, although one could always be mistaken for the other. Realising all this was a thrilling discovery. It also meant the end of their relationship as anything other than an arrangement – some sort of Jane Austen type partnership of convenience, but with fewer bonnets and more jokes about anal sex.

Brenda shifted as she tried to imagine this new reality – the crack at her feet had stabilised for now and she saw that she could in fact stand over the gap with a foot on each side. Eventually she would have to make a decision one way or the other but for now, and so long as the crack remained stable like this, she had a little time to play with. Her thoughts were her own business and she felt no compunction to share them with Jonathan for the time being. She was replete, like an egg – all was within, hidden and protected behind a smooth, inscrutable shell. The unwitting Jonathan may have been busy telling the world about the precise shape of her individual tits but, as exposing as that may be, in reality it was she who was, for once, in charge.

Brenda arrived home to a warm early evening in London. The smell of barbecuing meat turned Hackney into an open air restaurant and Brenda remembered that she had barely eaten since yesterday morning. The streets seemed mellow and lazy. Even though it was a Monday this part of town was populated by shift-workers, part-timers, working-from-homers and the unemployed and so there was no reason not to light the charcoal on such a beautiful evening. Weather like this should not be wasted, the people reasoned, and they were right. London had never felt more welcoming to Brenda and she did not feel that space around her as she usually did when she was alone.

She alighted the bus a stop early in order to pop into the small supermarket near her flat and buy a bottle of the palest Rose they had in stock, a packet of sausages, some finger rolls and a bag of salad. She had a disposable barbecue stashed somewhere from last year, she felt certain. The large stone sill on the outside of her kitchen window was wide enough, she had discovered, to hold it if she secured it by puncturing one side of the foil tray and winding an unbent paper clip through the hole and twisting the other end around a little protruding screw in the wooden frame. A large glass of water to one side was a precaution that she had never actually needed.

Brenda let herself into her flat and let the silence wash over her. She checked herself again for loneliness but found none, and smiled a little inside. An evening alone and this was not, for once, a bleak prospect. She did the necessary with the barbecue, opened her wine and twenty minutes later the smell of Brenda's cooking meat was mingling with the rest and she sat at the sash window, with it pulled right up, her toes over the frame next to where the hot foil tray sat and listened to laughter that curled up from gardens below. She felt warmed inside from the hot sausage bleeding into the soft roll, grease and tomato ketchup emulsifying in her mouth, cut through with sips of ice cold wine.

Happiness – this was what Brenda felt. She recalled her father saying once that he wished he remembered to be happy more in his life, to notice it, to mark it, and to understand that happiness is delivered in fleeting moments and the sane person seeks only to note it rather than strive to make it a constant state which is, ironically, the path to madness. Happy. This was happy. And she was alone. Brenda made a note of that too.

The sun went down, and a pleasant summer chill met the

air. Brenda remained in situ, letting her mind fly from one thing to the next without forcing it to alight on any moment in particular.

She liked Fenella, she was impressed by her. And she suspected Jonathan's dislike. She wondered, recalling Fenella's crack about him being 'good in bed', whether they had slept together. She considered the wisdom of asking Jonathan. In this moment of sanity, she decided not to, although she felt she may not always be so sensible.

She examined her feelings about Jonathan's show. It was exposing, that was a fact, but she didn't really know how to feel about it. She had no frame of reference, and no-one to ask. She couldn't call up any of her friends with the question, 'How did you feel when your stand-up comedian boyfriend used you for material in the most intrusive way possible?' She had to figure it out by herself and this was a lonely place to be. She couldn't even ask Jonathan as he took any interrogation of his artistic decision as evidence of disloyalty.

Brenda decided the thing she hated most was the feeling that people pitied her. That they thought she was abused, and exploited – that's what made her feel nauseous. She did not want to be pitied. That was the source of deep vulnerability and Brenda always reacted badly to anyone who asked to be pitied in order to get attention or manipulate those around them. Pity was the death of independence as far as Brenda was concerned. Once you are pitied, there's little chance to recover. And working as a journalist had certainly taught her that. You could be dishonest, depraved, downright immoral, but once the public pitied you, that was it. Perhaps it wasn't the intrusion she minded, perhaps it was the lack of control. Yes, she just wanted more control. Pouring the last of the bottle into her glass, Brenda decided she would call a halt to the 'thinking' for tonight, take a sleeping pill and go to bed. She felt calm, and checked her phone for the last time with a wry smile. Still nothing. Some boyfriends, she thought, might send a quick text to check she had got home OK. Perhaps it wasn't the fact that strangers didn't think she existed outside of the show that bothered her most; perhaps it was that apparently Jonathan didn't either.

4

Jonathan did not call the next day, or the day after that, and Brenda successfully resisted the urge to contact him. She was curious to see what he would do – she had never left it this long before. She got her answer on Wednesday morning when she answered the phone to him, and his first words were, 'why haven't you called me?' This made her laugh, which pissed Jonathan off. She didn't help matters by asking if he had forgotten how to use the phone and the conversation did not go well. She had his attention though, in a way she had not experienced since the first few months of their relationship. She felt dangerous and unpredictable and Jonathan, being a good comedian, was adjusting to his audience. If she was going to run away, he was going to have to come and get her – it was his instinct, he couldn't help it. It was when she stood still that the trouble started and this was all well and good, but Brenda wasn't sure she had the energy to spend her life running, especially when getting caught was becoming less and less interesting.

Brenda briefly enjoyed Jonathan's insecurity from an academic point of view – the tables so pleasingly turned – but heard the death rattle of their relationship. She had always provided the steady love that Jonathan could kick against, and if she was going to withdraw it, Brenda knew he would simply get it from someone else. God knows they were queuing round the block to provide it. But Brenda still felt she didn't want the drama of an actual break-up. She did not want to disturb the signs of life pecking their way into the world that she was nursing in her internal incubator. A break-up, however long overdue, would necessarily divert her attention, and she realised with extraordinary clarity that she need not do anything because Jonathan certainly wouldn't. When the time came the actual decision to stop this would have to be hers and she wasn't ready to make it yet. Not because she loved Jonathan, for she now knew she did not, but because she didn't have any spare energy to steady a rocked boat.

So she comforted Jonathan by saying she had been ill and allowed him to comfort himself by saying he wished he had known so he could have looked after her, which was a brilliantly deluded thing to say given that he was several hundred miles north and had been notable by his absence the last time Brenda had been ill and he had only been a short taxi ride away. But the conversation ended as it usually did, with Jonathan making promises he wouldn't keep and Brenda pretending to believe them. It was just that this time she was conscious of her pretence. It was an interesting sensation. She was taking that well-worn advice to 'fake it 'til you make it' and it felt sophisticated and womanly.

Wednesday was quiet, as was every other in these dog days of news. Many reporters could barely be bothered to come into work and those on casual and freelance contracts took advantage of the uncertain hours, and left the country altogether if they could afford to, leaving a skeleton staff to divvy up whatever did limp in. Today some distraction took the form of a new women's rights charity being launched by a soap star and a singer who was famous in the 1990s. They had chosen an

August launch so that they could be sure of some coverage, which served both to reinforce and undermine the premise of their cause. Brenda was sent down to the tea-party they were giving for journalists. She skulked around in the function room of the mid-level hotel in Mayfair that was now filled with trays of cupcakes and deliberately mis-matched tea sets one was meant to find both adorable and anachronistic and thought how much she hated events like this. There was a lot of earnest eye contact and nodding going on as a selection of 'strong women' (here the winner of a City-based sexual harassment tribunal, there an acid-scarred former model-turned campaigner who had been assaulted by a jealous ex-boyfriend, an actress who had written a long confessional article about racism in the film industry, Nancy Dell'Olio) discussed their work and themselves. A sense of great import was in the air, and no doubt it all was important, it's just that Brenda wasn't entirely sure what specifically this charity was fighting for or against, other than a general sense of injustice against women and girls all over the world. The facts of which Brenda did not dispute, it's just she had gone to three of these in as many months and they were all starting to blur together.

Spotting a friend from a rival newspaper, a very sharp and excellent columnist and profile writer named Emily, Brenda wove her way through the low-key-designer-clad power women to where she stood.

'What is this again?'

Emily turned and smiled.

'No idea. They're doing some sort of speech at 3, I think.'

Brenda checked her watch – ten minutes to go. She had a sudden and perverse urge to wait the ten minutes and then leave exactly when the speech started, but she knew this would not go down well back at the office.

'I interviewed that Fenella Lawrence last week,' Emily said. 'Do you know her?'

'I just met her this weekend in Edinburgh.'

'What did you think?'

'I liked her. She doesn't take any shit and she's good at what she does. Bit abrasive for some maybe, but I don't mind it.'

Emily nodded.

'So, were you seeing Jonathan?'

'Yeah.'

'I read a review of his show this morning.'

Ah, so that's why he'd been a bit off kilter. Brenda usually checked for his reviews online every day but she had overslept this morning and not managed it before his call. Emily continued.

'Sounds like he's getting the most out of you, eh? In more ways than one.'

'Where was it?'

'*The Times.* It was pretty good. Just said he had a lot of observations on relationships that seemed fresh and funny. They said the "girlfriend" was a great device that brought the show together into a coherent whole.'

'That's going to be his speech at our wedding.'

Emily smiled into her tea.

'Is it going well?'

'It's fine. Are you going to give Fenella a nice write up then?'

'Yeah, no point dumping on her now. She's tipped for the big award up there so best keep it positive, I think.'

'Did you want to dump on her?'

'Not particularly but it's always an option.'

Always a journalist first, feminist second, thought Brenda. But that was what made her so readable – Emily saw the many faces of her interviewees and made a judgment as to which ones to expose to the readership by assessing the prevailing wind and trying to get slightly in front of it. And this was interesting intelligence about the Edinburgh Comedy Award, which everybody performing up there expended vast amounts of energy pretending was not the focal point of the whole Festival. Once people made it into TV, film, radio, they mostly forgot about it but its significance to gigging comedians was huge. Brenda could tell how badly Jonathan wanted to win it by the fact that he had not mentioned it once. If Fenella took it home this year he'd be silently livid and impossible to manage. She didn't envy Lloyd that task, she thought, and then realised with a start that she was already painting herself out of the picture.

There was the sound of teaspoon on teacup which signalled the start of the speech. Brenda stopped listening around the 'we've come a long way, but we still have so far to go' mark, and without warning, an image of herself onstage popped into her mind.

She was standing in front of a small crowd in what looked like a classic New York fringe comedy club – a bare brick wall, a mic in a stand, a spotlit circle illuminating her face and upper-body. Brenda had never been to New York, so this image must have been created from things she had seen on screen. She couldn't hear what she was saying, nor the laughter from the audience, but she could tell from their faces that the gig was going well. What interested her most was her appearance. She had short blonde hair and she wore a black jumper.

Emily nudged her, and the image vanished, dissolving back into reality: this room, this tea cup and its non-matching but meticulously sourced saucer, this cupcake from that designer bakery.

'You were humming,' Emily whispered.

'Was I?'

'Yeah – just quietly, but it was getting louder.'

'Thanks.'

Out in the street, Brenda decided to walk. She was glad to be out of a room she had found unexpectedly oppressive. There had been a jangling sense of suppressed competition and hidden agendas that sat awkwardly with her after the straightforward fearlessness of Fenella's approach to conversation. And this part of London fascinated her. It was as unfamiliar to her as any foreign city, with its monochrome perfection. It was as if the rich preferred London in black and white, perhaps they thought it would befit its heritage, and so here, in the corner they controlled, this was how it appeared. Maybe they went to the Caribbean for colour; maybe they curated the whole world in this manner. Glossy black railings against pale white walls, ornamental trees in huge pots, pools of pearl grey pebbles in unused front gardens and even on one street, a pair of armed guards in black uniforms, loafing outside an apparently empty house, guns held softly. So silent, it was, silent and somehow sterile. Why did wealth suck the life out of everything? Or was it just that wealth meant you could inject life wherever you wanted it and so often that was elsewhere? A perennial state of 'elsewhereness' – that was maybe how it feels to be very rich, Brenda thought. This part of town suited the sunshine though. It made the walls glow like magnesium, and you could see your reflection darkly in the freshly painted railings. It was pleasant in its way, calming. Different to the money of Islington that seemed nervous, frantic, with bohemian pretensions, constantly trying to pretend it was all perfectly normal as property values increased around owners' ears, driving them half mad. This Mayfair money was cool and keen to remove itself from normality as effectively as possible, to cruise above it at an altitude of 30,000 feet in a soft tan leather interior.

Brenda thought again that she would like to be rich. Or rather, she would like to be free and riches seemed like a path to freedom, if you could be reasonable with your needs. Daydreaming as she passed a Chanel shop, she thought how well the black and white of the store's exterior, and interior for that matter, matched the general architecture. Everything matched here, and there was no shame about it. Money meant order and order was appealing. And of course, if you wanted chaos you could buy it and then pay someone else to restore order when you had finished. How successful would Brenda have to be to have all this, she wondered? And then she asked herself the next logical question: what should she try to be successful at?

This actually stopped her in the middle of the pavement. She had never asked herself that question before, not as baldly as that. She had asked herself what she wanted to do, or what her dreams were, to which the answers were vague and unconvincing. But now she asked herself what she should try to be successful at. And this meant she had to ask herself what she was good at. It was at this point that she discovered that she had absolutely no idea what that was.

This moment required a drink. Brenda sat down outside the grand Art Deco edifice that formed the exterior of a bar and restaurant – a local landmark. A curious, decadent tiled courtyard that held a stall of fresh shellfish on ice and a florist. Brenda couldn't see how these two went together, but somehow they did, perfectly. Everything here matched, she reminded herself with mock gravity, sometimes just by dint of geography. If it was here, it matched, that was the point. If you made it here, you matched.

Brenda ordered a glass of champagne – it seemed the thing to do. An expensive looking Lebanese couple sat in silence at the next table. He stared at his Blackberry, and who could tell what she stared at behind her £500 sunglasses. A heaving ship of fruits de mer sat incongruously between them, untouched. Brenda could not take her eyes off the woman's hair, though: a long slick of shiny, nutty goodness, with bronze, chestnut and mahogany strands glinting and flashing in the sun. Brenda remembered her daydream and touched her own sorry mop. She had still not rescued it from her own efforts, and was suddenly seized with an urgent need to get it cut and coloured. Hair – the window to a woman's soul, she thought, and took a swig of champagne.

An hour later and Brenda sat looking at herself in a floor to ceiling mirror, her head a patchwork of foils. An hour after that and Brenda left the salon with a short, sharp cut, peroxide blonde to the roots, giving her scalp a baby-pink appearance. She was delighted. It changed everything – her face, her sensibility, everything. A good haircut was no fucking joke. Brenda was no snob – she knew the power of a good look, and didn't sneer at those who made it their business to look, well, the business. Intellect could only get you so far and unless you were planning to be Iris Murdoch, which Brenda was not, this was a step in the right direction. She still didn't know what she was good at but she felt now at least she had the hair of someone who stood a fighting chance of finding out.

She didn't bother going back to the office, she had tapped out her piece on the women's charity on her phone and filed it remotely whilst she waited for the colour to develop on her hair. In any case Janet, her editor, was in Umbria for the next fortnight and barely bothering to check the content. She had left a deputy in charge who was just running press releases as articles as they came in, practically word for word and with lots of pictures. Brenda's phone buzzed: a text from her old friend Laura asking if she was around that weekend to make up the numbers on a trip to Cornwall. Someone had dropped out and so there was a room in a cottage going spare, starting the following evening through 'til Monday. Brenda texted back 'yes please' immediately and full of bounce, went home to begin washing clothes.

*

Another train journey then, and in completely the opposite direction. Brenda arrived at Redruth station around 6pm and the green smell of the earth rolled around her nostrils like fine truffles. Cornwall was a good place to come if you need to figure something out. This pagan land, too far even for the Romans, throbbed with unspoken but long held knowledge. Ley lines, secrets and cider; fertility, folk music and forgotten paths that could be re-opened with the thwack of a good sized stick. And the sea, the sea, shimmering in glimpses, caught between hills. A taxi took her the dozen or so miles to the coastal village of Coverack on the Lizard and a winding road that went first down and then up, met the cottage that was pushed into the side of a cliff overlooking the bay below. Laura opened the front door, and threw her arms in the air.

'Come here you silly bitch,' she shrieked and then laughed at the expression on the taxi driver's face.

Laura, in full hippy attire, held Brenda in a long hug and then pulled her inside. Laura's wife Susie reclined luxuriously on a blue and white striped linen sofa. Two men Brenda did not know sat at a dining table playing chess.

'Brenda, this is Dan and Pete. Dan's Susie's brother. I think you met him briefly at our wedding, he's lost a lot of weight since then.'

The penny dropped. Dan blushed slightly. Brenda smiled, but it was Pete that was catching her attention now.

'Pete was bringing his girlfriend but they split up yesterday, so that's why you're here and she's not. I mean, sorry, that sounded like you're supposed to shag each other or something, and you're not, I mean, you can if you want, but...'

'Laura, please stop talking immediately,' Pete said, but he seemed to be taking it on the chin.

Laura had shades of Asperger's syndrome and was unable to regulate everything that came out of her mouth. Those that had known her a long time just dealt with it as best they could in the knowledge that none of it was malicious, and it seemed that Pete knew this too. He had something about him Brenda liked immediately, something she responded to, a look in the eyes. It was probably the same thing she responded to in all the men she found attractive and it could not be defined according to physique or appearance. It was more just a sense that they would not be scared by anything that was true. Some men like artifice; some men like truth. On first impressions, Pete struck Brenda as a man who liked truth. She just fancied him, that was it, nothing complicated. A flutter inside – anticipation.

'We thought we'd go for a sunset swim,' Laura was saying as Pete smiled an open, friendly smile that revealed dimples in his stubbly cheeks and turned back to his chess game.

'OK, great.'

'I'll show you upstairs. We've rearranged the rooms now, so Pete and Dan are in a twin room and you're on your own in what would have been Dan's room, if you see what I mean.'

'OK.'

Brenda followed Laura up the small, steep staircase with the sense that perhaps she too had been noticed.

Upstairs there were three pretty rooms and a bathroom, all with magnificent sea views. The sky was beginning to pale and in the west, streaks of pink cloud hung lightly.

'This is you,' said Laura, opening the door to a room decorated in shades of fresh green. A double bed was pushed into one corner and a small chest of drawers and a chair against one wall. A pint glass with wild flowers sat on top of the chest of drawers. Brenda felt clean inside at the mere sight of this innocent little room. She breathed in and out.

'I'm glad you could come. It's £150 for the three nights – is that OK? You can do a bank transfer when you get back and we're all chipping in for food as we go along.'

'No problem.'

'OK, well, dump your stuff and we'll head out. We're going to take a dip and then eat at the pub.'

The beach was a perfect semi-circular bay, sheltered on three sides by the curve of the land and with the sea stretching out infinitely before them. By the time they waded into the day-warmed water the sky was a riot of pink, orange and red that reflected in the water like petals.

Brenda swam out beyond the line of the harbour wall so that the horizon expanded. Bobbing with her back to the beach, she felt her mind empty. Holding her breath and closing her eyes, she dipped cleanly beneath the surface, the cooling water closing over her head for a few seconds before she broke it again. Pushing her wet hair back off her face and pinching her nose, she opened her eyes again and felt drunk with the view. The horizon was now hazy everywhere the setting sun was not and the join between sea and sky was blurred, as if you could swim out and then just keep swimming up and up.

Brenda turned in the water and swam back to the rest of the group. Susie was already towelling herself on the beach and Laura was swimming to join her. Dan and Pete were chatting and treading water as Brenda reached them.

'It's a bit too perfect, isn't it? Makes me nervous...' Pete said, with a direct look that implied very little made him nervous.

'I was just communing with nature,' Brenda said and tipped her head back to wet her hair, perhaps unconsciously, or even consciously, aware that the stretch of her throat and the uncovering of the tops of her breasts in the water as she did so would have quite an effect.

'*For whatever we lose (like a you or a me), It's always ourselves we find in the sea,*' Pete quoted, and he was the kind of man who could get away with it.

Brenda smiled at the charm of it, and its prescience.

'That's lovely. What's that from?'

'It's an E.E. Cummings poem. I've always liked it.'

Dan swam away.

'So, you play chess, quote poetry. Do you also save puppies?'

'Of course and if you started drowning now, I could save you. I've done a course.'

'Well, aren't you just the perfect man? Why on earth did you split up with your girlfriend? She must be crazy.'

'Yeah, that's what I told her but weirdly it only seemed to make her more angry.'

Brenda laughed.

'So she dumped you?'

This was a little blunt and Brenda clenched her fist underwater as she saw him wince.

'Let's just say we both knew it wasn't working.'

'Are you very upset?'

A pause.

'No, I'm not. But that in itself is upsetting. Five years together, well, four and a half, and somehow I'm not upset. I have to wonder if there's something wrong with me.'

'You're probably in shock. You'll probably drink seven whiskeys and start crying at midnight.'

'Probably but I can always crawl into bed with Dan.'

A shout from the shore and Pete and Brenda swam to their piles of clothes.

The pub was busy but a table was available outside. The sun had set by now but the last remnants of colour still hovered just above the horizon. The sea was now a deep, still blue and the first stars were visible in the sky.

Pete and Brenda sat side by side opposite Laura and Susie, with Dan next to his sister. Brenda surveyed the group as she held a pint of Guinness in her right hand and a lit cigarette, cadged from Laura, that she wasn't really smoking in her left. Laura was large and her curly hair sprang joyously from her head and was littered with beads and pieces of multicoloured ribbon. She wore a heavy woollen zip up jumper with a pointed hood over her swimming costume and a pair of purple Thai fisherman's trousers and leather sandals. She had a pentagon tattooed on her wedding finger, which matched Susie's and was there in place of a traditional wedding band. Both practised Wiccan religious beliefs from their home in Totnes, although Brenda had never quite been able to ascertain what specifically these were and Laura and Susie seemed happy not to entirely explain. They had held a small civil service at the local registry office ten months earlier and then had a huge party in a field near their home, which Jonathan had said he would attend with Brenda and then pulled out at the last minute when he had been booked for a gig in Croydon hours before they were due to leave. Brenda had said she didn't mind. Their relationship had been newish at that point, and he had seemed genuinely sorry. She hadn't realised then that this would be the pattern for the rest of time and that Jonathan was in fact allergic to any social occasion that came from Brenda, or involved any of her friends.

Susie was an athletic build, with short hair flecked with grey. She had a handsome face which was starting to crinkle round the eyes. She wore Goretex walking gear and looked like she had no sense of humour which was in fact far from the truth. Brenda had met Laura at Nottingham University where they had both studied English, although Laura was three years older and seemed more so. Laura and Susie had been together for over seven years now, and Brenda admired their relationship. It was straightforward and mutually supportive and although they could be a bit earnest in their manner from time to time, they were good company: clever and enlightened. And whatever witchy stuff was going on was clearly working as they were spontaneous and welcoming and about as non-judgemental as a human could be, in Brenda's experience. She remembered being excited about Jonathan meeting them, feeling that they would all get on like the proverbial burning house. But in fact, the encounter had been stiff and awkward. Susie and Laura had barely mentioned Jonathan since, and Jonathan had jokingly referred to them as the 'witchy dykes' once afterwards which had sent Brenda into such a rage that the subject of her friends became a sticking point. Jonathan had punished Brenda by refusing to meet any more of her friends and Brenda had punished Jonathan by never inviting him anywhere again. It was an arrangement more unsatisfactory to Brenda than Jonathan and Brenda had the sneaking suspicion that in fact it suited Jonathan down to the ground.

It was a shame because Brenda was proud of her friends and had wanted to share them with Jonathan. She couldn't entirely understand what the problem was but she had a horrible feeling it was something to do with Jonathan's issues with outspoken women – something she squashed down inside herself as it didn't fit with her view of him, or his view of himself as an open-minded libertine with a sword of truth and shield of... ketamine? But enough of Jonathan, she thought, with the sense that he was unlikely to be thinking about her at this precise moment and so surely she did not owe him so much headspace. She observed Dan, dark haired and eyed with forearms covered in wiry matting that was almost black, who was squashed into a small space at the end of the bench. It was clear that he didn't mind. He was delighted with his newfound smallness and being hemmed into such a tiny area reminded him again of his massive achievement. He must be seven stone lighter, Brenda thought, and silently congratulated him. Brenda was an unremarkable size, average in most respects, but she had been plump as a child and could remember how it felt. She was also aware that she did not make the best of herself much of the time, but her new hair was doing an awful lot of the work for her. The sea had left her soft and tangy and the dying light would have flattered a camel. She could feel Pete next to her, he was tall and broad and she felt small. There was something proprietorial about the way he sat, but she felt that must be her imagination. He was emotionally shattered, she reminded herself, and she had a boyfriend.

A warm breeze kissed their faces as pub food was brought to them on large plates – scampi and chips for five, with wedges of lemon and a thick looking tartare sauce. Brenda couldn't imagine being anywhere else at this precise moment, or at least, wanting to be. She noticed Pete's hands. They looked strong, with nice, short nails and smooth tanned skin. A single leather band wrapped his wrist and she liked the hard, confident way he squeezed his lemon all over the golden scampi . Shit, she thought, she was going to have to get herself under control or she'd give herself away. Getting turned on by lemon squeezing was teenage crush territory and with Laura's gift for stating whatever was going on in front of her, the possibility of embarrassment hovered close by. Conversation was easy and free and Brenda did not have to make too much effort. These four knew each other well and had holidayed together before. It transpired that Dan and Pete had met many years before on a mutual friend's stag weekend to Amsterdam, and had bonded over the fact that they both preferred to get stoned than join in with the hiring of prostitutes. Pete had walked away from the prostitutes – Brenda filed this away in a small folder she had started called 'fantasy man' and was now enjoying the image of Pete hopelessly turned on by some incredible Eastern European beauty selling her body but refusing to do anything about it due to his unshakeable ethics.

Walking lightly back to the cottage, Susie and Dan strode ahead bickering about some family issue. Pete, Brenda and Laura trundled behind and it seemed to Brenda that there was some force of will being exerted by herself and Pete that was preventing them stopping still and kissing each other. She could feel the buzz of electro-magnetic activity between them and had learned to listen to that rather than deny or ignore it as she had when she was younger and still unsure of her sexual pull. One of the gifts Jonathan had given her was an understanding of this pull. A realistic understanding, that is, of her effect on some men, not some arrogant delusion. But right now he seemed a long, long way away and she suddenly realised, with a shock, that she was glad of it.

Susie and Laura went straight to bed, leaving Dan, Pete and Brenda to open a bottle and see where the night led. Pete produced a small lump of hash and began preparing a joint and Brenda settled back on the same sofa. It was large enough to accommodate both of them and leave a gap in between and so for now the certainty of physical intimacy seemed less heavy. Brenda wasn't sure she liked it.

'So, Laura said you go out with a comedian?' Pete asked.

'Yes, in a manner of speaking. He pumps me for material. Literally.'

Pete laughed, and so did Dan, although Dan was shy and said little. Brenda watched Pete's fingers working the hash, crumbling it into the cigarette paper beneath.

'So he talks about you onstage, then?'

'He talks of little else.'

'How does that feel?'

'Well, it can be quite helpful. Whenever I'm wondering how our relationship's going I can just go along to one of his gigs.'

Pete laughed.

'But seriously though…'

How does that feel?

Brenda couldn't remember when she had been asked so simply. She was more used to people covering their embarrassment by telling her how she probably felt.

'That must be weird for you.'

'It's very flattering, I imagine.'

'You must love it, secretly.'

How does that feel?

'It's a bit weird, I suppose. But I mean, it's flattering in a way. I suppose I like it, deep down.'

Pete nodded. She could tell that he had seen through the inauthenticity of her answer, the automatic nature of it. Brenda realised she needed to do better.

'The truth is, I hate it but I'm intoxicated by it. I know it's destructive, but somehow I can't look away. And when I tell him to stop it, he doesn't believe me because I don't entirely know if I want him to stop it, because I like the attention and if he stopped then I suppose I worry, deep down, that I won't exist anymore. Or that I won't matter at least, and I want to matter. I have an ego, even though it's not me on stage. It makes me feel important, but at the same time I know it's doing damage to my… my… me.'

Pete stopped crumbling hash for a moment and blinked a couple of times.

'I'd hate it. Just, properly hate it,' Dan volunteered. 'If I was going out with someone and they did that, I'd dump them immediately.'

Brenda absorbed this somewhat damning assessment of her relationship, but she didn't really care what Dan thought. All her attention was focused on Pete who just steadily continued preparing the joint. Brenda watched as his tongue slid over the gummed side of the paper to moisten it before sticking it down and she felt hopelessly turned on. She could feel the tightening between her legs. He exuded some kind of sexual health and strength, some kind of goodness, that fitted with this place, with its green smells drifting through the open window, mingled with salt from the sea. To have sex with Pete tonight, here in this place, seemed like the right thing to do. The healthy thing to do. The natural thing to do. To reject it would be to reject nature. At least, that's what Brenda was telling herself and there was no-one here to tell Jonathan.

She recalled a sleazy old man chatting her up in a bar three years before, when she was in the death throes of her university relationship.

'You're a sexy little bitch, aren't you? But then, you know that, don't you?' he had said, three double gin and tonics to the good. 'Let's go to my flat and fuck. It's enormous, and so is my cock.'

'But I have a boyfriend,' Brenda had protested, thrilled by the sheer force of his directness.

'Well, where the fuck is he then? Not here, that's where.'

Brenda had seen the logic, but declined anyway, though she sometimes wondered, given that the university relationship was now long over, whether she should have gone with this man, just for the experience alone – it would have made a great story. And as for Jonathan, she asked herself now, 'Where the fuck is he then? Not here, that's where.'

Pete lit the joint.

The three smoked in silence and then Dan made his excuses and went to bed. Brenda took a long drag and leant back gently as Pete moved his arm up to the back of the sofa, creating a nook for Brenda to drop into. They lay like that, quietly, for some time until Pete stroked her hair, moved his fingers down over the side of her face and then ran his thumb along her lips. She tipped her chin upwards and Pete kissed her softly. The tenderness of what followed shocked Brenda more than anything else. She hadn't been expecting it to be so gentle. Pete led her up to the innocent double bedroom and made what Brenda could only describe as love to her. That's how it felt. And then he fell asleep.

Sleepless, Brenda crawled out of the bed at around 5am, crept downstairs, was violently sick into the toilet, then sat on its lid and cried as silently as she could. She called Jonathan and got no reply. She gathered up her things, scribbled a quick note to the effect that she had a family emergency, called a taxi and left.

5

The rest of August passed exactly as Brenda expected, and was no more eventful for her than it had been prior to her trip to Edinburgh, only now she had plenty to think about. The big news was that Jonathan was nominated for the Edinburgh Comedy Award, and the bigger news that Fenella Lawrence won it. Brenda called him that night and he answered on the third ring. She pictured him holding his phone, waiting the three rings in order to not look too eager.

'Hi.'

'It's me.'

A pause. He always insisted on a short pause in order to convey to Brenda that she was not necessarily the most important person in his life at any given moment and therefore not the only 'me'. They both knew perfectly well that her name showed on his caller ID but it was a charade she allowed because it would require too much effort to challenge. She was now simply irritated by it.

'Oh, hey.' His voice was flat and pouty.

'Where are you now?'

'At the flat with Lloyd.'

'You didn't want to stay at the party?'

'You're fucking joking, aren't you? Anyway, it's her party now, not mine.'

Brenda thought he sounded about ten years old, but didn't say so.

'Anyway I'm surprised you haven't rushed up here to congratulate her, what with you two being new best friends and all.'

She stifled a laugh.

'Oh Jonathan, stop. We're not new best friends. I've met her once.'

'Yeah, well.'

'Listen, you'll get it next year.'

'I probably won't come next year.'

'You said you weren't bothered about awards.'

'Look, Brenda, I'm tired, OK? I don't need this interrogation. I just want to go to bed.'

Brenda genuinely felt sorry for him. But she couldn't quite bring it into focus to the extent that she could provide any real comfort. Something was making her scratchy, as if she would like to shake her hands hard and be rid of all this.

Brenda and Jonathan spent one night together in early September and then he flew to New York. He would spend a month there and then fly on to Los Angeles. He hoped to be back for Christmas he said, but would see how things went. There was no mention of Brenda coming out to visit him and she dared not bring it up it in case he said no and she would have to stop pretending to herself that it might happen at some point and admit that they were, to all intents and purposes, over. The award was not mentioned once, although it was the only subject of the entire night, and the idea of it sat elephantine in one corner, sulking and huffing and puffing. Jonathan was edgy and restless and they did not have a good time. It felt like the end, although neither would admit it. Brenda wasn't quite ready to say it was over and Jonathan never liked to say anything was over in case he changed his mind at a later date. So they watched a film and had OK sex and Brenda wished him luck as he left the next morning. He hugged her warmly and told her she was very special and by the time he got into the waiting taxi he was already on the phone.

So, September was here with its fresh stationery and sense of a new beginning but Brenda was bored as hell. Pete had sent her a couple of messages having found her on Facebook and Brenda had stared at them and then ignored them and then heard nothing since. She was still horrified at the care he had taken over her in bed. It made her feel nauseous, but she didn't know why. She felt somehow compromised, and she did so loathe her own vulnerability.

She was having a particularly dull Monday, trying as she was to write a piece on whether or not women are oppressed by fashion. It was a boring topic on which there was little new or of interest to say but some designer had got himself in trouble by using teenage boys to model his women's clothes in a high-end photo-shoot and so obviously this required a sharply delivered response from every mid-level female journalist in the UK, including Brenda. She was just writing a sentence she hated herself for more than any other that morning when an email announced its arrival with a metallic ping.

'Hi Brenda Monk. I am doing a gig tonight in Shoreditch. Just a very low-key new material night to try out some stuff. I have 20 mins. Do you want 5 of them? Fenella.'

Brenda read this three times because essentially it made absolutely no sense to her. Why would she want five of Fenella's twenty minutes? Was she suggesting they have a drink, and then she would do the remaining fifteen? She went to the loo for something to do and to see if a change of scene would clarify this email. She was mid-piss when she realised: Fenella was asking her to go on stage. To perform. For five minutes.

'Hi Fenella. Thanks for the offer but I'm not a stand-up. Congratulations on your win by the way. Brenda.'

She decided not to add the customary kiss. Fenella hadn't put one and to be honest, Brenda had never really liked this rather cutesy protocol that seemed to have grown up in the media before anyone had the chance to offer an opinion about it. It was now at the stage where it seemed rude not to add a kiss to a business email to a complete stranger, especially if you were a woman. Even the men were at it and Brenda had actually changed banks six months earlier when a junior financial adviser named Keith had added a kiss to the bottom of a message about extending her overdraft.

Brenda clicked send and regretted it. She felt disappointed somehow, though for what she didn't know for she was not, as she had said, a stand-up. But nevertheless it seemed that the lights had dimmed a little over her head and everything looked a shade darker.

'OK. Come down anyway and see the show. I'd like your opinion. F.'

Now Brenda was flattered, and she could never resist someone she respected blowing a little smoke up her arse – who could? Anyone who believes they are themselves immune has perhaps never had the experience.

Later that evening, Brenda found the small room above a pub just off the now eye-gougingly trendy Shoreditch High Street. Brenda fought the urge to vandalise the rows of customised fixie bicycles chained to the dirty railings up and down the road, and pushed open the door to the ironically traditional English pub, serving ironic lager and ironic wines and spirits. At least they were not serving cocktails in jam-jars yet although the now ubiquitous fish-finger sandwich was being consumed by a small table of hipster TV researchers, one of whom wore a child's Mickey Mouse sweatshirt from 1986, at a table towards the back. Brenda had an image of them all eating turkey dinosaurs and potato faces twelve months from now and wondered whether they ironically went to one another's houses for tea and had their mums cook it for them. But there was no time to enquire as Fenella was ordering a drink and waving at her.

'Nice hair, very good.'

Brenda touched her head. She'd forgotten that not everyone had seen the short blonde style she had now adopted as her normal hair.

'Here, drink this.' Fenella handed Brenda a glass of what looked like coke but turned out to also contain a double shot of vodka.

'It'll make everything funnier. Have you dumped Jonathan yet?'

'No.'

'But he's fucked off to America in a huff, hasn't he?'

'I wouldn't call it a huff. It's been planned for months.'

'His face when they called my name at the ceremony. Christ, it was a picture.'

Brenda smiled thinly.

'Why do you hate him so much?'

'Because he's a prick,' Fenella replied simply. 'He wants to act like he's on some kind of imaginary team of stand-up comedians, but in reality he's only in it for himself. Which is fine. I mean, we all are. Stand-up is not a collaborative thing. I just wish he'd admit it. He makes a big deal about being "honest on stage" but he's anything but honest about himself. He's plenty honest about you though, isn't he?'

Brenda chose to ignore this. August and Edinburgh were over, and as far as she was concerned so was Jonathan's show.

He was already working on new material and he hadn't won the award so the momentum for that collection of jokes was gone and they might as well not exist now. He'd still use some of them, of course, carved up and re-allocated into a 'best of' set for the American market but the intensity of that hour would not exist again. The jokes had been lit and had exploded in the sky, and the crowd had ooh-ed and aah-ed and moved on.

In the venue above the main pub around a hundred seats had been roughly put out facing a small temporary stage and a microphone. Although it was a secret gig word had clearly got out that Fenella Lawrence was doing some new material and it was already two thirds full. Brenda had bought another drink and now sat at the back of the room, as was her habit, waiting for the start of the show. The rest of the seats were filled over the following ten minutes and finally, at five past nine, the MC for the night, a comedian named George who prided himself on being an intellectual, hopped onto the stage block and started the show.

He did a couple of warm-up jokes, and drew the audience out of themselves with a little participation – a favour to the other comedians who now hovered to one side of the room, as it meant they could get a sense of what type of crowd was in, and perhaps adjust their material accordingly. Or perhaps not. There was a move towards deliberately contrary material at the moment and then pointing out to the audience that it wasn't working, which often led to a laugh. You had to have a fairly sophisticated bunch for this to come off but there were several high profile comedians playing sell-out rooms in decent theatres with this style of comedy and amongst the 'comedy connoisseurs' it was widely considered to be a 'bit meta' and therefore of higher quality than your average gag-smith. How long the self-appointed taste-makers would venerate this style was hard to say but its practitioners would continue with or without them and in the end, Brenda thought, perhaps it hardly mattered what the reviewers and commentators said. Perhaps all comedians were just trying to find what suited them and sod the rest.

Two comedians passed across the stage with some success. They held notebooks by way of apology or explanation, and the fact that this was billed as a 'new material' night made the crowd forgiving. They felt they were being let into a secret, that they had access to the process, rather than just paying to see unprepared comedians doing half-thought through jokes they hadn't yet bothered to learn, and so the atmosphere was generally supportive.

George brought Fenella on last, and the crowd cheered and whistled. Fenella quietened them down quickly and effectively.

'Don't do that – I'm planning to be shit tonight.'

And then this happened.

'Before I start reading out of my own pathetic little notebook, I'd like to introduce a brilliant new comedian who is going to do five minutes. Please give her a warm welcome as she's new to this game. Ladies and gentlemen, Brenda Monk!'

The crowd applauded and so did Brenda.

And then she realised what was happening.

Fenella pointed to her at the back of the crowd.

'Come on up then, Brenda. You're making me look like a dick.'

Brenda's eyes widened in horror and shook her head vigorously, trying to pass it off as a joke. The crowd laughed, and then lulled expectantly, and then started to wonder what was going on.

'Come up here, Brenda Monk, and tell these good people your story. Come on, come on, come on. We want to see her, don't we?'

'Yes', the crowd called, feeling they were witnessing some comedy moment they could talk about for a good few days.

Fenella got off the stage and walked over to Brenda, took her arm, and pulled her to the front. She walked her up to the stage, shoved the mic into her hand and stepped off, applauding with the rest of the whooping crowd.

Brenda stood and looked out at the expectant faces, and felt nothing so strong as that she was facing the wrong way. Any previous stage experience she may have had from a decade earlier may as well have never happened. Her mind was blank and as a hush fell over the room, nothing was coming to her. The crowd shifted uncomfortably, and the air-conditioning unit buzzed. Someone cleared their throat.

Fenella stood to one side with her arms folded, unwavering, unmoved.

Brenda lifted the microphone to her lips.

'Hi.'

The audience tittered. Brenda adjusted her stance.

'Hi,' she said again.

'HI!' shouted a man at the back, from the semi-darkness and the audience laughed out of relief more than anything. Brenda smiled too, and breathed hard into the microphone, amplifying a great huffing noise across the room.

'I'm Brenda Monk. And, ummmm, I'm going out with a comedian. Well, I say going out, he has sex with me and then writes jokes about it.'

A laugh. An actual laugh. Not a big one, and it was more generous than genuine, but still, there it was.

'He literally pumps me for material.'

Another laugh, a little bigger.

'He says I'm an arsehole, but you know, maybe I am an arsehole.'

This received a minor murmur. Strange – it worked so well for Jonathan. Brenda floundered a little, mind racing, trying to find a grip as she fell down the black hole. And then, from nowhere,

'We're getting married next month to make sure he has enough jokes for a tour.'

Another laugh, a little smaller than the first, but enough.

Brenda glanced at Fenella out of the corner of her eye, and Fenella nodded.

'Ummm, I don't... I don't know if I'm going to stay with him much longer though, as he met my mum last week and I haven't heard from either of them since.'

Pause.

'My dad thinks he's hilarious though.'

The biggest laugh yet.

'Ladies and gentlemen, Brenda Monk!' Fenella was already beside her, taking the mic out of her hand and gently pushing her off the stage to the sound of kind applause.

'Wasn't she great? That was her first ever gig, people, and you saw it here. So, look, what am I going to talk to you about tonight? I haven't a fucking clue...'

Brenda floated to the back of the room in a daze. She didn't hear Fenella's set, and was only vaguely aware of people around her rocking with laughter for the next quarter of an hour. She took a deep drink and sat still until her heart stopped racing.

The gig finished and Fenella bought Brenda another drink.

'That was good. You were good.'

'No, I wasn't, don't be ridiculous. They were laughing out of charity and they weren't even laughing that hard.'

'No, it wasn't just charity. Some of it was them just being nice, but you had a couple of pretty good shots, and you looked right up there. Not everyone does, you know. You stood right, and that's just pure instinct. I knew you had it.'

'Oh come on. I made a few awkward, crap remarks about

Jonathan and got off.'

'OK, the jokes could use some work. You liked it though, didn't you?'

'No, it was awful. I can't believe you did that to me.'

'Brenda, you liked it.'

'No.'

But she had liked it. And the reason she knew that was that she hadn't felt this alive for months. On the bus on the way home she stared out of the window, tingling all over, thinking about what she'd said onstage and how she could improve it. She was already 'working on her material.' It had felt good and powerful up there and it wasn't just about getting some control over her own life, her own story, back from Jonathan. There was something more than that. One moment stood out in her mind, as if it were made of diamonds: there had been a second where she had looked out at the faces of the audience and thought, 'I could say anything I want to. I could say anything I want to.' She was reeling from that one moment alone. The rest was just a matter of writing some jokes.

Brenda lay in bed trying not to ring Jonathan. She felt on some level that he would not be pleased to hear about it, even though he would pretend to be delighted.

'I always said you were funny, Bren,' he would say sweetly, 'you should go for it. I'll help any way I can.'

There, she already knew what he would say, so no need to call. And she knew what he would mean, too: 'Let me control this so that it doesn't get out of hand. And also, what are you using for material? Because I might need it.'

So, if you know what someone will say, and you know what they mean, why do you need them at all? Brenda wondered consciously.

She sat up and pulled an old, empty envelope and pen out of

her handbag and scribbled down what she had said on stage that night. Then she placed it carefully on her bedside table and went to sleep.

She woke to a text from Jonathan. Sometimes she wondered if he was telepathic as the few times he initiated contact always seemed to coincide with some seismic shift in her world.

'I miss you. I hope you miss me.'

Interesting. He'd only been gone a week.

Another text, from Fenella.

'When you going back on then? Got 5 for you tomorrow in Ealing. Don't say no.'

Brenda amused herself for a moment with a little imaginary farce involving sending the wrong reply to the wrong text, and then decided to send the same text to both.

'Yes.' Yes.

One felt right, one felt wrong, because if she was brutally honest, she didn't miss Jonathan all that much.

*

Ealing was a pain to get to. A bus, and two tubes, then a walk to the club. Fenella met her at the door and walked her in.

'I'm giving you five of my minutes again. I've cleared it with Jo. I'm also giving you fifty quid which is a quarter of what I'm getting. Don't get used to it, I just want to give you a sense of how it feels.'

Brenda's mind boggled – she was getting paid? This was extraordinary, she wasn't even that funny.

'Have you been working?'

'Not really, I can't concentrate in the office.'

'No, not that. I mean, working on your jokes?'

'Oh, yes, constantly, I can't think about anything else.'

'Have they improved?'

'I don't know.'

'Well, we'll find out tonight, won't we?'

'Yup.'

Brenda steeled herself. She decided not to go to the green room backstage. She'd sat in enough green rooms with Jonathan to know how it would be – too much psychological warfare for her liking and she didn't feel ready to cope with it. She ordered a drink and sat at the bar, watching the audience drift in. It was a Thursday night so this was an after-work crowd looking for something to make an early start into the weekend. It wouldn't be rowdy as they would be mindful of hangovers the next morning, but it would be cheerful. They would listen, that was the thing. In many ways the Thursday night crowd was the ideal audience for stand-up: in a good enough mood to laugh, but not so drunk they didn't care what you said and often they were real comedy buffs who themselves preferred to avoid the weekend crowds. Jonathan had taught her that, and at the thought of him, Brenda's stomach tightened. Why did she feel like she was cheating on him here, and yet not when she had slept with Pete?

The lights went out.

Brenda watched Fenella come on and give a few opening warm-up lines. The crowd were on her side immediately. She put them at ease and opened herself to receive the laughter she knew would erupt when and where she wanted it. Brenda knew what was coming, and nervously looked around the upturned faces that stretched between herself and the front of the stage. In a moment, Fenella would bring her on to do her five minutes. Then she would be up there, and the space she now occupied would be empty. Amazing how even the most banal and simple of thoughts now took an eternity to ticker across her mind. She felt that she was watching Fenella through glass and the words were muffled and unreal. Then she heard her name and forced herself off the stool and up to the low stage.

She took the mic from Fenella and faced the crowd.

Something was wrong, she could feel it immediately. There was not the warmth she had picked up from the audience at the new material night, this was more like a cool, detached interest. 'They've paid money to see Fenella,' Brenda thought rapidly, 'they don't want me. This isn't fun and cute for them – I'm annoying them just by being here.'

She looked into the face of a young woman at the front. She was looking straight back at her. She felt she had disappointed her already and nothing she could say now would change her mind. This thought process felt as if it had already stolen at least half of the now seemingly endless five minutes that stretched in front of her. 'About a pop song and a half,' she thought unexpectedly. In reality it had lasted about four seconds, but that's enough to put people off. She opened her mouth to speak.

'My boyfriend's a stand-up comedian. He thinks I'm an arsehole, literally. But I am, so it's OK... It's OK. He pumps me for material, literally.'

Silence, actual silence.

She'd totally screwed that up. The pacing was off, there was no charm to it and she was now staring straight up at the bright white spotlight that illuminated her, way over the heads of the crowd. She was not engaging them, or even communicating with them. Blood pounded through her head and a rushing was in her ears. It felt unreal, like the most clichéd of anxiety dreams. 'We're getting married next week so he'll have enough material for a tour.'

A polite laugh from roughly three people.

Nobody believed her. Of course she wasn't getting married next week. The set-up had no foundation so the punch had nothing to build on. By this point there was a tell-tale hum rising from the back of the room – people were starting to chat to one another in the darkness. A faint beeping sound and the chink of glass told Brenda that the bar was doing business. She had officially lost the audience.

Five and a half minutes later, Brenda practically ran off stage to sarcastic applause, face burning, acid in her throat. How she had stayed up there and even run longer than her allotted time was a mystery she wasn't interested in solving.

Fenella muttered to her as they crossed, 'It's OK, it's OK. I'll see you after my bit,' and tipped up to the stage.

'Ladies and gentlemen, that was our rookie comedian Brenda Monk doing her second ever gig. She's got guts, hasn't she?'

The audience cheered, relieved to have someone on stage who knew what they were doing.

Fenella delivered her fifteen minute masterclass and found Brenda skulking outside.

'That was a fucking horror show,' Brenda blurted. 'I'm never doing this again. What the fuck was I thinking? What the fuck were you thinking?'

Fenella pressed £50 in cash into Brenda's hand.

Brenda tried to give it back but Fenella wouldn't allow it.

'No, you take it. You earned it. A new stand-up would snap my arm off for fifty quid. You did your five minutes. You stayed up there.'

'Don't be fucking ridiculous. I haven't earned anything. You gave me five minutes and I totally screwed them up.'

'OK, you were too mannered, too prepared, you stared up at the lights instead of looking at the audience and your voice went all weird and shrill. But apart from that, it was good.'

Brenda laughed and handed back the money.

'Seriously, I'm not taking this.'

Fenella held it in her hand.

'I'll take this back on the condition that you do one more gig. Without me. Just one more. I'll set it up for you and we'll meet twice before it to work through your stuff. Then just do the gig and if you still hate it then I'll leave you alone.'

Brenda considered this.

'Why are you even bothering with me?'

'To annoy Jonathan.'

Brenda laughed.

'No, really, why?'

'To annoy Jonathan.'

'Ha ha. But seriously?'

'Seriously, to annoy Jonathan.'

Brenda did not make any attempt to control her face. She was defeated and annoyed – did all roads lead back to Jonathan? Fenella adjusted her posture and looked Brenda straight in the eye, focused now.

'OK, not just to annoy Jonathan. Although that will be a pleasing by-product when he finds out. I think you could be good, that's all. There's something about you, you know there is. Jonathan wouldn't be with you otherwise. He might be a wanker but he's not an idiot. And since he's been with you, he has improved no end. I think it would be exciting to see you take back your material – I've never seen anyone do that before. So many comedians mine their relationships for jokes, but when do you ever hear the other side of the story? Never. It's an experiment, think of it like that. I'm Frankenstein and you're my monster, and I love comedy, that's the truth. I love seeing something new happen in comedy. Aren't you curious, Brenda? Haven't you always been just a little bit curious, all those times you sat watching Jonathan, hearing your words come out of his mouth? Didn't you wonder whether you could do it too?

Maybe even do it better?'

Brenda stared at her shoes. She had wondered that. Many times.

6

Brenda met with Fenella twice over the next fortnight, and together they got ten minutes of material to some kind of standard. Brenda would stand in front of Fenella and deliver the jokes, a process she found excruciating. They picked over the precise wording of every line. Was it funnier to call Shrek a fascist rather than just racist? Or was fascist too much, and would kill the joke? Maybe right wing was better, funnier to give the audience the image of an old Tory buffer than some German mass-murderer? But then, racist had more punch. They found the rhythm in each set up, and the beats so that an extra unexpected line might get tagged on to the end which would flip the original premise nicely. They tried different versions, and grouped ideas so they flowed – a move from Shrek to Jane Austen in a way that felt conversational and natural, if such a thing were possible.

When Fenella decided she was as ready as she could be with almost no actual stage experience, Brenda vehemently disagreed, but resistance was futile. On their second date Fenella announced she had got Brenda an unpaid ten minute slot at a second tier comedy club in Balham two nights later. Fenella herself would be in Birmingham but she would call Brenda after the show. Brenda took this information home with her in a tightly wrapped little parcel of anxiety and sat fiddling with it sleeplessly for the next two nights. At work she stared at her computer screen, until the moment arrived when she could leave on the day of the gig, at which point she bolted out of the door and went to a nearby bar where she sat until it was time to get on the tube and head to the south east of the city. She had made the tactical decision not to go home, knowing somehow that she would not leave again that night if she did.

Brenda arrived early to the club. It was an affectionately regarded subterranean dive which had hosted a raucously successful monthly comedy night called Snort for years, booked and overseen by a grizzly monument of a man named Marvin. Brenda tentatively pushed open the door. Inside the room was empty and expectant. The main lights were on, and so somehow it felt naked and exposed – this was a room designed for darkness. There was a girl behind the bar with green hair, wearing a T-shirt with the name of a band Brenda was not cool enough to have heard of printed across it. Brenda had met this girl before when she had accompanied Jonathan to a gig here but she didn't know her name. She didn't like Brenda, she remembered that much though. Brenda didn't know exactly why but she had a vague idea that there had been some kind of one-night-stand with Jonathan back before he had met Brenda.

The girl was currently engaged in emptying a dishwasher of glasses and stacking them on the shelf below the optics in preparation for the evening's show. As Brenda approached the metallic smell and cloying warmth of the steam from inside the dishwasher hit her full in the face like a vomit cloud. Brenda stopped for a moment and gagged. The girl looked up.

'Jonathan's not here,' she said and turned away.

'Yes, I know he's not,' said Brenda. The girl shrugged.

'Broken up, have you?'

'Is Marvin out the back?' Brenda asked.

'Dunno. It's a bit early for Marvin...'

'OK, thanks.'

Brenda walked past the bar, fighting an urge to mess up the arty arrangement of beer mats advertising liquorice-flavoured shots and went over to the matt black door laid discreetly into the matt black wall to the side of the stage. Ah yes, the stage. There it was. Four black blocks on steel legs, each around a foot high, jammed together in front of a heavy black drape. A microphone in a microphone stand, its long wire snaking away down to the side, and off. And that was it. Nothing funny about this stage. Nothing funny at all. The only funny thing about this stage was who was on it. And in about an hour that would be Brenda, for a full ten minutes.

Within the rush that suddenly surged through her brain she managed to note a tiny tingle. A kernel of madness, as yet unpopped by the heat of the stage. A sliver of thrill. She would either make this room funny tonight or she would be enveloped in its silent blackness, buried alive in the softest of shrouds. She would either kill or die. For that was the language of stand-up comedy and where she used to roll her eyes at the overblown, absurd masculinity of these war-like epithets suddenly, in a white flare, she got it. She was a warrior, a gladiator, a...

'Mini-Egg?'

Brenda turned round to find Marvin standing behind her, holding a yellow bag of sugar-coated chocolate. Brenda took a handful and started crunching them hard, grateful for a new noise inside her brain.

'Still up for it, then?' Marvin raised a wiry grey eyebrow.

Brenda tipped her chin to a scornful angle and sucked her teeth.

'Of course. What do you think I am? I'm going to fuck this

place up. You'll never have seen anything like it in your life. You'll be begging me to stop before someone ruptures something...'

Marvin raised a hand to stop the flow and Brenda abruptly shut up. Aware she was now breathing heavily through her nose, she felt her breasts rising and falling – too big, too big, too cumbersome, not flat and swift and aerodynamic enough for this – and a redness creeping up around her neck. She was a fraud. She was sure they both knew it, and her pathetic imitation of the combative style of the more established stand-ups as they psyched each other out backstage only served to underline the point. This was a terrible mistake. She could leave now and no-one would think any the less of her. Well, except for Brenda herself, but what did that matter? She'd let herself down before. Jesus, if you can't let yourself down from time to time then we're all doomed, and anyone who says different has clearly never been on a diet. Marvin knew she would fail. It was obvious. She'd be on stage, the yawning silence threatening to swallow her whole. She'd forget all her jokes. Word would get out that she, Brenda Monk, Jonathan Cape's on-off-on-fuck-buddies-as-an-experiment-on-off-let's-just-try-being-friends-for-a-bit-on-off-definitely-now-off-ooops-on-again girlfriend had actually thought she was funny. That would be the biggest laugh of the whole evening.

She framed herself to turn and leave just as the doors swung open and in swaggered Rossly Barns, a rangy, long-haired Australian comedian in grey jeans, studded belt, large boots and a leather jacket, whose own personal confidence, won from years of experience, appeared to know no bounds.

'Hey, Brenda. Is Jonathan on tonight, then?'

'No.'

Brenda jumped as she heard her voice come out deep and low, with a strong West Country accent. Then she realised it was

Marvin talking.

'Brenda is.'

Rossly's reaction said it all. He pretended to collapse and die on the floor. It was a long, loud, drawn out death and when Brenda looked round, she could see the girl behind the bar laughing ostentatiously.

'Get up, Rossly. A woman pissed herself right there last week,' Marvin said.

Rossly stopped and leapt to his feet.

Brenda smiled at him sweetly, offering her hand as he steadied himself.

'So you're going on, are you, sweetheart?'

'Yup. So you'd better dust your best jokes off or you're going to look pretty amateur.'

'Strong words, female, strong words. No Jonathan?'

'Nope.'

'Well, let me say this. If you're funny tonight I'll fuck your brains out, how about that?'

Rossly had a glint in his eye that was not unappealing. He had a reputation for somehow getting away with the most profoundly crude material, and not for nothing. Brenda looked at him, breathing in the thickened atmosphere produced by a combination of recklessness and control – a comedian's two principal weapons of choice. She could learn from Rossly.

'And if I'm not funny?'

He paused. Perfect timing.

'I'll still fuck your brains out. I'd say that's a pretty good deal for you, babe.'

And then Brenda started to feel excited.

'And for you too,' she said, 'you get to fuck me either way.'

'Either way, eh?' Rossly arched an eyebrow. 'How about both ways?'

Brenda let out a shout of a laugh. Rossly regarded her for a second, clearly assessing the impact of his little witticism and then, having made a mental note of the gag and rated it according to his own personal criteria, he moved off with Marvin, striking up a conversation about the running order. Brenda followed them to the matt black door in the matt black wall that led backstage and walked through.

The door led straight into a small shabby room with a toilet cubicle to one side and another door at the far end. Beyond which lay an even smaller room that served as Marvin's office where Marvin and Rossly were bending over the desk, scrutinising the order in which the comedians would go on. Brenda guessed that Rossly was trying to make sure he had the sweet spot: the first act on after the interval when the crowd would be nicely warmed up, refreshed from a short break but not too tired to listen and laugh. This was surely why Rossly had turned up early. A comedian of his calibre would never normally bother to arrive until half an hour or so before the show started, at the earliest, so Brenda idly wondered what his agenda was. Perhaps he knew something she didn't. Perhaps there was to be someone important in the audience that night.

Next to the office was a man-sized space with a worn red velvet curtain hanging over it, slightly too short and too narrow, but big enough to enjoy a final hidden moment before stepping out into the full beam of the spotlight. The lack of a door here meant that the other comedians waiting their turn had to be quiet when the show was on, forced to listen to all the other acts, the triumphs and the tragedies. There was no escape from the pressing judgement of one's peers here and the awareness of this silent, hidden audience was probably the most intimidating aspect of performing at this particular club. In other larger venues the green room was a distance away from the stage, with a door or two in between. At those places the stage time was almost a relief from the constant scrutiny of other comics, as when they were not required by architecture to keep quiet they lost interest in the gig itself and set out to good-naturedly destroy one another instead. But not here. There was to be no such relief tonight. Beyond the curtain was the left wing of the stage. Beyond that, a microphone and the unknown. At some stage in the club's history a rather half-hearted attempt had been made to make this cramped, claustrophobic space feel like a comfortable green room for several acts or a large dressing room for one. Perhaps when it was built there had been a sweetly innocent plan to have local theatre groups perform Tom Stoppard plays here but such an idea had been quickly stubbed out by the sheer force of economics. Stand-up comedy was cheap to put on and made a bomb at the bar. Local theatre groups required all kinds of expensive kit and attracted the kind of audiences that drank one slimline tonic and went home.

There were two mirrors edged with naked bulbs, or open sockets where the bulbs should be. They were never turned on. The room was lit instead by an old, brown-fringed table lamp on a small table in the far corner. It was dingy but necessarily so, in order to avoid any bleeding of light onto the stage from under the curtain during show time. Round the edge of three-quarters of the room was a waist height sideboard where actors might lay out their make-up and good luck cards. Given that no actors had ever entered this room and those comedians who considered make-up integral to their public image usually arrived with the mask intact, along with the fact that a good luck card at a gig would be a sign of weakness and therefore an open invitation to ridicule, there was nothing on this sideboard other than three or four stickily empty pint glasses, a barren ash tray or two – a hang-over from the days when smoking was legal back here – and a mysterious dildo no-one wished to claim, remove or touch.

There were a couple of cheap metal framed chairs with tatty red cushions half-attached and two small matching sofas which may well have looked inviting at some point in the mid-1980s. The carpet was stained in various hues and damp in the corner next to the toilet room. The toilet room had no door as such, just a wooden screen that could be dragged across the entrance, although the comedians usually didn't bother. Partly out of genuine laziness, partly out of a desire to appear unbothered by suburban concerns for propriety and privacy. In short, this was not the sort of place Joan Collins would feel able to prepare to meet her public.

Brenda had been in this room a couple of times before but only in her capacity as Jonathan's girlfriend. She had sat on the left sofa trying look self-sufficient and mildly disinterested, alert yet unimpressed – the demeanour of any comedian's girlfriend who knew the ropes. She had always felt she was there by invitation and could be ejected at any time and so it had been important that her presence take up as little of the room as possible. Now, it was different. Now she was an act. She had a right to be there on her own terms and she must show that she was worthy of it. She must expand to fill the space, or be crushed by the others. If comedy was 80% confidence she needed to increase her confidence by around 79% within the next... Brenda checked her watch... forty minutes.

Rossly sauntered out of Marvin's office.

'I've told Marvin to put you on after me, babe,' he announced. 'You're doing ten, right?'

'Yeah, ten.'

'You got ten?'

'If I take it slowly...'

'Better to do a fucking amazing seven and leave 'em panting than fuck it up with a slow ten.'

'Yeah, I know.'

'Not as if you're getting paid so Marvin doesn't give a shit if you're three minutes light, do you Marv?'

Marvin looked up from the desk.

'Suits me better if she doesn't go on at all. Ludo always runs long and people start to worry about their trains once it gets on for 11 o'clock.'

Rossly nodded.

'There you are, babe. You don't even have to go on, if you don't want to...'

He left that hanging in the air like a malingering fart.

Brenda smiled. Rossly couldn't help but try to psych her out, throw her off her stride. It was instinctive. No point getting pouty about it. It was part of the game.

'Nah, I want to go on. I've got some new material I want to try out at an intimate club like this. You know, not so much pressure, eye contact with the front three rows. I like a small crowd.'

Brenda marvelled at the level of bullshit coming out of her mouth. New material? It was all new material.

'Sure you do, babe.' Rossly smiled crookedly.

He was sizing her up, not as competition, but as prey. Brenda smiled back, realising just in time that appearing confident was more important than feeling confident. Lesson one.

Rossly broke the atmosphere by opening his bag, looking for the CD of music he wanted Marvin to put on when he walked on stage. Brenda breathed out silently and felt for her small notebook in her jacket pocket. She sat down on the left sofa and pulling out a pen, she opened the book and started copying her set order onto the back of her hand. It was a waterproof pen which meant that the set order would remain on the back of her hand for anything up to a week, but at least it wouldn't rub off when she started sweating. And she had already started sweating.

The door to the green room swung open again and a stocky man in his early forties grunted into the room. Rossly glanced up.

'Hey Mike, buddy – you look like shit – you got cancer or something?'

Mike, he of the tired and wife and faded dreams that Brenda remembered from the Attic Bar in Edinburgh, adjusted to the small but deliberate body blow, and dumped his rucksack on the floor.

'It's full blown AIDS – I think I got it when your mum let me butt-fuck her in Melbourne last year.'

Rossly smirked and nodded, and went back to looking for his CD. Brenda sniggered to herself. Mike noticed her sitting on the sofa and frowned.

'I thought Jonathan was in New York or something.'

'He is,' said Brenda.

'So...' Mike looked at her with a quizzical expression.

'I'm going on.' Brenda heard herself say these words, and once again, the reality lurched in her stomach like a bad prawn.

'She's got some new material she wants to try out, right, Bren?' Rossly's voice leaned in to Mike's mounting confusion.

'Oh, right. I didn't know...I mean, I never realised...'

'You'd better not fuck it up tonight, Mike. Brenda's bringing the good stuff.'

Mike narrowed his eyes for a fraction of a second. He'd been on the circuit for over ten years now, and never got above club level. Never even made it to headliner. To Mike anyone was a threat, regardless of experience. Mike had seen enough people start after him, climb past him, and never glance back down the crevasse to see if he was OK, so he couldn't afford to be generous.

Brenda studied her hand while Mike walked into the toilet room and unbuttoned his awful black jeans. As the sound and smell of piss, fermented on the long tube ride down from Acton, filled the room, Brenda gagged again.

Was this really what she wanted? Rossly's words played in her head, 'You don't even have to go on, if you don't want to.' Did she want to? Did she?

She closed her eyes. She imagined getting up, making her excuses, walking out of the black door, through the bar, past the security guard and back out onto the street. She pictured hailing a cab and climbing in. She pictured telling the friendly, fatherly cabbie her address and sitting back, watching London slide past, not knowing, not asking, not caring, not judging. She would pay the cab, open her front door, slip inside and pour herself a glass of wine. She would put the TV on. She'd be home in time for *The Apprentice* if she left now. It would be as if this had never happened. Marvin wouldn't care, Mike would be relieved and Rossly would certainly find someone else to fuck whichever way he pleased. She could hide from Fenella, and what did she even owe her anyway? They barely knew each other.

She was drifting in a sea of sweet relief, when something gripped her inside, an unwelcome clench of regret and disappointment. A feeling that her life would continue without her if she stepped off now. All she could picture was herself sitting at home, bored, sadly downing a bottle of wine alone and wishing she was back at the club. That couldn't happen. The possibility of it was worse than the current reality. She was going to stay here, she knew now, and wait her turn and walk through the curtain, and with the screaming silence of the green room behind her and the potential actual silence of the crowd in front of her, she was going to tell her jokes.

Ludo Kinkovic's arrival brought her back into the room. He

pushed open the door and stood still, letting it swing back to a closed position in his face. For a brief moment he was framed by the open door, a frozen clown, bright pink hair gelled into a high quiff, a diamond in each ear, heavy black eye-liner and a shock of neon lipstick and a lunatic smile on his face. Rossly smirked, Mike grimaced and Brenda laughed in spite of the fact that it was not cool to do so. Marvin briefly looked up, and then looked down again. Ludo then entered the room as if nothing had happened.

'Evening all. What's the plan for tonight then? Anyone fancy doing a spot of the comedic, like?'

His mockney accent grated, but Brenda couldn't entirely hate him for it as it wasn't entirely inauthentic, just embellished a little round the edges. Ludo was bi-sexual, which formed the greater part of his act. Furthermore, he was perfectly willing to accuse fellow comedians of homophobia if the mood took him.

'Ludo, you appalling queer, you've gone pink. Just when I was getting used to the green,' Rossly drawled at him in his favourite 'straight-talking Bruce' voice.

'Queer is still a pejorative, Rossly darling. So unless you've ever sucked cock, I suggest you leave that language on the plane from Oz-land.'

'I find the term "Oz-land" deeply offensive, Ludo, to me and my fellow countrymen.'

'But not countrywomen? Tell me, do ladies even have the vote in your native land?'

'Yeah, that's why I had to leave.'

Ludo smiled benignly and slung his handbag on the sofa beside Brenda.

'Hello dear, have we met?'

'No, I'm Brenda Monk. I'm doing ten minutes.'

'Lovely. I shan't do any of my periods and mascara material

then, so you'll have something to talk about.'

Brenda gave him a chilly smile, but her stomach seized. She wished Fenella was here. She even wished Jonathan was here. She knew green rooms could be like this, but this was unusually arctic.

Ludo laughed to himself.

'No, really, I love lady-comics. You're so *brave*. MIKE! I didn't see you there, why must you always be so *invisible*. Really, last week at *The Last Laugh* I thought you were going to disappear from the stage entirely.'

Mike ignored him.

'Are you going to be a cunt all night, Ludo?' Rossly asked.

'Oh, I should think so, yes. I've got some friends coming and that always brings out the worst in me.'

Friends seemed a very distant concept to Brenda now. Friends couldn't help her here. Marvin stood up.

'OK, let's go.'

And Ludo strode out onto the stage.

'Come on, then, if you're coming, come on. Sit down, look there's a lovely seat right on the front row here, put your bottom there, bring your drink, oh is this your friend? Hello, friend – what's your name? What? Shout it out. What? Hilfer? Hilfer? Ah, das is gut, mein Hilfer, kommst zu hier and sitten das backsiden downen. What? *Heifer*? Your name is *Heifer*? What's the matter – didn't your parents like you? Oh HESTER! Hester, that's my favourite name, did you know that? I wish you'd said that to begin with, we could have had a lovely chat, but it's too late because I have to start the show. GOOD EVENING LADIES AND GENTLEMEN and WELCOME to SNORT! Yes, you're right to cheer because this is the bloody best comedy night in South London and we've got a fantastic line-up for you. There's ME. Thank you for that, much obliged. There's my favourite

Antipodean anteater – what? He's got a big nose and those funny little eyes – he has! Wait til I tell you... it's Rossly Barns! Oh you like him at the back, sir? Good, good. How long are you planning on staying in the UK, Mr Barns? We've got Mike Smith – no, not that one, he's going down on Sarah Greene as we speak. No, Mike Smith, the famous comedian. Yes, he's going to be whinging about his marriage I should think, but in an hilarious fashion. And then we've got a gorgeous little newcomer called Brenda Monk who you all have to be extra nice to. So, look, before I bring on the first act, I need to talk to you about my vagina. No, seriously, my figurative vagina is in a LOT of pain...'

Backstage, nobody spoke.

Ludo had fucked them all up in turn, just as he was known to. Rossly was grinding his teeth. Mike furiously scrolled through his phone. Brenda was sat white-faced, frozen to the sofa. Only Marvin smirked to himself as he worked through some accounts. The gales of laughter from the other side of the curtain had secured Ludo another booking before he even came off stage. Ludo was wrapping up, and calling Mike onstage. As Ludo left he pushed the mic stand down hard so that the first thing Mike had to do on entering was raise it, creating an awkward pause and putting him at an immediate disadvantage. It was a cheap old trick but Ludo had revived it in recent months. Back in the green room, Ludo took a mirror from his bag and studied his eyeliner.

'Hey Ludo, you do that mic stand shit to Brenda here, I'll punch your lights out after the gig.'

Ludo bristled a little. Rossly had been known to throw a punch every now and again and so it wasn't an entirely empty threat. Rossly had a certain danger to him in any case. He was unpredictable and didn't always seem wholly in control of his long, spidery limbs. He was thin but he was also tall and he could get a good hit in from above if he was of a mind to. Ludo didn't answer, but he had clearly absorbed the warning. Mike's voice, amplified on stage, penetrated the frosty silence.

'Yeah, so like Ludo said, I'm married. No don't laugh at that, that's not even a joke. OK, seriously, don't laugh, now, because... yeah, I'm married. OK, that laugh was just patronising. I haven't even started yet. I'M MARRIED. I have to do at least one joke, that's not my only joke you know, my act isn't just coming out here and saying "I'm married". Well, it kind of is but I like to think there's more to it than that. So, I'm married and my wife is beautiful. No, don't laugh at that, she is! She's beautiful and kind and understanding and supportive and sexy... BUT... OK, I thought you'd laugh more at that to be honest, but perhaps you've used it all up on my NON-JOKES...'

Ludo peered through the curtain. He didn't need to say anything, the contempt for Mike poured out of him like sour milk tipped down a drain.

Rossly approached Brenda on the sofa.

'You OK, rookie?'

'Yeah. I mean... yeah.'

Rossly nodded.

'You like your jokes.'

'Uh, yeah.'

'Well, fuck anyone that doesn't then. You just say your jokes, and come back in here. No big deal, OK?'

Brenda nodded, mute with fear now. This didn't feel like the gigs she had done with Fenella. There was no well-established, utterly loved and trusted comedian going on to introduce her and guide her up to the stage. No, there was Ludo who had just walked straight past Mike's open hand in front of the whole audience, who were now laughing. Ludo had created the tone of the room with his caustic manner and sharp-ended jokes and people were now laughing at the meaner end of the gag spectrum. Rossly had the experience to adapt to this and mental archive of material to pull up now he knew how the evening was shaping up. Brenda had precisely ten minutes of material she had never performed before. Brenda felt a chill of certainty that she was going to bomb. And now the idea was in her head, it was even more likely to happen. She would carry it on stage with her, an invisible backpack that would give her a slight stoop and a suspicious eye and the crowd would sense it instantly, in its animal way, and not like her.

Mike sighed, picked up a brown envelope with his name on it and dropped heavily onto the sofa. He discreetly opened the package and ran his finger across the banknotes and then, satisfied it was all there, opened a beer. Ludo was announcing that there would be a short break and they would be back with more in ten minutes and with that he bounded back into the room. Mike stared into the middle distance and drank his beer steadily. Ludo pulled out his phone and Tweeted his whereabouts and general feelings about them. The door was pushed open shyly and three very beautiful androgynous looking boys who could not have been more than nineteen years old drifted in.

'Here you are!' shouted Ludo. 'Come and save me, my pretties, look what I have to put up with.'

Ludo gestured around the room and the boys nodded awkwardly to no-one in particular.

'I've got a treat here, but you have to be under twenty to enjoy it,' Ludo said extravagantly.

'Guess that rules you out,' Rossly retorted.

Ludo just tossed his head and pulled a bottle of Prosecco out of his bag. He pushed his three boys into one corner, popped the cork and began whispering to them as he poured out four glasses.

Brenda looked at her hand and the thick blue printed words in a list that covered the back of it.

'Boyfriend, hair, shaved vagina, Shrek, Jane Austen, nipples, glue.'

Rossly was standing behind her, reading them out quietly.

'Stop it. Don't jinx it.'

Rossly smiled with some unexpected warmth.

'Let me tell you a little secret about comedy, Brenda Monk. You can't jinx it if you do it right.'

'Well, that's easy for you to say.'

'Yes it is, but it applies to you too. Here's my best piece of advice for you, are you ready? Always acknowledge what's happening in the room.'

He paused to let this sink in.

'Always acknowledge what's happening in the room. Do you understand what I mean by that?'

'Kind of.'

'It's rule one. You don't just go out there and say your jokes as if there's no-one there...'

'But earlier you said...'

'Yeah, I know I said you're just going to say your jokes and then come back in here, and that's true at the very basic level. I said that because you looked like you were going to puke your neck up or run away, and I can't fuck you later if either of those things happen.'

Brenda laughed sharply.

Rossly continued, 'But a properly good gig, like the kind of gig we all dream about? That's a conversation. You might do most of the talking but it's still a conversation. So like when you are talking to someone, you have to listen as well as speak. It's just the same in comedy, except you have to do your listening at the same time as you're doing your speaking, you get me? The audience will shift and change in front of you. Not physically, unless everyone leaves, which may and does happen. I mean their non-physical form will shift, like waves of dark matter, and you have to tune your antennae to them so that you can accommodate it. The best comedians can marginally shift their material so they still get to say what they want to say but present it to each audience according to the signals they are picking up, so that every audience has the same but different experience. So if you are open to that you can't jinx it. Because if you were jinxed you would just tell the audience you were worried about being jinxed and that in itself would become a joke. Do you see what I'm saying?'

Brenda was captivated by him. He had delivered this speech leaning over the back of the sofa, looking into her eyes. His were dark blue with small, uneven yellow flecks in them, so that they seemed like pools of deep water with sunlight playing on the surface.

'Look, Brenda Monk, I'm not saying you're going to pull that off tonight. Essentially, whatever happens tonight can be written off. If you have a great one, it's beginner's luck. If you have a shocker, it's because you're new. So you don't need to worry about tonight. What you need to ask yourself is, are you planning on doing this for real? Because if you are you need to start thinking about your antennae, not that list of words on the back of your hand. I like the sound of the shaved vagina, by the way.'

And he gave her a look so filthy Brenda felt a dollop of moisture expand in her knickers.

'OK?'

Marvin indicated that Ludo should get back on and start the second half. Rossly gave him a wall-burning look and Ludo didn't mess about. He brought Rossly on without too much ado and left the microphone stand at its correct height. Rossly practically jumped the distance between the curtained gap and the centre of the stage, grabbed the mic before the applause for Ludo's exit could die down and started singing into it in the voice of Elvis Presley.

'Ah well ah bless mah soul, ah what's wrong with me, I'm itching like a man on a fuzzy tree, I can't seem to shake these tiny bugs, I'm in love, I fucked your mum, oh-oh-oh. Oh don't act shocked, for god's sakes, grow up, this is a comedy club. If you want a nice innocent evening go and find some nice old kids' TV presenter to entertain you... Jesus, it's hot under these lights. Seriously, I'm sweating like a 1970s comedian up here... so this Yewtree thing's getting a bit out of hand, isn't it? I was looking for an old episode of *Top of the Pops* on YouTube yesterday and I couldn't find any 'cos of the new porn filters my internet provider's put on.'

'Nurghhwahhhhlngggggoh,' came a shout from the crowd.

Brenda tensed immediately. Heckling was always awkward.

Rossly stopped and looked out into the room with a curious half smile.

'Hello friend, I didn't quite catch that. Care to repeat it?'

Silence.

'Oh come on now, don't be shy. This isn't TV, we can be interactive...'

Silence. And then,

'WOUHGHHAH!'

'Awww, look, I'm so glad they've let you out for the night. Stay behind at the end and I'll be happy to sign your straitjacket.'

Big laugh.

Brenda relaxed and made a mental note for the future. Rossly continued.

'Now, where was I, ah yes, sexual assault, my favourite topic. It's weird to me though, people keep saying "women didn't mind it back then", you know, in the seventies when feeling up females was every old man's favourite hobby. But I don't know, surely women did mind, it's just they didn't say anything until now, what with feminism and all that. So that means for centuries men have been thinking women LOVE being groped at work. Spare a thought for us poor men, ladies, with our uncontrollable desires and URGES. I'm so frustrated these days I've had to start touching up pigs, but it's OK because they really do love it. Well, they must do, they never say anything.'

Ludo was not watching Rossly, he couldn't bear to. Ludo was slick and confident but Rossly was the better comedian and he knew it. They both knew it. Brenda felt his restless eyes alight on her.

'I remember my first gig,' Ludo's affectedly wistful tone was far from comforting. 'God, I thought I'd never leave the house again, let alone do another gig...'

'Thanks, that's really helpful.'

'Oh darling, you're not nervous, are you? Not down here in this grot-hole. Their IQs are in double figures out there.'

Marvin did not react, even as Ludo's eyes slid over to where he was sitting to check for a reaction. Brenda shrugged.

'What kind of comedy are you aiming for?'

'Funny comedy, I think, mainly.'

Ludo emitted a small, involuntary laugh from somewhere inside his right nostril.

'Yes, I always think that's the best kind.'

His attention flew to the stage.

'Well, good luck, dear.'

And Ludo moved across the room, ready to take over on stage.

'Thank you, dudes, you've been great, and listen, we've got a fantastic new act coming on next. She's a great friend of mine, she's really hilarious and she's finally decided to try some of her jokes out here for you lucky people. So please, give a really warm welcome to the hottest new comic this side of Balham, it's Brenda Monk!'

Ludo froze, one foot on the edge of the stage but still hidden by the curtain. He whipped round to look at Brenda, who was still sat on the sofa.

Rossly called her name from the stage.

'Brenda Monk, come on out here babe. You're making me look like more of a dick than I usually do!'

The audience laughed.

'Well, get out there then,' Ludo hissed at Brenda, eyes glittering, lip curled.

Brenda leapt up and crashed through the curtain, as Ludo slithered back. Rossly hugged her warmly and quickly and put the microphone straight into her hand. He waved at the crowd, igniting a further round of applause and cheers on his departure, giving Brenda a sound cushion to rest on for a second as she got her bearings.

'Hi, I'm Brenda Monk and I am trying this to see if I'm better at it than my boyfriend, who is a really successful stand-up comedian who does jokes all about me. Yes, you may well laugh nervously. That's what I do every time I go to one of his gigs. At the last one I went to, I found out he loves anal sex. And there's me thinking he just had a really big finger all this time. I tell you, I always face the front now – yup, missionary all the way for me. But I don't mind him talking about me, I just think maybe I should get paid for it every so often. Not that I'm getting paid for tonight. Yeah, that's right – I'm exploiting myself for a change. He doesn't have the monopoly on exploitation of this vagina. He's been talking recently onstage about the time he shaved his pubes to make his cock look bigger. I thought I'd give it a try too. Yeah, now my vagina looks HUGE! I'm so proud. He seems less keen, though. He's away at the moment, so I'm cut loose. Thank you, sir, meet me outside in nine minutes.'

'WOOUUGHHHHHAAAAALLLL!'

Shit, it was happening again – same guy.

The crowd laughed at the idiocy of the incoherent drunk at the back, and then quietened down, awaiting Brenda's response.

Brenda froze. She just stared into the blackness and all she could think was, 'I can't handle this like Rossly.'

And then by some miracle, she found she was saying, 'Hey, I'm working here – I don't come to McDonald's and knock the broom out of your hand.'

A huge laugh that rolled from the front of the room to the rear and back again, like two oceans meeting.

Brenda was delighted and then, on reaching for the next piece of material, found her mind was entirely blank. Free-wheeling in featureless mental space, she simply made noises whilst grasping at anything that seemed solid.

'Ha. Ha ha ha ha. Ummm... OK, so, so... what was I saying?'

The audience shifted a little.

Brenda became aware of a screaming voice in her head, 'Hand, hand, hand.'

'Hand,' she said, and the audience blinked back at her, as confused as she was. And then she remembered to look at the back of her hand.

Shrek. There it was, Shrek. That was next.

'Oh, yeah, so I was watching *Shrek* on the TV the other day, and it struck me that it's basically a right wing allegory. It's all about race, right? Yeah, I said it – Shrek is a massive racist. No listen, all the displaced fairytale people come and live in his swamp because they have been sent away from their land, so they are basically refugees from an oppressive regime subjecting them to torture. So Shrek, or Shrek W. Bush as I like to call him, does a deal with the leader of the oppressive regime that if he finds him a girl to marry, he can get rid of all the fairytale refugees from his swamp, or what I like to think of as Florida. I mean, it's right wing propaganda. Yeah, so Shrek is a racist. OK, then I was going to talk about... Jane Austen. YES, sorry, speaking of massive racists, who here likes Jane Austen? Only three of you? Come on, there must be more than that. She's on your ten pound note, for god's sake. There was a big fuss about that, of course. Lots of people thought she wasn't a good person to represent women because she basically ignored the existence of black people. But Queen Victoria ignored the existence of gay people and she was on all the money for decades. I like Jane Austen but I do worry about how white her world was. Although who can blame her. I mean, have any of you been to Bath recently? If I lived in Hampshire and only went on holiday to Bath I probably wouldn't believe in black people either. Oh, oh – the red light is on, so... So, I had a bit more but... but I have to wrap up now, so thanks very much, I'm Brenda Monk. I said that at the beginning. Oh it's flashing now so, you can't see it I know but, OK great, thanks, thanks very much! Goodnight sorry.'

Brenda flew off the stage as Ludo passed her.

'Brenda Monk, everyone. Isn't she sweet? Who else is still thinking about her vagina, though? I know YOU are, sir...'

Silence from the heckler but the crowd went nuts.

Brenda's hands shook as she rummaged in her handbag for nothing in particular, she just wanted something to do with them. Adrenaline pumping through her veins made her legs wobbly and her head light.

'Wasn't too bad,' Marvin said gruffly from his office cubby-hole. 'You can have another unpaid ten next month, if you want it.'

Brenda thought she might be sick, and could barely take

in what he was saying. She looked up a little wildly and caught
Rossly's eye. He smiled.

'How do you feel about that?'

'I... don't know. OK. I don't know. I can't remember anything
about it... I...'

Rossly pushed a beer into her hand.

'Drink this, OK? And just calm down. It was fine. It was fine.
You have a couple of nice ideas and you got a few laughs and you
did your full ten. It wasn't a disaster, so just chill.'

'Yeah, yeah. Chill, yeah, just chill. I'm chilling.'

Brenda gulped the beer which fizzed and frothed around her
nose. She wiped it with the back of her hand. She felt out of
bodied, as if she was looking at herself from above. Every part
of her jangled with discombobulation. She could barely feel her
hands although she knew one of them held a beer and was not
dropping it, so they must still be connected. She was finding it
hard to focus on anything at all.

'It's just adrenaline, it'll clear in a minute. Sit down.'

Brenda sat down. Mike was still sat on the other sofa, making
his way through a third beer. He was frowning slightly.

'Does Jonathan know you're doing this?' he asked, in a neutral
sounding voice.

'Uh, not really. I'm going to tell him.'

'That was his heckle put down, wasn't it?'

'Uh, yeah, yeah it was. It was all I could think of to say.'

Brenda went hot and cold at the very idea that she might
have stolen something.

There was an awkward pause, an unspoken accusation of
that most heinous of crimes – joke thievery – hung in the air,
before Rossly tutted.

'Fuck's sake, Mike. That heckle put down is older than your
mum's cunt. It's community property by now. When you're up

there and in the shit, you use whatever you can. We help each other out, right?'

Mike nodded slightly, his mouth a straight line. He stood up.

'Well, I'm going to hit the road. Got to be up early for the kids.'

'The pram in the hall, Mike, the pram in the hall.'

'Yeah, thanks.'

Ludo had wrapped up the gig and re-entered the green room, prompting Mike to gather up his bag and leave without particularly wishing anyone good-bye.

Ludo stared out Rossly, fury packed down like ice at his commandeering of the roll of MC.

Rossly simply muttered, 'Sorry mate – couldn't trust you to do it properly,' cracked open a cold can of beer from the tiny fridge and sank half of it in one.

Ludo stood with his arms folded, icily surveying him as he did so.

'Got a little crush, Rossly, darling? You do always let your cock get the better of you, don't you?'

'I am restraining myself from putting it in your mouth just to shut you up.'

Ludo stalked away, and as he opened the door to the green room, a tall, serene looking woman walked in. Rossly went over to her, pulled her to him and kissed her softly. Brenda gawped – she had, in spite of herself, been looking forward to being pursued by Rossly as he tried to make good on his promise to 'fuck her', even though she had been planning to turn him down. Now she felt foolish. It had been a joke, it seemed.

'Brenda, this is my girlfriend, Nina.'

Nina smiled lazily.

'Oh yeah, you were on tonight, weren't you? Yeah, well done. You were good.'

'No, I wasn't good. I forgot half my stuff and I didn't finish and people didn't laugh that much and I didn't connect it all properly and I screwed up the end.'

Nina paused and nodded, then seemed to realise that Brenda had finished speaking.

'Yeah, OK. Well, well done anyway.'

'Thanks.'

Something about this woman made Brenda feel like a teenager. She was elegant, dressed like a grown up, Middleton glossy hair tousled down her back and she wore no make-up. Rossly's over-attentiveness suggested that this was a relatively new relationship, and that furthermore, despite his over-confidence, Nina was way out of what he considered to be his league. Nina stood, unspeaking, a far-away look in her eyes and a small Mona Lisa smile on her shell-like lips. Rossly was already gathering up his stuff, anxious not to keep this extraordinary woman of his waiting.

'Hey, good luck, Brenda Monk. You're initiated now. Just got to keep working. You're not bad, you know? Not bad. Do as many gigs as you can.'

Brenda nodded dumbly and tried not to look disappointed and deflated. All the energy had now gone from her body and she wanted nothing more than to eat a trashy Chinese takeaway and go to sleep for a very long time. Rossly left, guiding Nina through the door, whispering in her ear so she giggled attractively.

'So, do you want this ten or not?' Marvin asked gruffly.

'Uh, yes. Yes please,' Brenda replied before she could change her mind.

7

Brenda awoke in Pete's bed to the sound of her phone ringing. Blearily, she reached to pick it up and Pete stirred beside her, then rolled over. Jonathan. Sliding quietly from the bed, Brenda took the call as she descended the stairs after closing the door carefully behind her.

'Hi, it's... It's early.'

'So, Brenda, have you got summin' you like to tell me?'

He sounded drunk. Despite the fact that they had barely communicated in almost a month, she still went cold. Her brain worked as fast as it could given that it was only a little past 6am, and she had been awake until 4.30.

'Ummm... look, I don't know who told you, but...'

'Good ole Mike Smith tole me. Good ole Mike Smith. My buddy Mike Smith, Mike Smith, my only frien'.'

How the hell did Mike Smith know she had got drunk at the gig after Rossly left, then thumbed through her Facebook messages and essentially booty-called Pete, who had been a little bewildered by her appearance at his door twenty minutes later but had stepped up to the occasion admirably, delivering over three hours of solid gold shagging until they had both fallen asleep in his clean, white bed. For a start, Mike had left the venue before she had. Had he followed her? Brenda held the phone away from her ear and stuck her head under the kitchen tap, lapping the cold water like a cat and hoping it might miraculously cure her hangover and get her out of whatever trouble she was clearly in. She turned the tap off and gave Jonathan her attention.

'Mike Smith doesn't know anything.'

'About comedy, no, but he seems to know an awful lot 'bout you, lil Brenda.'

'Like what?'

'Oh no, I wanna hear it from you.'

Brenda took a deep breath and decided to be honest. Jonathan was always talking about the value of honesty, so she bit the coin to see what it was really made of.

'Well, I've been lonely and...'

Jonathan didn't even let her finish.

'Lonely? So you decided to steal all my jokes and go out and try being a comedian, did you?'

Ah, so that was it. Relief flowed over Brenda.

'Brenda? Did you? Thought you'd get out there and try an' be funny while my back's turned?'

'I was interested... to see... how it might turn out.'

'Who got you the gig?'

'No-one. I got it myself.'

'No you fuckin' didn't. Someone got you the gig. No-one gets to play Snort on the third time out. Not even for an unpaid ten.'

Wow, Mike had lost no time in giving Jonathan the details. Brenda felt a plume of irritation rise inside her.

'Fenella Lawrence got me the gig. She's been helping me with my material.'

Silence. Ominous. Brenda took the opportunity to drink again.

'Fenella fuckin' Lawrence. Your material. It's my fuckin'

material.'

'No it isn't. I wrote it, it's mine.'

'But it's about us, isn't it? And I do jokes about us.'

'Yeah, well, last time I looked, I was an equal participant in us, so I don't see why I shouldn't do jokes about it too.'

'BUT YOU'RE NOT A FUCKIN' STAND-UP COMEDIAN ARE YOU?'

'Says who?'

'Says me. Says everyone. You're not.'

'Well, maybe I am now.'

'Are you funny?'

This was put with such childlike simplicity that Brenda actually laughed out loud.

'I think I might be, Jonathan – I think it's possible that I am.'

'Was it a good gig, then?'

Brenda knew he was asking this in spite of himself. He couldn't help it. He was an obsessive and when it came down to it, nothing else mattered.

'It was OK. I mean, plenty of room for improvement but I think I might have something... I think I might have something to say.'

Silence again.

And then, so quietly she could barely hear it, 'I love you, Brenda.'

This was so unexpected that Brenda thought she must have misheard. She held her breath.

'Did you hear me?'

'I think so.'

'I said I love you.'

'Yes, that's what I thought.'

'Well, aren't you going to say it back?'

Brenda was floundering now. She had never heard him

so pathetic, and yet a month ago this would have been all her fantasies. She closed her eyes and rested her throbbing head on the cool door of the fridge.

'Bren?'

It sounded like he was crying a little bit. She answered softly.

'I do love you, yes, in a way. OK? Have you been drinking, Jonathan?'

'I don'know. A bit.'

'Is it going well over there?'

'I don'know. It's different. They like different things. But I'm getting used to it.'

'OK, well that's good. You, er, you must be tired. Why don't you lie down?'

'OK, I'll lie down.'

Brenda heard him collapse onto what she assumed must be his bed.

'Can you come and see me, Bren? I want to see your face.'

Brenda made some fast calculations – how much paid holiday did she have left?

She also had a flashback to Pete's hands gripping her buttocks as she climbed on top of him.

'I'll ask at work and see what I can do.'

'Are you going to do another gig?'

Brenda weighed up her response, but she didn't flinch now.

'I think so. Yes, Marvin said I could have another unpaid ten next month, and I might look for some more open spots. You know, any advice would be really... helpful... Hello? Jonathan?'

A snore told her he was asleep. She pressed the red button on her phone and saw three missed calls from Fenella from last night. She'd deal with that later.

She crept back up the stairs to Pete. He was awake, and smiling.

'Everything OK?'

'Yup.'

'Are you getting back in here?'

Brenda got back under the covers and Pete ran a flat palm down the length of her body.

'I'm concerned I'm being used for sex.'

'No you're not,' Brenda replied.

'Being used for sex?'

'No, concerned about it.'

Another session marked by surprising tenderness, although it was over quickly. It felt for all the world like the kind of sex Brenda imagined married people must have. It was uncomplicated and quick, but not meaningless. Pete was the kind of man who was used to being in a relationship and so even when he was ostensibly engaged in something approaching 'fuck-buddy' sex, he couldn't help but fall into patterns that men used to commitment and longevity practice. There was no overwhelming sense that she should leave, for example. And so, like a trained pigeon recently set free, she implemented that for herself, rolling out of the bed after a polite gap and starting to get dressed. Pete watched her.

'Why are you leaving?'

'Well, you've got things to be getting on with, I'm sure.'

'Not really.'

'Don't you have a job?'

'Yes, I'm self-employed. I can award myself the morning off.'

'Ah, well, I'm not. And the news won't wait for me. Imagine if I didn't go in today, no-one would know what was going on.'

'Why did you come over last night?'

'To see you.'

'Did someone else turn you down?'

Brenda was startled by this. He had nailed it.

'Yes, I thought so,' Pete said but he didn't seemed bothered.

'Do you mind?'

'Not really. I can live with second choice if you're going to be that crazy in bed.'

Brenda couldn't remember much about it, so this was a pleasant surprise.

'So, can we meet up away from the bed?'

Brenda hesitated. She was technically still in a relationship, although the current set-up hardly merited the description. She thought about Jonathan and how he made her feel that she was begging for his time, how complex everything felt, and wondered whether she put up with it because she was simply bored and it gave her something to think about. She wondered why she felt less keen on dealing with it now and suspected it had something to do with this new flirtation with stand-up she seemed to be embarking on. A good person would officially break it off with Jonathan before going on an official date with a new man. But again those words, 'where the fuck is he, then? Not here, that's where...' echoed in her mind. She suddenly felt that this moral code she was so keen to stick to was ridiculous and irrelevant and so restrictive that she was missing out on her own life while others lived theirs however they chose. It was also silly to imagine herself to be some kind of right and moral woman, given the fact that she had now had sex with this man several times. She would have him inside her and yet refuse him a drink? The mark of a true Brit, she thought wryly.

'OK.'

'That took a while – I've never known anyone think so long about meeting for a glass of wine.'

'Well, I'm very intellectual. You'll learn that about me.'

Brenda kissed him and left, feeling good despite the fact of her apparent badness.

She returned Fenella's calls from her desk.

'I heard already – Rossly texted me. He thinks you're my little protégé.'

Brenda blushed at the remembrance of Rossly and her foolish assumption about his desire for her.

'What did he say?'

'That you did OK for a beginner. That Ludo was being a cunt but you took it in your stride. And that Marvin offered you another ten.'

'He did.'

'Did you accept?'

'Yes.'

'Good girl.'

'I don't know what I'm doing with all this. I spoke to Jonathan. He took it... oddly.'

'Well of course he's not going to like it.'

'I wouldn't say he didn't like it exactly, but it freaked him out.'

'Jonathan likes his women to be characters in his story rather than playing the lead in their own lives.'

'Hmm. He wants me to go and see him in New York.'

'Well, don't. You've got work to do here and you can't waste time flying over there just to listen him whinge about the faster pace in American comedy clubs or whatever his problem is.'

'That's a little harsh.'

'Unless you're going there to gig yourself you need to stay here and get on with getting better.'

'Look, I've never said I'm going to be a stand-up comedian, you know, as a life choice. I said I'd try it out a few times and see how I felt.'

'Yeah, but you feel great, don't you?'

Fenella was creepy, with this ability to read people so accurately and with such confidence. Brenda was impressed, but cautious too. As a weapons grade comedian, Fenella necessarily shared some personal attributes with Jonathan, though she'd rather stick a knife in her spleen than admit it. Some voice inside Brenda warned against jumping from one overpowering personality to another. She could not congratulate herself on extracting herself from Jonathan if she was simply going to allow Fenella to assume the role of chief Brenda controller, even if her motives were undoubtedly better than Jonathan's.

'I do feel better, yes. I feel excited.'

'Good, then get online and find an open spot for this week.'

'Yeah. I will.'

'I'll text you later to check you did.'

Brenda submitted, both grateful and grumpy for the push. Googling the various websites that held comedy listings for London, she found the small club nights in pubs that advertised open spots, picked up the phone and called the first five on the list. Within fifteen minutes, she had three gigs booked for the next fortnight: a five-minute spot, a ten-minute, and a gong show. This had now taken on a life of its own. She was doing stand-up, she was doing it, or perhaps it was doing her, but either way, they were in it together. Checking nobody was watching she then clicked through to the most high profile of the comedy websites, Gag.com, noted the closing date for the most prestigious of all the new act competitions, and clicked through to the online application form.

She stared intensely at the screen for a moment, half hoping words would simply appear in the gaps, absolving her of the responsibility of filling it in herself. She shut her eyes and heard a female voice screaming within. She minimised the screen and opened another: an American online gossip site that prided itself on its more sophisticated tone, and hoped it would distract her. It didn't. She was reading the same sentence about a young reality star who had been arrested on a DUI charge over and over again. She checked her phone: nothing. She looked round again. All about her faces glowed in the light of monitors delivering twenty-four-hour news coverage.

She brought the application form up again and just let her fingers type out her entry while she sat and watched the words jump onto the screen. She clicked 'Submit' before she could even check the information she had given was all correctly spelled. A confirmation message flashed up, informing Brenda that she would hear about regional heats in due course.

She sat back hard in her chair and let queasiness take hold. She was out there – she had plugged herself in, flicked the switch and brought her own monster to life.

8

A busy day passed – an internationally famous female pop star had posted pictures of herself to Instagram showing her sharing a bed with a top model, along with the caption 'Me and the Missus' and the media world had gone nuts. Brenda had done her duty and written a piece on the merits of lipstick lesbians. A somewhat dated phrase, but one that got as many clicks from male readers as female and so was still included in the headline. She also covered a press release from the Cabinet Office announcing their intention to find more women to bring into the government, as if all the women were currently hiding. And finally a quick blog for the paper's website responding to an actor's remark about British women having too high expectations in relationships that had clearly been taken out of context but filled a gap in the afternoon lull nonetheless. She replied enthusiastically to a text from Fenella about her progress, and more coolly to a text from Pete asking her to meet him for a drink the following night. She wanted to go, but she still instinctively played a little hard to get for some reason. She thought he could handle it. He didn't seem fragile and Brenda liked that, it certainly made a nice change. And yet her habit of running when someone showed an interest was too hard to break and frankly, she couldn't be bothered to analyse it much further – she had higher priorities than romance now.

Brenda felt a sudden and powerful urge to work on her material. She wanted to be good at this and she realised with a flash that this was the first time she had wanted to be good at something, or to work on something until she became good at it. At school she had been a perfectly fine student, and higher grades had come relatively easily. As had the 2:1 she had got without especially trying at University. She had always been perfectly capable and she now saw she had coasted along like this ever since. A newspaper traineeship came, the offer of a permanent position back when newspapers were not losing money hand over fist, her comedy reviewing which she enjoyed but didn't devote herself to. It had all just been sort of... *Fine*. And nothing more than that. She had listened in wonder to others talk about their ambitions and wished she could point herself at something in the same way. But whenever she had tried (a homeopathy course had been a particular low point when she was politely ejected on the third evening for laughing) it had fallen short.

Now, by some miracle, here it was. And to think she had been living alongside it for the past year without even realising – she had been watching, *helping* others achieve the dream she should have been keeping tight hold of for herself. Her phone rang: Laura. She let it ring out and checked her diary. They had a dinner arranged that night, she had completely forgotten. Perhaps Laura was cancelling. Her voice message told her different.

'Just checking we're still on for tonight. See you about 7 at Millicent's'.

Millicent's: a vegetarian place in Soho. The kind of place that put daisies in tiny flowerpots on every table and proudly told you which village the couscous came from.

Brenda met Laura and Susie but was distracted throughout.

They were in London for an exhibition at the Royal Academy of Art of Tracey Emin's line drawings, which they both enthused about whilst Brenda sat and tried not to look as if she was thinking about something else. Specifically how to develop her bit on Shrek, which she thought had some further potential she had not realised at the gig the other night.

'Are you even listening?'

'Yes!'

'What did I just say?'

'Something about Tracey Emin.'

'But what?'

'That she's... better... than... people say?'

'What's on your mind, Brenda? Because if it's not Pete then forget it because that's what I want to talk about next.'

And so the conversation turned to Pete, as Brenda had known it would at some point. Laura was characteristically blunt.

'What's going on, then?'

'Nothing. I mean, no, nothing official.'

'Are you a member of the Royal Family?'

'Not as far as I know but I haven't researched that far back.'

'So official, unofficial... What's the difference? You're either shagging or you're not.'

'OK, we're shagging. Or rather, we have shagged.'

'How many times?'

'Laura!'

Brenda smiled to see Susie stepping in to remind her wife of social norms.

'What? Sorry. OK. I don't need to know how many times.'

'You don't *need* to know anything,' Brenda said.

'Agreed, but I love you and I like Pete. So I want to know.'

'I like him, he seems... reassuring. I'm meeting him for a drink tomorrow night.'

'Good, good. I've got a good feeling about it.'

'That's... great. Don't do any spells.'

An awkward pause.

'I mean it, guys. *No spells.*'

Susie shrugged and stirred sugar into her coffee. Laura looked out of the window. Brenda was defeated.

'OK, but don't tell me about the spells. Can you at least promise me that?'

'No problem,' Laura and Susie said in unison.

Brenda shook her head in amusement.

'What was his ex like?'

'Awful.'

'No, not awful. Damaged.'

'She cheated on him all the time.'

'She had serious issues.'

'How long were they together?'

'About four years, on and off.'

'So they might get back together again?'

'No, not now. Pete's done with it. I can tell.'

Laura said this with such finality and Susie did not contradict her, so Brenda believed it.

'What does he do for a living?'

'Why haven't you asked him that, if you've done all this shagging? God, straight people are awful.'

'I dunno. I was doing other things with my mouth.'

Susie's hands went up to her ears before she could stop herself. Brenda knew that Laura had had affairs with men in the past but Susie had never seen a man naked and aroused in the flesh, and had no intention of ever doing so. Brenda laughed at her squeamishness.

'He imports furniture.'

Brenda's lip curled slightly and she tried not to look derisive.

'Don't be mean. It's beautiful, the stuff he gets. It's all Scandinavian design. That huge wooden table we've got in our dining room that you like so much? He got that for us at a 75% discount, so button it.'

'OK, sorry. I just had images of him going on dreadful research trips to Bali and droning on about supporting the local communities over there by massively overpaying for antique chairs that were built last week by local men who laugh at him as soon as he's on the plane.'

'Ooh, you'll cut yourself on that tongue one day.'

Brenda nodded with a glimmer of remorse.

'Sorry, I'm too quick to judge, I know. As long as he's not a hobby carpenter who's *so in touch with the earth* in his spare time, I'll cope. But if I catch him whittling on a Sunday afternoon I'm leaving.'

'Just give him a chance, Brenda, OK? You're used to pricks. It'll take a minute for you to acclimatise to a non-prick.'

As soon as Brenda got home she poured herself a glass of wine and reached for a newly acquired Moleskine notebook (blank pages, always blank pages) and a pen and began to work on a set she could feel vaguely confident in. Her mind kept drifting back to Pete, with his mad, bad ex-girlfriend and his beautiful Danish furniture. Now she came to think of it his flat had been spectacularly tasteful, to such an extent in fact that Brenda had felt a little grubby even being in it, as if she spoiled the aesthetic.

What Brenda did next was the first act that marked her out as a comedian: she wrote it down. She made a note of this seemingly idle thought on how it felt to stand in the home of a man she was sleeping with and started toying with how she might turn it into a joke. This more than anything was the turning point – not the gigs she had done, not the gigs she had booked, but this. This act of writing down whatever was on her mind to see if it could be turned into material. She became immersed, making spider charts, circling words and drawing emphatic arrows from one to another – *Monk; Orgasm noise; Furniture; Whittling* – and it was 1am before she realised the time. For the first time she wanted to speak to Jonathan about something other than the status of their relationship. She wanted to talk to him about comedy. The trouble was, she was pretty certain he had no interest in talking about comedy with her unless it pertained directly to himself, and that was going to be a problem.

*

Pete was reading a book on his iPad when Brenda arrived twenty minutes late. He looked up and smiled as she apologised.

'I got stuck in a meeting at work about digital policy for the next year and phones have to be turned over when the editor's talking,' she said, which was the truth.

'It's OK. I quite like it when people are late. It instantly gives me the upper hand.'

His eyes had a twinkle in them and Brenda sat down, relieved and pleased. For someone so apparently straight down the line, he did have the ability to surprise her and the mixture was enticing. Wine was ordered.

'So, you import furniture.'

'Yes, it sounds extraordinarily boring, doesn't it?'

'Well... No... I mean... You don't do carpentry in your spare time, do you?'

Pete laughed.

'No, do you?'

'No. Well, I like DIY but no, I wouldn't call myself a carpenter, no.'

'Do you have anything in particular against carpenters?'

'Maybe it was going to a very strict, oppressive Catholic school as a child. Jesus put me off them.'

'You went to an oppressive Catholic school and it was carpentry you came out hating?'

Brenda laughed now and then immediately pulled her notebook out of her bag and wrote it down.

Pete watched her, amused.

'What's that?'

'It's my new book for jokes. That was a good one. Can I have it?'

'Yes, you can have it. I can't think what I'd do with it. Except maybe pull women and you're here already, aren't you, so what would be the point?'

Brenda blushed against her wishes and was annoyed with herself. Pete pretended not to notice.

'So, have you got any more gigs booked?'

'Err yeah. I mean, nothing big... Just a couple of open spots...'

'Can I come?'

'Oh, no, no. I'm not ready for that. I don't want anyone I know there, it'd be too off-putting.'

'OK. Can I still have sex with you afterwards, though?'

She wasn't expecting that. She was about to object and then realised she liked it. And the tell-tale tightening between her legs confirmed it.

'Maybe.'

'That'll do for now.'

'Hey Pete, do I... do I... make a weird noise in bed?'

'You snore a bit if that's what you mean.'

'It wasn't what I mean, but now I feel even worse.'

'What kind of noise?'

'You know, like a noise at the end, like a strange one...'

Pete frowned a bit.

'I can't say I've noticed. I mean, you certainly sound like

you're enjoying it but frankly by that point I'm kind of caught up in what's happening to me, so...'

Brenda nodded. She didn't know if he was lying or just being a gentleman and though she would usually heap scorn on the concept of old fashioned courtesy, she suddenly found herself a little relieved that this man might spare her a little. That he had no desire to expose her any further than she wished to be exposed. Pete topped up her glass.

To say the evening went well would be an understatement of gross proportions. Two hours passed easily, turned into dinner and moved to Pete's immaculate flat via the kind of taxi ride that would distract even the most conscientious of cab drivers. From taxi to hall, from hall to living room, from living room to dining table: the finest Swedish pine and strong and well built as one would expect with such a provenance, they certainly tested its structural integrity to its limits. Brenda didn't ask about the ex-girlfriend and Pete didn't ask about Jonathan. Brenda begged an early start and left Pete and his beautiful flat around 2am in a minicab, an arrangement to meet before the end of the week tucked into her smile.

The following morning Brenda sat down with her notebook again. Ten minutes. That was all Brenda needed for now: ten good, strong minutes. The journey proper started here. She had spent time going over and over her set, putting in the hours, tweaking it, honing it, trying to know it well enough to forget it. The idea that this ten minutes would become twenty, then an hour and so on seemed unreachable for now. A couple of texts with Fenella calmed her down a little, but she knew that in the most essential sense, she was on her own. No-one could go on stage for her – she could not send a replacement version of herself out there if the nerves got too much. And no-one was begging her to do it, either. There may be supporters, and in time even fans, but this was a path she would tread alone. If she had the precise combination of character traits that made it more appealing than frightening, the nerves would be overcome although perhaps never wholly conquered. The executioner is as lonely as the executed, but at least in comedy one could choose which to be. Brenda chose executioner, and this would inform everything she did from now on. She would kill. She would not die. At least, not if she could help it.

But when the next gig day came and Brenda found herself trudging down a rainy, wind-swept street in North London, she felt bleak. It was a cheerless late November weekday evening and people carried themselves as if braced for the winter that lay ahead. She suddenly felt that she did not want to do this. All the blood seemed to have drained from her body, leaving a joyless, desiccated husk. It seemed impossible, but she was here now and she knew deep down she had no intention of going home. She remembered Fenella telling her not to expect to feel excited or even nervous every time.

'Sometimes you'll just feel flat, and the idea of being on stage an hour later will seem inconceivable, and the time you have to wait until your name is called is interminable, with every moment an opportunity to leave, and every moment passing that opportunity lost. But in those times you just have to sit there. Physically force yourself to stay. And then suddenly, almost without warning, you will be standing on stage, doing your set, and then nothing else will exist and the light will warm you inside and out, and then you'll be finished and you'll feel amazing again, even if it went badly. It always does feel good when you've done it, you just have to trust it. You just have to dig in and mentally strap yourself to the club so you can't leave, however much your whole being is screaming at you to walk out and go anywhere else but here. And you know what else? Sometimes the

147

gigs you least feel like doing can end up being your best ones.'

Brenda held this in her mind as she arrived, introduced herself to the MC, and expressed her gratitude at the ten minutes she had been allowed in his club. She got herself a drink. She sat down in the green room and used every part of her being to force herself to remain there. She greeted each nervous new comic as they came in and chatted lightly with a couple of them. She went to the toilet, just for a moment to herself. She came out and quietly ran over her set in her mind. And then, just as Fenella said, there suddenly came the moment when it was her turn.

She walked on stage as if in a dream, her legs taking her there, her mind shut out of the proceedings in case it let her down. This would become muscle memory soon and though her mind would still produce the fight or flight chemical that was so powerful, she would teach it that flight was an impossibility and so fight was the only option available and that energy would be turned into what is called 'stage presence.' Or what is really the audience's instinctive ability to sense fear and be entranced by the will to overcome it and even to beat it back into submission by looking relaxed and natural and in control.

And then the lights were on her and the beam warmed her chest and her face and there were upturned faces and they were laughing and she felt confident and open and invincible.

'Hi, I'm Brenda Monk. Yeah, I know, my dad didn't want a girl – he really wanted a Scottish TV detective.'

First laugh. They were on her side. She had a certain amount of credit now that would last a little less than a minute. The follow up needed to be good to prolong it.

'I think he's proud of me though, now that I'm a comedian. To be honest, I think he's just pleased I've finally got a boyfriend who thinks I'm funny. Yeah, my last boyfriend was a comedian too and didn't think anyone was funny apart from him. It was a good arrangement while it lasted though. He used me for laughs, and I used him for sex. Yeah, people always want to know what it's like dating a comedian. "Did he pump you for laughs?" they ask. Yeah, I say – literally.'

Second laugh.

'The worst thing was he would do impressions of me on-stage, you know, my orgasm noise... I never knew I sounded like a dolphin trying to impress Simon Cowell...'

Third laugh.

'My current boyfriend's much nicer about it, much more gentlemanly. He doesn't like to talk about my orgasm noise because it's too personal. No, he prefers to tell everyone about my snoring instead. Apparently that's more like Simon Cowell when Cheryl Cole's trying to impress him...'

Brenda walked off stage knowing she'd had a good one. She wanted a drink badly and she grabbed a large glass of white wine from the bar and drank it quickly. She stood at the back of the room to watch the others come on and go off and had a sense that she was probably the third best out of eleven in total. She savoured the feeling of being here on her own terms. She had stood at the back like a good girl, waiting for Jonathan to do his exemplary turn, so many times but always felt that the space around her was rented.

Now she owned it. She had bought her place here with sheer bloody minded determination, and she liked it. And she had done well, too. The audience had laughed consistently, but more than that, they had liked her. They had been on her side, she had made them feel relaxed enough to sit back and enjoy themselves. She silently congratulated herself on this achievement and was already thinking of how she could replicate it as many times as possible in the gigs to come.

Brenda walked the three miles home. She felt too massive

inside to squash herself into any form of public transport and the excess energy had to be got rid of somehow. She knew she wouldn't sleep, but for some reason she resisted calling Pete. She had a strong instinct that she needed to be alone for this, and in any case she didn't especially want to discuss the gig in depth. The material about her and Pete was still fresh in her mind, and actually talking to him might confuse the issue. At least, that's what she told herself. The gig had been good, that was the main thing. She had been good. For the first time in a long time she didn't feel the need to call anybody at all. She was enough.

9

The Gong Show is not a format to be trifled with. A dozen or so new comics, one MC and an audience who actually want to see humiliation on stage. Unlike most stand-up shows, where people come expecting to laugh and are annoyed if they don't or become paralysed with cringing horror when a performer has a bad night, a Gong Show crowd actively wants to see something awful happen on stage. It's part of the fun. Each comedian takes their turn and has to try to last a full five minutes without being 'gonged off' by the MC, who hits the brass cymbal with barely disguised glee if they feel that the act is failing to ignite the audience. It's brutal but the survivors know they have passed a rite of passage and it spurs them on.

Brenda was up for it. She felt good today, but tried not to trust that feeling too much as she knew it could lead to complacence. She had bunked off work for the afternoon claiming an appointment at the dentist and sat in a coffee shop over the road from the grotty West End venue holding tonight's horrors, drinking Americano after Americano and trying to keep her mind still. As the hour approached, the good mood vanished, until finally she rose from her seat, caffeinated to the eyeballs, shivering with nerves and sick with anticipation. She tried to tell herself that this would be the same five minutes of material that she had performed three times in the past fortnight, and that each of those times it had gone perfectly well. One gig had been great and the other two fine, but nothing terrible.

It was the same jokes, she repeated to herself as she descended the red carpeted staircase into the club. But she knew that made no difference. You could perform the same joke over and over again and get a different result every time. She knew that it was her demeanour, her delivery, her attitude that partly made the material work and far from being a comfort, that knowledge made it more frightening. It was not her jokes that would be judged but herself and she knew she was far from consistent. In fact, she didn't know herself well enough inside yet to control the external version she projected on stage. When it was her turn, the ramped up atmosphere would bring out her most essential nature, and then 375 strangers would judge her on it. The sound of the gong would be the crash of self-realisation – has the insistence on self-awareness ever been so brutally delivered?

Brenda lasted exactly 3 minutes and 42 seconds. The first 3 minutes and 30 seconds went pretty well, certainly nothing to be gonged off for, and Brenda's burgeoning sixth sense of feeling how long she had been on stage told her the end was in sight.

'No, seriously,' she said, easing up to a bit she had worked on about her observations in the East London pub which she now considered a fairly safe laugh.

'I mean, where does it end? It's like kids' food can't just be kids' food. It's so ironic now...'

And then she caught his eye – a middle-aged man half way back in the crowd, burly to the extent that he nearly took up two chairs, arms folded across his large chest, chin tilted and a look of pure disgust on his face. She blinked a little, and then he was all she could see, obliterating all else like the Eye of Mordor.

'I wonder if they... if they will get ummm turkey faces, I mean

dinosaurs, turkey dinosaurs... and potatoes with their mums...'
She stammered a bit, and she couldn't remember the next bit.
How did this link? What did it link to? She knew she'd fucked
it up, and she knew she couldn't start again, so simply fell silent
for a moment. The man shook his head slowly and smirked. The
seconds ticked by. And then Brenda made the utter, toe curling
faux pas of apologising.

'Sorry, I... sorry... so the next bit is...'

She looked at the writing on the back of her hand for too
long, trying to make the words come into focus (fatal) and the
gong sounded.

The audience cheered with pavlovian simplicity. Brenda
waved as her heart plummeted and she tripped off stage in a blur
to the conciliatory glances and gestures of everybody backstage.
A drink to take the edge off, and then the door opened and in
walked Rossly.

'You were doing alright til you fucked it up,' he slurred. He
smelt of beer.

'Why are you here?'

'Thanks.'

'Sorry, that came out wrong. I mean, why are you *here*?'

Rossly shrugged. 'Us old timers like to pop in on a gong show
every now and again. I just did my early set at the Store and
thought I'd see what was going on over here before I go back to
close the late one.'

'Well, you've seen it now.'

The last act had just been gonged off after twenty-two seconds
to blood curdling cheers. The crowd had become medieval; the
executions came thick and fast.

'Why did you just grind to a halt like that? You were going well.'

'I don't know. I just suddenly clocked this guy three rows
back and he looked like... like he hated me. Like nothing I could

ever do would ever please him. Like he was disgusted by me. And it was like my brain froze and I was sort of sucked into a vortex of cold, black nothing and I couldn't remember what I'd just said or what I was going to say next.'

'So you had your first Stone Waller?'

'Uh, I suppose so.'

'Everyone gets a Stone Waller every now and again, Brenda. For fuck's sake, you can't let them get to you. If you just crash into a Stone Waller headlong you'll only hurt your head. You've got to look round them, look over them, look anywhere but them. Either that or you take them on directly. Ask them why they're not laughing, but you have to be pretty on top of your game to do that because you can risk losing everyone. But whatever you do, you can't just stop like that.'

'I know,' Brenda said miserably.

'You been gigging?'

'Yeah.'

'Good.'

'I entered a competition too.'

'Even better. All good experience. Come on, come with me. I've got to be back at the Store for the late show. Come and watch.'

Brenda walked across Leicester Square with Rossly to The Comedy Store, and entered the infamous building with the same thrill she always got. She let her eyes scan the numerous black and white framed pictures of comics past and present that covered the walls. The dark red colour scheme lent itself to the sense that this was the beating heart of stand-up comedy in London, Britain, maybe the world. It was certainly pumping tonight. The late show was already underway and the room was hot and heavy with bodies, booze and laughter. Rossly bought Brenda a Jack Daniel's and coke and they stood along the far side of the room, next to the raked seating, and leaned against the wall with the other comedians that had been on, would go on, or had just popped in to see what was going on after they had finished their own gigs around town.

They silently greeted Rossly and turned their attention back to the stage where a young comedian was having an extremely good night. His material concerned race mainly and how it felt to be one of only a small number of black people growing up in a remote area of North Wales. He stood in the middle of the stage, very still, holding the mic to his chest, leaving one arm and hand free to provide all the movement he needed. He was so relaxed and confident that it seemed the laughs came from nothing, just bubbling up to greet whatever remark he casually chose to make. Brenda had never seem him before, but she'd heard his name a lot recently: Bradley Wilson. As he embarked on a spoof rap in a broad Welsh accent, Brenda felt the shame of the gong show lift and the joy of a good gag engulf her. Here, in the dark, she let it go, just... let it go. Rossly, sensing that this must be Bradley's closing bit, whispered, 'wait here' and then weaved through the chairs that surrounded the stage and disappeared behind a concealed door that led to the green room.

Five minutes later he was on stage, having what appeared to be the time of his life. He was closing – the most senior role – and the added prestige suited him. He danced around the stage, his long, wiry limbs wheeling and pointing and striding. He could cover so much ground in one step, it seemed he could jump over the whole audience with one leap if he wanted. He made his act seem improvised and spontaneous, but Brenda had seen enough of his performances to know it was not. It was just that he had built up so much material over the years, that he could pull anything out to fit whatever was going on in the room – 'always acknowledge what is happening in the room' – so it seemed he was making it up as he went along. Brenda noticed that he barely flirted, though the women were rapt almost without exception. He was crude, sexually aggressive in his language and ideas, but it never felt threatening – why? Brenda couldn't say for sure. There were certainly other comics that used similar language and in their mouths it was off putting. Maybe it was some instinctive sense that Rossly liked women, he fundamentally liked women. He was not furious with them because of fear, which was an affliction some other male comics laboured under, and it leaked out of them unconsciously.

Twenty minutes later and Brenda was outside with Rossly, smoking a cigarette.

'So, how's Jonathan?'

'OK, I think.'

'You haven't heard from him?'

'A bit. He's busy, I'm busy. You know, different time zones and all that.'

Rossly nodded, obviously taking this in.

'How's... yours?'

'Nina? Nina's great. Yeah, she's something else. She used to be a model.'

'Uh-huh.'

Rossly suddenly seemed slightly embarrassed, as if he knew he'd exposed something of himself he hadn't been intending to. But he shook it off quickly.

'If those girls I was at school with could see me now, with her... Christ, that'd give them something to think about.'

'Were you not a sexual hit at school, then?'

'On the Gold Coast? Nah, you had to look a certain way to get any there, and trust me, this isn't it.'

He gestured to his long thin form, black hair, rock-gothic style.

Brenda didn't know what to say, but it didn't seem that Rossly was after any particular reassurance from her. Nina clearly provided what he needed in that regard.

'Once I got good at stand-up though – fuck. If I could go back and tell my fifteen-year-old self the kind of pussy I'd be getting aged thirty-six, he'd have dropped dead on the spot in a pool of vomit and involuntarily ejaculated semen.'

Brenda laughed.

'You liked that, Brenda Monk? OK, well, I'll have to try that out at my next gig. Could work. Yeah, could work nicely.'

'Is there anything you wouldn't say on stage?'

Rossly thought for a minute.

'My mum was in a wheelchair practically all my life. She had MS. I guess I wouldn't... well, I haven't up to now. That's the only thing, I think. Never say never, though.'

'You'd joke about your mum's disability?'

'If I had something to say about it and I could make it funny, yeah.'

'So why haven't you?'

Rossly considered this for a minute.

'I guess I just haven't found a way to make it funny yet.'

Brenda nodded.

'So you think nothing should be off limits?'

'That's correct.'

'What about hurting people's feelings?'

'That's not my concern.'

'Shouldn't it be?'

'No. I'm a comedian. I work in comedy clubs. I'm not a kids' show presenter. People who come here are grown-ups. If they can't handle it, they shouldn't come. Or they should just go and see the big tours of the nice, safe stand-ups they know they already like and will never say anything that will challenge anything they already think and feel.'

'But surely not everyone has to be out there, shocking people all the time. There's nothing wrong with just being funny.'

'Yeah there is. It's a waste of talent. If you can deliver truths whilst being funny, that's a powerful place to be.'

'I don't know, I don't know about that.'

'Look, Brenda Monk, being a stand-up comedian isn't just about being funny, it's about talking about things people won't talk about in their everyday lives. Things that they're too scared to look at. Anyone can get laughs, I mean, look at you...'

'Thanks a lot.'

'No, I mean, think about it. You got up on stage for the first time and people laughed, didn't they? I mean, maybe they weren't like constantly hysterical, but you did make them laugh.'

'Yes, I suppose so...'

'So, it's easy to make people laugh. That's what no-one gets about this job until you do it. Anyone can make people laugh at least once. Most people are nice and if you get up on stage they will laugh just because they're expected to half the time. Getting the laughs isn't the challenge. It's getting the exact type of laughs you want to get, that's the difficult part.'

'So, all the laughs I've got so far are just... meaningless?'

'No, not all of them. Some of them are, though. Think about what you want to say then try and work out how to make it funny. If you can do that, you're worthy of the word comedian.'

This was slightly blowing Brenda's mind and so she didn't quite notice Rossly was very lightly kissing her until it was already happening. She pulled back.

'Oh, hey, no. I don't... I don't think I want that... just at the moment...'

'Sure, no problem.'

Rossly lit another cigarette as if nothing had happened. He seemed so unfazed that Brenda also brushed it aside, even wondering if she had imagined it. He smoked silently for a moment. Something was bothering Brenda.

'Can I ask you a question?'

'You can ask me anything you like, babe.'

'That gig when you said you'd fuck me afterwards and then your girlfriend was there and it was like you'd never even said it... what was that? I mean, what was that about? Did you mean it?'

'Dunno. Maybe.'

This was a maddening response but Brenda gave him the benefit of the doubt. She had effectively just rejected his advances, after all.

''Cos it seemed like in the end, you were just taking the piss out of me.'

'I don't know what I was thinking, really. I just said it 'cos I felt like saying it. I was interested to see what your reaction would be.'

'Oh, right.'

'Me and Nina, you know, we've only been together a few weeks. It's not like we're married or anything.'

'No, but still...'

'So do you want to fuck tonight?'

'No, oh no thanks. I think... I think, Rossly, that I would just like to be... friends with you. I mean, I think somehow I need us to just be friends.'

'Easy, girl. I was just suggesting we fuck tonight. I wasn't asking you to start a relationship with me.'

'I know, I know you weren't. But I need help with comedy. if I'm going to do this properly and I think if we had sex I wouldn't get that help.'

Rossly grinned. And then grinned some more. He whistled and put his hand on her shoulder.

'Oh Brenda Monk, Brenda Monk, Brenda Monk,' he crooned

softly, much as Brenda imagined he would if he were moving inside her, ready to come, 'you'll be a true stand-up yet.'

10

When Brenda wanted sex she went to Pete, and he was happy to oblige. This was a great arrangement until one day, she realised that when she wanted a bit of company, she also went to Pete. And when she wanted comfort she went to Pete, and soon it would be Christmas and there might have to be some sort of discussion about the exact nature of their arrangement so as to properly define how they would spend the festive season. Pete had made it clear that he wanted Brenda to be his girlfriend. Brenda had said it was still too complicated with Jonathan and until she had the chance to break it off with him officially she couldn't really start a new relationship as that was immoral. Pete said that was bullshit, and he was right.

In truth, Brenda hadn't heard from Jonathan for three weeks. The drunken 'I love you' chat was never referenced again and Jonathan clearly had no idea he'd said it. Their last conversation had been snatched, with a promise to catch up properly later which never happened. Brenda knew it was effectively over but neither could really muster the energy to kill it properly. Brenda had no doubt that Jonathan had slept with other women in New York or that he had continued to do so now he had arrived in LA. And as for her... Well, she could hardly claim to have been faithful to whatever it was they had sort of had when he left.

But she knew she was being unfair to Pete. If she could get a gig, she was there and Pete was hassling her to come along and watch. She had no idea how he would feel about her talking about him on stage, however oblique the references may be, and she hadn't confronted it even to herself. Easier just to avoid the issue by making sure he was never there to see it in the first place. And she could justify it to herself on a number of grounds, including the needs of 'art' and the sense that she was perfectly entitled to use her own life in her jokes as long as she never mentioned anybody by name. It seemed the best policy for now. Or at least, the easiest.

Brenda was preparing to leave for a gig in High Barnet, when her mobile went – Pete.

Calling to wish her good luck perhaps? Or suggesting he come along to watch? Brenda's instinctive response was to ignore it. She was in pre-gig mode now and not looking to chat. But some other kinder impulse took over and she pressed 'Accept', planning to say she couldn't talk now, but would call later. She didn't even get a chance to say hello.

'So, I hear you're talking about me in your act,' Pete said, his voice devoid of its usual warmth.

'Ummm... well, I... where did you hear that?'

'A friend of mine happened to be at your gig last Tuesday and she recognised your name from when I told her about you.'

A long pause.

'I don't know what you want me to say.'

'Well, you seem to know exactly what to say on stage. Why don't you start with that? Come on, I'd love to hear it.'

'You don't sound like you'd love to hear it. You sound like you've already decided you hate it.'

'Don't be a bitch.'

Brenda's stomach lurched. He'd never used language like

that to her before.

'I'm just trying to find my voice.'

'Your voice? What's that?'

'My style, my comedic style. The thing that makes me "me" as a comedian. I'm just... exploring.'

'Well, that's nice for you but do I get any say in this?'

Brenda hesitated. Pete filled the gap.

'You know you're doing to me exactly what Jonathan used to do to you, don't you? You do realise that?'

Brenda did realise that but she didn't want to admit it. If she did, she'd have to stop doing the jokes she had written about them and frankly, they were working better than a lot of her other stuff.

'So, what, are you asking me to stop? Because... because I don't know if I can.'

'Of course you can. You can stop anytime you like.'

'But it's good material. It's working.'

'So, write some other stuff that works instead.'

'It's not as simple as that. I want to talk about what's important to me. And my relationship is important to me, so I have to talk about that.'

Pete was quiet. And then he spoke steadily, and with control.

'So, are you saying we are in a relationship?'

Brenda felt cornered. She couldn't deny it now. She'd pretty well said as much.

'I... think so, yes, I think so... I mean, are we? What do you think? What do you want?'

'You know what I want, Brenda. I mean, you know what I wanted. But I'm having second thoughts now. I don't know if I want every conversation we have served up to Friday night drunks in some grotty old stand-up club.'

'Well, technically I'm not actually good enough to gig on a

Friday night yet, so...'

'YOU KNOW WHAT I MEAN.'

'Yes, sorry, yes. I know.'

'Oh shit. Shit, shit, shit, shit, shit. Why do I always do this? Why do I always fall for the nutters? With the damaged ones who can't just settle down and have a nice, loving, straightforward relationship, I mean, WHAT IS WRONG WITH ME? WHY DO I ALWAYS FUCKING DO THIS?'

Brenda reeled. She'd never heard Pete like this before. This was pure animal anguish pouring down the phone and it sliced through her like the sound of a dog in pain. She left a gap to see if there was any more and then softened her voice.

'Are you OK?'

'Yeah,' Pete said as if all the life force had left his body. 'Brenda, I think I'm going to just have a bit of time to myself, if that's OK. Say what you like on stage. I don't want to limit you. Say what you like. I just don't want to give you anything... new.'

He hung up. Brenda felt desolate. But she had a gig to go to and if she didn't leave now, she would be late. She walked around her flat gathering up her things as if she was made of lead. At least the relationship status issue had been resolved, she thought drily, in the sense they were now definitely not in one. She thought she might suddenly cry but then gulped it down and fought it back. She needed to be harder than this. Tonight would be the biggest challenge she had ever faced – she would perform her set feeling like she'd had her heart kicked out of her body and though the full impact had yet to hit her, she could already glimpse the loneliness to come. She knew a normal person would cancel the gig, but she couldn't conceive of doing that. She needed to be there, and if nothing else the distraction would be welcome.

She arrived at the club with five minutes to go. No time for nerves. No time for anything. Her name was called. She walked out onto the stage and scanned the audience. She felt untethered from something, and mildly crazy. She knew her set inside out by now and the words came out naturally. But this time something was different. She was reckless and honest – painfully so. The material she had done before was given a new flavour by the earlier phone call with Pete, and then without warning new words were tumbling out of her mouth.

'He said I was a nutter for talking about us on stage, and he didn't want to give me anything new, which is fair enough. It's just I'm pretty sure I can get a fair few jokes out of that...'

She felt slightly hot and sick in the moment, but the laugh came and soothed her like a cooling balm.

Brenda walked off stage, went straight to the bar and ordered a large glass of wine. She downed it and ordered another. She no longer felt heartbroken or lonely. She felt vindicated. When she had admitted on stage that the relationship had ended that day, she had actually got a cheer. She was funny. Her failed relationship was funny. The laughter of the crowd had suggested that it didn't really matter what had happened with Pete, with anyone – that in the end, it was all just material.

The club promoter found her after the show and offered a paid ten the following week.

'My woman comic just dropped out and you have to have one these days otherwise people give you shit.'

Brenda didn't even bother arguing with the sentiment; she just accepted the work. She would get £80. Her first paid gig. She was now technically a professional stand-up. She wanted to call Pete, but of course she couldn't. She didn't want to call Jonathan. She stood in the street outside the club and called Fenella.

'So, I got my first paid gig.'

'Fucking yes. That's my girl. When?'

'Next Thursday. Someone dropped out and I did OK, and I think he just thought it was the easy option. Eighty quid.'

'Eighty quid's a fucking fortune for someone just starting. This is superb news. Does Jonathan know?'

'No. I've barely spoken to him. It's basically over, we're just torturing the puppy now. Someone's got to end it but neither of us can be bothered.'

'Ha. Amazing. So look, now you're a real stand-up come to one of our women in comedy drinks nights. Monday, The Blue Pillars, you know it?'

'Yeah.'

'You'll come?'

'Yeah.'

'We're gonna take good care of you, Brenda. We need another soldier on the ground.'

'Cannon fodder?'

'Fresh legs.'

'OK.'

'You don't sound very happy about it all. I'd have thought you'd be more up.'

'Things are a bit fucked... personally.'

'I thought Jonathan was old news.'

'No, someone else.'

'Well, get over it or use it. Don't let it slow you down. Men come and go, but comedy's forever.'

The tone was mocking, and Brenda smiled and felt momentarily lifted.

'Nobody keeps a relationship going at the start of a comedy career, Brenda, seriously, plenty of time for all that later. If he loves you, he'll come back. I'll see you Monday.'

If he loves you, he'll come back. If he loves you. Brenda had never considered the possibility that Pete might love her.

It seemed far-fetched, and yet now she remembered his exact words.

'Why do I always fall for the nutters?'

Fall for. As in, fall in love.

'For the nutters...'

Nutters. That was her. She was the nutter. Or the latest in a line of nutters, in this scenario. She remembered Laura and Susie's description of his ex.

'Awful,' they'd said. 'Damaged.'

Was that her, too? Was she awful and/or damaged?

Brenda suddenly recalled reading a press release she had been sent at work about all comedians having some form of psychosis. She had laughingly passed it round, before saying that it was too loaded for her to cover. Its glibly compiled checklist had described Jonathan to a tee. But now it chilled her to the bone. Did it also describe this new Brenda? She felt for the first time how cold it was outside.

The door to the club opened and a couple tumbled out, laughing. They stopped dead in their tracks when they saw Brenda.

'Hey, it's you. You were on tonight,' the man said, smiling into Brenda's face.

'Yeah.'

'You were fucking great! And I don't normally like female comedians, do I babe?'

'No he doesn't. He normally hates them, but he really liked you. Didn't stop laughing.'

'I didn't. I literally didn't stop laughing. Brilliant.'

'Thanks,' said Brenda, not feeling entirely complimented but pleased to take it nonetheless.

'I liked it too,' said the woman, pulling her white puffa jacket around her and zipping it up, 'but I'm not as in to comedy as he is. He loves it, don't you?'

'Yeah, I love it. I love *Mock the Week*. Have you ever been on that?'

'Uh no, not yet.'

'You should. You'd be good and I wouldn't normally say that about a woman comedian, or comedienne, should I say?'

'No.'

He nodded without listening. Brenda felt she would never have anything to say to this man.

'You should do *Mock the Week*, though.'

'OK, well, I'll call the BBC in the morning.'

Brenda felt ashamed of her sarcasm, but couldn't help it.

'Yeah, well, we'll come and see you again, won't we babe?'

'Yeah, and your ex sounds lovely. Sorry he dumped you.'

'Yeah, me too,' Brenda said, unsure as to which one of the three of them she hated the most at this precise moment. The couple tipped off towards the Tube station, laughing together, happy. Brenda hailed a cab and went home to her empty flat.

That night she couldn't sleep, a problem she was finding increasingly tiresome. After gigs she was too pumped to relax for hours, no matter how much she drank or how much weed she smoked. At least when she had been with Pete she could release some of the pent up energy through sex and he was usually willing to stay up and chat for a short while, but when she was still awake at 3, 4 even 5am he would be fast asleep and she would lie next to him, staring at the ceiling, going over every part of the that night's gig. But now she didn't even have him to help her out.

Brenda put the TV on and found a late night American sitcom that used to be good on an obscure channel and sat in front of it. Tonight she was confused – it had been a great experience, going out there and just winging parts of it and yet now she felt thwarted somehow, unfinished in some way. She wondered if she could masturbate her way out of it but didn't feel the urge, 'I'm telling myself I've got a headache,' she thought wryly, and then reached for her notebook to write it down. She tried to think back to the gig. If the promoter was willing to pay her on the basis of it, then surely she should try to distill what was good about it and recreate it. Logically it seemed like a winning formula, although Jonathan had told her time and again that a good comedian makes each gig unique – once you are working to a formula, you will officially become a 'hack' and that is the beginning of the end of any legitimate artistic endeavour.

Brenda knew she ought to examine what had gone well, though. She closed her eyes and put herself back on stage: the full length curtain with a bare brick printed design, the high stool she hadn't used, the round spotlight illuminating her top half and allowing a little room to move. It had felt like proper stand-up, that was the thing. She had controlled the room, even though she had been a bit out of control herself. The usual material had gone well but she had surprised herself with the ad-libs.

'I said it was OK to dump me as long as I could still have sex with him after gigs, you know, to blow off steam, or blow off something. You know, all this talking, it's actually quite relaxing for a female comedian to do something else with her mouth after a show.'

It had got a nice laugh, and though it had come out a little clumsy, there was something in it. With a bit of tweaking it could work much better. She made a note of it. She had talked about her lesbian friends' disgust for straight people, and the line she shot back at Laura at dinner about how straight people don't talk in bed had been said somewhere and might lead to something. A bit about her Catholic school and hating carpentry taken from her first proper date with Pete had come from nowhere, but she liked it. And then the blurt that had taken her by complete surprise.

'I don't want to give you anything new...'

It had left her vulnerable because it was so clearly real and recent, and yet it had felt satisfying, purging. Did it need that raw energy behind it in order to make it funny? Or could she recreate it? Brenda would have to experiment to find out so she wrote it down too, and then suddenly tiredness came down on her like a twenty foot black drape and she fell asleep on the sofa with the TV on and her pen still in her hand.

11

Fenella had explained that the Women in Comedy drinks happened with haphazard regularity – maybe three times a year, and was often prompted by an occasion, such as Christmas in this case. So Brenda found herself in an upstairs room in a central London pub at the Women in Comedy Christmas Drinks. Three tables in one corner had been noisily shoved together and the new mega-table was surrounded by fifteen or so women of varying ages, sizes and abilities. In the opposite corner of the room were three middle-aged men, clutching pints and trying to work out what was going on. Fenella saw Brenda hovering in the doorway by the upstairs bar and shouted her over.

'This is the famous Brenda Monk I was telling you about. She's just started doing stand-up about three months ago – got her first paid gig next this week.'

'Congratulations,' said one of the three women Fenella was standing with at that precise moment.

'This is Josephine Pascal,' said Fenella.

Brenda recognised her from a gig she had been to years ago, before Jonathan was on the scene. She was a distinctive looking woman, not easily forgotten: very small, like a twelve-year-old boy, but with defined muscles in her arms that she showed off to great effect in a loose pale pink sleeveless vest. With dark gleaming skin, black, black eyes and very short hair, shaved up the sides and back with the just the beginnings of a tight afro on top, the beauty was arresting and slightly intimidating.

'Hi,' said Josephine, sticking out her hand to be shaken. Her manner seemed a bit chilly, though Brenda didn't know why.

'And Nellie Dibbot and Katherine, who works as Miss Linger the Librarian.'

'Ah yes. I didn't recognise you without your... clothes, uh, make-up, I mean, sorry,' said Brenda, frantically trying to re-member which acts she had seen on stage over the past few years. Miss Linger was, as far as she could recall, a woman who performed an aggressive feminist burlesque routine and then painted her naked body red whilst shouting a reasonably funny monologue about her observations of animal behaviour.

'I prefer it that way. I'm not as scary off-stage...'

'So, you're working as a stand-up,' said Josephine.

Brenda was in no doubt now, her tone had a frost to it.

'Yes, I've only just started. I'm not very good at the moment.'

'No-one's very good when they first start,' Nellie said smiling, clearly eager to be liked, playing with her nicely highlighted shoulder length blonde hair.

Fenella, who had disappeared to the bar, returned with a drink for Brenda which she swigged gratefully, wishing she'd had a drink before she arrived. This suddenly felt intimidating.

'I've known stand-ups socially for ages though and I used to review comedy a lot so I've seen loads of it. But of course, it's very different when you're actually up there.'

Nellie laughed for no particular reason and Katherine nod-ded in agreement.

'How's it been going?'

'Not bad. I've done about thirty gigs now...'

'And you've got a paid one already? You must be good. Or you must know someone good...'

This seemed unnecessarily barbed from Josephine, and Fenella nudged her.

'I got a her a couple,' Fenella said, 'and the rest she got by herself.'

'I only got the paid one because they had a gap because a woman dropped out and they need another one.'

This elicited a great peal of laughter from all four of the women in front of her.

'Need another one. Brilliant. Where's this?'

'At the Craic House in Croydon.'

'Who dropped out?'

'I don't know, he didn't say.'

'At least he's trying to book one woman per show. More than you can say for some of them.'

'Most gigs have at least one woman on the bill now though?' asked Brenda, tentatively.

'Not most, but definitely more. It's getting better. But it's still only one per show usually, even when they have a policy to get more women in,' said Nellie.

'That's why we have these drinks things,' said Fenella. 'We'd never see each other otherwise. Only one of us ever gets booked for anything. If we left it to professional work to catch up personally we'd never see anyone else with a vagina...'

'It's better once you get beyond the circuit, though?' Brenda asked.

Stony faces.

'Not really,' said Nellie.

'I'd say it's worse,' said Katherine.

'They fuck me off... especially the ones that come to my gigs, see me smash it and then don't book me for any fucking panel show at all.'

'My agent tried to get me on *Gagging Order* and the producer told her that they'd had a woman on last series and she hadn't talked enough, so they weren't really doing women that much now as they made them nervous.'

Derisive cackling.

'I did a pilot for a TV panel show once, got a beautiful thank you letter from the producer. They got a series and told me I couldn't do it because they were going for a more "blokey vibe". Can you believe it? I've blanked him ever since and you know what the real fucker is? I don't think he really understands why I'm pissed off. He says it's the channel and there's nothing he can do about it. ' Josephine rolled her eyes at the memory of it all.

'I thought stand-ups hated doing panel shows,' Brenda said.

'Don't hate the money, though. Couple of grand for a couple of hours work? Extra income keeps me gigging when it's costing me more to get to a gig than I'm being paid to do it.'

'And it helps pay for Edinburgh. They wonder why there aren't more women comics doing full hour-long Edinburgh shows. Well, I'll tell you fucking why. It's because that costs MONEY and if you give five out of six places on any well-paid TV show to men and leave one chair for women and even then we have to fight for that chair with a load of non-comedians, news readers and...'

'Ex-popstars...'

'Yeah, or whoever, how do you think we're going to get enough cash to PAY to go to Edinburgh. And they complain there aren't enough of us to fill the spots even if they did get more women, I mean, can't they fucking see the economics of it and how they dictate the outcomes? IT DRIVES ME FUCKING NUTS.'

There was an awkward pause. Josephine took a deep breath. Brenda looked into her drink.

'We're usually funnier than this,' Fenella said and broke the tension.

Josephine smiled slightly for the first time and went to the toilet.

'Don't be put off,' Nellie said, laying a hand on Brenda's arm. 'When it's good, it's the best job in the world.'

Brenda now recalled seeing her in action: Nellie was a pretty woman with a filthy mouth. Brenda had been impressed that her faux-naive stage persona let her get away with anything, and through a ditzy, tongue-tied act she actually addressed a variety of taboo issues with sharp observation.

'No, I'm not put off. It's all very interesting. Excuse me a minute.'

Brenda needed to urinate and also wanted a moment to herself. She always found groups of comedians to be intense company and though she loved it, she also required brief time-outs every now and again. Crossing the room, she found a steep, narrow staircase that led two floors up to the Ladies. These old pubs always seemed to put the female toilets in strange, out of the way places, an echo of a time when women were not welcome here and there was no need to provide them with conveniences. Brenda climbed the stairs and pushed open the dark mahogany door at the top of the building. As she entered the one cubicle locked snapped open and Josephine walked out, brushing a light dusting of cocaine from the end of her nose. She paused, then knowing she'd been caught, smiled grudgingly. Brenda smiled back. They both hesitated.

'Want some?' Josephine said.

Brenda considered for about a second.

'Yeah.' Josephine palmed Brenda a tiny paper wrap and a rolled up five pound note and stood aside as Brenda slipped behind the door and locked it. The top of the cistern was flat, which was good. A lot of pubs and clubs in London had installed sloping cisterns now in order to stop this kind of thing. Brenda tapped out a small hillock of white powder and took out a credit card. She chopped it quickly into two small, neat lines and bent to suck it through the fiver, one into each nostril. She sniffed once, then again, pinched her nose together, let go, sniffed one more time, and opened the door.

Josephine was leaning against the sink.

'Thanks.'

'So, you're going out with Jonathan?'

'Oh god, I don't know. Not really. We were, I mean, it's a bit up in the air at the moment with him being away.'

'I was with him for nearly five years.'

Brenda hadn't seen that coming.

'Has he never mentioned me?'

'Well, he might have done and I just don't remember... I mean, of course, I know he's had girlfriends in the past and stuff...'

'We were engaged.'

This was news. Brenda, momentarily winded, did not know what to say.

'When did you break up?'

'Two years ago. I got pregnant by accident and I knew I couldn't cope with it and we talked about it and he kept changing his mind about whether or not he wanted me to have an abortion.'

Brenda felt that like a kick to the gut.

'So, what happened?'

'I didn't want to keep it. I'm younger than him for a start and I wasn't remotely ready. I'd only just started gigging. But he kept crying and saying he didn't know what we should do. He couldn't even say the word pregnant for a week. He just kept on calling it the "Terrible Mess". At one stage he wanted me to have it and he said he would look after it on his own. Then he said he couldn't do that and be a comedian at the same time and comedy had to come first. Then he said we should get married. That's when he proposed and I said yes even though I didn't want to – stupid fucker I was. Then he said he'd made an awful mistake. Then we booked the abortion and we got to the clinic and he stood in the car park outside and told me he didn't think I should go through with it. I was right on the threshold of legal termination by then. He left me there and I went in and had the abortion on my own. Then I went home and moved all my stuff out – he wasn't there. I haven't seen him since.'

Brenda was silent and sick inside. The coke was starting to sharpen her brain and highlight her senses, and she thought she might cry or punch the mirror or just start shouting. She didn't trust herself to say anything out loud and felt relieved she had not put more of Josephine's gift up her nose – she still had the ability to control herself, at least. And she was shocked to the marrow. She needed to let the full horror sink in a little.

Josephine went back into the cubicle with her package.

'I don't know what to say,' Brenda said, then clenched her jaw together to stop questions or platitudes tumbling out against her will.

'Just thought you should know,' replied Josephine through the door.

Two big sniffs, and Josephine reappeared. She checked her nostrils in the mirror.

'Is this why Fenella hates him?'

'Yeah.'

'It's pretty much over between us.'

'I heard about his Edinburgh show.'

Brenda nodded, her mind burning now, heart racing. She had a wild urge to dance which would be highly inappropriate.

'Did he used to talk about you, too?'

'Yeah, until the Terrible Mess, then it was like I never happened.'

Brenda remembered seeing a short set of Jonathan's on the TV some years before where he had referenced a girlfriend, but the material had not been especially original or memorable.

'I'm over it. I'm glad I had the abortion. Can you imagine trying to bring up a kid with him? It wouldn't be fair – on anyone.'

Josephine shuddered and Brenda had no intention of admitting that until relatively recently she had day-dreamed semi-constantly about having a baby with Jonathan. She looked straight into Josephine's eyes, which was a mistake. It was like staring into an abyss. Brenda felt light-headed.

'Do you ever talk about it on stage?'

'No. It's not funny. Not to me, anyway.'

'Does everyone know about it?'

'Not really. Only Fenella knows the real extent of it. And my family and stuff, but I kept it pretty hidden. I mean, people knew we were together, obviously, but the Terrible Mess never really got out.'

'If people knew...'

'Yeah.'

'It would ruin him.'

'Yeah.'

'So why don't you tell? If you hate him.'

'I don't want to ruin him, not comedically. He's already ruined inside. I'm not interested in destroying his career, he's a pretty good comic. And I'm not vindictive. I do mindfulness training and shit like that, and I've just let it go. I never wanted kids anyway, so you know, I'm not all cut up about it... if you pardon the expression.'

This suddenly struck Brenda as impossibly hilarious and she started laughing. And once she started, it was like a stopper exploding out of a bottle of cheap cava and heaving hysteria was sprayed all over the tiny toilet room. Josephine caught the bug and also started laughing from somewhere deep within, great sobs and snorts, until both women were helpless and bent over.

'It wasn't that funny,' Josephine pushed out between laughs.

'No. It was shit.'

'I didn't even mean to do a joke,' Josephine said.

'I know.' Brenda gasped and came to a stop.

'Oh god… my stomach hurts, shit, that's got to be better than an hour of yoga.'

They calmed down, taking deep breaths and letting out sighs of relief.

'Listen, Josephine, I'm really sorry that happened, and you know, if there's anything I can…'

But Josephine waved a hand in front of Brenda's face.

'Oh stop, seriously. It's OK. I had loads of therapy, I'm OK, honestly. You should know what you're getting into, that's all.'

'Trust me – it's more a case of what I'm getting out of now.'

Back downstairs, last orders were being called at the bar. But Fenella had a better idea.

'Let's wrap this up and carry on at The Magpie,' she suggested to the half dozen or so women who were still there.

Fenella led the way down Newman Street, turned onto Oxford Street and then right onto Charing Cross Road. After a few minutes she ducked down a side road, wet and shiny from rain and street lights, and pushed open a door Brenda had never noticed before, though she must have walked past it many times.

Down a wide flight of stairs, a few chatty words exchanged with the woman on the door and a flash of Fenella's membership card, and Brenda was able to survey the scene. The room was cavernous, like a sunken empire, and was decorated somewhere between a traditional pub and a set from *Oliver!* The scale and style of it was a delightful surprise, and gave it the feeling of a speakeasy – a whole world suddenly there in front of you with just a push through one unassuming door. Fenella ordered shots of Tequila and bottles of beer for everyone.

'Up and in,' she shouted, and then all put their shot glasses to their lips and flipped them.

'OH YES, THANK YOU,' Josephine cried and took a swig of her beer.

'I had no idea this place was even here,' said Brenda.

'Yeah. It's great. It's cheap to join, it's open 'til three and pretty much anything goes as long as you don't break the furniture.'

Brenda looked around. It was full but still felt roomy. There were strange homely touches like Edwardian style lamps and rugs, but the wooden chairs and tables were solid and bereft of style. All over the walls were framed posters from shows long since over, and black and white pictures of dead British theatre stars. There were Art Deco prints and in one corner a collection of bandanas had been incongruously pinned to a cork board and hung above a sofa. On one wall was a painted mural of a classic pub scene from a hundred years ago. Brenda felt that she had walked into the part of Disney World called 'Pub Land' – there was something so self-conscious about it all, and yet it wasn't forced or pretentious.

'Loads of comedians hang out here after shows and stuff. I'm surprised you've never been before,' Nellie was saying sweetly.

'I've been with Jonathan mainly for the past year and it's not really his kind of place.'

'Jonathan and I used to come here all the time,' said Josephine with a factual tone.

'Oh.'

Brenda didn't know what to say to that so she said nothing and drank her beer.

Another three rounds of tequila and everyone was best friends.

'Why is it so shit being a woman?' Nellie was shouting, the ditzy little girl voice gone. 'I wish I was six foot tall and like, nineteen stone and then I could kick everyone in the FACE if they PISSED ME OFF.'

She stumbled against a passing male who tipped her back onto her feet and continued towards the exit.

'S'not shit,' Brenda said, 'I like it. I like my tits and my vagina.'

'Good for you,' Nellie said gaily, 'I'm sure they're very nice.'

'Thanks.'

'What's your comedy 'bout, then?'

'Dunno yet.'

'She's still finding her voice,' said Fenella, who had drunk more than anyone and seemed the least affected.

'Oh yeah. Good. Takes ages.'

'I FUCKING LOVE GOLDIE HAWN,' Josephine shouted as she caught site of an old TV that was turned on with the sound down behind the bar. On the screen was a film from the 1980s, *Bird on a Wire*, and Mel Gibson was flirting with Goldie Hawn as if from another lifetime.

'That's what I wanna be like when I'm old. Just like Goldie Hawn, all sort of buttery and sexy but at the same time not giving a shit about anything.'

'I wanna be like Katharine Hepburn,' piped up Brenda, 'I wanna live on my own on a farm and carry logs around and make my own kayak and tell everyone they're fucking it all up.'

Fenella and Nellie collapsed onto their table in a heap of giggly booziness.

'I'm going to live in a hotel in Berlin,' said Fenella, 'and take a young lover every now and again and smoke loads of hash. And then one day, when I've had enough, I'll end myself in the bath.

It's very considerate to kill yourself in a hotel room, you know. It means no-one you know has to find your body. And they have to clean it all up, too.'

'I want a nice little cottage by the sea and a husband and three dogs,' said Nellie, the little girl voice now back in place.

Fenella mimed sticking two fingers down her throat and Nellie belted her across the arm with surprising strength, and then seemed to collapse a little, her forehead beading with moisture.

'I'm gonna be sick.'

Nellie bolted for the toilets.

'She's not one of us,' Fenella murmured as she watched Nellie go.

'Shuddup, course she is,' Josephine said, suddenly annoyed. 'She goes up there, she does her act. Just 'cos we hate it, doesn't make her any less of a comedian.'

'Yeah, maybe,' said Fenella with an insincere tone.

Brenda was quiet and tried to squash thoughts of having her own comedy appraised in this way if she ever had need to lurch off and find a friendly toilet bowl.

'For fuck's sake, Fen. Not every woman who gets on stage has to advance the fucking cause, you know. We're not all obsessed with the fucking *sisterhood*. This life's hard enough as it is without insisting that everyone with XX chromosomes has to like, stick to some kind of feminist script, or whatever.'

'It's alright for you. When you get bored of the sisterhood, you get to talk about being black – what the hell am I supposed to do?'

This made Josephine roar with laughter. Brenda jumped.

'Nellie's good and that's all you need to know,' she said when the laughter attack subsided.

'Yeah, I know... But still. It'd be nice if she wasn't so... Submissive on stage. She could be better, don't you think? If she wasn't trying to be so *likeable* all the time. I mean, what does she think's gonna happen if, like, one person thinks she's a bitch? LOADS of people think I'm a bitch and my career's going fucking marvellous.'

Josephine rolled her eyes and looked drunkenly at Brenda.

'And what about you, Brenda Monk? Are you gonna *advance the cause?*'

'Yeeeaaah,' drawled Brenda, barely able to operate her mouth, 'I'mnachaaangeevrything...'

'Good,' Josephine drawled back, ''bout time someone did.'

''Bout fuckin' time,' said Fenella.

12

Brenda couldn't specifically recall a dog shitting in her mouth but it must've happened at some point, for her saliva was turd flavoured. The alarm on her phone had been screaming with increasing hysteria for some time and she managed to turn it off without looking at the screen, the brightness of which she thought might actually blind her. She lay back and groaned. The sharpness of the pain that lay in a straight line across the tops of her eyebrows was intolerable and though she knew she needed water as a matter of urgency, the taps seemed impossibly far away. She lay very still, waiting to die. After five minutes it was apparent that death was not going to save her and she rolled out of bed and crawled to the shower.

Brenda sat curled up on the bottom of the shower cubicle and let the hot water wash away her sins, aware that she was drinking too much on a nightly basis now. She turned her open mouth upwards, hoping that hydration inside and out would make it all go away, but she knew this was going to be with her all day. She desperately wanted to take the day off but knew that would mean trouble. She had already taken two days off the week before and a few more before that, and people were starting to notice. It was still a week until Christmas, and the office was busy. She couldn't get away with being absent. Her editor needed the newspaper's blog sites constantly updated after an edict from on high regarding 'digital strategy', so she was basically writing double the number of words compared to the same time the year before, although without the benefit of double the number of ideas. Or double the income.

Brenda got dressed as if it were the last thing she'd ever do on earth and stumbled out into the world. It was cold and frosty and this offered some relief. She could finally stand to look at her phone and saw a text from her dad:

'Will I ever see you again?'

There was also a missed call from Jonathan along with a notification of new voicemail. She pressed the button and held the phone slightly away from her ear.

'Hi Bren – so it's all going really, really well out here, but I'm popping home over the holidays for ten days or so and thought it might be nice to hook up. Let me know.'

She couldn't let him know because she didn't know herself. The memory of Josephine's Terrible Mess story was still vivid and though Brenda did not want to confront Jonathan with it she also didn't want to sit with him, pretending she didn't know about it. And in any case, she had no idea of the state of play of their current relationship status. Neither had ever been inclined to give Facebook the satisfaction of having its insistent 'About Me' section completed in full, so there was no external marker for how things stood. Brenda did not believe they were still a couple. She certainly didn't feel that they were, but they had yet to officially 'split up'. So what should she do about seeing Jonathan? Now that she knew his horrible secret could she even bear to talk to him again? There was no way this could be resolved before coffee, an almond croissant and a poo. So Brenda cleared her mind and got on the bus.

She knew something was up as soon as she sat down at her

desk because her editor asked to have a word at lunchtime. She never asked to have a word. When Janet wasn't delivering instructions verbally, she was typing out instructions via email. Janet never asked for anything. She decided what she wanted to happen, who was going to do it, and then issued the afore-mentioned instructions. That was how Janet did things and she had been around newspapers for a long time and it wasn't going to change. In any case as a working method, it was reasonably successful, Brenda had observed, so you couldn't really com-plain. She got results and she kept people employed, which with journalists falling around everyone's ears at rival papers, was not something to be sniffed at. But today Janet had a gentle tone that Brenda had not heard before and if anything it freaked her out more than the usual bollocking. Brenda resolved to keep a low profile for the morning and just deal with whatever this lunch-time 'word' was about as the situation became clearer. She wrote a quick blog on a silly little story that had come that morning regarding a poll carried about by Pedigree Chum suggesting most women would rather have a dog than a boyfriend, was sick twice, ate a fried egg sandwich, felt a bit better, and tried not to fall asleep on her keyboard.

Lunchtime rolled around and Janet took Brenda to a small cafe round the corner from the office. This was ominous indeed.

'I'm not going to fire you,' Janet said as her opening gambit.

Brenda genuinely wasn't sure if she was pleased or disap-pointed.

'But I would like to know what's going on.'

'I'm trying to be a stand-up comedian,' Brenda said simply, too hungover to lie. Que sera, sera – that was the only way forward when dealing with a blinder like this.

Janet sat back hard in her chair.

'Thank god for that. I thought you were pregnant, and we

just don't have the budget for another maternity leave.'

Brenda smiled, happy to have given some relief. Janet pressed on.

'A stand-up comedian? What on earth for?'

'Don't know, just wanted to try it.'

'Are you funny? You don't seem funny. You've never struck me as funny.'

'Well, it's not a very funny place to work.'

Janet seemed mildly insulted by this.

'How many gigs have you done?'

'About thirty.'

'Are you any good?'

'Getting better.'

'Huh.'

Janet pondered for a moment and Brenda forked in hummus and chips with a tomato salad dripping in oil and vinegar.

'Do you want to write about it?'

'Not really,' said Brenda.

'Why not?'

'I don't know. I can't explain it, just feels a bit... private.'

'*Private?* Oh I've fucking heard it all now. You're doing stand-up comedy and it's *private?* What, do you do all your gigs in your own bathroom with the door locked or something?'

'No. I just mean I don't know what I'm doing yet and I don't want to tell everyone about it in a national newspaper while I figure it out.'

'Well, fine then, but don't waste any more of our fucking time being late and hungover. If you can't turn it into a regular blog, you're on your own.'

'OK.'

'You're on notice, Brenda. If you change your mind, let me know. We can do some kind of big thing about women in comedy and whether or not girls can be funny. Tie it in with some other shit about being a woman in a man's world, or something.'

Brenda nodded, thinking that sounded like precisely the kind of thing she was trying to avoid.

'Alright then, good. I'll see you back at the office. I've got to see Tony before he fucks off on holiday.'

And with that, Janet got up, paid for both of them and left Brenda to her hummus.

The rest of the day was a write-off, and Brenda started to wonder whether she actually wanted to get fired. Her first paid gig was forty-eight hours away, and Brenda knew she needed to concentrate: this could be the real beginning, and set her on the road to the rest of her life.

*

In the end the paid gig was uneventful, mundane even. She stretched her material to the required fifteen minutes, and although it had felt solid there had been no particular magic. Brenda was disappointed. She had wanted something special to mark her first booking as a professional stand-up, but in the end it had felt flat. She had tried the post-Pete row material again but somehow it hadn't quite hit the mark, it had felt calculated and false, which was annoying. After all, Brenda thought, she couldn't go through an actual break-up every time she needed to do a good gig. Falling back on old material – 'When is the right time to do a shit at your boyfriend's house? Let me tell you – it's not right as he's reaching climax...' – felt boring and cheap, as though she was cheating someone. But they'd laughed, and so she couldn't have been cheating them. Then who? Herself? Did that matter, if the crowd liked it?

Brenda's artistic catastrophe was broken, and somewhat

relieved, by the promoter handing over her money, and she couldn't deny the thrill of receiving that brown envelope, with four £20 notes inside and her name scrawled across the front: *Brenda Monk 80*. She knew she'd keep it forever – the envelope, not the cash.

Over the next few days, she considered the maths. If she could get three paid gigs a week, that would be £960 a month. Not quite enough to live on, but she had one credit card she barely used with an £8,000 credit limit, pristine and ready to abuse. She could use that to supplement the low income, and as she improved she would get more paid gigs. She would be given larger amounts for the gigs she did, and then one day she would be a headliner making three or even four thousand a month, like Jonathan, and that was plenty for anyone. In fact, that was way more than she was making now. She wondered if her dad could lend her a bit to tide her over. He never had much, but sometimes he was able to magic up a few hundred pounds if the tide was right. There were no guarantees though and she didn't expect it. In fact she had always refused his help in the past on the basis of her pride and need for independence. But perhaps if it was offered, she could force herself to accept this time. Comedy, it seemed, was more important than pride and in any case it would be good to see him. Brenda picked up her phone and texted.

'Sorry, lots going on. Lots to tell you. When you free?'

'Christmas Day.'

Brenda laughed and replied instantly.

'It's a date. See you for lunch x'

Brenda checked her diary – ten days away. Why did Christmas always come around so fast? One minute it was months away, the next it was here, and then over again. Sometimes she wondered whether it was even worth the bother. Scrolling back through her messages she came across an unanswered one from Jonathan.

'Hey did you get my voicemail? Call me on my cell.'

Cell. Annoying. He was affecting Americanisms already. Perhaps he was back in the UK now, Brenda thought, sharing her time zone, breathing her air. Did she want to see him? Not enough to call, but she was curious. She made a note to text him back... At some point.

13

Brenda parked the comically tiny car she had hired on the small street that was in fact the main thoroughfare for the village, got out and crunched up the frosted mud on the lane that led to her dad's house: an old pile of bricks roughly formed into the shape of a house, but surrounded by inexpertly built lean-to type structures made from wood frames and nailed in sheets of corrugated iron and hard, clear plastic. The whole confused building sat in a Wiltshire field that had once been a garden. It was overgrown apart from a very large vegetable patch, currently dormant, which was clearly meticulously tended. Brenda put her rucksack and small bag of presents on the ground and knocked on the door.

'Happy Christmas!'

Brenda's dad hugged her tightly and looked her up and down. 'Nice hair.'

It really had been too long. She'd had this hair since the end of August. She stepped inside her father's home, or what had once been her parents' home until the death of her mother ten years previously. It was relatively clean, and she breathed a sigh of relief. She turned to look at her dad. He was also relatively clean. His clothes looked a bit tatty, but then they always had. His hair was long but freshly washed and he had never really been a short back and sides man in any case. Brenda only worried about him when he was actually stood in front of her, but she found nothing amiss here.

'Is Amanda coming over?'

'No, she's seeing her kids today.'

'OK, that's nice.'

Amanda had been on the scene for about three years and lived in her own cottage about a mile away. They were clearly happy with the arrangement and no mention of moving in together had ever been made. Brenda and Amanda had little to do with each other but there was no great animosity – more a lack of interest on either side.

'I can smell food. Good food,' Brenda said moving towards the kitchen, thankful (and not for the first time) that her dad could cook.

'I brought this,' she said, pulling a bottle of half-price supermarket Champagne from her bag.

'Very good. Let's open it now.'

Two hours later and they were pissed, a third bottle open on the table and empty plates in front of them.

'You were a funny child.'

'Was I?'

'Yeah. Show-offy, though, and a bit rude sometimes. Your mother got embarrassed when you said things that made it awkward.'

Brenda nodded and sipped her wine.

'Like the time you told her boss you were an acquired taste.'

'Did I? How old was I?'

'Eleven.'

'Jesus.'

'Never imagined you getting up on stage though, for real. You were shy in your way, too. Wanted the attention when you wanted it, then didn't want it when you didn't want it.'

Brenda smiled. This felt as familiar a description of herself as another could make.

'Dad, I think I might try and do it, like, full time...'

'Oh yeah? Must be going well, then.'

'Yeah...'

A pause while her dad pretended he didn't know what was coming next.

'I mean, it takes a while to really make any money.'

'Mmm.'

He wasn't going to make this easy. He even seemed faintly amused.

'If I left my job, I wouldn't have any money coming in.'

'Yes, that's how it usually works.'

Christ.

'So...'

'So?'

'Is there any way you could... maybe...give me a bit of...help?'

'Why, are you having trouble getting up?'

Brenda nodded to herself.

'No. It's OK. I'm fine. Don't worry about it.'

'What's the comedy thing about, then? Where's it come from?'

'I don't know, but I tried it and now suddenly I feel like... me. Or like someone I thought me was... or might be, would be if I... I'm not making sense... I...'

'I've got two grand in a box upstairs. You can have that.'

Brenda thought she might pass out. This was double, even treble, what she had dreamed possible.

'It's the last of your mother's life insurance. I withdrew it from the bank when those cunts stole all our money.'

Brenda had heard this often enough to know he meant the international banking community.

'I only need my pension now. Mortgage is paid off, such as it was, and I grow all the food. Got my pension, fuel allowance and whatnot. Only need money for meat and condoms.'

Brenda laughed with a snort.

'And to be honest, I only wear the condoms to flatter Amanda. She went through the menopause years ago so I don't know why I carry on with this little charade. It's my own fault. I did it on the first date so she'd feel younger and now I can't get out of it.'

Brenda's heart was bursting out of her body. Two thousand pounds would be a hefty contribution if she kept her outgoings low. That was nearly three months' rent. She didn't have to eat anything fancy, just beans or whatever, and people always bought comedians drinks after gigs so she wouldn't need money for booze. With the credit card and this she could live for six months if she was very careful, without earning a penny from stand-up, and she didn't anticipate allowing that to happen. She could effectively resign tomorrow, which was Boxing Day, so the day after. She could live for six months. OK. No guarantee of being able to live after that six months with no official job and if she didn't manage to earn anything through stand-up she would be in an horrific amount of debt but she would be able to travel to gigs outside London because there would be no day job to get back to, and that would surely increase the opportunities for work.

'Are you OK in there?' Brenda's dad said, knocking on her head.

'Yes, really good. Thank you, Dad. Thank you.'

She beamed at him and he smiled lopsidedly back. He poured out the rest of the wine into their glasses.

'Shall I open another?' he asked, rising out of his seat.

'Always,' said Brenda.

As her dad wandered out of the room she looked down at her phone and saw an email from Pete.

'Hi! Happy Christmas! I hope all is well with you and we get a chance to catch up in the New Year! Love Pete.'

This was tricky. It was the first she'd heard from him since he told he wanted some time to himself back in November, a request Brenda had respected and made sure she did not violate by calling him. It read like a template or general message Pete had sent to everyone in his contacts list, but how could she be sure? And if it was personal to her it would look bad to ignore it. On the other hand, if she responded to it and it was just a general mail-out she would feel foolish. Her resistance was low though. She could hear her dad returning from his make-shift wine cellar and hoped the bottle he was bringing up was not homemade. She tapped out a reply before she had time to decide not to.

'Happy Christmas to you too, Pete. I also hope all is well with you and that we do get a chance to catch up in the New Year! Love Brenda.'

She clicked send, re-read and saw that instead of sounding light and breezy and slightly teasing, it sounded glib and a bit sarcastic. Shit.

A message appeared almost instantly.

'Sorry. Forgot to take you off my mailing list. Won't happen again. Pete.'

Brenda re-read that little turd of a message, and then started typing a reply she already knew she would regret.

'No problem. You're already off my material list. Old news. Brenda.'

She clicked send and hated herself.

Another instant reply.

'Am I?'

Brenda ached for him. She ached for sex with him, all warm and strong and healthy feeling.

'Yes. I'm sorry about that message. It was meaner than I intended. Happy Christmas, seriously. B.'

A long wait while her dad talked about something she wasn't listening to. Her phone buzzed. Her dad rolled his eyes.

'Go on, have a look. I'm sure it's something earth shattering...'

Brenda opened the message.

'Shall we have a drink in the New Year, then? It would be nice to chat. Pete.'

A sunbeam opened inside Brenda. Yes, YES.

*

Brenda would have knocked on the door but it was already open and the party was raging inside. Loud hip-hop music was being broadcast to the surrounding area but since it was New Year's Eve it seemed unlikely that anyone would mind. Brenda stepped over someone who was lying on the ground in the front garden and bent down to ask him if he was OK.

'I'm perfect.'

'I'm worried you'll freeze to death.'

'If the ice fairies come for me, I will be powerless to resist.'

'Come inside soon, OK?'

'What is "soon"? Does an owl have any concept of soon?'

Brenda went inside. Wall to wall comedians. This now legendary and somewhat traditional New Year's Eve party was a staple of the comedy year and Brenda had been twice before. Once by accident with a one-night-stand she had met at a gig as a student and once with Jonathan. Held in a run-down, old Victorian terraced house owned by an ex-circuit comedian who had bought it in the 1970s and now lived in Spain with little concept of his property's current value, it stood in an otherwise unassuming residential North London street and the pull of the party was felt throughout the comedy community. Every year comics from far and wide heard the siren call of the beckoning Bacchanal and swung over, like giants crushing the landscape. The five bedrooms were always occupied by stand-up comedians who needed a place to rent for however long and its status as a kind of glorified hostel for working comics had a far longer pedigree than any of its current tenants. As indeed did the party, which seemed to take place automatically without anybody actually organising it. The party always got going late as most comedians worked on New Year's Eve if they could – the audiences were awful but the money was good. No-one would book someone as inexperienced as Brenda for such a big night but she still left it until 11.30pm to arrive. The party usually lasted around three days, with people coming and going and staying and crying and laughing and coming and going for all that time. In fact it was hard to tell when the party stopped for sure as this house was always full of comedians and so the only real way of telling whether the party was going on or not going on was by the volume of people in the house and since there were always quite a lot of people in the house, there was one argument to say that the party had basically been going on to a greater or lesser extent for the past ten years. In short, this house had become a sort of informal drop-in centre for stand-up comedians, with an especially busy period around New Year.

There was no part of the house that was not available, no mealy mouthed shutting of bedroom doors here. Brenda opened her own bottle of wine, greeted a few people and went upstairs to where Fenella had already texted Brenda to come and find her on arrival.

When Brenda entered one of the bedrooms, which though it belonged to a thirty-year-old man looked like that of a fourteen-year-old, she saw Fenella lounging on the bed with Katherine and Rossly. To one side a woman with a shaved head and multiple piercings sat on the floor gently cradling a baby, who slept happily in clean swaddling. The baby's father was stood to one side talking quietly with another man, but kept looking down at his new baby with awe and pride. In fact everyone was talking very quietly in here so as not to wake the baby. But it was a slightly empty gesture as the music was thumping through the floor. Perhaps the persistent steady beat aped his mother's heartbeat in the womb, but for whatever reason, the infant slept soundly.

'Jonathan's downstairs,' said Fenella.

Brenda missed her stride a little, but managed to keep control of herself. She didn't know how she felt about this news and so anything that wrote itself across her face at that very moment would not necessarily reflect the true scope of her feelings. She cursed herself internally for not realising sooner that of course he would be here. She also realised she had not responded to his request to see her a couple of weeks earlier. A muddle of emotions flashed by in a matter of seconds, but she was grateful for the warning. Fenella seemed to divine this.

'Just wanted you to know so you're not, you know, caught off guard.'

'Thanks.'

'I've been hearing good things about you, Brenda Monk,' Rossly said.

He took out a packet of cigarettes, pulled one out, then remembered the baby and put it back.

'You've been gigging.'

'Yes. I've also given up my day job.'

'Round of applause,' said Rossly. 'What are you living on?'

'A loan and a credit card.'

'All good incentives to get better.'

Brenda drank and regarded Rossly. She liked him. A lot. He was undoubtedly a monumental fuck up, but she liked him. And the way he was looking at her now, she was fairly certain he liked her. Properly liked her – not just to try it on with, but in some emotional sense too. She had felt it before but dismissed it, still slightly embarrassed at that first encounter and also painfully aware that she was nothing special to look at compared with Nina.

'I think I'd better get Jonathan out of the way,' said Brenda and left the room.

Always this urge to walk away whenever a man seemed to show interest. She couldn't account for it. Why did she always require them to follow her, figuratively or otherwise? It was a pathological behaviour pattern but she didn't seem to be doing anything about it: she was already half way down the stairs.

Jonathan was in the sitting room at the back of the house, sat on a large sofa and holding court. He looked extremely good: tanned and clear skinned, with a new gloss on him that Brenda didn't remember from before. The contrast with the pallid, winter worn, semi-nocturnal comedians around him was striking. It was four months since she'd last seen him – the day he left her flat to get on his plane to New York – and there was no way of pinning down her feelings in one easy sentence. So much had happened in those four months she almost felt like an entirely different person now – when he had left she had been just another angry, neglected girlfriend. Now she was a stand-up comedian.

Yes, she really was. She had resigned three days earlier to a stony faced Janet, whose partings words had been, 'Call me when you've finished fucking it up, you're a slightly above average journalist and we always need a few of those to do the basic stuff.' Since then she had done two gigs and booked several more for the New Year. The first regional heat of the competition she had entered took place in less than two weeks and she had not allowed herself the option of picturing failure.

The first surprise was that she did not want to have sex with Jonathan. That was a relief. The second surprise was how pleased she was to see him, and when he looked up and saw her his face split into a wide grin and he stood up immediately.

'Here she is!'

He opened his arms wide and embraced her fully, kissing her neck behind her right ear.

'My Brenda.'

Confusing – his Brenda? No, not his Brenda. She pulled back.

'How are you, Jonathan?'

'I'm so fucking well you wouldn't believe. Joan has been getting me so many meetings and auditions and shit. I've done a bit on *Comedy Central* over there and got great buzz. I've got a call back for a part in this shit hot new sit-com written by a couple of ex-*Simpsons* writers next week. Apparently they told Joan the audition was just a formality, they know they want me.'

'Amazing. It all sounds amazing.'

'Yeah. It is.'

'And you look really well.'

'Thanks. So do you.'

And that was it and in an instant the pleasure Brenda had initially, instinctively felt evaporated. What the hell had they ever talked about? It appeared that, as far as Brenda was concerned, without the sexual attraction there was very little conversation to be had. She stood awkwardly in front of him for a moment. Then she suddenly remembered Josephine and the abortion, and had to steady herself. It was so unrelated in her mind to the man that stood before her, she could hardly comprehend they were the same person. She had an urge to bring it up, just to see what he would do. But then Jonathan spoke.

'So, you're really doing stand-up, then?'

'Yeah, it's what I do now.'

'You still doing material about us?'

'A bit, sort of. I'm doing stuff that's more what's on my mind at the moment though.'

'Oh. Right.' Jonathan looked a bit hurt and Brenda realised she had been insensitive, though she hadn't meant to be. The sudden frosty atmosphere was broken by Rossly calling out from across the room as he loped through the door way.

'Ah, Jonathan Cape, the prodigal returns.'

'Rossly Barns, the convict never leaves.'

'Cheap, Jonathan, cheap.'

'Cheap is OK by me if it works.'

Brenda was instantly bored. She hadn't come here to stand around and listen to comedians willy-waving. That was her old life.

'OK, guys, I'll see you later.'

'Hang on, I haven't finished with you yet,' Jonathan said with unexpected authority.

'Oh, sorry,' Brenda replied, feeling anxious where she once would have been thrilled by his insistent attention.

'So, look, I've had this idea, Brenda. I think it would really work.'

'What's that?'

'We do a double gig.'

'What?'

'What the fuck is a double gig?' Rossly said, not liking being excluded.

'Yeah, what are you talking about?' said Brenda, eager to maintain some kind of control of the conversation.

'We have half a show each to talk about our relationship. We do our material about the same topics, but from our own perspectives.'

That shut them up.

'Are we...in a relationship?' Brenda asked.

Jonathan shrugged.

'In as much as anyone is...' he replied, which was no kind of answer.

Brenda's mind raced. She could see the potential benefits to her: a highly publicised gig with Jonathan, slightly taboo subject matter, fascination for punters to see a couple effectively having a highly deconstructed row live on stage. It would definitely get reviewed and it might be the punch through into a wider consciousness that she needed to get more paid work. And it was interesting comedically. No-one had ever done it before, in her experience. Yes, she could see all that. What she couldn't see was the benefit to Jonathan. There must be one. He never did anything without some direct benefit to himself, but it was not immediately apparent in this case, and that made her nervous. She didn't want to show her neck though and she certainly wasn't going to ask with Rossly standing right there, so she tipped her head to the side in what she hoped was a blasé fashion and considered the suggestion.

'Sounds interesting,' she said with great nonchalance, her mind already skipping over all the material she could use and work on.

'Yeah, it does,' said Rossly, grudgingly. 'Never seen that before.'

'I know, right? It's sort of ground-breaking,' Jonathan said with the beginnings of an unbearable trans-Atlantic twang.

'Who wants some MDMA?'

And that was the end of that for the time being.

Brenda was sitting with Rossly, Fenella and Jim John, who had turned up sometime around 1am with his guitar, having driven all the way from Nottingham after his gig in order to be at the party. Fenella had rolled a very nice joint and they were all pleasantly high. The MDMA felt kinder this time but Brenda suspected it was just because she was more relaxed generally than when she had last had some in Edinburgh. Everything was soft round the edges and welcoming and harmonious. And so when Brenda spotted John Nunn sitting in one corner, talking earnestly to another comedian, she felt that it would be the most natural thing in the world to approach him. Rossly, Fenella and Jim sat back to enjoy the show.

A year ago John Nunn had been a high end circuit comedian earning a decent living with the odd TV appearance to his name. He was now a millionaire with an arena tour booked for the year ahead which would make him millions more. His rise had been meteoric, and yet he had also been around forever. He must have been forty-two, but the money had lifted some of the ageing worry off his shoulders and he'd clearly been on holiday somewhere hot. He looked more expensive than anyone around him – success dripped off him. It was strange to see him here, but in fact twelve months earlier he had been at this very party with £60,000 worth of debt, one pair of shoes and, according to gossip, an application for bankruptcy on his coffee table at home. Then he had changed agents.

His new representation had the biggest and best client list in comedy. They controlled everything. They represented comics and also created, produced and owned the primetime TV shows these comics performed in. They had a DVD distribution business and a live tour promotion team. They created and sold merchandise and dealt with international licensing agreements. It was what was known in the music business as a 360 deal, but these guys were the pioneers in terms of comedy. The earnings of their top seven comedians in any given year dwarfed the combined income of every other gigging comic in the UK.

You gave them your life; they gave you your money. It was as simple as that.

Brenda recalled how Jonathan had followed John Nunn's career with a mixture of contempt and envy. She knew every last detail of his meteoric rise. He had signed up with his new agents in January. They had immediately paid off all his debts and booked him onto their flagship live stand-up show on BBC1, where the viewing nation would see him perform his best seven minutes of material. He was ready. He'd been ready for years.

Next they booked him as a guest onto the primetime chat show they also produced, which was fronted by a comedian turned presenter they also represented who referred to him as 'one of Britain's best loved comedians' and set him up for all his best jokes, as planned beforehand with the producer. They then booked him on a mid-range tour of a hundred dates across the country. The TV appearances meant that he sold out all but seven of these dates and they had a DVD ready to come out off the back of it in time for the Christmas market. A couple of appearances on the main panel shows, one of which was also produced by his agency, meant that he was now cemented in the public's mind as someone who was a rock solid ticket to laughter. His DVD had gone to number one in the comedy charts and stayed there for two weeks before slipping down to number four. It was still at number seven and didn't look like moving out of the top ten for some time. He was now making his agency a lot of money with his highly sellable family-friendly, light observational comedy. The £60k debt had been repaid several times over. Brenda felt warmed through with a chemical love for humanity and was suddenly overwhelmed with the desire to congratulate him on his success. His £2.4 million success, if the rumours were to believed.

Brenda walked over to him and stuck out her hand.

'Hi, you're John Nunn.'

He completely ignored her. She tried again.

'Hi, you're John Nunn.'

He stopped and looked up and his pale blue eyes told her he was stone cold sober.

'Do you know it's rude to interrupt people when they're talking?'

Brenda absorbed this and pressed on.

'Yeah, I do, but it's that kind of party, isn't it?'

'It certainly seems to be for you.'

'Yeah.'

He turned back and carried on talking to his friend, who seemed embarrassed and unsure as to what to do next. Brenda didn't move. John stopped talking and turned to her.

'Can I help you with something?'

Brenda was feeling bold and facetious – a terrible combination.

'You could give me twenty grand.'

'Would that make you go away?'

'For a bit.'

'I'll call my manager...'

'OK, cool. Hey John Nunn, why come to a party if you don't want to meet new friends?'

'Because I barely see the old ones as it is. I don't have time for new people.'

'That's sad, that's very, very sad.'

'Yes, it is. What's your name?'

'Brenda. Brenda Monk.'

'Well, Brenda Monk, it's been wonderful meeting you. Seriously, life-changing in many respects.'

Brenda beamed at this.

'But I'd really like you to go away now so I can carry on talking to my friend here, OK? I can't stay here long, I'm on a flight at 7am so I have to leave here in about ten minutes and I don't want to waste any more time talking to you.'

Brenda nodded and felt overwhelmed with the desire to hug him. Which she did. He froze in her arms and when she had finished, he looked her straight in the eye and spoke with deadly but contained fury.

'Seriously, fuck off, OK?'

Brenda walked back over to where Rossly, Fenella and Jim were eating their fists.

'That was diabolical to watch,' said Fenella. 'I literally cannot believe what I have just witnessed.'

'He seemed so sad and angry and stressed, I thought he needed a hug,' Brenda said dreamily.

'No more drugs for you, babe,' Rossly said. 'He's an uptight prick anyway. Always has been, even before the money and whatever.'

'Must be weird for him though, suddenly getting famous and rich.'

'Yeah boo-hoo, my heart bleeds.'

Brenda left around 3 o'clock the following afternoon having talked constantly for hours. No comedic stone was unturned and though she had felt Rossly's eyes on her almost all the time, she had made sure to spread herself around the room. She felt part of it all now. This was family time for many of the comedians there, especially the handful of old-timers in their fifties and sixties with estranged wives (several in some cases) and children, who had spent Christmas alone and looked forward to this night as the most festive they were likely to get. There was talking shop, one-up-manship, laughter, drug taking, enlightening conversation, advice, comfort, the odd small half-hearted fight and a little sleep. Brenda had napped around 10am for a cou-

ple of hours, lying half under a bed, and woke to find that someone had put a blanket over her. She would never find out who.

Wandering down the road in a daze, blinking in the light
like a recently born creature, Brenda faced the New Year with
excitement. She couldn't stop thinking about Jonathan's offer.
Though they had barely spoken for the rest of the party (she was
fairly certain he had left with someone else around dawn) he
had made sure to take her to one side in the early hours and told
her he may be high, but he was serious. He said Lloyd would be
in touch with her to arrange the details. Brenda got the feeling
he knew far more about her recent comedic activities than he
was letting on, but she wasn't particularly inclined to make any
inquiries. Whatever he was hearing must be broadly positive,
otherwise he wouldn't want to share a stage with her. He
obviously expected to be the better comedian on the night but he
wouldn't want to devalue his currency by appearing with someone in a dedicated show if that person was out and out crap. His
motivation for wanting to do the show in the first place was still
a complete mystery but she was so excited by what she could
get out of it she decided to ignore any niggling little doubts
she may have. This was an extraordinary opportunity and they
didn't come along very often. When met with an extraordinary
opportunity, there is only one answer: yes. You figure out all the
other stuff later. The nature of Brenda and Jonathan's relationship couldn't be fudged forever but for once, in the face of a truly
amazing professional offer, Brenda could use his vagueness to
her advantage.

'BRENDA!'

She turned to see who was shouting and saw Rossly striding
up the street. She waited for him to catch her up.

'Why are you leaving so early?'

'Early? It's the next afternoon.'

'Yeah but still... Why are you going? You haven't got any-where to be.'

'I just felt like going home.'

Rossly took this in.

'Shall I come with you?'

'No thanks.'

'Are you OK? You're not feeling weird? You were pretty mashed in there for a while.'

'Honestly, Rossly, I'm fine.'

'OK, give me your number then so I can check on you later.'

She gave him the number and kissed him on the cheek. He looked vulnerable for a brief second and then he was striding back to the house.

Brenda felt liberated and strong. She arrived back at her flat, had a bath and then went to bed. She slept long and soundly, barely stirring until she woke disoriented and incredibly hungry at 11pm. She got up and made herself a plate of scrambled eggs and toast and sat eating in her dark kitchen, contemplating the future.

Jonathan had indicated that he would be back in the UK in February and would like to do the show then. They had both agreed that performing it for one night only on Valentine's Day would be a stroke of genius. That gave her six weeks to prepare. Heat One of the competition was in two weeks and she had to make sure she did well. The rest of the time she had other gigs booked. All of which were unpaid apart from one, where she was offered a percentage of the box office, though what percentage had yet to be determined and Brenda was fairly sure she wouldn't be buying her first Rolex with it.

She had work, though, even though she was effectively paying herself to do it. Or rather, MasterCard was paying her to do it and she was paying MasterCard to let her. So in a sense she was currently paying to be a stand-up comedian. She had a hot flash of terror at what she had done and suddenly wanted so badly to see Pete she could barely stand it. She picked up her phone, held it for a moment, and then sent a text.

'You know that drink? Do you want to have it now?'

And then waited.

'No.'

So Brenda went back upstairs to bed and masturbated, orgasmed in less than fifteen seconds and then fell asleep again.

She woke at 6am to a second text from Pete that must have been sent shortly after the first one, by which point Brenda was dreaming.

'Don't booty-call me, Brenda. Let's have a proper drink and a conversation first. When are you free?'

She felt heartened by his use of the word 'first'. She texted him back.

'Tonight, but early.'

14

Brenda arrived at the pub they had picked because it felt 'neutral'. She was early this time, the result of the joke Pete had made about lateness giving him the upper hand, Brenda didn't relinquish the upper hand quite so easily these days. She bought a large glass of white wine and sat in a quiet corner with a high wooden panel on one side. It felt private, which was good. If they were going to have a difficult conversation she didn't want to feel self-conscious. Pete arrived and she watched him looking around for her. She felt nervous, although she couldn't honestly say she knew what she wanted tonight. Apart from sex. She definitely wanted that, but not at any cost. But it was more than that. She had missed him, but she couldn't detangle the reasons why. Did he simply provide comfort when she was feeling lonely? Or was there more to it than that? She hadn't really allowed either of them the time to find out because she always fitted him between other things. Pete saw her, smiled in an attempt to look relaxed, and came over.

'Oh, you've got a drink.'

'Yes, I thought I'd start early with the lady petrol so I can achieve total irrationality by last orders.'

Pete laughed but this remark certainly didn't quell his anxiety and Brenda kicked herself inside for saying it – it wasn't a helpful way to begin. Pete got himself a pint of Pilsner and sat down opposite Brenda. Brenda realised she had no idea what Pete wanted either.

'You look well,' he began, for the want of something better to say.

'Thanks,' said Brenda, 'so do you.'

'Did you have a good Christmas?'

'Quiet but nice. You?'

'Yeah, just family. Saw my sister and my nieces and that was... nice.'

This was awful. They both sat with engines revving but not in gear. How could they get this started properly? One of them would have to be bolder than the other. Brenda spoke first.

'So, you said you wanted some time to yourself. How's it been for you?'

Pete looked at the table and frowned.

'It's been... uneventful, I guess. I don't know what I was expecting to happen, that I would have some revelation or something, but it never came. I just got used to not seeing you.'

That was a punch. A bleaker sentiment Brenda could not have imagined.

'I've stopped talking about us on stage. Well, mostly. I mean there are three jokes that just work every time and, you know, at this stage I do need guaranteed laughs so that I can safely extend my set with new material. If something doesn't work, I can pull out one of my trump cards and get the gig back on track, so... sorry, I'm rambling.'

'No, it's OK. I want to understand.'

Brenda nodded and felt sick, the way she always did when a man she was attracted to was extremely nice to her.

'It's hard to explain. I ditched my job. I'm doing stand-up full time now.'

'That's a brave move. Must be going well.'

'Yeah, it is. I mean, I'm not being paid but I'm getting better at it, so I hope it's only a matter of time...'

'What are the three jokes you do about me?'

'It's nothing awful. I mean, the joke's on me really. You're always the hero. I say, my boyfriend...'

'My boyfriend? How am I your boyfriend?'

'Oh, well you're not, I know that. It's just that the joke works better if I say it's my boyfriend.'

'Isn't that a bit weird? To do material that sounds as if it's real but the basic premise is a lie?'

'It's not a lie, it's just a *framing device*.'

'A framing device? Stop, please, you're killing me with romance.'

There was some humour in this remark and Brenda was encouraged by it.

'It's blurred with comedy, Pete. I don't think people really believe you're talking about a real person. When Jonathan was doing his show about me, I used to meet people and they'd say, oh, I didn't think you actually existed...'

'But you did.'

'Yes I did.'

'And you had feelings, real feelings that aren't just part of a framing device.'

'Yes, I know. But my feelings were all fucked up because I respected the comedy. And I suppose I now know, because I wanted to be up there doing it too. So even though sometimes I felt violated in a way, I never really put my foot down about it. It wasn't why I left him.'

'So, you have left him now, then?'

'Yes. I mean, we haven't had the official conversation or anything but it's pretty clear it's over. He wants to do a show together where we each do material about the same relationship issues. Like a kind of comedy his and hers perspective.'

'Sounds like a very unorthodox couples therapy.'

'Yeah, except the aim is not to get back together...'

Pete nodded and drank his pint.

'So, the jokes, then...'

'Oh, yeah. OK, I mean, it's hard to tell a joke and make it funny like, here, now, like this...'

'I'm not here to laugh, Brenda. I'm aware that this is not the world's smallest and most awkward comedy show. I just want to hear what you're saying about us... me.'

'Ummm, well the first one is about going out with someone who imports Danish furniture...'

'It's not just Danish.'

'I know that, but the joke works better if I say Danish.'

'OK.'

'And it just leads into a bit about couples getting obsessed with watching Scandinavian box-sets, and how it's creepy that every time we watch an episode of *The Killing* I come home the next day and there's a new piece of furniture from the TV show and I'm scared that one day I'll look over into the corner of the room and see a really tastefully designed wooden coffin and you'll be standing in the dark with a knife.'

A glimmer of a smile passed across Pete's eyes.

'It sounds shit when I say it like that but it works when I do it properly.'

'I can see that,' said Pete generously. 'Go on.'

'The next bit is really short, and it's just a silly little gag about the first time you do a shit at your boyfriend's house.'

'I remember it well. I'm still in treatment.'

'Shut up!' Brenda laughed, and Pete smiled properly and those kinks in his cheeks that Brenda had not seen for so long melted her from the inside.

'It's not massively original but a certain sort of crowd likes it, so it's got me out of difficulty a few times. And then the last bit is about...'

Brenda stopped and frowned.

'Is about?'

'Sorry, I've just realised the third joke is actually about Jonathan, it's just I ascribe it all to the same man.'

'Hmmm.'

'It's nothing bad. It's just a thing about shaving all your pubes off to make your cock look bigger.'

'Hah, great.'

'No, it's a joke about me. It leads into a thing about me shaving all my pubes off to make my cunt look bigger. That's the gag.'

Pete cleared his throat and took a long draught of beer.

The disabled toilet was big enough for them both to lie down, and as Pete put his face between Brenda's legs she knew this wasn't going to take long. After less than thirty seconds she pulled his head up, indicating that she wanted him inside her now and he obliged fully. It lasted a minute and a half at a driving pace and then he rolled off and lay beside her, head twisted slightly under the bars that lay along the side of the toilet bowl to help more legitimate occupants.

They regained their breath.

'Oh shit, I needed that,' Brenda sighed.

'Me too.'

Pete pushed up on his elbow and kissed Brenda softly and gently on her mouth. She smiled dewily up at him.

'I really fucking love having sex with you,' she said and he kissed her again.

'Come home with me,' he said.

'I can't. I've got a late gig. I could come over after though.'

'I have to be up early, I need to get to bed.'

And there in a nutshell was the problem. They lay quietly side by side, staring up at the ceiling which was covered with bits of dried toilet roll someone had once soaked and thrown up for unknown reasons.

'I'd like to try and make this work, Brenda. I missed you. I was surprised how much I missed you. Can you do something for me, though?'

'I'll try my best.'

'Do you think you can just stick to those three jokes about us? I mean, any other stuff you say, can it be made up or based on other relationships, or about an ex or something? I think I can take a lot, but I can't feel comfortable about our private things if I feel they're just going to be used for material. I'll start to watch what I say and then it'll be dishonest and we might as well not bother.'

Brenda felt an instant knee-jerk reaction to being told to limit what she could talk about on stage. She had started doing stand-up so that she could whatever she felt like saying, and now someone was telling her she couldn't. And yet, she could see the sense of it, and honestly, it was the reasonable position to take. She knew that would be the objective view. And so if she wanted to have a real, adult, relatively functional relationship with another human being this would always be an issue. So was Pete worth it? That was the real question. Was he worth it?

Brenda turned to look at him.

'OK. We'll try it like that and see how we go.'

Pete nodded.

'Let's take things very slowly then. When are you next free?'

'Sunday.'

'You have gigs every other day this week?'

'Yes, and two of them are out of London.'

'Jesus.'

Brenda didn't speak. She had no plans to cancel them.

'OK,' Pete conceded ground. 'Sunday it is then. Come to my flat and I'll cook us lunch.'

'Late lunch?'

'OK.'

'Sounds perfect.'

'It will be.'

'I love your confidence.'

'It masks my deep existential angst.'

'I imagine visiting Denmark on a regular basis helps with that.'

'Funnily enough, it doesn't.'

'OK, see you Sunday,' said Brenda, standing up and pulling on her jeans.

'I think I might stay here for a bit, soak up the atmosphere.'

'Soaking up piss is what you're doing. This toilet is unisex.'

'That is a thousand per cent correct.'

Pete got to his feet and Brenda slipped out and away.

'Do you have a website?' a fellow comic had asked her at that night's gig, and Brenda had bashfully admitted she did not. In fact, she was embarrassed that it hadn't even occurred to her.

'Then how is anyone supposed to find you?' He had continued, possibly, it seemed to Brenda, slightly enjoying watching her squirm, 'Or are you keeping yourself a secret?'

No, she was not keeping herself a secret, not at all. Brenda had arrived home around 1am and immediately set about creating one. She blessed the era into which she had been born, for without a great deal of technical know-how Brenda had created a website using an online template that would cost her around £12 a month to maintain. With it came an email address. Now she felt she was in business, even if any business had yet to find her.

A part of the internet belonged entirely to Brenda Monk. That alone was a statement, and another weapon in her arsenal.

A few days later as she was preparing for the first heat of the new act competition, Brenda had a call from Lloyd, just as Jonathan had said she would, asking her to meet him at Soho House the next day. She turned up to the private members' club and climbed the steep, narrow wooden stairs to a large restaurant area with big sash windows and an atmosphere of deals being done. Lloyd sat in the far corner and waved to her as she approached.

'Brenda! You're looking great. Sit down, what can I get you?'

Brenda ordered a coffee and took the chair opposite Lloyd. On the table in front of him was a small pile of papers stapled together and an envelope stuffed full of cash.

'So, how's things with you and Jonathan?' Brenda asked politely.

'Oh fantastic, couldn't be better. The buzz around him over there is immense.'

'Yeah, he said.'

'Oh, you've seen him?'

Lloyd didn't look altogether pleased with this information.

'Yeah, at a party.'

'Well you know all about it then, our little idea.'

'Yeah.'

'I think it's really interesting. He's so innovative and with you on board it could be really special.'

'I don't see how you could do it without me on board.'

'Quite. Clever Brenda. So, to business. Here's your contract.'

'I need a contract?'

'Well, we want to pay you, Brenda, so it's for your protection as much as anything.'

He smiled creepily and Brenda suddenly felt she needed to

get away from him as fast as she could. He seemed contaminated in some way.

'You want to pay me?'

This was welcome news, she had to admit, however much she hated the messenger.

'Yes. Five hundred quid. There it is, all in there.'

He patted the envelope.

'I hope you might find it useful.'

Useful? It would mean she could buy a cheap little car for a start, which would allow her to drive to gigs outside of London. It was more than useful.

'Just sign the contract here and here and take the money.' The cash looked good enough to eat – fat wads pushing its way out of the open side of the envelope. Brenda saw that Lloyd had two copies of the contract open in front of him, laid side by side on the table. The had both been turned to the signature page and Brenda could see that both Lloyd and Jonathan had already signed their own names. The only gaps left were for her.

'It's just a standard thing – nothing controversial. We'd also like to film it, if that's OK, just for our own internal use, but you'll be welcome to have a copy for your website if you like – I see you have a website now, which is great – you're really having a good go at it all, aren't you? Fantastic.'

Brenda thought she might actually become ill if she spent any more time sitting here, and the money was practically talking to her now. Lloyd proffered an expensive looking pen – his 'signing pen' as he liked to call it – and Brenda took it, scribbled her name twice, picked up the envelope and her copy of the contract and downed her coffee.

'Great to see you, Lloyd. See you in a few weeks,' she said and exited fast.

First Regional Heat and Brenda took a corner of the green

room and spoke sternly to herself: nearly fifty gigs under her belt by now. She had a very solid fifteen-minute set that succeeded more often than it failed. There was no way she wasn't going to get through.

She heard her name being called and she stepped out onto the stage with a confidence that even surprised herself, and held the microphone with ease and familiarity. She was even now able to pull it out of its cradle and move the stand as she delivered her opening line so no momentum was lost.

'Hi, I'm Brenda Monk,' she told the excitable crowd, 'but please don't be scared. My name means nothing. I'm not religious, although I did go to Catholic school. The nuns were really uptight, and as you can imagine, they weren't keen on having a Monk in the class. The Priest liked me a lot though, especially after I had my hair cut short...'

She was enjoying herself now, delighting herself even from time to time and it showed on stage, as she moved around naturally and freely, finding she wanted to maintain eye contact with the audience.

'Yeah, I don't think being forced to learn about Jesus on my knees in front of a pervert has left me with any lasting psychological damage though, so that's good. But enough of that. What I'd really like to talk to you about is my deep and pathological fear and hatred of carpetry... Carpetry? Sorry, I meant to say carpentry! Wow, I really fucked up my own joke there, all that set up and for nothing. What the hell is carpetry anyway? Did Jesus spend his life laying carpet tiles around the office buildings of Nazareth? I think not...'

Brenda felt high – even a stumble couldn't stop her now. She acknowledged it and turned it into a joke, getting a bigger laugh than she may otherwise have done. She felt unstoppable. She sailed through.

That evening, back at the flat alone, Brenda took stock. She got out her notebook and listed her accomplishments so far... Having died on her arse a few times, she had learned not to fear it. She had also learned how to turn a gig round if it wasn't going well and Rossly's advice – always acknowledge what's happening in the room – was used to great advantage. She now knew how to deal with a heckler. She knew how to make herself perform when she was flat and tired. She knew she could still come up with the goods when she was sad or upset, she knew how to slightly rearrange material on the fly according what was going well, and once or twice, she had even experienced the thrill of improvising entirely new material on stage mid-gig if something occurred to her as she was talking. This was truly the mark of someone who knew what they were doing, and though she wasn't confident or consistent enough yet to do this on a regular basis, the fact that it was happening at all was very encouraging.

15

Brenda barely saw Fenella, Rossly or anyone else in her life apart from Pete, and the hundreds of strangers she entertained around the UK. She bought an old Nissan Micra from Ebay for £450 and used it to drive to gigs outside London. It was a far cheaper way to travel, and meant she could always get home afterwards, thus saving money on hotels. Paid gigs were still highly elusive. She had got £35 for a set in Liverpool, and it had cost her more to get there and back than that. But a club she had played in Cardiff had intimated that they might be willing to book her for proper money at some point in the future if her next few unpaid gigs there went as well as the first. Sometimes she was able to split the petrol money with other comedians going to the same gig, and the long journeys back with a 'carful of cunts' as one comic put it were immensely enjoyable and informative. And with all this, Brenda had never been happier, she felt she was flying. She felt in charge.

The money was a worry but she still had a good four and a half months to change things, and she knew she was building a reputation. Following her success in the regional heat, she had now actually got her name onto the list of working comics that was curated by gag.com. That was a huge deal. It was just a stub at the moment, but she had been acknowledged on some level by the comedy industry. She was real and in comedic terms, she existed.

And she had Pete. He was officially her boyfriend, and the newness of it all meant they were on best behaviour. He did not complain that he mainly saw her between the hours of midnight and 3am and Sunday afternoons. He was able to entertain himself at the weekends, just as Brenda had when she first got together with Jonathan. This was, after all, the first six months of the relationship and they were both delighted with how much they had in common. He didn't ask too much of her and she asked almost nothing of him, except that he adapt his sleeping patterns to accommodate her work. Although Brenda usually did not wake until gone lunchtime, Pete's self-employment meant that they could sometimes steal an afternoon together and join the retired and the unemployed in the simple pleasures afforded by the hours between 2 and 6pm – a late lunch, a film in an empty cinema, an afternoon in a quiet pub.

And now, with the start of February, the double gig with Jonathan approached. It was laughable at this point that they were in a relationship and they both knew it, but as Jonathan was never one to draw a line under anything in case it suited him to pick it up again at some undefined future moment, it took a clarifying text from Brenda to really lay it out.

'Just to be clear, we're not actually going out anymore. The relationship is for gig purposes only, OK?'

To which she had received nothing, which was typical. If he acknowledged it he could of course be held to it. But it didn't matter. She had made the move she needed to make and that was that. And ironically, extracting herself personally meant that she could now fully concentrate on the job in hand.

A venue had been booked for the 14th. By a stroke of luck, Valentine's fell on a Sunday this year and so most places were dark that day anyway, and the low maintenance nature of the show meant that it was simple to open up, have one junior technician to operate basic lights and sound, and make a little extra cash at the bar. It was a West End theatre just off Leicester Square that was known for holding stand-up shows that were slightly more ambitious than the average club put on. It held around four hundred punters and the show was already selling well.

The show had been advertised in the listings and had a couple of preview puff pieces in London newspapers. Her name was on a poster. People were talking about her. This was a leg up in the industry of magnificent proportions, and if it went well it would propel her to the next level. The gig would certainly be reviewed by someone. This might provide her with a useable quote for any future publicity material, and would look good on her website. The whole thing was just thrilling. Brenda had even agreed that Pete could come after he had quite reasonably argued that she couldn't shut him out forever and it wasn't fair to prevent him from coming to events that were open to everyone but him. And given their circumstances, he had in fact been extraordinarily understanding. When he had pointed out that Brenda was spending Valentine's Day on stage pretending to be another man's girlfriend she had seen his point, and checked herself.

Brenda communicated with Jonathan by email about the list of topics they would both cover and the format was nailed down: they would both start the show sitting side by side on a large leather sofa in the middle of the stage. Instead of a microphone in a stand they would use radio devices, with packs clipped to their waistbands, and looped over their ears. They would have five loose topic headings and each perform five minutes on each, taking it in turns. One watching the other from the sofa, standing up when it was their turn to perform; sitting down when they were watching.

It was all going incredibly well, until the moment two days before the gig when Brenda was at Pete's flat, working on her material and Pete picked up her contract and casually flicked through it.

'Uh, Brenda, did you read this before you signed it?'

Brenda looked up from her notebook.

'Yeah. I mean, I skimmed it. Lloyd said it was just a standard deal.'

'So you know they will own everything you say on the night, then? I mean, you're happy with that?'

Brenda frowned – this was news.

'In what sense will they own everything?'

'Well, this clause says that the show format is theirs and all the material performed by either party will be wholly owned by them in all countries in perpetuity.'

Brenda was across the room slightly faster than the speed of light and was looking over Pete's shoulder.

'Where does it say that?'

'Here, on page five.'

Brenda snatched the contract out of Pete's hands and tried to read the words, but her head was spinning. First of all, she couldn't believe she'd broken rule one and signed a contract she had not read.

'You know rule one is...' Pete began.

'Yes, I know,' Brenda snapped, and tried to focus.

Second of all, she didn't quite know what the implications of their ownership would be. Was it a really terrible thing? They'd only own the precise material she used on the night. They wouldn't own anything new she wrote and didn't perform. Or anything old she didn't perform. The trouble was, of course, that she would want to use her big hitters for such an important show. It would be all her best material that she had spent the past six months trying out, honing, improving, testing and modifying. All her top jokes would be unusable after this one gig. She could do her second best stuff, but then she risked being reviewed badly and she'd lose everything good about it in the first place.

'Those little fuckers.'

'I can't believe you didn't read...'

'I KNOW THAT, PETE, YOU DON'T HAVE TO KEEP SAYING IT!'

'Well then, why didn't you?'

'I don't know, I don't fucking know. Lloyd had a bulging envelope of cash right in front of me on the table and he was just going to give it to me as soon as I signed, and I knew it would buy me a car and OH SHIT, shit, shit, shit, shit, shit. Can I renegotiate, do you think?'

'No, you've signed it.'

'Can I back out?'

'You could, but they could sue you. They probably wouldn't, but they'd put it about that you're the kind of comic that backs out of big shows at the last minute and that's not going to help you, is it?'

'OK, OK. Let me think. Let me think, let me think, let me...'

Brenda's mind was racing, but she wasn't going to take this lying down. She dialled Lloyd's number and he answered straight away.

'What's this bit about you owning everything?' Brenda asked as soon as she heard his voice.

'It's just a formality,' he said, unconvincingly.

'A formality for what?'

'Well, in case we wanted to take anything further, you know, down the line. It's best to cover all eventualities. It happens all the time in LA. It's totally standard.'

'Yeah, well, taking fat out of your arms and injecting it into your labia happens all the time in LA. Doesn't mean I want it in my life.'

'Never say never.'

'Don't fuck around, Lloyd. What does it mean?'

'You signed the contract. You could have read it first. Maybe it's time to get an agent if you can't be bothered with the admin?'

'An agent takes 15%, and since that would currently be 15% of nothing, they're not exactly queuing down the street to take me on.'

'That's not true. You've just been paid £500. That would be £65 for an agent. A nice bottle of wine at lunchtime at least...'

'Fuck you.'

'Now come on, Brenda. This gig is going to be good for you and your...new career. So let's not be like that. Why shouldn't we own it? We're paying for it.'

'You'll make it all back on the box office.'

'Well, that's our risk. Here's a lesson for you gratis. You can either work for free and own everything, or get paid and give something away. That's the choice you've made.'

'But it wasn't an informed choice.'

'Then you should have informed yourself better. It was all there on the page in front of you, you just preferred to look at the money.'

'That's a dirty trick, Lloyd. You know I'm broke and you put that money there to distract me.'

'Then learn some self-control.'

There was no way she was going to win this. He was totally correct on every level except the one involving basic human decency. Why had she ever expected anything else? She modified her tone.

'OK then, Lloyd. You win this one. Just tell me one thing. What are you going to do with the tape?'

'We might develop it into a show in LA. Some TV execs are interested in the format for Jonathan, so we said we'd get them a tape.'

'What about me?'

'Oh, we'd get someone else to play you.'

'Why not just use me?'

'They'll probably want an American girl. That's usually how it works.'

Incredible.

'OK, fine, I'll stick to the contract. But only to the contract, to the letter of it, and nothing else, OK?'

'Sure. Sorry Brenda, I've got call waiting.' And he hung up.

Brenda worked solidly for the next two days on new material – effectively burner material that she would use once and then throw away. Pete fed and watered her and apart from using the toilet, basic hygiene maintenance and one brief shag, she did not move from his lovely pine dining table, sitting hunched over her notebook, scribbling away and occasionally chuckling to herself. Jonathan was in touch, checking there was no overlap in their material, which made Brenda smile darkly to herself. She found it surprisingly easy to lie to him. She had a couple of missed calls from Laura but that could wait until much later. Fenella called, but Brenda managed to fob her off by saying she was in a creatively concentrated mindset and didn't want to dilute it too much – a line Jonathan had used on her frequently if he didn't feel like seeing her while they were together. Fenella and Rossly wanted to come along to watch (out of a ghoulish curiosity apart from anything else) which didn't bother Brenda. The more the merrier, as far as she was concerned. As the remaining hours dwindled, Brenda began to feel increasingly pumped, a combination of coffee, lack of sleep and gimlet eyed determination not to allow Lloyd and Jonathan to walk all over her.

The night before the gig, Brenda let Pete make her some proper food and she actually sat down and ate it with him, knowing full well that she would be unable to consume anything the next day. A bowl of spaghetti carbonara had something of the flavour of a final meal about it, and though Pete was not allowed to know the content of Brenda's jokes, he assured her that he had no concerns about the quality. Brenda smiled queasily. What was once a most exciting opportunity had become something toxic. Her new objectives were to use material that would garner a great response from the crowd but that she would never feel inclined to perform again, get a couple of good reviews to use in the future and to destroy Jonathan, comedically or otherwise. These were not impossible aims, but he had four years' worth of experience and 99.9% of the crowd were his fans, meaning that they were already on his side before they even entered the building. She had six months of experience and no fans whatsoever, unless she counted Pete, who had never seen her perform, and Fenella and Rossly who were on her side but would still always come out in favour of comedy itself, rather than any particular comedian. She would know instantly from their faces whether they thought she had given a good account of herself.

Brenda knew she would barely sleep but resisted the sleeping pill Pete offered her in case it made her sluggish the next day. She knew she could perform with abject exhaustion – she'd done that several times before – but she couldn't perform medicated, or at least, she had to yet to try. When she did sleep, she dreamed literally: she was on stage and did not know her jokes, the audience all had their backs to her, she was shouting but no sound came out, she was blind. There was no expert interpretation needed here. Her subconscious mind and her conscious mind were so in tune that the mysterious filter was nowhere to be found. This was a problem that required every part of her mind, body and soul; she was consumed by it. Every hour or so, she got up and returned to her notes, checking again and again, obsessively making additions and corrections. Around 4am, Brenda sat down at the table for the last time that night and opened up her notebook. She looked through her material. It was good, but was it good enough? Was it strong enough, challenging enough? She picked up her pen, wrote down a line. Looked at it. Scribbled it out. This was a fight, not just between her and Jonathan, but within herself. She picked up the pen, wrote the line again and forced herself up the stairs.

Brenda woke up around 7am having slept in half hour bursts for the previous three hours. It was still dark, but the light was beginning to show and some early birds were singing. Brenda got up, left a sleeping Pete in the bed, and opened the door to his tiny roof terrace. The air was cold but dry and soothed her aching head. She needed to cool down, step back for a moment and get her mind right. The birds were singing louder now and a new dawn was creeping in. Brenda looked down and caught sight of a fox weaving its way between the gardens of the ground floor flats below, stealthy and silent, watchful and wily. It was a solitary creature, wholly responsible for its own well-being. It was careful not to get injured. If it could not hunt, it would not eat and no other fox was going to stop and look after it if it could not keep up. No, other foxes had to take care of themselves – that was the reality of being a fox – you were on your own. A fox only picks a fight if it's sure it can't lose. Brenda shivered and went back inside.

16

Brenda picked up the bunch of flowers Lloyd had left in her dressing room and put them in the bin. She didn't need these patronising overtures to femininity. She needed to remain highly focused. Performing jokes she had never used before in front of a large crowd on such a high stakes night was crazy but it was the only thing she could now do in order to protect her best material, which she would need to make her way through the competition. The ultimate prize for the winner of the competition was a guarantee of paid work for six months, and that could be a launch pad to anything. She had to keep her eyes on that prize and simply survive tonight. If she could give a good account of herself here, and not destroy herself, that would be all she needed. She pulled a miniature bottle of Jack Daniel's out of her handbag and drank it in two swigs. She had never performed drunk before, and didn't intend to start now, but she needed something to calm her down, her hands and legs were shaking hard from too much adrenaline. She had to find a way to give less of a shit in order to raise her game – the ultimate stand-up paradox. Alcohol was her best option.

She had banned everybody from her dressing room. She didn't want Pete around her right now, and she didn't even want to see Fenella or Rossly. She didn't want friendly, concerned faces making her feel that what she was about to do was any more frightening than it already was. The fact that she had a dressing room at all seemed faintly ridiculous. For the first time she actually longed for the uncaring cut and thrust of a busy green room where she could warm up a little, bounce off some other comics, even if the chat was barbed and occasionally undermining. Stuck in this room that had seen better days, with a brightly lit mirror and an empty metal clothes rack, just felt weird. But this was technically a theatre and was equipped to accommodate groups of actors in larger productions. So there was room to give Jonathan and Brenda a dressing room each, on either side of the stage. They would meet in the middle, in front of several hundred strangers, and begin.

Through the loudspeaker mounted high on the wall Brenda could hear the audience coming in to the auditorium. The hum of excited chatter sounded like bees swarming and Brenda felt sick to her stomach. She wished she'd bought another JD, and so when a helpful young backstage assistant popped her head round the door and asked if there was anything she needed, Brenda ordered a shot from the bar. The assistant nodded and disappeared. Brenda looked at herself in the mirror. The short blonde hair was still in full effect, the black eyeliner was skilfully flicked and black mascara increased her eyelashes by at least 30%, but the effect was subtle. She wore no other make-up. She wore a black V-neck jumper and a pair of black skinny jeans. On her feet she wore a pair of red patent leather lace up brogues. She looked good tonight. That at least, she could be sure of. This outfit had come together well and gave her some confidence.

The assistant reappeared with Brenda's drink and set it down on an opened ironing board that hadn't been used for years. Brenda thanked her and waited until she had left the room before she necked it in one. A rustle on the loudspeaker and a voice spoke.

'Five minutes until showtime, thank you very much.'

It vanished with another rustle and the swarm of bees returned, punctuated by clinks of bottles and glasses as they buzzed around the bar, hastily buying drinks before the show began.

'Oh shit,' Brenda breathed to herself, 'shit, I can't do it, I can't do it, someone make it go away.'

She sat down and put her head in her hands for a minute. Her phone vibrated – had her prayer been answered? She opened the message.

'Good luck – you'll be amazing x'

Pete had texted her from the other side. She smiled a bit but it came out like a grimace. She was nauseated to the core and even smiling made it worse. She had a very bad feeling about tonight. The assistant knocked and then stuck her head round the door.

'OK to mike you up, Brenda?'

'Yeah, come in.'

The young woman had very cold hands as she passed a long thin microphone lead down Brenda's back and left the end to trail out by her bottom like some kind of tiny tail. She looped the moulded wire structure around Brenda's ear and bent the microphone along her cheek so that it lay flat against her face about an inch from the corner of her mouth. She was strapped in now, getting further entangled, making it harder to escape.

'Phil will put your pack on at the side of the stage, OK?'

'OK. Thanks'

And she was gone again. Brenda felt dizzy with sickness. How could she get away? There must be a back exit. She thought she'd conquered the urge to fly rather than fight a couple of months ago, but here it was, back with a vengeance. Every insecure thought she had learned to suppress in the previous six months of gigging seemed to flood her entire being now, and she experienced that tell-tale urge to lie down and go to sleep – a sign the mind is dealing with the knowledge of impending trauma. She recalled being told by a serious face she could not place at the New Year's Eve party that the impact of a gig on the human body had been found to be akin to being involved in a medium sized car crash, and that years of dealing with the shock and subsequent adrenaline surge was what made comedians crazy: you get up and walk away from the wreckage every time.

The stakes were high with this gig, and Jonathan's presence was no comfort, no comfort at all. Did he even think she was any good? Did it matter? Did she think she was any good? These thoughts were as unhelpful as they were insistent and they had to be controlled by force of will. And Jack Daniel's.

Rustle.

'Act One beginners to the side of the stage please, Act One beginners to the side of the stage.'

Brenda laughed out loud – Act One beginners? She hadn't heard that since she was a member of the chorus in a slightly over-ambitious production of Stephen Sondheim's *Company* at university. This was two stand-up comedians who would walk out, talk, and then walk off again. Not a cast of thousands who needed corralling at the appropriate moments. This slightly officious stage manager was getting on her nerves. He clearly felt this gig was somewhat beneath him and another production, such as *Les Miserables* or *The Phantom of the Opera*, would be much better served by his skills. Brenda took one last look at herself in the mirror, raised her eyebrows twice and opened the door.

She walked the short distance down a grubby, narrow corridor to a door with a laminated notice on it that read 'STAGE

RIGHT'. She pulled it open, jumped up three small black steps and greeted Phil, who was waiting with a radio mic pack. He pulled out the end of her tail and he plugged the jack into the pack.

'Where do you want it?'

'Where do people normally have it?'

'Dunno, depends. Middle of the back of your waistband's traditional though, I suppose.'

'OK, put it there then, please.'

He tucked the pack into the back of her jeans with a well-used, professional 'excuse me', and clipped it onto the waistband of her jeans, fiddled with a couple of knobs and then vanished.

Brenda turned round to face the side of the stage. There was no curtain between the front of the stage and the audience. Peering round the huge black curtains that hung around her on stage right that were there to cover any activity during a performance, she could see the far corner of the audience, who were sat down and chatting. Brenda felt vomit rise in her throat. She looked over to the left wing and saw Jonathan standing with Phil, having his own mic pack fitted. She saw Phil laugh and Jonathan laugh with him. Brenda hadn't made Phil laugh. She felt horrible. Why had she ever agreed to do this? How could she ever have thought that this could possibly work to her advantage?

Jonathan saw her and blew her a kiss. She smiled weakly. He looked excited. Brenda didn't think she looked excited. She thought she probably looked like she'd just been diagnosed with herpes.

'OK?' whispered the backstage assistant.

Brenda nodded. It was all she could manage. She felt the house lights go down, and the audience quieten and vibrate with an expectant hush. She lifted her head. Showtime.

Brenda walked out on stage and in that instant nothing else

existed, as if she had passed through some invisible permeable membrane that divided horror from happiness. The horror lived in the wings, the shadows, the 'before'. Here was only light and warmth and 'now'. She smiled at the audience as they applauded. She gave a little wave to show how relaxed she was, and she almost felt it too. She sat down on the sofa next to Jonathan who was already flirting with a middle-aged woman on the front row, who sat with a younger woman who was her spitting image only thirty years younger. Brenda guessed that they were mother and daughter and had come out together on Valentine's night at the daughter's suggestion. She guessed they were both single. Brenda had got good at assessing audiences. She had a joke about divorced mothers somewhere. If she was right about these two, she could have a little chat with them from the stage and then drop it in. It would look spontaneous and the crowd would love it. An audience would always laugh hard at a mid-range joke if they thought you'd just made it up on the spot. Her nerves had evaporated. It was as if they had never existed. She was now in survival mode – kill or be killed.

Brenda and Jonathan had decided to begin with a little bit of banter sat side-by-side on the sofa. The plan was for this to degenerate into a staged row. Then Jonathan would leap up, apparently incensed by the conversation, and deliver a short monologue to the audience from his perspective. After about five minutes, Brenda would interject, as if she could stand it no longer, and get up. Jonathan would then hand over to her and sit down while she did five minutes. This would then be the pattern for the next hour or so. There would be no interval. The venue had fought this. They always made money at the bar in the interval, and so Brenda and Jonathan had agreed to allow the bar that was built in at the back of the auditorium to remain open throughout. It didn't bother either of them. In fact, it was preferable as it lent a certain 'comedy club' vibe to this strange hybrid show. They were both so used to people getting up and down to go to the bar at the gigs they usually played that far from being off-putting, it actually put them both at ease and reduced the intensity of the room.

'Good evening, good evening,' Jonathan began. He turned to Brenda and leant in a little in mock seduction, 'Good *evening...*'

First laugh.

'Good evening, Jonathan. How are you feeling this evening?' Brenda replied with arch courtesy.

'I'm fresh as a daisy, Brenda, and you?'

'Well, I'm a little bit under the weather today because I didn't sleep very well...'

'Oh dear and why's that?'

'I guess I was waiting for you to come home.'

Jonathan looked at the audience with a 'boys will be boys' shrug.

'But you said you prefer to sleep alone...'

'I prefer to sleep alone, yes, but I wasn't planning on sleeping.'

The audience murmured a laugh at the innuendo.

'I'm concerned I'm being used for sex,' Jonathan said, as planned.

'No, you're not,' Brenda said, as planned.

'Being used for sex?'

'No, concerned about it.'

A huge laugh erupted through the room.

Brenda was glad of it – she had ripped this little exchange straight from a conversation with Pete, and it had worked. She felt the audience settle in. They were more comfortable with Jonathan, who now got to his feet and began his solo piece, but they could see Brenda was perfectly capable and would deliver. They didn't need to feel sorry for her or nervous on her behalf, and with this realisation, they gave themselves permission to laugh at what she said – she was not the abused party, they could see that, and she wasn't some shy little woman who would be dominated by this comedy titan she shared the stage with. It would be a fair fight, and a good show. The room eased back into itself, heads turned up like smiling seals in the water.

Jonathan stood up on cue and walked to the front of the stage to start his first solo flight. Brenda reminded herself to look at him and not the audience, and to laugh at what he said. It was all material she'd heard before, much of it culled from his Edinburgh show. Of course he had the luxury of doing his best stuff as he would own it all with Lloyd anyway once the show was over. Brenda felt a fresh wave of resentment rise over her, but did not surf it – she had to stay focused. Looking out over the tops of people's heads for a brief stolen moment, she caught sight of the black camera mounted behind the back row, recording everything. Its red pin prick of light the only point of true focus in the darkened fuzz of the room. She also knew that somewhere, out there were Pete, Fenella and Rossly. She quickly turned her attention back to Jonathan in case she saw anyone she knew and caught their eye, which could prove fatal.

Jonathan was wrapping up his bit. The audience were laughing warmly. The mother and daughter on the front row, which Brenda decided to use as the litmus paper for the whole crowd, were giggling moistly. They'd probably double team him if he asked them to, she thought grimly and placed a mental bookmark on that thought to ensure that it would not come out of her mouth under any circumstances. If she lost them, she'd lose the audience and she'd look like a woman-hating, bitter bitch. She regretted letting Jonathan go first as it now meant that she was catching up rather than setting the tone. It had made sense when he first suggested it. He had said he would warm up the crowd on her behalf so she'd get an easier ride, but she now saw her mistake all too clearly. Brenda got ready to leap up and take exception, as agreed.

'So I ask you, can there ever be a *right* way to do Valentine's Day? Seems like anything I do for my girlfriend will be the wrong thing...'

A couple of men cheered. Brenda arranged her face into outrage.

'Hold on, hold on,' she said, getting up and the crowd laughed.

Jonathan mimed looking surprised and then apprehensive as he backed away from the front and took his seat on the sofa, giving Brenda the floor. She instantly felt better. She may not have as many gigs as Jonathan under her belt but she'd done enough for this to feel familiar, and the brightness of the lights obscured the size of the room.

'I never asked for anything on Valentine's Day except a card and a kiss. But my boyfriend?'

Jonathan pointed comically to himself from behind and got a bonus laugh off it.

'My boyfriend assumes I want the full works, and then gets grumpy with me for apparently demanding something I never even wanted. Then he goes out and buys a big, expensive bunch of flowers and says he'll take me for dinner. I'm a grown woman. I'll get my own fucking dinner, thanks.'

The crowd laughed a little, but not with any enthusiasm. It had come out too hard, and too charmless. She had misjudged the tone and the pacing was off and she'd forgotten a bit in the middle so it didn't quite make sense.

Jonathan shrugged behind her with a 'see what I mean?' look and got another laugh.

Brenda was floundering. Jonathan was getting laughs off the back of her fuck up. She tried again.

'And what is it with diamonds? Who wants diamonds? Diamonds are just hundred million year old dinosaur turds, packed down over centuries...'

Brenda caught sight of the sparkling rings on the fingers of the mother and daughter and knew this wasn't going to work, but it would be even worse not to finish the joke.

'So why would I want that on my finger?'

A small laugh, polite more than anything. She decided against doing the follow up gag which suggested that if she wanted a turd on her finger, she'd be willing to tickle his prostate during sex – it didn't seem like that kind of crowd. She needed to change pace and very, very fast. She had to use one of the tried and tested jokes she was trying to keep back in order to retain ownership. But needs must and if she had to sacrifice one or two in order not to lose the gig entirely, it seemed a small price to pay at this juncture.

'I know I sound bitter,' she admitted and the room silently adjusted in her favour. She felt it – good – always acknowledge what's happening in the room.

'But I can't help it. When I asked my boyfriend if this outfit made me look fat, he said, "no babe, it's your fat that makes you look fat"...'

Big laugh. Massive laugh. She had them back, she mustn't lose them again. If in doubt, be self-deprecating, another lesson she had learned over the previous six months. She turned to look mock-accusingly at Jonathan and caught his flash of annoyance just before he covered it up.

Jonathan took his next turn with ease, and there was no indication that he was rattled by Brenda's unflattering joke at his expense. After all, what else had he expected? He may not be used to being challenged on stage but he wasn't an idiot and he squashed his instinctive reaction and continued like the consummate professional he was. He launched into a funny bit about how you have to pretend your girlfriend's bum is small even when you prefer big bottoms and got the crowd back on-side. Brenda followed with some material about how men can be any size but women have to look the same, which she then deftly reversed by offering her sympathies to all men who were now being battered by the beauty industry in the same way women had been for years. This took the 'tub-thumping feminist' sting out of the tail and brought the more conservative men and women round, including the mother and daughter on the front row who were perhaps naturally averse to female comedians but were warming to her. Jonathan would always be their favourite, but she was making good progress. Jonathan countered this with a rundown of the average woman's bottles in the bathroom – a bit he'd been doing for years and was always popular – and then began the segment they had roughly titled 'Bedroom Politics' with his material about Brenda's sexual preferences.

As Brenda sat and listened, she could practically feel Pete wince through the dimmed room. She nodded along with Jonathan and even put two thumbs up at the mention of her favourite position. That elicited a wolf whistle from the dark, which in turn got its own laugh.

Brenda stood to say her piece. The show was drawing to a close now, and she had also agreed to let Jonathan close it. This would be her final segment and she knew she had to yet really make an impression. Some kind of nascent professional pride was rising in her, along with a sense of injustice at the ease with which Jonathan created his own laughs and then took hers, too. He was so smooth, so confident, so unflappable and now he would walk off with this gig in his perfectly distressed £200 denim pocket, loved by all but those who knew him best. Brenda couldn't bear it – when would something, anything get to him?

When would he have a real, honest, in-the-moment reaction to something he couldn't hide from, or turn to his own advantage with a loveable, floppy fringed shrug? When would there be consequences? And who would deliver them?

Brenda knew, and she knew just how to do it. A joke, somewhere, back there, written on a page, with a line through it, dormant but with a faint pulse, was about to be brought to life.

Brenda smiled coolly at Jonathan and turned to the crowd.

'Unfortunately, my boyfriend's favourite sexual position is anything that will get me pregnant.'

A laugh.

'On our first night together, he asked me how I wanted eggs in the morning, and I said "fertilized". It was meant to be a joke, but unfortunately he took me seriously. You know the worst place to find out your boyfriend is indecisive? An abortion clinic car park.'

This achieved that particular type of laugh which included shock – an aspirated laugh, equal parts gasp and giggle – pleasure and pain, and what could be sweeter?

The woman and her daughter exchanged a glance and looked uncertainly at Jonathan.

Brenda followed their gaze and looked him straight in the eye. She laced the punch with an extra shot just for him.

'Talk about a Terrible Mess...'

He visibly froze and they tumbled into a wide abyss, falling down and down with nothing to hold on to but each other. Except neither was reaching out.

Everyone was looking at Jonathan now, expecting his response. With an almighty wrench he pulled himself back through the years and into the room. He shook his head twice, and then forced that smile up his cheeks. She'd got him, that was for sure. 'Nothing's off limits with relationships and comedy,' that's what he'd told her a year ago, never expecting it to be reciprocated. But even still, he was too practised to miss the next beat. He did not stand up, perhaps fearing a tell-tale wobble, but spoke from his spot on the sofa.

'And you know the worst place to find out your girlfriend's been cheating on you?'

The laugh anticipated the punchline.

'You got it. An abortion clinic car park.'

A respectable sized laugh, but not the kind Jonathan would usually be happy to end a show on. Nevertheless, before Brenda could say anything more, Jonathan was walking towards her, towering over her, an arm firmly round her shoulders.

'Ladies and gentlemen,' he had abandoned his closing set and was wrapping up now, eager to get off, 'we have been Jonathan Cape and Brenda Monk. And remember, don't believe everything you hear in a comedy club. Happy Valentine's Day!'

And he led her off stage, giving her just enough time to catch the appalled looks of the mother and daughter. Brenda, a little wild, managed to wave at them and then was bundled into the black.

His cold fury was quite something. He looked at Brenda with a mixture of fear and disgust, and walked away, murmuring, 'I'll deal with you later.'

Brenda walked shakily to her dressing room. She sat down in the chair in front of the mirror and tried to process the show.

She looked at herself – who was in there? Her cheeks were flushed and her eyes were impenetrable. She hardly knew how she felt, and her reflection gave no clue.

There was a loud knock at the door, and anticipating a visit from Pete, she rose to greet him. She barely had time to stand up before Josephine was at her, a hand round her throat, propelling her backwards until her head hit the wall with a crack. So much strength in that tiny body. Josephine kept her hand round Brenda's neck and pushed her face right in close. Her eyes were dark and hard and full of fury, like chocolate covered espresso beans. She breathed hard through her nostrils and Brenda, noticing a small amount of foam at the corners of her mouth, remembered her cocaine habit and wondered if she might actually kill her. When she spoke, her jaw was so clenched she could barely push the words out through her teeth.

'Don't you ever fucking use my life as material again, do you understand?'

'I'm sorry, I didn't know you were coming...'

'Don't you ever fucking use my life as material again. Do. You. Understand?'

'Yes, I'm sorry, I'm sorry, please...'

Josephine pressed her thumb against Brenda's throat, cutting off the air for a moment. She began to choke.

'If I ever hear you do that again I will find you and kill you. Is that clear?'

'Yes, yes. I'm sorry, I'm so sorry, I just wanted him to know that...'

Brenda was trying to speak, but it came out gargled and scratchy.

'I don't care what you wanted him to know. Use your own sorry little life if you want something to talk about, OK?'

'Yes.'

Thumb pressed harder.

'OK?'

'Yes...'

Josephine let her go.

Brenda dropped to her knees, coughing and spluttering and desperately trying to catch her breath. Josephine stood over her for a moment.

'You stupid little cunt,' she said softly and walked out.

Brenda stayed on her knees until Pete entered the room and found her there. She looked up, still profoundly shocked and shaken to the bone.

'Hey,' he said, 'well done, why are you down there? Do you have to make a sacrifice to the comedy gods, or something?'

'Something like that,' said Brenda in a voice that sounded very far away.

Pete held out a hand and she got up unsteadily.

'Are you happy with how it went?'

'Mostly,' replied Brenda faintly.

'That last joke was a bit near the knuckle.'

Brenda gave a hollowed laugh at the unintended irony, and felt her neck. She wondered if it would bruise, and then hoped she would be able to pass it off as a love bite.

Lloyd stuck his head round the door.

'Great show, Brenda. Just what we were after. Hope you enjoyed it,' he said rhetorically. 'Jonathan wants to shoot off as he's got some friends in, but he said he'd catch up with you before we fly back to LA.'

'OK.' Relief flooded Brenda. She couldn't be bothered to account for herself to Jonathan tonight. She couldn't believe she had been so stupid as to think the abortion gag was a good idea. And she really couldn't believe that she had been so naive as to think that Josephine might be pleased she'd done it. Writing jokes at four in the morning with no opportunity to test them first had been a huge gamble and she wasn't sure it had paid off. It had certainly lost her a friend, although in truth, she had never really thought of Josephine as a friend. There was danger about her, and that coke habit was not to be trifled with. She felt bad though. She knew she had walked all over some basic stand-up etiquette. In fact, forget stand-up etiquette – she had trampled on basic human decency. She felt like shit.

'Are you alright?' Pete said, obviously realising that this was not just post-show wobbles.

'I don't know.'

'What's the matter?'

'I said something I shouldn't have said.'

'Oh don't worry about it. I don't mind as long as people think you're talking about him. And like you said, most of it isn't true anyway.'

'No, not about you. About someone else.'

'Who?'

'Someone Jonathan used to go out with.'

'Which bit?'

'The last bit.'

Pete let this sink in and Brenda saw the change in his eyes. It was something like disappointment and she couldn't bear it.

'So, that was true, about the car park?'

He couldn't bring himself to say abortion – oh god, why did he have to be so decent?

'Yeah.'

'Shit.'

'Yeah.'

'Does the real woman know?'

'Judging by the fact that she just tried to strangle me, I'd say she does, yes.'

There was a long pause.

'Is this stand-up, Brenda? I mean, is this really what it's all about?'

'I don't know anymore,' Brenda replied truthfully. She leant against her dressing table. 'Listen, please don't take this... I... I think I want be on my own tonight. I need to think about it all.'

Pete did not protest, which was sickening in its own way. He put his arms round Brenda, kissed her head and left her alone in the dressing room.

Around 2am, whilst Brenda was still curled up on her couch staring blankly at the wall, she received a text from Rossly. It contained only a link to gag.com, and Brenda braced herself and clicked through. 'Comedian couple dance around the blurred lines of reality', the headline read. In an exhaustive review that detailed and analysed almost every word that had been uttered, and evaluated it until the frog was well and truly dead, the writer concluded that it had been a draw. He wrote that though Jonathan was clearly the more accomplished comic, Brenda had a raw energy that that particular crowd did not always warm to, but held a promise of things to come. 'While Jonathan had charm, Brenda had punch', the reviewer concluded, with the clear meaning that he found the punch more exciting than the charm. Amongst the deep shame Brenda was experiencing, a small shoot of hope pushed through. She texted Rossly.

'Thanks for that. I needed it.'

The reply came right away.

'You OK?'

'Yeah, just glad Josephine didn't actually kill me.'

'Yeah, she was pretty furious – Fenella filled me in and then went off with her.'

'I feel awful.'

'Oh come on kid – you ever seen her set?'

'No.'

'She slags off everyone she's ever met.'

'So why won't she talk about the thing with Jonathan?'

'I don't know – she's ashamed?'

'No, don't think it's that.'

'Well, we all have our blind spots. You know mine.'

'I totally violated her though.'

'She'll get over it – nobody knows it was her.'

'Yeah, but I still shouldn't have said it.'

'Maybe not, but you'll know next time. And to be honest, it was fucking dynamite comedy.'

'Was it?'

'Fuck yeah.'

'Thanks.'

'Tonight I actually thought you might have potential.'

Brenda smiled for the first time in what felt like days.

Brenda woke up the next morning to a text from Fenella.

'Look at the *Guardian*. And Josephine wants to meet you for a chat.'

'OK x 2. Will meet Josephine anytime. Feel awful about it.'

'It'll be OK. Have you ever seen her set?'

Brenda nearly laughed as Fenella unconsciously echoed Rossly's words.

'No, but I've heard. Let me know when's good.'

And she slid off the sofa and went to the toilet. After making a cup of hot, strong coffee, Brenda opened her laptop and clicked on the *Guardian* homepage. Nothing there she could see related to her in any way. She clicked through to the dedicated comedy page, and there it was: a review in an actual national newspaper. This was unexpected. Their show had been a one-off and reviewers never usually bothered with those as there was no opportunity for anyone who read it to go and see for themselves. Brenda closed her eyes and prepared to read it. Fenella wouldn't have been so cruel as to flag up something really horrible. At least, Brenda didn't believe she would now she knew her friend was not furious with her about Josephine. Brenda made a fist inside, breathed in, breathed out and opened her eyes.

'Two comics who are, or at least appear to be in a relationship staged a highly experimental comedy stand-up show at the

Newport Street Theatre last night. Jonathan Cape, an Edinburgh Comedy Award nominee and circuit regular took to the stage with his "girlfriend", a relatively unknown comedian called Brenda Monk. They proceeded to take it in turns to critique their own relationship with mixed, but mostly positive results. Cape has form for this type of confessional stand-up which has become fashionable in recent years. His nominated and much praised Edinburgh show was an hour devoted to talking about his girlfriend, although there was no indication that Brenda Monk was that same girlfriend as details of the exact status of their relationship were not forthcoming. With that said, this reviewer would put money on "It's Complicated" coming close to the truth. The material was mostly strong, especially from Cape who drew heavily on his previous work. One could accuse him of being lazy, and though the new stuff was no doubt welcome to his more loyal fans, he probably thought, as far as material is concerned, "if it ain't broke". And it isn't, even though his love life might be. Monk had a slower start, with a few bum notes early on, but once she hit her stride she showed serious promise. And if her closing bit was anything to go by, it will be interesting to see how this sharp, funny and at times painfully honest comic develops. But the real star was the format itself, which was fascinating and original – expect more of this kind of thing to start popping up all over the comedy scene.'

Brenda read it once without stopping, absorbed that she had not been given a total trouncing, and then read it again properly. She got up and walked around the flat for a few minutes, and then returned to the sofa to read it again. Her phone buzzed. It was Fenella.

'Can you do tomorrow night with Josephine? I'll come to referee/bodyguard.'

'Tomorrow night is good for me. And thanks for the

Guardian tip.'

'Good isn't it? You've got your poster quote!'

Brenda took a minute to understand what a poster quote was, partly because she didn't have a poster. Then she realised – she would have a quote she could use for publicity. She read the review for a fourth time and found the words she was looking for.

Sharp, funny and painfully honest.

There it was. She could use that for the rest of time.

The gag.com review was meaningless now in publicity terms, although Brenda was grateful for it, knowing as she did that it would be the one read by all her peers. But for all its credibility, it had been superseded in the hierarchy of opinion by a respected national newspaper. She did indeed have her poster quote. All she needed now was a poster.

17

Brenda arrived very early at Josephine's address and found a coffee shop nearby to wait in. Pete had told her on the phone that she should not under any circumstances be late for this appointment, and Brenda knew it too. As she sat drinking her Americano Brenda ran back over the conversation she and Pete had had the night before. She had still wanted to keep her distance. She knew she had scared Pete a little at the show but he did not seem to be running. The fact that she was so ashamed of herself reassured him that her moral compass had not completely melted in the comedy furnace, and her arrangement to clear the air with Josephine also told him there were some parameters for social behaviour that he could relate to still in play. He had asked to come over but she had declined his offer, saying she needed to prepare for the showdown with Josephine. She had agreed to come straight to his flat when she finished, whatever time that was. She was also aware of how badly she had neglected her friends, her real friends, over the past half a year and texted Laura, begging forgiveness and asking if she could come and stay for a weekend soon.

The appointed hour arrived and Brenda knocked on Josephine's door – a council flat in a small estate on Brixton Hill. Brenda rarely came to Brixton but had in past occasionally met friends who lived south to see a film at The Ritzy, and then drink Pina Coladas until 3am in a bar on Electric Avenue. But it wasn't her place. It was so unfamiliar, with its kiosks selling multi-coloured braided hair, poker straight bobbed wigs, the market with two dozen vegetables she couldn't name on display on one stall alone and the sound of patois being spoken on the streets – she felt out of sorts.

Fenella opened the bright red door and stood aside to let Brenda in. She very slightly rolled her eyes, and Brenda's mood lifted a little. She entered a tastefully furnished living room dominated by a vibrant Swedish rag rug that covered the whole floor like a carpet. Two sombre west African wooden masks hung on walls, looking blankly through empty eye sockets at Brenda as she sat down opposite Josephine.

Josephine was quite still, her legs tucked under her, a cup of camomile tea in her hands. She watched Brenda as she sat and offered her nothing. Fenella sat on one of four cheap looking dining chairs that surrounded an oval dining table, in the middle of which was an artfully arranged vase of dried flowers with bright orange seed pods hanging off some of the stalks. Brenda sat on the edge of her seat, wondering who was supposed to speak first in situations like these. Josephine cleared her throat, and Brenda realised she was the one who was expected to start.

'First of all, I'd like to apologise...'

No movement from Josephine.

'I had no right to do that material.'

'Then why did you?'

'It's complicated.'

'Isn't it always?'

'Yes, and it's no excuse.'

'No, it's not.'

'Well, Jonathan backed me into a corner.'

'Really? You looked pretty in control on stage to me.'

'No, I mean beforehand. I stupidly signed a contract Lloyd gave me for the show without reading it...'

Fenella instinctively sucked her teeth. Brenda pressed on.

'And I didn't realise until the day before that I'd basically signed away all the rights to anything I said on the night.'

Josephine raised an eyebrow at this and glanced at Fenella, who pursed her lips. Brenda was minutely encouraged.

'It meant that if I did my best material he would own it and I wouldn't be able to do it again. So I decided I would write all new stuff and just hope it worked. I wrote that abor... That joke about you while I was in a kind of frenzy in the middle of the night, and I crossed it out because I knew I couldn't use it. Then I felt the gig going away from me and I knew reviewers were in, and I had to use something and part of me knew, just knew, that it was a good joke and so... And so I said it. And I regretted it instantly. And like I said, I'm really very sorry.'

Josephine sat silently. She very deliberately sipped her tea.

'It is a good joke,' she said finally. Brenda was not expecting that.

'Uh, thanks.'

'Don't do it again.'

'I won't. I won't ever do it again.'

'Good. Because I'm having it.'

Brenda's brain was working slowly. She didn't quite comprehend, but was just happy not to be pinned to the wall by her throat.

'But the contract says...'

'He doesn't own it if I say it.'

'Well...'

'I'd like to see him try.'

There was silence.

'You can go now.'

Brenda sat still for a second, hardly believing what she'd just heard. Fenella stood up and walked her to the door.

'OK?'

Brenda breathed out.

'Is that it?'

'What you've got to understand about Josephine, my little friend, is that she is quite, quite mad. Which is why I love her. But I'm afraid you got a taste of the famous temper last night, and as I am sure you can imagine, the world looks a little different once the cocaine's worn off and you've had some sleep.'

Brenda nodded, speechless with gratitude.

'You talked to her, didn't you?'

'A bit, but it didn't take much. She gets it, you know, and her material... My god, I don't think there's a man in London that hasn't been lashed in some way or another.'

'So why doesn't she take down Jonathan?'

'Well, two things. First of all, she genuinely loved Jonathan. And second, it was a very traumatic time and no matter what she says, I don't think she's over it.'

'I feel so bad.'

'Don't. It is a good joke. And look, you may have to live with this... I wouldn't be wholly surprised if it was heard again in the not too distant future.'

'Oh no. I'm never doing...'

'No, not you. Her.'

Brenda gaped.

'You're not serious. She meant it?'

'Yes,' Fenella significantly lowered her voice, 'I think, now she's calmed down, she can see a way to use all that stuff for herself. I think you showed her how it could be made funny. I don't know for sure, I'm just saying it wouldn't amaze me.'

Brenda really didn't know how to respond to this. Comedians were truly a breed apart, she thought, even though she was now one herself.

'And my god, you should've seen Jonathan's face behind you when you said it. Oh Christ, Brenda, that was truly wonderful to behold. And for that, I can only thank you.'

Fenella gave Brenda a quick hug and shut the door. Brenda walked back through Brixton, wishing you could still buy bags of weed on the street as easily as ten years ago, and descended the wide stairs into the Tube station.

Twenty minutes on the Victoria Line and Brenda was out in the air again at Finsbury Park. A short walk down three residential streets, and she found Pete was waiting for her at his flat.

'That was quick. I wasn't expecting you 'til at least 10,' he said.

She fell against his solid warmth, wrapped her arms round his body and started crying. He squeezed her and then held her away from him to look at her properly.

'Did she try and strangle you again?' He asked.

'Oh no – I think that was just her idea of a playful tiff,' Brenda replied and wiped her nose on her sleeve. 'Sorry, this is just tension release, or PMT, or something. I'm stopping now.' And she did.

'At least you're making jokes. That's a good sign,' said Pete and led her through to his immaculate living room area. He opened a bottle of wine and poured it into two beautifully made, exquisitely understated glasses. Brenda pulled herself together and drank hers until she felt like talking.

'It was totally bizarre. It lasted about three minutes. Fenella was there. I sat down and apologised and explained a bit about why it had happened. And she just sat there like some sort of fucking sphinx and then basically said, you can't do that joke again because I want to do it myself.'

'What?'

'And then she told me to go away.'

Pete was dumbfounded.

'She wants to do the joke herself? But I thought she never spoke about all that stuff.'

'That's what she told me, although I get the impression that sometimes it's the coke talking. The problem is no-one quite knows when it's the coke talking and when it's Josephine, and maybe there isn't really any difference between those two things.'

'So you're off the hook then?'

'It looks like it.'

'And you're not bothered about her using your joke?'

'She's fucking welcome to it. I never want to say those words again. You know, I remember thinking at like my first or maybe my second ever gig, "I could say anything I want", and it was so intoxicating that I thought I'd be high off it forever, but now, I don't know...I don't know if I want to just blurt anything without thinking. In fact, I'm pretty certain I want to change my style entirely.'

'In what sense?'

'Well, you know, I started getting into comedy when I was a teenager, and I liked all kinds of comedy then. I'd hoover up anything. And when I started reviewing, it was the same. There wasn't any one kind of comedy I thought was "the best", or the "real comedy". And then I started going out with Jonathan and I met all his friends and went to all their gigs, and they were all into this confessional stuff. You know, talking about their lives all time, no boundaries, no rules and I sort of absorbed this idea that that was the "true comedy" and all the other kinds are inferior somehow, because...because that's what they think.'

Pete nodded supportively, though he had no experience of what she was describing. Brenda paused and frowned, trying to force her thoughts into one place, and continued.

'But I don't know if I think that. I don't know. And when I started doing gigs, I just sort of slipped automatically into that style. But now I don't think it's what I want. It feels... cheap. And lazy. And I mean, where does it stop? That's the trouble – it's like a snake eating itself, and then when there's no more snake left and you've cannibalised your whole life and put it on stage, what's next? You have to start doing awful or crazy things just so you've got something to talk about. Or you start talking about other people and then, you know, things start to get messy. I don't know. I remember the look on Diarmuid Coyle's face... sorry, Diarmuid Coyle is this really amazing comedian who's always trying new things, and doesn't rely on anything personal at all. I remember the look on his face in Edinburgh when he met Jonathan, and he just had this vibe of total contempt. And I got it, you know? I got it, even though I was Jonathan's girlfriend, I got where Diarmuid was coming from.'

Pete nodded more enthusiastically now. This he could understand. Brenda reached over and touched his knee lightly – an instinctive need to connect with him, though she barely knew she was doing it.

'And I think I realise now... I think I realise that I don't actually want to do that kind of stuff. Rossly said to me, oh sorry Rossly Barns is this Australian comedian I'm friends with, he said to me months ago that it's not about just making people laugh, it's about how you make them laugh. What do you make them laugh with? How do you control the laugh? And I didn't understand at the time, I just thought he was being pretentious, but I see it now, I see it. I want to do something different. I used to have this bit about Shrek being right wing that I really liked, and I felt good doing it but it never quite worked so I dropped it because other stuff was going better, and now I see that I dropped it because I couldn't be bothered to work on it. Because it was easier to do the other stuff, you know about boyfriends and whatever. It was easier to do that than work on my Shrek bit, but I don't want to do this because it's easy. I want to do it because it's hard.'

Brenda took another sip of wine. Pete sat quietly next to her.

'I think I understand.'

'It's hard to explain to a non-comedian...'

'Yes, but I think I understand. I think it sounds like exactly the right thing to do.'

Brenda smiled at him and sniffed some snot.

'Do you want to come to Devon with me for the weekend to see Laura and Susie?' she asked quietly. It was a spontaneous offer, but it felt good.

'Yes, sure. That sounds fun. When?'

Brenda still couldn't quite believe how easy it was to make arrangements for the future with him. It seemed marvellous and strange after all that time with Jonathan.

'Dunno. In the next few weeks. I haven't got a gig for a fortnight, so I'm going to write a whole new set and try it out. Might as well take advantage of not being paid...'

They ordered an Indian take-away and ate it in front of the TV with the rest of the bottle of wine and then went to bed, and Brenda briefly remembered how it felt to be part of a normal couple, and liked it.

*

Brenda had not known Pete had a car, and she had also not known that it was a very nice car. He was obviously proud of it, and she found this curious and endearing but also slightly unappealing. She never in all her life had imagined that she would be with someone who was proud of their car. He pulled the Mercedes S-Class round to the street where she was waiting to get in, and she noted that it was pristine inside. Most of the cars Brenda was familiar with, including her own, were carpeted with a thin layer of fast food detritus, used tissues, a torn map book, some empty plastic drinks bottles and old cardboard coffee cups. But Pete's car didn't even have any weird sandy gravelly stuff in the folds of the leather gear box cover. She didn't really know what to make of it, though obviously it was no hardship to be driven in it. Pete was waiting for her to comment, but she couldn't quite bring herself to play it straight.

'Your cock is perfectly adequate, you know.'

'I do know, yes, but it's my balls I'm worried about.'

'Well, I'll check them later for you.'

'In Laura and Susie's house? I assumed I'd have to leave my dick at the door.'

'I'm sure they'll let you bring it inside as long as you can control it.'

'I can't guarantee that, Brenda. I simply can't guarantee it. I wish I could, but you know what I get like around the gay community. I get a liberal erection that will not go down.'

Brenda giggled and watched London become not-London out the window.

The journey passed happily, and Brenda had to admit that being chauffeured in a smart car to Devon for the weekend was a very grown up way to go about things. They arrived four hours later and stepped into another world. Every other shop front was either a brightly painted, fiercely independent coffee shop or a brightly painted, fiercely independent health food store-cum-alternative medicine practice advertising Reiki massage, homeopathy, Wiccan healing rituals. Reflexology and acupuncture were considered orthodox, mainstream medicine in this town, and the more extreme end of the spectrum had barely been heard of in other parts of the country. Laura and Susie had a sense of humour about it all, thank god, but they were still very much a part of a community that did things entirely their way.

The street that held Laura and Susie's house was too small to park in, and so Pete expertly parked his hunk of German metal in a tight spot on the high street and they walked the final few minutes to the door. Laura was beside herself at the sight of Brenda, whom she'd given up for dead. She flung her arms around her with childlike force, not really taking into account her size, and swamped Brenda with a hug.

'Come in, come in, the spare room's all ready. I've made some beer. No don't laugh, Susie bought me a kit last year and I've only just got round to it. Brewed some beer I suppose I should say, that's the right term, isn't it? Just step over the cat, he's so disgustingly fat these days he can barely move. I honestly don't know what he eats, I'm pretty sure he's being fed somewhere else, we've put him in a diet but it doesn't seem to make any difference, the vet's getting terribly cross with us. Oh god, I think I sound like one of those cat women. I don't, do I? Here you are, just dump your stuff, is the bed big enough, do you think? I don't know how much space you're used to...'

'Take a breath, Laura, Jesus,' Brenda said, though delighted to be here.

She felt more herself already, as if she had rediscovered the light side and was now basking in it.

'I'm sorry, I'm just so excited to see you and I'm no good at hiding things. We'll eat in tonight. Susie's cooking a roast chicken, which I'm fairly sure even she can't fuck up completely.'

Brenda caught an edge in Laura's voice but chose to ignore it.

When they all sat down for dinner it was clear to see that Laura and Susie were not getting along very well, and Susie felt like a stranger to Brenda. Then again, she felt so hyper-aware of everything and everyone these days, she had to check herself every now and then. But no, as the meal wore on Brenda became certain there was hostility in Susie's gaze, and she and Laura barely made eye contact all night. Brenda had always experienced them as a tactile couple, but there was no touching tonight. Once a perfectly passable roast chicken with home-grown potatoes and various organic salads had been served, conversation turned to Brenda's new profession. Susie, who had been agitated and bad-tempered all night, was in no mood for soft-pedaling.

'Don't you think it's a bit irresponsible to just leave your job before you're earning?' Susie asked, her voice harder than Brenda had ever heard before.

'I suppose so, but I think sometimes you have to make the leap,' Brenda replied in as even a tone as she could muster.

'Quite right,' said Laura.

'But what will you do at the end of this six months?' Susie pressed on, ignoring her wife.

'Well, hopefully I will be earning by then.'

'And if you're not?'

'God, just leave it would you, Susie? You're not her bank manager.'

'I think it's important. And I never thought *you'd* be the one telling *me* not to be socially insensitive.'

It was meant to be a joke, and maybe at another time it could have been taken that way if delivered with some affection, but this sounded harsh and irritable and everyone shifted slightly. Laura blinked, trying to take in what she'd heard. Susie had never shamed her with her Asperger's before.

'So, Brenda? What will you do?' Susie was not letting this go.

'I... I guess I'd have to sign on for a bit.'

'So the state would have to pay for you to be an unpaid comedian?'

'Since when have you ever said things like "the state would have to pay"?', Laura asked, aghast. 'You'll be using phrases like "taxpayers' money" next and then I really won't know who I've married.'

An awful moment. And then Susie turned her attention back to Brenda.

'Jobseeker's Allowance would barely cover even the monthly minimum payments on the amount of debt you'll have racked up by then...'

'So I'd get another job.'

'So why leave your job in the first place? It was a good job. It was the kind of job a lot of people would kill for. Do you know how many thousands of people would love to work as a journalist?'

'Well now they can, there's one more vacancy. Look, Susie, what's your problem with this? You sound so pissed off and I have no idea why. I'm just doing what I want to do.'

'But why should you get to do what you want to do? When you can't even support yourself? I mean, maybe there's a thousand things I'd like to do but I can't just stop working because I have bills and responsibilities.'

She gestured at Laura, who looked at her lap. Her condition made it hard to get a well-paid job, and so Susie had always basically supported them both while Laura brought in what she could. While they were happy, this wasn't a problem. Obviously now things had changed. Laura was very quiet and Susie seemed to know she had crossed a line.

'I'm sorry it pisses you off that I'm trying something new,' Brenda said, a little annoyed herself and so less charitable than she might have.

'It doesn't piss me off that you're trying something *new*. I'm just asking why you have to be so *extreme* about it.'

'LEAVE HER ALONE,' Laura exploded. 'JUST LEAVE HER ALONE, LEAVE HER ALONE, LEAVE HER ALONE.'

Laura was screaming now, locked into her anger and frustration. This had clearly been building for some time and Brenda wondered how easily Laura could have substituted the word 'me' for 'her' in her outburst. Susie got up from the table and walked out. They all heard the door slam.

Laura looked desolate.

'I'm sorry, guys, I don't know why this is happening. I thought we could keep it together for the weekend, at least.'

'I'll clear up,' Pete said in a saintly fashion and tactfully left the room.

Brenda turned to Laura.

'How long has it been going on?'

'Since before Christmas. Something just seemed to change, I don't know, around Hallowe'en. We had our usual coven gathering at Drusilla's house and Susie was all prickly on the way home. She said Hallowe'en was all about "out with the old, in with the new" and that had a special resonance for her this year. When I asked her what she meant she wouldn't go into it. She's been like this ever since.'

'She won't talk about it at all?'

'No. Not to me anyway.'

'And you have no idea what's bugging her?'

'No.'

'Honestly?'

A pause.

'Oh come on, I thought all lesbians did was talk about their feelings. I thought that was the whole point, a never-ending emotional chat and no sex...'

Brenda nudged her playfully, and Laura smiled a bit.

'Bed death was never our problem.'

'I know. So what is?'

'Well, I don't know...'

Laura began and then stopped. Brenda waited. Laura took a deep breath.

'I know she... I know she's always wanted to travel more, and you know, I don't like new places all that much. Totnes is so nice, I don't see why anyone would want to leave and we go to Cornwall if we want a change of scene.'

Brenda bit back a remark about Cornwall not being the most remarkable change of scene one could imagine for a Totnes resident but she understood that Laura felt anxious when in unfamiliar surroundings. Once again, this had not been a problem while they were happy.

'I think... I think she's started to feel that I've been holding her back. And now she's nearly forty, she wants to... do some of that stuff...'

'And I... what I'm doing has made her feel that all the more?' Brenda asked, tentatively.

'Yeah, maybe. Although she's right, you know – it is pretty reckless, what you've done. Although I support it, I mean, everyone should live their dreams and things, but still... I don't you to end up in debtors' prison 'cos I haven't got any money to bail you out and nor does anyone else.'

'I know that. I take full responsibility.'

'You don't have any responsibilities.'

'I do to myself.'

'That's not a responsibility, that's a life-style choice. You only have responsibilities when other people are involved.'

Brenda processed this, and felt the prescience of it given the previous couple of weeks.

'Sorry, I sound judgmental, I don't mean to be.'

'It's OK, but look, I'm fine. Don't worry about me. What about you and Susie? Are you going to be OK, or is it over?'

'Honestly, Bren, I don't know. I really don't know.'

Pete and Brenda lay side by side in the double bed in Laura and Susie's spare room. Laura had taken a herbal sleeping pill and gone to bed. Susie had yet to come home.

'Do you agree with her, then?' Brenda asked.

'About what?'

'You know what.'

'No, not doing this. You tell me what you want to know. I'm not going to guess.'

'Do you agree that I'm reckless and stupid for wanting to be a comedian?'

'No, I don't think you're reckless and stupid for wanting to be a comedian.'

'So what do you think?'

'I think it's great that you're following your dream.'

'But...'

'But nothing.'

'No, there was a but there, Pete. What comes after it?'

'I come after your butt.'

'Don't make shit jokes, I'm trying to have a proper conversation.'

'Oh god, Brenda, please... I don't want to do this now. I thought this was going to be a nice weekend away, not some sort of Relate conference.'

'Do you think I should have quit my job?'

Pete pushed himself up on one elbow and looked Brenda straight in the eye.

'Do *you* think you should have quit your job?'

'I... I don't... yes, yes I do, of course I do. Otherwise I wouldn't have done it, would I?'

Brenda was aware she sounded defensive but this only

aggravated the situation.

'OK, fine, good. If you're fine with it then what does it matter what anyone else thinks?'

'Oh fuck off, Pete, don't be all like that.'

'Like what?'

'Like all Mr Perfect and rational and whatever.'

'Oh, OK, sorry. What shall I do? Throw something out the window and scream "if anyone wants me I'll be in the lake?" Is that the kind of thing you're after?'

'Well, it would make a nice change. Not everyone can be so in control and sorted and perfect with all amazing, tasteful furniture and white sheets that make everyone feel dirty all the time.'

'What are you talking about now?'

'Just leave me alone. You clearly don't understand, so there's no point me trying to explain. Just stop judging me.'

'I'm not judging you.'

'But you are, though. You are. Everyone is.'

'No, not everyone. You may be surprised to learn that most people couldn't give a shit what you do. Most people aren't even aware you fucking exist.'

Brenda flared her nostrils and rolled over. Pete waited a moment and then picked up his pillow, got out of bed, took a blanket from the top of the wardrobe and settled down to sleep on the floor.

When Brenda woke up the next morning, a cold, blue Northerly light filled the room. Pete was snoring, spreadeagled on the carpet. She slipped out of the room and went downstairs. Susie was in the kitchen making toast. She looked up as Brenda came in and then looked back down at her plate.

'Morning,' said Susie.

'Morning,' said Brenda.

There was no further speaking while Brenda made herself

a cup of tea. Then Susie broke the silence.

'I'm sorry, I may have... over-reacted a bit last night.'

Brenda shrugged, though was not inclined to make nice just yet. For one thing, she'd slept very, very badly and felt like shit.

'It's OK. Forget it.'

'I'm just in a bit of a funny phase at the moment. Laura and I haven't been... having the best time.'

'Yeah, she told me.'

Susie nodded, though she had obviously already made the assumption that Brenda knew.

'There's no-one else.'

'It's none of my business.'

'I just feel life is... draining away somehow. I feel like I'm going to suddenly be old and I won't have done anything I wanted to do.'

'It's not about making lists and ticking things off, you know.'

'Maybe not for you. You don't need to make a list, you can just do each thing as it occurs to you. For most people, that's not the case. For me it's not the case. I have to have a list otherwise I'd never do anything. I have a job I don't like that takes up most of my time. I have to prioritise.'

'You do prioritise. You felt like getting married to Laura, so you did. That's a choice – no-one forced you. Just because you don't like it anymore, I don't see why you have to take it out on anyone who is doing what they want to do, or *need* to do, to be happy.'

'Life isn't just about being happy.'

'Then what is it about?'

'Saying you'll do things and then doing them.'

'Jesus, Susie, that's depressing.'

'We can't all live as selfishly as you, Brenda.'

Brenda didn't react, Susie looked regretful.

'I'm sorry, that came out wrong.'

'Look, Susie, if you want to do things, just do them. If you're unhappy in your marriage, then get help or get out. I'll be here for Laura.'

Susie raised a sceptical eyebrow. Brenda saw it.

'Well, I'll do my best to be. And Laura's got all her other friends, and the coven, and things like that. The world won't collapse if you say you want something different. You can't sit around being miserable all the time. Well, actually you can, just don't go around telling everyone else to be miserable too.'

Brenda's back was really up now, and she stalked out of the kitchen with her tea and stood in the tiny garden, inhaling the fresh country air. She wanted desperately to leave but she'd have to wait for Pete to wake up. Once he did though, she had no doubt they would be on their way fairly quickly. And then there would be a four-hour journey in which to sort out their own relationship. Brenda asked herself if she could be bothered. The next round of the competition was next week, and now she had had her epiphany about the kind of material she wanted to perform, she really needed to get to work.

An hour later, and after muted goodbyes all round, Pete and Brenda were on the road.

'I don't want a row,' Pete said as they joined the motorway.

'Nor do I,' said Brenda, with a slightly combative tone.

'Good, then can we just forget last night? I support you completely. You know that. Please don't make me work so hard.'

'OK.'

Pete genuinely seemed happy to drop it after that and Brenda wasn't going to pick a fight. As he automatically drove them both back to his flat, his clear assumption being that Brenda would be staying the night, she once again marvelled at this new, grown-up relationship she seemed to be having. A relationship where every argument did not result in one or both of them threatening to end it, or leaving or one even actually dumping the other, only to return at some later date for a completely draining chat and then over-heated sex. It seemed that Pete had just absorbed the row and moved on – Brenda thought it might actually be a miracle, but realised she had never experienced life as a real couple, so what did she have to compare it to? Nothing – she was learning as she went along, throwing down track ahead of the speeding train she was driving all by herself. Perhaps it was time to let someone else help.

18

It was the fifth weekend in a row that Pete was spending alone in London. As March turned to April Brenda worked ever harder, driving around the country to any gig she could find, consuming service station sandwiches, pasties, all night fast food and developing the attendant constipation known as 'Comedian's Dodgy Gut Syndrome'. She was managing one paid gig a fortnight now, but still nowhere near enough to support herself, or even a small hamster. She had told an increasingly frustrated Pete to stop nagging her, that she was spending all her free time with him. To which his response was that if all her free time basically amounted to the hours between 3 and 6am on Sunday nights, then she might as well not bother. Brenda couldn't stop gigging, though. Her need was manifesting itself as something like an addiction and Pete clearly knew that if he forced her to make a choice she would choose comedy and so he never pushed it that far. She had, after all, begun the two relationships around the same time and was not ready to give up either one. In fact, in some respects, the relationship with comedy was less complicated and more rewarding. For though Brenda knew she didn't currently make much of a girlfriend, she was improving as a comedian with every gig that passed. She had a solid twenty minute set and more material to rotate in as and when she felt like it. She had plastered her *Guardian* quote across her website, joined Twitter and set up a Facebook page. People were starting to notice her.

The hard work she had done in the weeks since that night with Josephine was paying off. There had been days, of course, where she sat staring at a blank computer screen all afternoon or doodling in a notebook creating great cityscapes of interlinking, carefully shaded cubes, unable to think of a single word in the English language let alone a fully-formed joke. The monstrous self-loathing that accompanied these apparently wasted afternoons (mornings were a distant memory now) could only be managed by telling herself everyone experienced it, there was nothing wrong with her, even that it was creatively necessary. But still, the impotence and pointless frustration that engulfed Brenda when nothing was forthcoming was lonely and miserable. A walk around the block sometimes cured it but not always, and that was when she could even be bothered to leave the house (which of course meant getting dressed). Brenda wondered what people had done before Twitter, Facebook and the million and one blogging sites you could while away several hours continually reading and re-reading, driving yourself half mad, wondering if time had slowed down. Brenda found that a really bad day could be defined by the sense that the MailOnline's TV&Showbiz section was not being updated often enough.

But it was a necessary process and once she adopted a new method she had read in an interview with a favourite comedian of hers of thinking of topics that interested her or she felt strongly about and then trying to make them funny, rather than just writing lists of potentially hilarious scenarios, it had come a lot easier. Be interesting first, then add the funny – this was her new mantra.

Since she had ditched all the material about her specific

relationships she had felt more at peace with herself, too. She liked her comedy, that was the difference now. Before she had felt at war with her material but now it came out of her as if it had always been there. Not all of it worked, of course, but the process felt good and that was half the battle. And the more she wrote, the more she found that Holy Grail, her 'Voice' – the sound, the attitude, the way of viewing the world that was uniquely hers. She knew the total realisation of this 'Voice' was a long way off, would be years in the making, in fact. But the suit she was tailoring for herself was slowly moving from off the peg, to fitted, to bespoke. Brenda was getting acquainted, then comfortable, with her particular type of funny.

She knew she was neglecting Pete, but felt unable to do anything about it. She'd been open to him coming to her gigs now, but he'd decided against it. The comedians just talked shop all the time, including Brenda, and pretty much ignored Pete. The punters just wanted to buy Brenda drinks and also pretty much ignored Pete. It wasn't much fun, and Brenda sympathised – she had been in that position once herself, she just wasn't going to slow down to make more time for him. Her attitude was that he could either like it, lump it or leave. He was lumping it. For now.

'When stand-up comedians start earning loads of money, you know touring and stuff, they often end up employing their partners as like a PA, or manager or something,' Brenda had said idly one night, as she ate pasta in Pete's flat at 4am, having driven straight back to London from a gig in Leeds.

'Yeah. I'm not going to be your fucking PA, Brenda. As you may have noticed I have my own business. And identity,' Pete had replied tersely, red-eyed and scratchy with need for sleep, and that was the end of that.

Brenda had to push any niggles she was having with Pete to one side and concentrate on the next round of the new act competition. It was imperative that she made it to the semi-final. Failure was not an option. She could see from the success of previous winners that it was the fastest and most efficient route to an agent and paid gigs. The competition was sponsored by a large chain of comedy clubs that would then invite the winner to six months' worth of regular gigs at each of their venues around the country. This was the ticket to a more stable existence, at least from a financial point of view. Brenda was well aware that she was now halfway through the money she had available to live on, and already knew that there was no way she could remain in the flat she had rented for the past five years. She had opted to stay there based on the fact that it was home, and it was affordable, as long as everything went to plan. However, as she was learning, almost nothing in the comedy world ever went to plan. Any money she did make from gigs went straight into buying petrol for the next one. Pete had suggested on one occasion that she might move in with him, but her horrified silence had nipped that idea in the bud.

The second heat took place in Birmingham, and when Pete said he wanted to come along, she felt too guilty to say no. He had been patient and easy-going for the most part, and how could she refuse him what was a very simple request? She still recalled the misery of being excluded from Jonathan's gigging life as and when it suited him and didn't want to emulate the worst of his behaviour, at least as far as she could help it. Into the deal Pete had offered to drive Brenda to Birmingham in his grown-up car and even pay for a hotel so they didn't have to rush back afterwards. Brenda had agreed, and so they drove away from Pete's flat on a beautiful, sunny spring afternoon.

Blossom frothed the trees and that special English light that clarifies made every shade of green known to the human eye softly glow. The countryside looked radiant as they drove past it, and things felt more hopeful. Arriving in Birmingham was something of a comedown, but the hotel was smart and the room was high up in the building with a view that lifted their spirits. The door had barely closed before Pete had pulled Brenda down onto the crisp bed and gently lifted her T-shirt to kiss her breasts. They hadn't had sex for a while and as Brenda ran her hands up Pete's thigh, he was already unzipping his fly. He pushed her skirt up around her waist and she sat on top of him, rocking back and forth as he kissed her neck.

Brenda showered smiling. Maybe she had just been sexually frustrated and that had led to a general irritability that had now vanished. She felt better disposed towards Pete than she had in weeks and suddenly she felt full of confidence and vigour, certain of victory tonight and a place in the semi-final assured.

She dressed quickly in what was now her stage uniform of all black with patent red lace-up brogues, and applied her make-up with the dexterity that comes from experience. She had a routine now, and though she was not superstitious like many comedians she knew, she still liked things to follow a certain pattern. Pete was good at making himself invisible before gigs and she felt flooded with sudden warmth for him as she came out of the bathroom to find him calm, quiet and ready to go. She had taken him for granted and she felt sorry for it. Amazing what five minutes of reasonably satisfying sex can do.

They arrived at the venue – one that belonged to the competition sponsors – and made themselves known to the organisers. After being ushered backstage, Pete made his excuses and said he would see Brenda later. He was not wild about green room dynamics and had now found that he preferred to sit at the bar reading a book until the show began, rather than listen to a load of neurotic comedians (including Brenda) jangle themselves and each other into a frenzy that could only be remedied post-performance by alcohol or drugs or both. Those comedians who were teetotal had other ways to relax that took place away from the prying eyes of their peers, and were, it was speculated, less healthy than intoxication rather than more so.

Brenda helped herself to a glass of wine and sat down to skim over her notebook. Brenda checked the running order and found that she was going on first, a fact she was not delighted about as she would now effectively be warming up the crowd for her rivals. She had planned to hover at the back for the first couple of acts so that she could get the measure of the crowd and adapt her material a little if necessary but she would have no such opportunity now. She could listen to the ten or fifteen minutes the compere did at the top and try to get a sense of it but it wasn't much to play with and she was still effectively going out there cold. The five other comedians in her heat were unknown to Brenda but were all, like her, now veterans of countless open mic spots, thrumming with ambition, vibrating at a higher frequency than the average person in the street.

Brenda noted the names of the judges, and had a momentary flashback to a brief confrontation Jonathan had had with one of them at a party a few months back. Brenda had hovered quietly next to him as Jonathan jabbed his finger. But the now-judge had looked her right in the eye as she had left in Jonathan's turbulent wake, and she hoped he did not remember her. Would he penalise her for having been with Jonathan? Or reward her for putting up with him? Brenda tried to shut down this most unhelpful of internal monologues, but she was in the eye of the storm now and it was weirdly still and silent and desperate to be filled.

There was not much chat to be had – this meant too much to everyone in the room. And whilst green rooms were never usually a nursery for collaborative work, this was an actual competition, rather than merely a perceived one, and so there was never going to be much love. They were all polite though, and civil, apart from one very young-looking girl Brenda had noticed as she walked in. This girl couldn't have been more than nineteen years old but she was trying to look older, or at least wiser. She was affecting a jaded air and with dyed black hair, heavy fringe, thick glasses and pierced sulky mouth, she was not exuding approachability. Brenda stuck out her hand in any case, not wanting anything more than a brief introduction. She was surprised when the girl just stared at her outstretched hand and sniggered nastily.

'Sorry, I don't do hand-shaking, because I'm not a fucking banker.'

'Oh, OK, fine. I'm Brenda Monk.'

'Yeah, I know who you are.'

'Oh right. I don't know who you are.'

'Why would you?'

'Well, yeah, I'm not claiming to know everyone in the world.'

'Yeah, right.'

'So, what's your name?'

'Cody.'

'Cody what?'

'Just Cody.'

'Just the one name for you, is it?'

'Well, I was in care til I was fifteen and I don't want my real parents finding me when I get famous.'

'Oh right. Fair enough.'

Cody scowled at Brenda.

'So, how come you know who I am?'

'Because you're Jonathan Cape's girlfriend. So we might as well all go home now, 'cos obviously you're going to win.'

Brenda felt two other nearby comics prick their ears up at this.

'Actually, I'm not Jonathan Cape's girlfriend.'

'OK, you were then. Whatever, sorry I don't know every detail of your life, I'm not your stalker. You're not that interesting, you know.'

'I didn't say I was.'

'Well, anyway...'

'My relationship with Jonathan won't have any impact on the result of this competition.'

'Yeah, right.'

'He's not here. He's in LA.'

'Yeah, but you know all the judges, don't you?'

'No. I've met one of them once, and I can guarantee he won't remember me. He barely looked at me at the time.'

'That's 100% more than I've met.'

'Well, I can't help who I've met.'

'No, but they can help you, can't they?'

Brenda had not immediately disliked anyone as much as she immediately disliked Cody for a very long time. They were now glowering at each other, both clearly hoping the woman standing opposite her would crash and burn and be sent home with singed wings.

'I haven't had a leg up from anyone. I've done it all myself.'

'If you say so.'

'Well, who else says so? *You?* You know fuck all about me.'

'I know more about you than you know about me. *A hell of a lot more,*' Cody replied with an infuriating smirk.

Brenda knew she was talking about Jonathan's Edinburgh show and controlled an urge to smack her in the mouth.

'You might know what I like in bed. You have no idea what kind of comedian I am.'

'You're no kind of comedian. You're a comedian's girlfriend trying it out for a hobby to get his attention.'

That struck a nerve. The gloves were off it seemed.

'Oh I see. You're one of those silly little emo girls who thinks they're "so fucked up". What do you do every night? Masturbate over your Bill Hicks poster and fantasise about getting raped by the ghost of Lenny Bruce?'

'At least I know about comedy.'

'Listen you *child*, I know about comedy.'

'Only by sucking its dick.'

'Who made you the fucking comedy police? You think you get to say who's a comedian and who isn't just because you did a bit of self-harming when you were fourteen?'

'I was in CARE.'

'Good, then you'll have plenty to talk about on stage. Spare a thought for the rest of us who don't have great lakes of self-important teenage pain to draw on.'

Brenda wasn't sure where all this was coming from but she had a sense that it had been building up for a long time. She was suddenly shaking with rage and before her eyes Cody became every comedian, every *person* who had ever undermined her, insulted her, belittled or just plain ignored her since the day she first met Jonathan. She tried to get herself back under control. She would be on stage in less than twenty minutes and this was not the vibe she had been hoping for.

'Look, I'm sorry I said that. Have a good gig, OK?' Brenda said with immense will power.

'Fuck you, Gag Hag,' Cody replied and turned her back on Brenda, who fought every single fibre in her being to not shove her very hard against the table. If this little bitch didn't get thrown out of the competition tonight she would give up comedy on the spot, Brenda thought, knowing full well she wouldn't.

The show began. The compere did fifteen minutes but he was not on form and his warm-up was lacklustre. For this reason it was impossible for Brenda to get a true feel for the crowd before she walked on. It took every single ounce of mental strength, skill, determination and suppression of a natural instinct to panic and run away that Brenda had to give a performance that vaguely represented her ability. At one stage, as she let a medium-sized laugh roll back through the room, she had glanced at her feet and entertained herself with the idea of clicking her red shoes together and instantly being at home. And then remembered with a sickening jolt that she was on stage, competing for her livelihood, and she really needed to fucking concentrate.

In the end, she had been good, well, competent, but she knew she could have been better and that really pissed her off. To add torture to terror she would also now have to sit and watch all the remaining acts whilst trying to figure out if she stood a chance of going through. She had gone down well, but someone could easily top her – it wouldn't take much.

Cody stomped out fourth and did exactly the kind of material Brenda had known she would, full of achingly self-conscious anecdotes about how she didn't fit in with anyone in her bleak home town, twisted fantasies about killing people designed to appeal to the kind of men she was desperate to be attractive to, and liberal use of the phrase, 'I guess I'm just wrong in the head'. She got some laughs though, and had one joke that Brenda had grudgingly enjoyed. But she was nowhere near as good as at least three of the other comics. Four if Brenda included herself, which she daren't at this stage. Given that only two could go through to the semi-final it seemed obvious that Cody would be going home disappointed, which was of some comfort to Brenda.

The format of the competition allowed the judges to eliminate three comedians, then choose one from the three remaining for a guaranteed place in the semi-final. As the six stood along the front of the stage to face the judges and the audience for a second time that night, three names were called. Brenda's was not one of them.

Cody's was though, and she clumped off the stage with a scowl and a middle finger upturned to the judges, clearly feeling that this was just another in a long line of injustices and that these tossers would live to regret their decision when she was famous and they were in need of a job. A fantasy she would surely nurture in her bedroom that night until it was as real to her as anything else was. Brenda did not change her facial expression, but inside her a plank fell. First hurdle just about cleared, but she wasn't home and dry yet. She was glad to see Cody go, but still couldn't help but empathise - it could, she felt, so easily have been her.

The head judge, having been schooled by TV talent shows, left as long a pause as he dared before naming the person who would definitely go through: an extraordinarily eccentric twenty-two-year-old art college graduate who dressed like an Edwardian dandy but did truly hilarious material about the contents of all the various gossip magazines, in triumphant vindication of never judging a book by its cover.

Brenda's guts sank to her shiny red shoes – click, click, click.

She stood next to the man in his fifties who had retired from his day job as a county council admin assistant in order to pursue his dream to be a comedian and waited to see what the result of the very unscientific public vote would be.

For the only remaining place in the semi-final would be decided by audience cheers. The compere stood by the plastic 'Laugh-o-meter', a garish construction with a manually operated dial in the middle. As Brenda's name was called, the compere mimed listening to the crowd as they screamed and applauded and whooped and pretended the arrow was quivering under his touch. The audience responded by increasing the volume and two very loud shouts of support from a group of rugby players allowed the compere to push the arrow up to the line that divided 'Side-splitting' and 'Gut-busting'. That was as much as she was going to get.

It was now the turn of the fifty-year-old. Though he had been good, the audience liked Brenda better, and the cheering was markedly quieter. This was obvious to everyone and though the compere tried to introduce tension by making the arrow rise high, then fall, then rise, then fall, it eventually settled in the part of the Laugh-o-meter called 'Stomach-clutching' and so Brenda had won. She had won. Well, not won exactly, but scraped herself a place in the semi-final, and tonight that felt like winning. It took a moment for it to sink in. The light fractured and the sound distorted. She was through to the semi-final by a whisker. Or a side-split, depending how you chose to quantify it. Brenda was subdued and Pete could see that she wasn't happy. They left the venue fairly rapidly after the result was called, but not before Brenda had smiled with entirely faked sincerity at Cody who stuck up her middle finger again and carried on drinking.

Brenda was quiet in the taxi back to their hotel. She was quiet in the lift on the way up to their floor, and she was quiet as they walked down the corridor to their room. Pete swiped the key card several times before he got a green light. 'Do it more slowly,' were the only words Brenda uttered during this time and they walked in to a turned down bed and a chocolate on each pillow.

'I shouldn't have had sex,' Brenda murmured to herself.

'Sorry?'

'Um... I... I think maybe, maybe it's not good to have sex just before a gig.'

Pete looked hard at Brenda and went wordlessly into the

bathroom. She sat on the bed in a daze until Pete came out.

'What do you mean?'

'I mean I think having sex just before I go on stage is a bad idea.'

Pete let out a laugh that was not especially filled with mirth.

'What, like Rocky? Or Frankel?'

'Yes, yes, maybe a bit like that. It is a bit like being a boxer or a racehorse. You know, you have to keep all the energy inside, so it just comes out on stage.'

Pete blinked and did not conceal the fact that he considered this pronouncement to be horse shit of the highest order. Brenda continued sitting on the edge of bed, her hands in her lap like a Buddha.

'I know you think it sounds stupid.'

Pete did not respond immediately. Brenda continued:

'The trouble is if I have sex before a gig I'm too... content, or, I don't know exactly, all I know is that I was soft when I went into that green room and so I wasn't prepared for that little bitch and it threw me off and I didn't do enough on stage.'

'You got through!'

'Yes, but not safely, it wasn't a done deal.'

'So when can I have sex with you, Brenda? When?'

Pete's irritation popped its cap.

'You know, this never used to bother you. We used to have sex all the time whether you had a gig or not. But now... now, when can I see you? Or talk to you? Or introduce you to my friends? Or eat dinner with you at a normal human time? I can't on a gig day, I can't after a gig, I can't on an off day... when? When's the magical time when you can take a short break from this great and noble pursuit of comedy? This vocation of yours, this *wonderful vocation?*'

A distant echo of a conversation long forgotten filled Brenda's head.

A voice... Her voice... Saying this thing, this exact same thing, to Jonathan.

She smiled to herself.

'Why are you smiling? What's funny?'

'Everything', Brenda said softly, 'everything's funny.'

Pete looked defeated. He sat down next to her on the bed they had been physically joined together on four hours earlier. Brenda looked at her hands, her ears now deaf with realisation. When she spoke her voice was muffled in her own head. But still the words came out, though she wasn't sure exactly who was forming them.

'I can't do this any more, Pete. I'm sorry.'

'Can't do what?' he said remotely, though he knew perfectly well.

'I can't do comedy and us. I can't do both. I can't make you happy like this and I can't make myself happy either. I want to be the sort of person who goes out with the sort of person you are, but I can't. I'm not. You're miserable and I don't want that.'

'I'm not,' said Pete in a broken voice, 'I'm not miserable.'

'But you are though. You are.'

He couldn't contradict her.

'If I'm going to be a comedian, like properly a comedian, I can't be in a relationship at the same time.'

Pete nodded, he'd given up, all the energy he'd expended 'not minding' suddenly deserted him and he crumpled inside.

'I'm really sorry. I really am... I wish it was different.'

'Maybe one day it will be,' said Pete.

'Maybe,' said Brenda, and they lay down together quietly and went to sleep.

19

Brenda now realised with horrifying clarity how crazy she'd been to think she would be making a living out of stand-up comedy within a year of her first gig, which made it all the more important that she win this competition. Money was ever-dwindling with little prospect of a radical turn-around any time soon. If she won the competition, she would be guaranteed paid gigs pretty much overnight. She knew now she was not going to stop doing this, so she had to make it work somehow. She had no time for the self-doubt fluttering round the windows and perching on the sills. She must simply press on, girded within, blind and deaf to the crushing arm of reason and rationale.

The semi-final was around the corner, and by coincidence fell on her thirtieth birthday – time was marching on. Brenda was looking forward to being thirty, or rather, 'entering her thirties'. She had never felt right as a twenty-something, she was not light-hearted enough by nature to do that traditionally hedonistic decade justice and though she'd had some very debauched nights, she had always felt she ought to be getting on with something else. And the thirties were now considered to be the period in a person's life when they really started working hard, making something, building something that would last a lifetime. In many cases this would be a family, but for Brenda that was so far on the horizon it might as well be off the chart. What Brenda was building was a career. She was raising a brood of jokes that would serve her for many years to come, and it was a full-time occupation.

With Pete out of the picture Brenda could devote all her time and energy to comedy. As May began, the month of both seminal birthday and semi-final, she was riding a wave of good gigs and feeling high. She felt the need for stage time all the time and was scratchy and restless on nights where she had no booking. On these evenings she would often go down to a stand-up club just to hang out and watch the show and she now counted several dozen working circuit comedians as friends. So she was always welcomed and hours were spent after gigs just sitting in green rooms shooting the shit, obsessing about jokes and trying to say the most fucked up things they could think of in order to amuse one another. These were jokes that would never see the light of stage – they would likely offend the most broad-minded of punters – but were a way to let off steam and explore boundaries of taste, or lack thereof. Nights like these felt like home to Brenda. They had when she had been Jonathan's girlfriend, but then she had always been behind a piece of invisible glass, not really one of them. Now she was firmly in place, one more cousin in the extended family.

Brenda was thinking about the semi-final constantly now. She still had horrified flashbacks to the second heat, and how close she felt she had come to missing out. She was grateful to the audience for putting her through, but she distrusted it too. Audiences could be fickle, and she had a suspicion that the loud cheer from the table of rugby players that had pushed her to victory had been more mocking than genuinely supportive. It could so easily have gone the other way. She needed to be the best, incontrovertibly the best, and leave nothing to chance. She was now consistently gigging four or even five times a week and would happily do more if she could get them. She had at last played some weekend gigs in smaller clubs for small amounts of money, box office splits (the most she had made like this was £12.50, which felt like a fortune) and sausage rolls. One promoter had even attempted to pay her with a bag of raw chicken wings, which she had declined on basic health and safety grounds – they had felt warm to the touch.

Brenda woke one afternoon to a text from Jonathan who seemed hilariously unable to comprehend that she, or indeed anyone, was in a different time zone to him. Although to be fair she now had her own personal time zone that bore little resemblance to anything a normal working person would recognise.

'Call me now. I mean it. Call me.'

It had been sent nine hours earlier, around the time Brenda was going to bed. She must have just missed him. She made a cup of coffee, ate a slice of toast, had a quick perusal of the papers and various websites she regularly checked and then picked up her phone and dialled his number. He answered straight away – possibly a life-time first.

'Brenda, where the fuck have you been?'

'I've been asleep?'

'Asleep? It's the middle of the afternoon.'

'Well, yes fair enough, it is now, but you actually texted me at 5am my time. I assume you weren't expecting an immediate response then.'

'Whatever, look, you have to come out here as soon as possible.'

'To LA?'

'Yes! Where else?'

'Well, I don't know where you are at any given moment.'

'When can you come?'

'I can't come.'

'You have to. Seriously, Brenda, I need you here. If what we had means anything to you, you have to come.'

'Why? What for?'

'It's Lloyd, he's totally fucked me... us over.'

'How?'

'The double-gig thing, he's just... look, I'll explain it when you get here.'

'When I *get there*? What's the matter with you? It's not a quick ride down the Northern Line.'

'So how soon can you come? You might be able to get on a flight this evening. There's usually one around eleven.'

Brenda amused herself with the thought that there was a time when she might have actually considered flying to LA with this amount of notice, just because Jonathan asked her to.

'Jonathan, listen to me. I'm not coming, I've got things to do.'

'What things?'

'Gigs, writing.'

'Yeah but not real gigs.'

'They're real to me.'

'Brenda, I need you. For god's sake, I don't ask for much.'

'You don't ask for anything and neither do I. What the hell is the matter anyway?'

'Lloyd... I mean, that fucker, I literally can't believe, him... Lloyd has sold the fucking double gig format to some big TV company.'

'But I thought that was the whole point?'

'Yes, it was. But it was supposed to fucking well have me in it, the slippery little bastard.'

Brenda was struggling to comprehend what Jonathan was saying, but if she was right in her first guess a wide, rich seam of uncontrollable laughter was opening up inside her.

'Jonathan, are you... are you telling me he's sold the show

and *recast you?'*

'YES! At last she gets it, yes, that's what the slimy cunt's done. Can you fucking believe it?'

Brenda was now fizzing with mirth and she struggled to keep her voice even.

'But... But how? I thought you co-owned it.'

'I thought so too, but apparently there's some fucking "key man clause". Some LA lawyer type bullshit I didn't know about that gives him the right to override me in the event of a deal. And apparently the fucking shit-hole TV execs want a "name" in it for ratings purposes, or ad revenue or whatever. It's all fucking bullshit.'

'I don't see what I can do about it. My contract signed everything over to you and Lloyd. Well, Lloyd, as it turns out.'

'You need to come out here and we can present a united front. If we go in there, and Joan's totally on board with this, she says she'll even consider repping you if she sees you gig over here. Don't worry, I can set that up. Anyway, if we go in there together and say we're going to sue, you know, or that Lloyd has stitched us up, then they might get cold feet about it all and drop it. It's got to be both of us though they won't care if it's just me. And you should see who they've got to play you, Bren. Honestly, it's like some LA actress who's about as funny as lung cancer. And they're even giving us different names, for GOD'S SAKE. I mean, it's not right, Brenda. We're the artists, we're the ones writing the material. It's just totally against everything for them to just steal it like this. You have to come out here and defend your right to your own material. It's a matter of principle.'

Brenda stopped laughing. She regained control of herself and spoke firmly.

'Listen, Jonathan, you didn't give a shit about me and my rights when you knew I'd signed that contract giving you and

Lloyd ownership over everything I said that night. Do you have any idea how badly that fucked me up?'

'But that's exactly what I'm talking about, Bren. You can come out here now and reclaim your rights. You can reclaim your material.'

Brenda thought back to all the stuff she'd said on stage that night and shuddered.

'Jonathan, let me explain something to you. I don't want any of that material back. I don't care what you do with it. As soon as I realised what you and Lloyd had done to me with that contract I wrote a whole book of burner jokes to use once, and once only. My style's completely different now. None of that stuff is of any use to me. As far as I'm concerned, they can have it. And if they've called her something else then so much the better. It's nothing to do with me. It's not my problem.'

Jonathan was very quiet before he spoke.

'So you're just going to leave me to sort all this out?'

'Yes.'

When he spoke again, his voice was full of reproach.

'You've really let me down, Bren. I never... I never thought this of you. I thought we were tight, I thought we were simpatico. I thought you were on the team.'

'I'm my own team now, Jonathan. I don't have time to be on yours. And to be honest I never felt terribly valued even when I was, except as some kind of vaginal joke generator.'

'You've changed,' was Jonathan's final gambit.

'Yes. I have,' was Brenda's response.

And she hung up.

*

Semi-final day. Birthday. D-Day, as in Do or Die Day. The semi-final was in London, so no need to travel. This was good. It meant Brenda could devote all her energies to preparing herself. There was a school of thought that said the less preparation you do, the better you'll be on the night, but Brenda's temperament did not bear this out. She liked to be as prepared as possible so that if anything went wrong she had a well-constructed, reliable launch pad to take off from. If she had to go in another direction spontaneously, she could but only, she had found, if she was settled and sorted mentally beforehand. She woke around noon and made herself some breakfast: one hard-boiled egg sliced onto a piece of toast, economical and delicious. She then allowed herself an hour or so of messing about online, replying to a couple of Facebook messages and even responding on Twitter to three people who had taken the trouble to tweet her positive feedback from gigs they had seen her at.

Then she had a shower, put on a pair of yoga pants that had never seen any actual yoga and a T-shirt and around 3pm she sat down with her notebook to go through her set list. She broadly knew what she wanted to do but it never hurt to go over it again. Around 5pm she got changed into her show outfit, put on her make-up and left the house.

She arrived at the venue just before 6pm, but instead of going in she went to a pub nearby and killed another forty-five minutes with a small glass of wine and a last check of her material. She then took out a pen and wrote a list of words on the back of her hand. She had experimented with performing with no prompts and ideally wanted to wean herself off this habit in due course but tonight was no time to start changing the routine. At 6.45pm she left her table and went two doors down to the club that would decide her destiny.

Inside were three other comedians. Two would go through to the final. There was another semi-final taking place tonight in Manchester and so a total of four would become finalists that night. The final itself would be held at the Edinburgh Festival in August and for one person it would change everything, every single thing. The three comics sat in the green room were clearly sick with nerves and Brenda felt glad she didn't look like them, until she caught sight of herself in a mirror and realised she did. This being London, it was likely that more established comedians who were not gigging that night would pop in to see how the evening went and to cast judgement on each act, reporting back to others in the days to come. Brenda had performed here before and that gave her a small advantage. She knew how this room absorbed laughter rather than amplified it and so she wouldn't be put off when the crowd's reaction sounded more muted than it did in other places. For anyone else who had not had the benefit of this experience they could easily lose their stride a little while they worked out that it was the acoustics and not necessarily their material that was at fault.

Brenda nodded and smiled to the others and they all exchanged some light pleasantries. Apart from the odd self-appointed combatant like Cody, these competitions were softer backstage than most normal gigs. No-one had much spare energy to put into impressing each other, it must all be ploughed into the stage time. The MC was a well-liked, youngish circuit comedian and former runner-up of this very competition who was just beginning to get the odd spot on a TV panel show. This had instantly given him more money, and more hunger for success – he had now seen what could be done if television came knocking for real and he also enjoyed a very minor amount of celebrity that he wore with a self-conscious shrug, trying to seem weary of it though he was secretly giddy with this new-found recognition. He was excited to be here with these novices, able to dispense words of wisdom and comfort from the relative lofty heights of his mid-range status. He assured them all that he would give them the best introductions he could and prepare the crowd so they wouldn't walk on cold.

Brenda was on third. She was the only woman in this semi-final and so third on was the expected spot in order to break it up, in terms of gender. She didn't mind. Third was fine by her, though she felt a flare of ego at not being last – was this the beginnings of a desire to headline, she wondered? If so, she was pleased: ambition was to be encouraged at all times. Brenda had no intention of being one of those who were considered great by their peers but never troubled the wider public consciousness. Not for Brenda that dread moniker the 'comedians' comedian' – no thanks. There were ways of remaining true to yourself and having some degree of success, Brenda felt sure of that. She wanted to be a working comedian, not some kind of life-long human art experiment.

This particular green room was cut off from the actual stage, meaning its occupants could not listen to one another's sets without moving out to the audience seating area. Brenda decided she would watch the MC do his warm up, just to see what the crowd was like and what they responded to, and then creep back to the green room to get her mind right to perform. The show began, and as ever took on its own life. Everyone in the venue became elements within its body – organs, arteries, parasites – each with their part to play.

From the moment Brenda walked on stage, took the mic out of its stand and turned her smiling face to the crowd, the room was hers.

She could feel it immediately, something warm emanating from the darkness, a molecular shift in her favour. Unconsciously she carried herself with confidence and the walk from the side of the stage to the centre was as casual and unaffected as moving from her kitchen to her living room. Every joke she made she timed to perfection, every piece of meticulously prepared material that came out of her mouth sounded as though she had genuinely just thought of it. The rhythm was right tonight and she pictured herself with the audience in space, embedded in Quantum Foam, waving and curving as they were held together, pushed towards each other from within a soft cushion of mutual understanding. Every move she made was received with openness and loving warmth as though it was always meant to be, that it was simply the natural progression of a conversation between minds and she was in complete control. When she did something, everything realigned to her advantage – she controlled it. It was her space, and the audience became a part of her, until she was the space itself. It was as close as Brenda had ever got to a religious experience. She didn't believe in God; she was God. The pure exhilaration of becoming one with her audience was enough to obliterate any other concerns. She had come close to this a couple of times in the past, and had heard other comics describe it, but this was her first direct hit. She had worked hard for it too and now she knew what it truly meant to be in the magic zone.

It was golden and powerful and she was dizzy with it as soon as she re-entered normal space/time. The green room appeared to be sparkling, the very molecules around her like glitter. This was some kind of drugless high that no amount of money could buy.

Perhaps, thought Brenda, this is my reward for loneliness, for leaving Pete, for never seeing my friends, for having no money, for giving it everything I've got – I made the sacrifice and the comedy gods are pleased.

If that was true, she mused, it was worth it.

Brenda went through to the final on the judges' vote. No other outcome was possible, and Brenda had to remind herself to look surprised when her name was called. She grinned so widely she felt her lip might split, and then floated away, unable to properly focus on anything and anyone for the following half an hour. The other finalist was chosen by the crowd, and Brenda congratulated him mistily. She knew she would have to re-introduce herself at the final in Edinburgh as she had forgotten him instantly.

Edinburgh – and now that little shockwave hit. She would be going to the Edinburgh Festival not as a student, not as a punter, not as a girlfriend, but as Brenda Monk, comedian. That was a pretty astonishing feat in itself. Not yet one year on from her first gig, and here she was. The vertigo forced her to sit down on the sofa. Yes, sitting was good. Why had she not thought to sit before? She would sit for a while.

The door flew open and in walked Rossly. Brenda's heart leapt – this was her instinctive reaction to the sight of him, and that was a surprise to her. He pulled her up and hugged her hard, and she felt a tingle of arousal in her body. If there was ever going to be a night together, it was going to be this one. That's what Brenda thought as he pushed her away from him and smiled into her face, those blue and gold eyes full of pleasure.

'Jesus, you were fucking great. Jesus. All that new stuff too... I mean, great. And the Shrek bit's working and it's real and interesting, and just fucking great, Brenda. Just fucking great. I'm gonna stop saying fucking great.'

Brenda felt beside herself, as if she really had split into two people in order to accommodate this much happiness.

'Did you feel it?' Rossly said.

'Yeah,' said Brenda. 'I can still feel it.'

'Fucking great. Let's get out of here.'

Rossly took Brenda to a bar he liked down a narrow side-street in Soho. It was decorated like a Moroccan souk, with wall hangings and a tented ceiling and low leather cushions the colour of fire to sit on. He ordered a bottle of champagne.

'Steady on. I haven't won the thing.'

'But it's your birthday.'

'Is it? Shit, yes it is. How did you know that?'

'You said it on stage.'

'Did I?'

'Yes, you said you were excited about getting older because it meant you could stop pretending you don't masturbate.'

Brenda laughed.

'I did, didn't I? God, I'd completely forgotten that. I just thought of it on stage, it wasn't planned.'

'You were so fucking on it tonight, Brenda. Just beautiful to watch.'

Brenda was glad of the dim red light because she blushed. And the more she became aware of the blushing the worse it got. And Rossly was not the kind of man to miss the moment when it arrived. He put his hand behind Brenda's head and pulled her towards him. She happily acquiesced and his sharp face was suddenly out of focus. Their lips met, and his were soft. He made a tiny moan as they both rose into the kiss, the coal suddenly lit within, the heat jumping up. Brenda broke away and sat back into her cushion.

She blinked a couple of times and took her champagne. Rossly did the same.

'How old are you today?'

'Thirty.'

'S'good age. I liked being thirty...'

But he couldn't get any more out because Brenda, warm and full of bubbles, wanted to kiss him again. And as she did so, he ran his hand up her back, so that every vertebrae became electrified under his touch.

They kissed in the taxi all the way back to Brenda's flat, breaking off momentarily for Rossly to pay and Brenda to get the door open. They kissed all the way along the hall and into the bedroom where they fell onto Brenda's unmade bed and continued kissing. It was as if they needed to get ten months' worth of kissing done as soon as possible before they could move on to second base. In time, Rossly's hand slid under Brenda's black V-neck jumper and over her breasts, pulling the lace of her bra down as he did so. His other hand undid her top button, pulled down her zip and slid into her knickers to find a slippery opening inside. Her hand ran down the front of his shirt and cupped over his crotch to find... Nothing. Flaccid.

Brenda pulled back and looked at him quizzically. He looked down and shook his head quickly.

'Don't worry about it, it'll come,' he said.

And continued kissing her, pulling her top over her head and unclipping her bra in an impressive display of expertise.

Half an hour later, and still nothing. The kissing had stopped, as had the blow job Brenda had begun, only to be halted after five minutes by an apologetic Rossly. They now lay side-by-side in an uneven state of undress.

'It's not you.'

'OK.'

An awkward pause.

'It really isn't.'

'I said OK. Don't worry about it.'

'I've wanted to fuck you since I first saw you.'

'Well, here I am...'

'It's not you.'

'OK.'

Rossly sighed in frustration.

'Want me to go down on you? I mean, I'd like to...'

'Oh, no thanks. Don't worry about it.'

'Shit.'

Rossly stood up abruptly, ran his fingers through his hair and kicked the skirting board. Brenda stayed where she was, trying to think of how to manage the sexual frustration raging inside her. She burned for him now, she burned for straight hard him inside her. She clenched her internal muscles to try to lessen the discomfort.

'I'll get us a drink.'

'Do you want me to leave?'

'No, I don't.'

Brenda rolled out of bed and found the bottle of Jack Daniel's she had been eking out since Christmas. She poured them a large shot each and they sat on her sofa drinking.

'So, you really don't mind?'

'Of course I mind. I was horny as fuck by the time we got home, but I'll get over it.'

'You do believe it's not just you, don't you? I mean, I've had this problem before. It did for me and Nina. She wasn't hanging around to chat once it happened with her, I'll tell you that.'

Brenda nodded.

'Why?'

'I don't know. I've always had it in some way or another. I think it's tied to my family life when I was a kid.'

'You seem remarkably sorted about it. Most men would rather eat their own balls off than talk like this.'

Rossly pulled out some joint-making equipment and started skinning up. The activity alone made it easier to talk, let alone the contents of the spliff he was creating.

'Yeah, well... I've had a long time to think about it. And in any case, I believe in no bullshit. I practise what I preach, babe.

I'm trying to be a better human.'

He licked the joint shut.

'So, what have you concluded?'

'I don't know for sure. But my best guess it that it's because sex was off-limits in my house when I was growing up. In all senses, you know... With Mum being in a wheelchair, Dad wasn't getting any but he was too Catholic to go elsewhere, so you know, I always felt guilty about it if I got a piece of nice pussy, which by the way, was *rare* back then. Whenever I had a wank as a teenager, I'd cry after I came.'

'That's fucked up.'

'Yeah. Hey Brenda... Are you going to talk about this on stage?'

'Uhh, god, that hadn't even occurred to me. No, I shouldn't think so. It doesn't really fit with where I'm going at the moment, jokes wise.' She sipped her drink. 'Are you?'

'Probably. It's all good stuff. Do you mind? I won't identify you. No-one will know. I'm always having one night stands that go wrong.'

'Thanks.'

'That came out different to how I planned. I meant to say, I'm always having one night stands that go *right*.'

Brenda laughed but then was quiet. Did she mind if he talked about it in his set? She could see how it would fit Rossly's style of comedy perfectly – it was honest and self-deprecating and slightly taboo, and that was what he did.

'No, I don't mind. You'll do something good with it.'

They sat in companionable silence. Nothing was off-limits with Rossly and it was relaxing.

'I thought about doing some stuff about my mum dying,' Brenda said, out of the blue.

'Really? That'd be interesting.'

'Yeah. I don't know though. I can't make up my mind.'

'When did she die?'

'When I was twenty.'

'What was she like?'

'Quiet, that's what I mainly think of when I think of her. She was just... Quiet. She never really expected anything to happen, she never really wanted anything to happen.'

'Maybe she was just happy with what was already happening.' Brenda was ashamed to find that this had never actually occurred to her. She had always assumed that her mother must be desperate to escape the humble, settled life she had with her dad, but had given up trying. Brenda had certainly been up and out of it at the first possible opportunity. The idea that her mother had simply been happy was a revelation.

'What did she die of?'

'A brain tumour. They didn't know she had it for years, and then she started having mood swings and bumping into stuff. And when she finally went to the doctor it was too late. Inoperable. She was dead three months later.'

'That's rough.'

'Yeah. It was rough on my dad.'

'He still around?'

'Yeah.'

'You get on?'

'Yeah.'

'I'll get my coat.'

Rossly mimed getting up to leave as Brenda laughingly asked why.

'Rule One, babe. Never date a girl who gets on with her father, they won't put up with any shit.'

Brenda glowed a little.

'You're dating me now?'

'That's not what I said.'

'Good. Because I'm not up for that stuff at the moment.'

'No, you've got more important things to be getting on with. I get it, babe. Don't panic.'

They talked, swapping stories and experiences on and off stage, until they fell asleep on the sofa.

Brenda woke first in the afternoon light and saw Rossly's erection as he slept. Careful not to startle him, she unzipped his fly and removed her jeans and knickers. He woke just as she was swinging her knee over his body and smiled sleepily at her as he figured out what was going on.

'I hope you were going to seek consent, Miss Monk, otherwise I'd have to report you.'

'May I?'

'Would you?'

He allowed her to slip him into her warmth and they started moving together, softly, softly, then harder and harder until they shuddered to a stop.

Brenda bent down to kiss him.

'That was a very nice way to wake up,' he said.

'Yes, lovely,' Brenda replied.

'And there was I, thinking your favourite position was the reverse cowgirl.'

Brenda laughed out of habit, and then examined the laugh. Jonathan's Edinburgh show of last year felt so long ago, it seemed that he must have been talking about someone else. The detachment she was experiencing now was eerie – that Brenda Monk was gone.

Rossly seemed to read her mind.

'Hey, you wanna hear something funny?' he said.

'You think you can manage it?' replied Brenda

And then Rossly offered her a golden nugget of gossip he had heard on the comedy grapevine. Jonathan and Lloyd had acrimoniously parted company following the double-gig double-cross and Lloyd was now executive producer on the TV pilot version of the show, starring two up and coming American comedians as 'the couple'. Joan had found Jonathan a semi-regular part in a mid-range American network-syndicated studio sit-com, in which he played an eccentric British guy who was a failed rock star. Jonathan had made a fuss when he had accidentally seen the casting memo asking for a 'Russell Brand type' insisting that he was only interested in parts that called for a 'Jonathan Cape type', but had quietened down when Joan told in him uncompromising tones that there was 'currently no such thing as a fucking Jonathan Cape type.' Jonathan had shut up and taken the part, scared there was nothing else around for him and unwilling to return to the UK without having conquered Hollywood.

Brenda was still laughing as she made the coffee.

20

August, King's Cross railway station, and Brenda was finally here, awaiting her platform for the train to Edinburgh. It was almost exactly a year since she had last stood on this very spot half-drunk, out of control, barely knowing what she was doing as she boarded the train to go and see a boyfriend who had not invited her, so little in her life that this had been genuinely the best and most exciting thing she could think to do with herself. This time was so different it felt as if it was happening in an alternative universe – yes, in fact it was an alternative universe, and one of Brenda's own making. She had created this reality. This sparkling, fresh, exciting reality, full of potential and throbbing with life force.

Her platform was announced and Brenda pulled her small suitcase to her carriage, found her seat and arranged herself for the journey. At the other end of the line was the competition final. She felt heavy with an awareness of its significance, but also glad of the length of time she would have to sit here and reflect a little. She didn't think she had sat in one place for so long since she gave up her job eight months earlier. As they moved off, Brenda settled back into the rhythm of the train, steady and rocking and let her mind wander.

June and July had passed quickly and though the weather

had been hot, it had made no difference to Brenda. She had been inside the whole time, sleeping all morning, pacing, writing, practising all afternoon, gigging at night or at least going to watch gigs if she couldn't get on herself. She begged stage time wherever and whenever she could. Rossly had been vaguely on the scene, but Brenda had kept him at arm's-length, she simply didn't have the mental energy for any kind of relationship with anything other than comedy. As the grey, graffitied walls slid past, Brenda thought of all the help and advice Rossly had given her since they met the previous October – so unexpected, and the sweeter for it.

The drinks trolley had begun its progress through the train, and though Brenda would have loved a G&T, she knew her wallet couldn't support it and bought a lemonade and a packet of nuts instead that would have to do for lunch. She was too wound up to eat properly anyway, and hadn't had a real meal for nearly a week. July had been her final month of having enough money to cover her bills and she had formulated a plan for the short term at least. At the last minute, on July 31st, she had withdrawn the final £200 which would keep body and soul together in cash terms for the month of August, even as her bills went unpaid one by one. Texts from her dad asking if she was OK were answered positively, regardless of the situation and she knew there was no point worrying him – the money he had given her was all he had to offer. She was totally on her own now. She could sell her car when she got back if she really didn't have anything to eat but she couldn't imagine getting more than a hundred quid for it. In twenty-four hours from now, her direct debits would start defaulting in turn and she effectively no longer had a bank account. After August, she would have to start looking for somewhere new to live as her current flat was completely unaffordable. She was literally living on her wits from now on.

As to more pressing matters of accommodation, Fenella had saved her arse. She and, somewhat terrifyingly, Josephine were sharing a place for the whole Festival with a couple of other comedians that Fenella had stayed with before. So she knew from previous years that the flat they had booked had a small cupboard in the hall and when cleared of the various things stored inside it would just about house a single mattress with a single person on it. Brenda was to stay in it free of charge and this would be her Edinburgh home for the week she intended to spend there. She was incredibly grateful. Rossly had offered to share his flat, his *bed*, with her for nothing but she had known immediately that this would be a terrible idea. She had to be a comedian at the Edinburgh Festival this year and a comedian only. Definitely not a girlfriend on any level, however informal and 'free' the arrangement might be.

As England raced by, whole counties breezing past, high clouds making shadows on the golden fields, Brenda thought back to the shimmering elation she had felt during and after the semi-final gig. But it had eluded her since that night. If she could recreate that for the final there would be no stopping her. Even if she never found it again she understood she would spend her life trying – anyone who ever experienced it would feel the same. There was no going back now. Even if she didn't win the competition she knew this was her for life. This was what she would do, this was what she would try to be successful at. The money was secondary. If she lost the final and had to get a job in September, so be it. She would still gig. She'd be knackered and have no time for anything else, but it would be worth it. Comedy had become Brenda – she couldn't imagine a Brenda Monk without it.

Brenda's reverie was broken by the buzz of her phone announcing an email. Laura, wanting to tell her that she and Susie had been seeing a counsellor and as a result had booked a weekend in Barcelona, a city Susie had always longed to see.

'It's going OK, for now I think. I'm trying to deal with new things and Susie seems better. More patient at least. Who knows what will happen. Relationships are hard, but we've made some progress. Good luck in Ed. See you when you get back? Lx ps what's going on with Pete?!'

Brenda felt instant relief, though she knew it was selfishly motivated as she had been scared of taking time away from gigging to go down and be with Laura in the event of a break up. She would have gone, of that there was no question, but the prospect of being away from the comedy clubs had given her vivid nightmares about forgetting all her material and even her own name.

As for Pete, well, she hadn't heard from him since the morning after that night in the hotel in Birmingham. It had been too painful to have even the most casual contact especially, it seemed, for him. He had driven her home and then driven away and that was that. Brenda's night with Rossly had confused her more than anything and she wanted to back away from any romantic entanglements altogether – it all felt too much to confront. She wished she could combine the two men into one perfect being but it was a childish fantasy, so for now she would have neither. Brenda idly wondered what such a creature would be like – a long-haired, strong-backed paragon of goodness with a dirty mouth, an innate understanding of the comedy world and great taste in furniture. Perhaps he existed, but Brenda felt relieved she hadn't encountered him yet, she'd never get anything done...

Brenda didn't attempt to reach Pete at all, for she knew what would happen if she did. They would end up back in bed with nothing resolved and there was no way that would help anything. She knew he knew it too, and she knew that was why he did not attempt to reach her either. And though she missed him, sometimes with a hard painful aching, she couldn't mess him around again – he was too good for that. He was an occasional daydream now, a version of some other life. Simultaneous to this, she felt excited to be in Edinburgh at the same time as Rossly, free and single, and able to stay up all night doing whatever with whomever she chose. And if that person was Rossly, then that was no problem at all. But she was mostly – no not mostly, wholly, yes, wholly here for the comedy and she kept this at the front of her mind. It was too important to fuck it up now over something, or someone, stupid.

Walking once again up the wide, tarmacked slope that led out of the station and into the fickle Edinburgh sunshine, the smell of yeast filled her nostrils and she felt excited. She looked down at her phone and found the email from Fenella with the address of her accommodation. It was on a street she was familiar with that ran behind George Square and she set off on the twenty minute walk feeling springy and invincible. All this couldn't quite remove one worry though, and that was the prospect of sharing a house with Josephine for a week. Fenella had assured her that it was water under the bridge. Perhaps Josephine had genuinely forgiven her. Perhaps she could simply manage to avoid her for the whole week.

Brenda found the building she was looking for, and pressed the button that was adjacent to the name of the unknown Edinburgh resident who had let their flat and fled the city for the month of August.

Fenella answered.

'Yes?'

'It's Brenda.'

'Oh yes it fucking well is. Come on up. Fourth floor, lots of stairs.'

The door buzzed, the catch released and Brenda pushed it

open. Inside was a dark concrete staircase with a dour front door on every floor that gave no indication of the luxury that lay behind each one. Brenda reached the fourth floor and was panting. She made a resolve to get fitter, though she knew she wouldn't carry it out.

Fenella was waiting for her.

'I'll have thighs like fucking nut crackers by the end of the month,' she shouted gleefully and hugged Brenda tight. 'Good to see you. Come on, I'll show you your cupboard.'

Six feet along the wall from the entrance was a door in the wall, and when Brenda opened it there was a narrow space with an inflatable single mattress on it and a pillow, purchased by Fenella. Brenda had brought a sleeping bag but nothing else would fit in her bag and she had resigned herself to the prospect of sleeping on a hard floor.

'You can pay me back when you're famous,' Fenella said.

Brenda felt overwhelmed with gratitude.

'The rest of the flat's fucking marvellous, if that's any consolation. You'll only be sleeping in here and you'll have your eyes closed then...'

Brenda threw her bag into the cupboard, secretly delighted to have her own space at all, and allowed Fenella to show her round. It was one of those beautiful Edinburgh flats – big airy rooms, wooden floors, huge windows and a generous kitchen with a dining table for six in it. This was how you lived up here when you were selling out night after night, Brenda thought to herself, glancing with renewed admiration at Fenella. She wanted this, she wanted this for herself. It was a sign of success, of hard graft paying off, and even to share a tiny part of it was a thrill.

Fenella seemed full of the joys of the Festival and as last year's Award winner the pressure was off and she could simply enjoy performing her new hour-long show, status assured and unassailable. It was a good thing Jonathan had kept his word and not come this year – the sight of Queen Fenella the First striding around her city might have finally forced him to break his cool in public, something he took great care never to do.

Fenella was in the kitchen when Brenda came out of the bathroom, having washed her face and cleaned her teeth.

'So, I thought we could see Rossly's show and then head out after that?'

'No, no way. I can't do that. I can't.'

'Oh come on, it'll take your mind off it.'

'Not even the second the coming of Jesus Christ could take my mind off it, Fenella. No. I'm staying in. Trust me, I will be in full effect after it's done. I'm here for a week.'

Brenda had made a promise to herself that she would not turn up to the final tired, hungover or generally off her game. and Fenella could see the sense in it so she left Brenda in the enormous living room – the living room of someone with an income so far in excess of most of the flat's current occupants that it felt a little cruel – and went out into the free-radical charged Edinburgh night.

Brenda sat with her notebooks, a bottle of wine and a delivery of Indian food from a place she had found on a menu in a drawer, and tried to assemble her set for the following night. She knew where the tentpoles were – the jokes that would support the whole structure, the jokes she could rely on to get a laugh at regular intervals. So she placed those in a running order first, spaced down the page with gaps to be filled in with personal favourites and other material that wasn't necessarily hysterically funny but leant shape and flow to the whole thing. She scribbled between the words in capital letters – 'Catholic; Kids; Wanking; Nancy; Shrek; Austen; Pope; Hole' – and this unintelligible scrawl was as important as the tentpoles. New comedians often made the mistake of excluding them, worried that they should be maximising laughs at all times. But Brenda had learnt the value of giving tiny rests to the audience – just the odd reflection or observation or linking sentence that wouldn't crack everyone up, but would inform the next joke, making it funnier and more satisfying somehow. It took a bit of nerve and some experience to include these moments, but Brenda knew it made the difference.

Brenda was packing it all up around half past midnight, when the front door slammed. A moment later Josephine was before her.

Brenda froze, as if caught in the act of something awful, though she was doing nothing wrong. Josephine stood very still in the doorway.

'Fenella said I could stay—'

'Yeah, I know,' Josephine said, cutting her off. Brenda nodded, not knowing what to say and certainly not wanting to say the wrong thing. She would like to live to see the final, whatever happened.

'The joke's working well.'

Brenda was baffled for a moment and then realised she meant the Terrible Mess gag.

'Good, I'm glad to hear it.'

'Maybe we can hang out a bit.'

'Yeah, maybe.'

'Well, good night then.'

'Night.'

Josephine hovered for a moment.

Brenda looked back at her notebook, trying to smooth the awkwardness.

'I'm glad you dumped him,' Josephine said quietly.

'I don't know if I dumped him exactly – he just wandered off and I didn't bother to follow...'

'Yeah, well, as good as. Have you heard what he's doing?'

'Yeah.'

'I Googled it.'

'Me too.'

'That costume...'

And suddenly Josephine was silently laughing.

'The beret?'

'Yeah.'

Brenda felt herself start to dissolve too.

'What the hell was that?'

'Some storyline about him pretending to be French so he could fuck a dumb American.'

They were both now laughing, eyes watering, wheezing and shuddering.

'He's always been such an authentic comic,' Brenda managed to squeal, as Josephine gripped the door frame.

They came to a halt.

'Yeah, well,' said Josephine, wiping her eyes. 'Yeah.'

And she left the room. The sound of a bedroom door closing followed a moment later, and Brenda poured herself the final dregs from the bottle of wine and knocked them back with medicinal haste. She got up, put on a pair of cotton shorts and a T-shirt, brushed her teeth and got into her cupboard. She fell asleep two hours later which was not at all bad, considering. It was a fitful, dreaming night of high, restless sleep – trapped in wooden boxes and kicking her way out, or standing in fields of golden corn under a hot sun, with low-flying aircraft buzzing over her head. Each time Brenda woke in the pitch black of her cupboard, she pressed a button on her phone and saw the hours passing, like some abstract conveyor belt she could not step off.

She had entered the tunnel and there was only one way to go – forwards. For the entrance had crumbled behind her, she had detonated it herself.

21

Final day, here at last, bright and sharp as a pin.

The show began at 9pm, and would take place in a medium sized venue within the temporarily erected complex of marquees in Bristo Square that housed fourteen individual comedy club rooms of varying sizes, three bars and a cafe. Brenda slept until midday, crawled out into the light to a flat that seemed empty but was probably sleeping, made some coffee and tried not to eat her own thumbs. She was nervous but more than that, she felt the weight of destiny on her. This evening's show was a lock and if she was the correct key, she would turn into a professional stand-up comedian overnight.

Brenda fixed herself a bowl of cereal but could barely eat it and threw it away, hoping no-one would notice that she was wasting their precious food. She would go shopping tomorrow and replace it. Today she could do nothing but think about tonight. There was no point in trying to control it, she just had to give in. There would be no relief unless she obliterated her mind with booze and drugs and although she was confident she could find enough of either in less than ten minutes here she had no intention of destroying her chances like that. She had seen comics, promising comics, do that before and it was not a pretty sight, especially when it was played out on stage for all to see. A big-match temperament, that's what she needed. She remembered reading about that in a Jilly Cooper novel as a student and not being a natural polo player, she had wondered what it was. Now she knew – the ability not to crumble when the stakes were high. And not only that, but to actually get better the higher the stakes got. Did she have the stuff? She would find out tonight.

In the meantime, Brenda had another problem, one she had been trying to ignore since she found out, but was now served as an unwelcome reminder as she perused the competition flyer that sat in a stack on the kitchen table. One of the judges was a well-known female comedy critic, Frances Weiss, who had said on record many times that she did not think women were naturally funny, or rather that she had 'yet to see a female comedian that really made me laugh' and so for the time being she was 'forced to conclude that there weren't any.' Why she had said this no-one quite knew. Perhaps it was simply the unpalatable truth that no-one with female genitalia had ever tickled her funny bone, perhaps she was just being provocative in order to get attention or attract more readers to her blogs and columns, perhaps she honestly felt that no woman could match her favourite male comedians. And she certainly did have her favourites. Jonathan was one, and just as she made no secret of her attraction to him, he did nothing to dissuade it – why would he? The reviews she gave him were out of this world. Maybe she just plain didn't like women, but whatever it was, this was not going to help Brenda tonight. Some had argued that her public remarks should bar Frances from judging a competition such as this, but in the end it made no difference. For actually as far as the competition organisers were concerned her presence on the panel spiced things up, sold more tickets and led to increased media coverage, publicising both the competition and the chain of comedy clubs that offered the prize. So there she stayed, in prime position. Brenda was determined not to allow herself an excuse for failure though. If she was good enough, she could overcome a bias against her.

And in any case, there was one further problem that might eclipse all the others in the form of John Nunn, the newly-famous newly-rich comic she had attempted to hug at the New Year's Eve party just eight months before. He was hosting tonight's final and Brenda was praying he wouldn't remember her. If he wanted to he could subtly turn the audience against her before she even stepped on stage. They wouldn't notice him doing it – they would laugh along – but he could just plant the idea in their minds that she was a bit sub-standard, or a 'token woman' or whatever it was that would make them a little nervous or pitying before she got to the microphone and that would be devastating. Brenda needed all her faculties tonight, and she congratulated herself on her restraint the night before.

It was a balmy evening as Brenda walked the short distance to the venue. She was early, very early, just as she had intended. She wanted to breathe in some of the atmosphere and let the excitement move through her. All around were people with somewhere to go, walking in groups, chattering, discussing shows they had seen or wanted to see, clutching Festival programmes or leafing through them to find something to see. There was dance, theatre, music of course but as far as Brenda was concerned, there was only comedy. There was the 'grown up' Festival too with its distant opera stars and guest conductors and the Book Festival in its tranquil garden. But comedy, comedy, comedy was all that flowed through Brenda's veins. The rest of it may just as well not exist. And if you kept to certain venues and streets and squares here, nothing else did exist – it was a world within a world, and as Brenda reached the conjoined marquees she could see that they had built an entire inflatable village for anyone who wanted to forget everything and just live in a place where laughter was the only currency.

Brenda chose the quietest of the three bars, bought a Jack Daniel's and coke and sat down at a wooden table with a small cactus in a flowerpot in the middle. She watched people for a short while and sipped her drink. There was a couple having a clench-jawed row about ten feet away from her and she felt a flood of relief that she was unattached at this very moment in time. A group of young men perused the large board which detailed all the shows going on in the fourteen rooms here and chose what they wanted to see. Any name that was familiar from TV was automatically put on a shortlist, Brenda noticed. Two girls sat on the floor drinking smoothies and taking pictures of themselves on their phones.

At that moment, Brenda's own phone buzzed. A text message. She hesitated before opening it, for the slightest thing could put her off her stride now, but saw 'Dad' in the ID and pressed green.

'Good luck chicken, break someone's leg, Dad x'

Brenda smiled, finished her drink and had a last look at her notebook before getting up to leave.

She walked to the front of the long queue of people snaking round the edge of the venue waiting to be allowed in. Brenda knew that none of these people had come to see her or any of the other finalists on the bill. They were here to see John Nunn, THE John Nunn. Brenda could only hope the punters knew the bulk of the gig would be taken up by unknowns like herself, otherwise this was going to be even tougher than she imagined.

She reached the front of the line.

'Sorry, doors aren't open yet,' said an unexpectedly officious student ticket-stub collector, already in position to marshal the crowds.

'I'm in the show,' said Brenda.

The ticket-stub collector looked her hard in the face.

'Well, I've never seen you before.'

'No, you wouldn't have. It's a new act competition.'

'What's your name?'

'Brenda Monk.'

'Hold on please.'

He lifted the radio he'd obviously waited his whole life to use to his mouth and clicked the talk function open.

'We have a Brenda Monk here. A Brenda Monk. Is she authorised to enter? Over.'

While he waited he looked her up and down, clearly not hugely impressed.

'Security's tight because we have John Nunn in the building tonight,' he said with great import.

'Yes, I know,' Brenda replied and congratulated herself on not kicking him in the shins.

The radio buzzed back.

'Yeah, over.'

The ticket-stub collector slightly reluctantly stood aside. Brenda wondered how long it would be until she was sufficiently recognisable to enter her own gigs unchallenged.

She passed the two black clad stagehands who were quickly sweeping up the debris left by the preceding show (it had clearly involved some kind of glitter cannon), walked to the edge of the stage and pushed her way behind the heavy black drape – these were makeshift spaces and did not have elaborate backstage set ups. Behind the curtain was a small area with chairs and a table of drinks and snacks laid out for the final, or rather, the final's VIP guest MC. John Nunn was nowhere to be seen. He was unlikely to fraternise with novices like them. But he was a professional and would no doubt turn up at some point to briefly familiarise himself with the people he was going to be introducing on stage. Brenda could not honestly say she was looking forward to that moment, but kept telling herself there was no way he would remember her. He must, she surmised, meet thousands of idiots wanting to hug him every week. She would just be another messy blur, morphing into the faces of the masses.

She appeared to be the first to arrive, and so took the opportunity to go back out and stand on the stage. This was a luxury the others would not be afforded, and she was glad of it. To get a sense of the space before the actual moment where she was performing, or rather, competing, would give her a very slight advantage and she knew she needed all the help she could get. The seats were on a steep rake – the best use of the space in order to maximise sales – built onto a large metal frame. The people furthest away from her on the back row would practically be above her head and she made a mental note to raise her eye-line high every now and again in order to include everyone. Too many comics made the mistake of only playing to the front three rows, and in so doing they effectively cut their audience in half. When this happened, as had been the case at one of Brenda's early gigs, she now recalled, it was a disaster. In a club if anyone felt excluded they would lose interest in the act and start talking amongst themselves, making a noise at the bar and generally creating disturbance. This couldn't happen here as it was a more theatrical set-up, but the principle was still a good one to stick to.

She saw the three seats half way back with 'RESERVED' signs stuck to them – the judges. She wasn't sure if she was pleased or not to know where they would be sat. She pushed it down inside herself where it belonged and tried to turn it into positive energy. Brenda felt the width and depth of the performance space too. It wasn't ideal for stand-up as there seemed to be acres of black floor for one person. But these venues were designed for as wide a variety of shows as possible and this also needed to accommodate, for example, a fifteen-strong university sketch troupe who played with great vigour every afternoon at 2.30pm to about a dozen people. Best to remain stationary in the middle when the time came, she decided, rather than draw attention to the extra space by trying to cover it walking up and down.

Two people came in while Brenda was walking the width of the stage. They were chatting happily, cracking jokes and laughing with a high, nervous sound that indicated a very new friendship. These were the two finalists from the Manchester semi, it turned out. They were young, male, one white, one of Bangladeshi origin, but judging his accent British by birth. They were dressed almost identically in checked, short-sleeved shirts, baggy-ish jeans and leather lace up shoes – the influence of Peter Kay was very clear here. Brenda wondered if they were also going to do all the same jokes.

'Hi, I'm Brenda Monk.'

'Hi, Brenda Monk,' the British-Bangladeshi Peter Kay said. 'I'm Adil Nawaz.'

'And I'm Davey Crockett,' said the white-British Peter Kay. 'It's not my real name though, it's a name I chose to piss off me dad. He hates Americans and...'

'Hi, nice to meet you. There's a backstage bit.'

Brenda sensed that Davey had been about to launch into his material and cut him off quickly. She couldn't stand comedians who did their material at you off-stage, always testing it, making everyone an audience and actually deluding themselves that nobody knew what they were up to.

Adil looked around.

'Rake's high, isn't it?'

'Let's hope there's no hoes in tonight,' said Davey, riffing off the word rake, 'or spades...'

An awkward pause while everyone wondered if that was racist and then Davey laughed it off with an ironic chortle that immediately made it 'self-aware meta-racism' (he hoped) and therefore OK (he hoped). He checked Adil's reaction, found none, and resumed normal service.

Brenda was bored with these two already. She just wanted the show to start, and to be standing on this stage for real.

A woman bustled in, all sensible hair, black slacks, black T-shirt and special curved-soled shoes that 'mimic the natural gait of a barefoot tribesman' in order to 'relieve back and muscular pain' that most people had now stopped buying on the basis that they looked awful and made one fall over on a regular basis. She seemed harassed and put upon, although Brenda suspected this was more of a lifestyle choice than a genuine reflection of any real stress.

'Hi, I'm Barbara, I'm stage managing tonight, are you my acts?' They nodded.

'We'd like to open the house. Where's my fourth?'

'Here,' said her fourth, sauntering in.

Brenda knew she was supposed to know this one from the semi-final, but could not remember him at all. She was relieved to hear him introduce himself to the others.

'I'm Sean West, no relation.'

'To whom?' asked Barbara.

'Fred and Rose,' he replied, twinkling to himself at his own 'wrongness'.

'Oh right. No, I didn't think you were.'

His high quiff and shaved sides gave him a punkish air, which he underlined with a checked shirt buttoned all the way up, skinny grey jeans with a chain running from his belt loop into his pocket. The jeans were so tight it was clear that nothing was attached to the end of the chain in his pocket, unless of course it continued through a hole in the denim and was tethering his cock. It was possible – Brenda had seen weirder. A pair of dirty white plimsolls completed the look. Brenda wondered what they thought of her own outfit: black V-neck, black skinny jeans, lipstick red patent brogues. She suddenly thought they might think she was referencing Jo Brand's early stage uniform in some oblique way. This had never occurred to her before – had it been a sub-conscious homage? Not deliberately, but she quite liked the idea. It felt... apt, somehow. It placed her in a continuum of female stand-up comedians that had worked their way to the top, fair and square.

Sean West turned to her and offered his hand.

'Hi, Brenda,' he said stiffly, warily.

'Hi, Sean. Good luck tonight.'

'Thanks.'

He seemed nervous, and was it Brenda's imagination, or was it her that was causing it? He was eyeing her now, as if she held some secret she wasn't telling him. She realised once again the effect that semi-final gig was still having. That powerful, golden time on stage she had experienced had clearly freaked him out as much as it had her, though for different reasons. Sean West clearly thought Brenda Monk was the one to beat and that made her smile inside.

Barbara hustled them all backstage, and the house was opened. People streamed in, finding seats, mostly avoiding the front two rows on the assumption that they would be picked on. Brenda stood in the make-shift green room with Davey, Adil and Sean. They all now clutched drinks they were not consuming – a beer for Sean, a Coke for Adil, and water for Brenda and Davey – and were trying to control their nerves.

A previously unnoticed door at the far end of the backstage area marked 'Fire Escape' suddenly opened and John Nunn was ushered in by a small group of people. He walked over and, with the aid of a young woman holding two phones hovering next to him, quickly went round the group.

'Sean West.'

'Nice to meet you Sean, best of luck for tonight.'

'Adil Nawaz.'

'Nice to meet you Adil, best of luck for tonight.'

'Davey Crockett.'

Slight pause. A joke instantly crossed John Nunn's mind, but he wasn't about to go giving them out for free.

'Nice to meet you Davey, best of luck for tonight.'

'Brenda Monk.'

He was trying to place her. She beamed at him to try to distract him. He frowned slightly and then stopped bothering to expend any energy on figuring it out.

'Nice to meet you Brenda, best of luck for tonight.'

And with that done, John Nunn moved to a corner of the backstage area with his team and spoke quietly to them until the show began.

Frances had sauntered in with her fellow judges: Mark Johnson, a veteran TV comedy producer who had long battled depression and was not working much these days, and last year's winner – a thirty-something comedian whose arrogance had led to a Messiah complex so strong he thought Jesus was him. The judges huddled to one side, and talked earnestly amongst themselves, enjoying the separation and the effect they imagined it was having on the competitors.

John Nunn was a different person on stage, of course – you would struggle to believe it was the same man. He bounced around, half-skipping, covering the ground as though it were nothing. People rocked with laughter as he flipped jokes high into the air, one after another, and let them fall onto the crowd like a warm summer rain.

Brenda felt a tingle as she watched him from behind the curtain. His fellow comedians may not be too impressed with the content of the material, but the skill, the precision, the control could not be denied.

Then suddenly Sean was on, and the competition began.

Brenda, being the only female, was on third again and was not going to examine the privilege too far. If there was another woman in the bill she wouldn't have been guaranteed this happy spot in the running order and so what meagre advantage she did have, she did not feel bad for. Sean did an unbelievably good set. Brenda couldn't remember it from the semi-final so it was all fresh to her. He did a great line in ironic metro-sexuality with a bit of left-wing politics thrown in, a couple of mentions of the *New Statesman* lest anyone mistake his intelligence and then he was off again, pumped and ready to drink that beer for real.

John Nunn was on for the second time now, the rain maker, flying higher than weather. And then Adil shuffled on to play the persona he had created for himself: a nervous Bangladeshi boy trying to make his way in this strange new world called Britain – he even put on a Bangladeshi accent. It was a fun device for essentially commenting on English culture, and here in Scotland it went down a storm.

Then John Nunn.

And now Brenda.

He said her name, she knew it was her name but it didn't feel like her name. She was detached from herself somehow and as she performed the miracle of putting one foot in front of the other to reach the mic, she marvelled at the fact that she did not simply fall down like a doll. All her energy was compacted inside now, pregnant with jokes, and she had to work hard to get any power to the outermost limits of her limbs.

'Good evening ladies and gentlemen, my name is Brenda Monk. My dad didn't want a girl, he wanted a Scottish TV detective.'

And so it began, as it always did, and seemed to continue of its own accord.

'But no, I like my name now. It's taken me a while, though. When I was a kid I hated it. Yeah, I went to a very strict Catholic convent school and the nuns hated having a Monk in the class, as you can imagine. The Priest didn't mind it though, especially when I cut my hair very short. He taught me a lot about Jesus, I'll give him that. And he taught me a lot about the value of very sturdy underwear. Lessons I still use to this day.'

A decent laugh, and she was finding their level. She was switched on now, the first joke the canary down the mine. She continually averted her gaze away from the judges' chairs, but momentarily, unavoidably caught sight of Frances's unlaughing face.

'Fuck you,' Brenda thought to herself, 'fuck you and the donkey you rode in on.'

Brenda caught a man looking at his lap in the front row and turned her attention to him.

'Oh sorry sir, you're shaking your head. Did you not like that one? You're not a priest yourself, are you? OK, good. I'm sorry, I don't mean to be paranoid but when you've had a Catholic school upbringing you get used to the feeling you're being followed around by a man, scrutinising your every move, trying to make you do stuff you don't want to do. No, not Jesus – Jimmy Savile. Was that a bit far? Did I go too far? I don't want to upset anyone, that's why I wear these red shoes, you see. If the gig goes badly, I can click them together three times and be back home. Or at least in Glasgow...'

This got a nice laugh, but Brenda was starting to feel uneasy.

It was going a little too well, a little too smoothly, and something within her was saying there was an edge missing. Perhaps bringing in something more real would redress the balance... She mentally slightly rearranged her set.

'Yeah, I once went out with a guy who loved woodwork. I came down one Sunday morning to find him whittling in the kitchen and I had to dump him right away. We'd been going out for three months and I never knew he whittled. But that's what we're like, isn't it, us British women. We'll shag someone for weeks before we even ask what they do for a living. I'd already slept with my last boyfriend twice before he asked me out for a drink. And I actually hesitated. You can put your cock in me, I thought, but don't try and control me with a nice glass of Chablis, oh no.'

Big laugh.

She had them back now. Keep it relevant, she thought, this isn't some art school crowd. They want proper laughs.

'I should really deal with my issues though because I'm getting older and I need to think about finding someone half decent to procreate with. I don't want a family, necessarily – it's not very compatible with my life. I just want to have had a kid, you know, so I can join in. I don't like feeling excluded and most people I know have had at least one so I think I ought to have one, you know, for slow days on Facebook. You know what I mean, when you've run out of Buzzfeed links with photos of weird Post-It notes people have left on fridges in communal houses or whatever, you can just post a picture of your kid in a funny T-shirt and take the rest of the day off. Yeah, that's what I want. Now I'm thirty, I need to start thinking about it. I like getting older though, I do. The best thing about it, as a woman, is that you don't have to lie about masturbation anymore. Honestly, remember at school, the women here know what I'm talking about...'

A quick glance at Frances – nothing. Stone Wall. Fuck her, fuck her, fuck her.

'You know, at school, when a boy would accuse you of masturbating and you felt like the world had ended? But they talked about wanking endlessly, didn't they? Well, the tables turn when you're in your thirties. The men don't want to be talking about wanking then, no they don't. Tragic to still be wanking in your thirties – that's what wives are for. No, but women! Women, oh yes, it's our masturbatory golden age. If you're not masturbating there's something wrong with you. And the best thing is, if you don't feel like it, you can tell yourself you've got a headache and just roll over and go to sleep. But I never knew until I turned thirty everyone was up to it. It's like a silent society where full membership is granted on your thirtieth birthday and everyone starts talking about dildos and handing round Nancy Friday books.'

A lull.

Nancy Friday was perhaps too niche a reference, although she had heard female laughter and so she had split the crowd. She needed to reunite them now...

'If you don't know who Nancy Friday is guys, ask your girl-friend. And if you don't have a girlfriend, find out who Nancy Friday is and maybe you'll get one.'

A cheer from the women in the crowd – always a nice sound. Brenda caught the eye of an amenable man on the second row who looked like he could take a bit of interaction.

'Tell me, sir, do you know who Nancy Friday is?'

He shook his head bashfully.

Good, thought Brenda, relieved. She sometimes got it wrong.

'OK, sir. I'm going to take pity on you. It's porn for girls, that's what it is, in book form. Yes. It's feminist porn. I'm sorry to get political, but that's what it is. I'm not political actually, not really, although I do find I'm definitely more politically engaged these days. You start noticing things more. Like for example, I was at home the other night and *Shrek* was on the TV and so I started watching it, and you know what? I used to love *Shrek*. I loved it when it came out, I really did, but now all I can see is a massive green racist.'

Ahh, her *Shrek* bit. It had been with her so long now, it felt like an old friend.

'Hear me out. You remember *Shrek*. OK, it begins with all the displaced fairytale people coming to live in his swamp because they have been sent away from their land, so they are basically refugees from an oppressive regime subjecting them to torture. They are asylum seekers. Forget they're from Fairytale Lane or whatever, imagine they're all from Zimbabwe. But does that move Shrek? Oh no, no no no. Shrek actually does a deal with the leader of the oppressive regime that if he finds him a girl to marry, some captive young virgin to be bought and sold, he can get rid of all the fairytale refugees from his swamp, or what I like to think of as Kent. And this is happily ever after? I know he ends up liking them all, but seriously, he's the main character. It's like making a kids' film with Goebbels as a sympathetic lunk who just wants to be loved. Although with Walt Disney you never quite know, do you? I mean, it's right-wing propaganda, it is. If Shrek were alive in Britain today, he'd vote UKIP, I'm telling you. And then I started to think, my god, are there these right-wing subliminal messages in everything I have ever loved? I know, I bet you never thought you'd hear a lapsed Catholic say that... but maybe my upbringing has made me susceptible to it, though, which is a worry. Like when I was a teenager, my favourite book was *Pride and Prejudice*. Yeah, I know, I mean the clue's in the title, Brenda. *Pride and PREJUDICE*. Am I just drawn to it? Without realising? I'd finished *Mein Kampf* before I realised it wasn't all about one man's love for his tent.'

Not Brenda's favourite joke, but she had found it got a certain section of the audience back in the game so it stayed. She felt two men to one side who hadn't laughed yet suddenly guffaw and realised its value once again.

'And I read the other day that apparently people now think Jane Austen was racist because she basically ignored the existence of black people, and you know what? I never even noticed that, so what does that make me? A subconscious racist? As if I didn't have enough to worry about with my conscious mind, turns out my subconscious is some kind of nineteenth-century slave owner. You can't blame Austen though. She was a victim of time and geography. It's not like she could have a week of winter sun in Sharm el-Sheikh every Christmas – I mean, have any of you been to Bath recently? If I lived in rural Hampshire and only went on holiday to Bath, I probably wouldn't believe in black people either. But I loved *Pride and Prejudice* – feisty Lizzie Bennet, stroppy Mr Darcy – honestly, these days I can't fancy a man unless he completely ignores me. Which is why my latest crush is the Pope. It's that convent school again – they put a poster of him on the wall, for God's sake, like he was George Michael. The thing about the Pope is he really does play hard to get, but I think I'm wearing him down. I'm very accepting of his transvestitism, and he doesn't pressure me for commitment, so it kind of works. Except for the abortions. He doesn't like those, does he? I mean, neither do I, of course, I'm not saying I'm a *fan* of abortions, I don't think anyone is, whatever the Republican Party tells you, but what's a girl to do? It's the only downside of going out with the Pope – he just won't wear a condom.'

A big, shocked laugh. Just the sort Brenda had come to love.

'Thank you ladies and gentlemen, you've been great, I've been Brenda Monk, goodnight!'

And she was off and behind the curtain in four seconds to loud applause and John Nunn was back on introducing Davey Crockett.

Brenda's ears were ringing. She had to check her watch to see that she really had done twenty. She felt uneasy though – sometimes a set can be too smooth. The magic she had experienced at the semi-final was not there. Though to the untrained eye the two gigs would be hard to separate, she knew, she knew in herself and she was worried she had been too slick. You needed a bit of edge to really push it to the next level. She didn't want to lose that punch, that raw energy the reviews had pointed out after her double-gig with Jonathan.

Davey Crockett was on and he was playing an absolute blinder. You could tell because everyone backstage was listening to him. Even John Nunn's assistant had stopped examining her two phones. It was not the most original act in the world, it was derivative in many respects: cheeky northern lad doing jokes about ordinary life. But the confidence was overwhelming, and the jokes were good. Brenda was not surprised to learn that this twenty-six-year-old had been gigging for nothing since he was sixteen in local pubs and clubs around his Lancashire home town. The only question was why he had waited so long to enter this competition. But apparently, according to Adil, it had been precipitated by the recent death of his father who had never approved of his stand-up career. Without the overbearing patriarch on his shoulder, he was now free to pursue whatever dream he chose, and he was wasting no time. The competition was wide open, Brenda felt, and success on her part was no certainty. Nothing to do now, though, nothing could be done. Nothing to do but wait and listen to John Nunn performing his contracted twenty minute set while the judges deliberated. Brenda's stomach went through all the colours of the rainbow in that time and back again, and then the four of them were stand-ing on stage, with John Nunn at one end, and the head judge at the other, holding his own dedicated, destiny defining micro-phone in his hand. Brenda knew Frances was out there, in the dark, and she wondered whether anything she said had managed to crack her face once.

'So, have you reached a unanimous decision?' John Nunn asked the head judge.

'We have indeed. But let me say John, it's been a really tough decision. The standard has been incredibly high this year and we felt any of these four could easily go on to a successful career in stand-up comedy.'

'But there can only be one winner, Mark.'

'Yes, that's right. But first we have to announce the runner-up.'

'Ah yes,' said John Nunn making a mental note to have a word with his assistant for not briefing him properly, 'of course, the runner-up. And you know, there's no shame in that. Many of the stand-ups we now know and love have been runner-ups, or runners-up should I say, in competitions like these.'

'That's right, John, yes.'

'Well, Mark. Lay it on us, which of these four newly-hatched stand-up comedy chicks – no offence Brenda – wasn't quite good enough to win?'

'Hah, well, we wouldn't put it like that, John. But yes, thank you. Our runner-up tonight is...'

He waited, looked around the room, waited again, and then...

'Brenda Monk!'

The crowd applauded.

Brenda's knees buckled a bit.

'I have not won, I have not won,' was all she could think, though she would rationalise this later into the more consoling and reasonable 'I did not lose, I did not lose.'

'Congratulations, Brenda!'

Mark was shaking her hand, and then John Nunn was.

The crowd were smiling and clapping as Brenda took a small bow – something she had never done before but did now. Why had she never bowed before? Her mind was reeling – why did I bow then? I have not won, I have not won, I know, I bowed because they are applauding me, I have not won, and I'm never usually on stage when the audience applauds, I have not won, they always applaud, I have not won, when I'm already off because, I have not won, that's when the compere, I have not won, says my name.

'Davey Crockett...' Mark was saying and the room erupted.

Brenda clapped along, pushing her mouth into a smile and nodding inanely. He had been good, there was no denying it. And he deserved it, even though his material was safer than a baby-seat in a Volvo. Davey raised his hands in mock triumph and hugged both Martin and John Nunn as though they were old friends. And who knows, given how long this young man had been performing comedy, they might have been. John Nunn quickly and efficiently closed the show, the audience applauded again, the comedians trooped off stage and the house lights came up, suddenly illuminating the strange black box they had shared for an hour and forty-five minutes.

They all shook hands back stage, but Brenda wanted to leave. She needed to be on her own now, just for a short while, to get her head together. Frances Weiss was chatting animatedly to Sean, who was clearly her favourite, and Brenda watched her grab Davey as he approached, in order to congratulate him. She completely and pointedly ignored Brenda as she walked past. Another one bites the dust, Brenda thought, and the search for a funny fanny continued. Brenda felt a surge of annoyance and toyed with asking her whether she felt her own innate prejudices against women could ever be fucked out her by the right man but decided against it – she was probably not in the right frame of mind to talk to anyone with influence and power just now.

Which was why she flinched when John Nunn's bomber jacketed, vaguely gangsterish, fifty-year-old agent, an industry legend called Steve Angstrom, approached her without warning.

'Brenda Monk.'

'Yes.'

'You were funny.'

'Thanks.'

'Needs a bit of work, but funny.'

Brenda nodded.

'Listen, here's my card. Come and see me when you're back in London. I can always use more women. Women are getting quite commercial these days. Lots of work out there for funny women who want it.'

He put the card in her hand and she closed her fingers lightly around it.

'Are you being looked after?' he asked, in a manner which managed to be both protective and menacing at the same time.

'I... Well...'

'Have you got a drink? Is someone getting you a drink? What would you like?'

'A white... wine...'

'Isabelle, could you find Brenda here a white wine, please?'

Isabelle, ostensibly John Nunn's assistant though clearly in reality answerable to Steve, looked up sharply and then went straight to the table pushed to one side, covered in drinks and snacks.

'I like your stuff. It's interesting but marketable, you know what I mean?' Steve said, matter of factly.

'Er, thanks.'

Isabelle arrived with the white wine. She handed it to Brenda. Steve nodded approvingly.

'Would you excuse me now, Brenda? I just need to check on John. Come and see me, OK? I'll look forward to it.'

'Of course,' Brenda said, not quite comprehending any of this, unsure what she even wanted out of it.

Of all the agents in the world, she had never imagined herself with Steve Angstrom. She wasn't sure she could, even now, but the offer was pretty amazing. And she knew what the result could turn out to be – the evidence was standing not five feet away from her in the form of John Nunn, who was now greeting Steve and introducing him to Davey Crockett. Adil stood with them, though was largely being ignored and Frances now appeared to have an increasingly uncomfortable Sean pinned up against the wall, talking animatedly into his face about her theories of comedy. As Brenda walked past she was in full flow.

'Of course, from a Marxist–Leninist perspective comedy is all about the veneration of the working class...'

Brenda made a poor job of concealing her smirk.

Just as Barbara clapped her hands and said, 'Guys, please do feel free to continue this in one of the bars but we need to clear the area now for the next show,' Brenda pushed open the half-hidden fire escape John Nunn had come in through and was surprised to find herself out in the open air.

The street was bustling. People walking past, up and down, places to go. No-one took the slightest bit of notice of Brenda, though she knew if John Nunn appeared here now he would instantly be mobbed. Aware that this was actually quite an imminent reality, she moved off fast, found a low stone wall that surrounded a large tree in the middle of the square and sat down.

She uncurled her fingers and looked at the business card she held. It was plain, expensive off-white with embossed lettering, bearing Steve's name and an office address in East London that had probably been bought for nothing twenty-five years ago and was now worth millions – this man couldn't help but make money. It found him. And now he wanted to represent Brenda, and that would give her access to every big TV show, every number one touring venue, every comedy club in the UK. Did she want to give him her life, though? She'd take the meeting, of course, but she wouldn't necessarily sign up with him. Not until she'd met other agents – Fenella's for one – she'd offered to set her up for a coffee in September.

The possibilities, though. My god, the possibilities – Steve would change her life in a snapped finger. Come to think of it, he probably had snapped a few fingers in his time if the stories were true, and Brenda had no doubt that they were.

Her phone buzzed. She looked down and read the message from Fenella.

'Runner-up. We can work with that. Fucking well done. With Rossly at Attic Bar. Come find us.'

Christ, news travelled fast in this business.

This business: her business.

Brenda tucked Steve's card safely into her back pocket and stood up.

Acknowledgements

Thank you to all the team at Unbound, and especially John Mitchinson, Rachael Kerr, Justin Pollard, Dan Kieran and Isobel Frankish who have been so hands-on with this book from the beginning. Thank you to all at Faber who have been incredibly supportive. Thank you to Elizabeth Garner for the great editing. Thank you to Emily Bryce-Perkins and Katie Phillips for the great PR-ing. Thank you to Mandy Ward and Kirsty Lloyd-Jones for all the help, advice and stalwart agenting. Thank you to Kate Gross for the fast reading and giving of feedback.Thank you to Bridget Christie for help with some of the details that were out of my reach. Thank you to Miranda Hart, Emma Kennedy, Victoria Coren Mitchell and David Baddiel for being willing to help with crowd-funding events. Thank you to all who pledged – you have made this book happen. Thank you to David for absolutely everything. And thank you to the comedians who are both in and out of my life for the inspiration and the laughs.

Subscribers

Unbound is a new kind of publishing house. Our books are funded directly by readers. This was a very popular idea during the late eighteenth and early nineteenth centuries. Now we have revived it for the internet age. It allows authors to write the books they really want to write and readers to support the writing they would most like to see published.

The names listed below are of readers who have pledged their support and made this book happen. If you'd like to join them, visit: www.unbound.co.uk.

Peter Alexander
Monty Alfie-Blagg
Bronwyn Allanson
John Allen
Kate Allen
Cheryl Anderson
Lucy Armitage
Lucy Armstrong
Jay Arrowsmith
Lucy Ashiagbor
Paul Baker
Laurence Baldwin
Paco Banos
Dana Barrett
Helen Bates
Katherine Beevers
Jessica Bolger

Hannah Booth
Joanna Bowen
Amy Bowers
Mark Bowers
Phil Brachi
Carol Brand
Jessica Brand
Jules Brook
Sarah Browne
Miranda Bunting
Julie Burchill
Ali & Tony Burns
Agnieszka Burza
Seymour Butts
Liz Cable
Martin Cain
Anthea Callas

Clare Cambridge
Lynn Canham
Elspeth Cannell
Xander Cansell
Ellie Cary
Tim Chambers
Pauline Chaplin
Anne Cheong
Benjamin Chiad
Kate Claisse
Jeannie Clark
Hayley Clarke
Chris Cody
Stevyn Colgan
Joy Conway
Rachel Cowie
Carol Croft
Diane Curtis
Holly Curtis
Ruth Curtis
Sarah Darling
Beth Davidson-Houston
Helen Davies
David Deeson
Bruce Dessau
Wendalynn Patricia Donnan
Jillian Dougan
Joy Douglas
Emma Doward
Bob Dowling
Anne Dowson
Lawrence T Doyle

Jane Dudley
Gillian Dykes
Mag. Dr. Helgo Eberwein
Cara Edwards
Hayley Edwards
Karen Elliott
Michael Elliott
Alice Emsley
Neil Erskine
Ben Evans
Ann Fenton
Sarah Fenwick-Stubbs
Elisabeth Filippova
Paul Fischer
Shannon Fitzsimons
Richard Flint
Michelle Flower
Sara Forfar
Ilana Fox
Isobel Frankish
Liz Fraser
Angelina Fryer
Merryl Futerman
Tania G.
Nick Galetti
Paul Gallagher
Tim Galvin
Chloe Gardner
Cyrus Gilbert-Rolfe
Mark Ginns
Wendy Goddard
Salena Godden

Elspeth Gonzalez-Skuja
Jo Gostling
Peter Govan
Voula Grand
Paul Greenfield
Mike Griffiths
Rose Grimond
Kate Gross
Laura Gustine
Geoff Hale
Andy Hall
Samantha Hall
John Harding
Gary Harper
Cathy Harris
Caitlin Harvey
David Harvey
Darren Havard
Clare Haynes
E O Higgins
Rachel Hillman
Paul 'Didymus' Holmes
Emily Hopkins
John Hopkins
Craig Houston
Russell Hughes
Deborah Humphrey
Lucy Hunt
Andrew Hunter
Cathy Hurren
Emma Jackson
Stephanie James

Stuart Jary
Louise Jenkins
David Jones
Julie Jones
Jez Kay
Gemma Kee
Lilian Keegel
Jo Anne Kennedy
Rachael Kerr
Feyaza Khan
Dan Kieran
Rosa Michelle King
Victoria Kirk
Lynsay Kobelis
Alexis Kokolski
David Kraft
Jenny Lambert
Andreas Lammers
Cher Langston
Tracy Laurence
Jimmy Leach
Natasha Leahy
David Llewellyn
Victoria Lloyd
Emma Longbottom
Thomas Love
Joanne McBride
Louise McCabe
Sean McCarthy
Barbara McCrudden
Stephen McGinn
Beth McGowan

Colleen McKenna
Alistair Mackie
Alex Marcou
Dawn Marshall-Fannon
Lorelei Mathias
Audrey Meade
Laura Meecham
Tom Meeten
Daniela Menezes
Gia Milinovich
Florence Miller
John Mitchinson
Danny Molyneux
Andrew Monk
Lorna Monk
Bernii Morgan-Langridge
Jonathan Morris
Peter Morris
Michael Mortensen
Rachael Morton
Anna Moss
Catherine Mulhall
Lynsey Murphy
Samantha Murphy
Anna Murray
Karina Nelson
David Nicholls
Rachael Nicholson
Amanda Nunn
John Nunn
Marion Nunn
Mark Nunn

Sara O'Donnell
Kayuri Odedra
Lesley Orrell
Courtney Owen
Jessica Pan
Nic Parkes
Jim & Adele Parks
David Parry
Rima Patel
Matt Patterson
Viggo Pedersen
John Pelton
Philippa Perry
Shayan Phaily
James Phillips
Kim Pile
Justin Pollard
Jude Powell
Lyndsey Pullen
Jennie Pyatt
Jeanette Ramsden
Emma Read
Sarah Vashti Rennacker
Joshua Reynolds
Gill Richards
Kate Richards
Rachel Richards
Gillian Riddell
Della Roberts
Emma Danielle Robinson
Jayne Robinson
Geraint Rogers

Alison Rogerson
Lorna Ross
Robert Ross
William Ross
Victoria Rowland
Deb Ruddy
Kirsten Salt
Katrin Salyers
Stephanie Sandall
Robert Sandler
Comedian Dan Schreiber
Donna Scott
Georgina Scott
Penny Scott-Bayfield
Brian Scranage
Michelle Semple-Morris
Roger Shaw
Justin Sheppherd
Helena Sherriff
Katie Shuster
Annetta Slade
Claire Slade
Mathew Smith
Matt Smith
Martin Southard
Melissa Stevens
Caroline Sturmey
David Tan

Faye Tan
Dror Tankus
Dan Tetsell
Feri Tezcan
Mike Scott Thomson
Chloe Thorn
Martin Togher
Mike Totham
Gemma Underhill
Charlotte Underwood
Kim Upton
Melanie Vallance
Mark Vent
Louise Vine
Jonathan Wakeham
Karin Wannemacher
Mandy Ward
Carole Warmington
Frances Watson
Arabella Weir
Rebecca Priscilla White
Yvonne White
Patrick Wilcox
John Wileman
Shona Williams
Jayne Woodbury
Stacey Woods
Nadim Zaman

A note about the typefaces

Jan Tschichold (1902–1974) was a German calligrapher, typographer, book designer and teacher. This book has been typeset using a digital representation of the Sabon, the typeface he designed between 1964 and 1967.

Sabon, designed by Jan Tschichold for both hand- and machine-composition, was issued simultaneously by the Linotype, Monotype and Stempel type foundries in 1967. The designs for the roman were based on the type designs of Claude Garamond (c.1480–1561) and the italics on those by Garamond's contemporary, Robert Granjon. Gill Sans was drawn on the basis of the classical Roman capitals (such as those found on the column of Trajan in Rome) and was inspired by Edward Johnston's sans serif 'Johnston' typeface designed for London Underground.

Tschichold, accused of communist leanings by the Nazis, was arrested shortly after their rise to power in 1933. He witnessed the seizure of all the books he had ever designed and only narrowly escaped by being smuggled out to Switzerland in August of that year.

During his time at Penguin he oversaw the design of 500 paperback covers and produced a four-page booklet of precise guidelines called the Penguin Composition Rules. It wasn't an easy process and Tschichold became the scourge of Penguin's typesetters and printers, demanding the highest levels of consistency: 'Every day I had to wade through miles of corrections (often ten books daily). I had a rubber stamp made: "Equalize letter-spaces according to their visual value." It was totally ignored.'